AROUND ELDRITCH CORNERS

Other books by Christine Morgan

Fantasy and Gaming:
The MageLore and ElfLore trilogies
The Silver Doorway series for younger readers
Ellis: A Kingdom in Turmoil (with Tim Morgan)
Naughty and Dice: An Adult Gamer's Guide to Sexual Situations (with Tim Morgan)

Thriller and Suspense:
Scoot
Caged
The Widow's Walk
Murder Girls

Horror:
Black Roses
Gifted Children
Changeling Moon
Tell No Tales
The Horned Ones: Cornucopia
His Blood
Spermjackers From Hell
Lakehouse Infernal
Birthright
The Night Silver River Run Red
White Death
Trench Mouth
Warlock Infernal
Damned Lazy
Homebody
C*nt-Kick the Witch Bitch (with Edward Lee)
Nympho Shark F*ck Frenzy (with Susan Snyder)

Collections:
The Raven's Table
The Wolf's Feast
Dawn of the Living-Impaired and Other Messed-Up Zombie Stories
Tombs and Terrors: Tales of Ancient Times
Visceral: Collected Flesh (with Patrick C. Harrison)
Dreadful Fancies: Steampunkish Stories
HorrorSmut
Rip Your Heart Out
Almost Normal Horror
Buzzards & Bone
None So Blind
Pulptastic Yarns #1: Martian Matinee

AROUND ELDRITCH CORNERS

CHRISTINE MORGAN

WORD HORDE
PETALUMA, CA

First Edition

ISBN: 978-1-956252-08-8

A Word Horde Book
www.wordhorde.com

TABLE OF CONTENTS

Dedication:

With thanks to the many awesome editors whose themed anthology calls inspired me to peer around some pretty weird eldritch corners!

THE ARKHAM-TOWN MUSICIANS

ow, it happened that there were, in the village of Dunwich, a series of strange events and dark atrocities,
centering primarily around the Whateley family, and
culminating on that most dreadful night when an inhuman voice
shouted an unspeakable name from the height of Sentinel Hill.

But this is not an accounting of those events.

For it happened that there was, also, a poor and humble farmer
who had been on occasion in the employ of the Whateleys. His
cattle, in the end, met the same grim fate as most others near-
abouts—missing at best, sore-ridden and sucked dry of every drop
of their blood at the worst.

The farmer himself, left further impoverished and shaken all but
to madness by what he had witnessed and the tumult following,
soon drank himself to an early grave. He was by no means the only
Dunwich resident to do so.

What went forgotten was that the humble farmer had also, for
many years, kept as well as his cattle a few donkeys to help with his
labors in the fields.

Or, a breed of creatures that might have been donkeys once...
might have begun as donkeys... but had, over time... changed.

Whether it was from feeding off what grew in Dunwich, or whether something else had responsibility, some hideous cross-breeding

1

that introduced unnatural bloodlines, perhaps as a result of the arts of which old Wizard Whateley was said to have been a practitioner, the farmer could not know. Nor did he care to guess.

Only one of these creatures was left behind when the farmer died. Though he did not altogether resemble a donkey, it was as a donkey he thought of himself. And so, as a donkey he shall be called.

After all, he did the work of a donkey. He had the general shape of a donkey, with four strong legs that reached the ground in addition to the myriad centipedal limbs protruding in rippling rows from either side. Where his skin was not mottled pinkish-yellow, the hide was as coarse and grey-brown as any other donkey. If the two long whiplike tentacles that sprouted from his withers were unusual, bristling with hair and ending in reddish sucker-mouths, his tail and stiff mane and upstanding ears were perfectly ordinary. And if the end of his muzzle splayed out into fleshy pink tendrils such as might be found on a star-nosed mole, what of it?

He was still a donkey, hale and healthy and hearty, and proud.

But, in time, the donkey had grazed the grass of his pen down to bare stubble, which seemed disinclined to grow back. He had long since finished the oats and corn stored in the hay-shed where he slept. It occurred to the donkey that he could not stay here much longer on his own.

"Dunwich is done-for," said the donkey, and brayed a laugh at his joke. But he quickly sobered. "And what of myself, then? My master is dead, and his masters as well. Hard-working though I am, I doubt I would find much welcome among the neighbors. They would not take me in even for all my tireless strength. I am a donkey, yes. But I am, after all, no ordinary donkey."

He kicked down the fence of ramshackle wooden sticks and freed himself into the wider world. There, he found more grass, brown and sour and dry.

"For that matter," he said, "why should I want to go on toiling at thankless work on a farm? Why should I plod in the mud, pull a plow, draw a wagon? Did I not just say how I was, to be sure, no ordinary donkey? Why, then, should I labor as one?"

The donkey ambled at his leisure through the blighted fields. He glanced about with interest at the domed hills surrounding Dunwich, and peered down toward the dark, tangled hollow of the glen.

"No, indeed," he told himself, "I am meant for greater and better things than this. I shall go forth from Dunwich to make my own way in the world! Perhaps I might become a musician. Yes! Yes, and why not?"

Here, he hee-hawed at the top of his voice, and found the sound pleasing. He stamped time with a hoof, and when he slid his hairy wither-tentacles one against the other, they gave off shrill, rasping notes like violin strings or a grasshopper's legs.

"Why not?" he cried again. "But these country-villages are no place for such a celebrity as I am bound to be. In Arkham-Town, however, I surely will find my fortune and fame!"

So saying, and very satisfied with his plan, the donkey set out.

Past scattered houses that wore a uniform aspect of desolate age and squalor, he went, and past the huddled cluster of the village itself until he reached the tenebrous tunnel of a covered bridge where his hoofbeats clop-clopped with hollow echoes.

The road then curved, dusty and sometimes flanked by crumbling walls of briar-bordered stone, through a landscape of sloping rock-strewn meadows, luxuriant weeds and brambles. In forest belts, the trees loomed too large and whippoorwills chattered. Chimney-ruins and ancient rough-hewn columns poked up through the undergrowth. At boggy places, fireflies danced in abnormal profusion to the strident but dissonant croaking of bull-frogs.

"They," said the donkey, scoffing with a snort, "are no musicians, that is to be sure!"

He brayed forth his own song, shaming the bull-frogs into silence from their raucous rhythms. He trotted over yet more crude wooden bridges of dubious safety, which traversed deep gorges and ravines.

Not far ahead, knew the donkey, was the junction where Old

Dunwich Road met Aylesbury Pike. And only a short while further on from there were the crossroads by Dean's Corners.

Ahead, at a spot where water trickled from a cleft boulder to form a pool by the edge of the road, the donkey saw a figure hunched over and lapping at the water. It seemed to him to be some sort of dog, or at least as much dog as he himself was donkey. In truth, the donkey had not known many dogs before; they had been scarce in Dunwich and unwelcome, for it was said they always set off with a terrific baying in pursuit of Lavinia Whateley's strange son.

This dog, if dog it was, had corpse-colored fur and loose skin that fell in rugose folds and wrinkles. His hind paws were paws proper, but his front ones gripped the rocks at the edge of the pool with long, narrow fingers. His face, when he raised his head, was oddly squashed of countenance, with an immense dripping scoop-shovel of jaw from which arose yellowish tusks.

"Good afternoon!" said the donkey, greeting the dog in all good manners and politeness. "How do you fare on this day, Brother Dog?"

"Wretchedly," the dog replied, giving its head such a shake that its jowls wobbled and droplets of water sprayed about.

"Wretchedly?" the donkey cried. "What a shame! Do you not have your freedom?"

"Oh, I have my freedom," grumbled the dog in a growl. "I, who was a huntsman's most faithful companion, I, who might have run pack-mates with the Hounds of Tindalos, I have all the freedom anyone could ever have, and two extra!"

"Then how is it you seem so displeased? I have only just gained my freedom, and could not be happier!"

"I'm sure that is fine and well for donkeys," the dog said. "But I did not gain my freedom. Neither did I choose it. I was, as I said, a huntsman's most faithful companion. Long years I went by his side into the dark woods. I faced any beast of the forest without fear, even the young of the Black Goat! I was ever loyal, and stalwart, and true!"

The donkey tipped his head, the centipedal limbs waving all down his sides in consternation. "Did your master, the hunstman, die? Mine did—"

"No." The dog snarled, grinding his yellow tusks against his sharp upper teeth. "He married. And his wife, you see, could not stand the sight of me in the house any longer. She feared what I might do to the children. As if I—I!—would bring them any harm!"

"The huntsman did not send you away!" said the donkey, aghast.

"Oh, no," said the dog. "He offered to, but that was not sufficient for her. *What if it comes back?* she said to him. *Even if you led it far into the woods and left it, it could find its way!* And so, he, the huntsman, my own trusted master, took up an axe and made to split open my skull!"

At this, the donkey gaped, then snuffled a breath so that the fleshy tendrils at his muzzle flapped and wriggled. "What did you do?"

"What could I but run? I would not have bitten him, despite his murderous intentions. So, now, here I am, with no home and nowhere to go."

"It is well that we found each other then," the donkey said. "For I am on my way to Arkham-Town, where I mean to become a famous musician. With a voice such as yours, so rumbling and resonant, you must make a fine singer yourself."

The dog considered this for a moment, and agreed that a famous musician sounded to him like a fine thing to be. They fell in most readily together, and soon reached Aylesbury Pike.

The air took on a fresher fragrance, bereft of the odour of mould so prevalent in Dunwich. Wildlife scampered unseen in damp drifts of fallen leaves. The day was crisp, the sky clear, though heavy clouds built over the hills. They saw no riders or wagons or other traffic, no one at all, until they came to the crossroads.

There, a signpost pointed in the direction of Dean's Corner, a sleepy but tidy and well-kept little village. Another arrow indicated Aylesbury itself, the distant smokestacks of mills and factories lost in a murky haze.

Most interesting of all, however, was the small mound of recently-turned earth where the roads met, marked with a rough wooden cross jutting up askew at an angle. But it was not the cross, nor the grave, that interested donkey and dog so much as what sat nearby.

It was a cat, large and queenly, of regal bearing. Her sleek coat was of many colors—umber, cream, russet, mahogany and gold. Her eyes were brilliant emeralds. She had a tail like a plume, and gloriously long, curling whiskers. Around her neck, on a silken ribbon, hung a bauble of Egyptian design.

The donkey greeted her as politely as he had done the dog. "Good afternoon, Sister Cat! How do you fare on this day?"

She gave a great yawn, showing ivory teeth. She gave a great stretch, back arching, needle-claws digging into the dirt. Then she sat primly again, licked her forepaw, and smoothed her curled whiskers.

"I am in great distress and despair, Brother Donkey," she replied. "Your companion does not mean to give chase, I should hope. I'll scratch him to the bone, if he does."

The dog grumbled. "I am a hunter, no chaser of cats."

"Good," said the cat. "For I am a cat of Ulthar, and will bring deadly punishment on any who try to do me mischief."

"We mean no such thing," the donkey assured her. "Brother Dog and I are merely traveling to Arkham-Town. But what do you do here? Whose grave is that you sit beside?"

"That of my mistress."

"She must have been tiny," observed the dog.

"It is only her head."

"Her head?" cried the donkey. "Where is the rest of her?"

"I will tell you," said the cat. "My mistress was, on her mother's side, kin to the Whateleys of Dunwich. Do you know of them?"

"Indeed," the donkey said. "I came from there."

"Well, after what happened there, her neighbors decided that she must be a witch. They set upon her, and beat her to death with sticks and with staves. Then they used the blade of a shovel to chop her head from her neck. Her body, they threw into the river. And her head, they buried here at the crossroads, so that even if her spirit somehow returned, it would be unable to find its way home."

"Barbaric!" the donkey declared, and the dog woofed his agreement of this assessment.

"They would have done the same to me, if they could," the cat went on, "for all it is forbidden to kill any cat of Ulthar. But I eluded them, and avenged my mistress."

"How so?" asked the dog. "You are only a cat."

Her ear flicked disdainfully. "I caught yuggoth-mice, which feast upon the pallid mushrooms in the deep groves. I carried their slick, bloated corpses to the village, and dropped one into each well and rain-cistern."

At that, the dog and the donkey exchanged an impressed look. Clearly, the cat was not one with whom to be trifled.

"And what will you do now?" the donkey asked her.

The many-colored cat uttered a sigh. "With no warm hearth to curl up by? With no mistress to put down dishes of milk? I have been sitting here all this day, asking myself that very same thing."

"Why, then! You must accompany us to Arkham-Town! Brother Dog and I are on our way there to become famous musicians. We have definite need of a soprano!"

"Famous musicians?" The cat preened. "I should like that very much, I think! Yes. Let us be off at once!"

So they were off at once. Though, as the cat had to frequently stop to wash her face or groom her magnificent coat, they made rather less good time than they otherwise might have done.

It was coming on toward dusk when they first heard the eerie, warbling cries. The noises sounded something like the hoot of a barn-owl, something like the dawn-crowing of a rooster, and something like nothing ever voiced by the throat of any earthly creature.

Along the road there ran a ragged line of stout old fenceposts, the fence itself now long gone. Atop one of these, the unlikely trio saw as they drew closer, perched the source of the cries, holding on by the grip of scabrous orange-brown talons. Matted-looking feathers stuck out in uneven clumps from black, rubbery flesh. A stinger-tipped tail waved from its hind end and it flapped wings of leathery membrane for balance.

Where a face should have been found, there was none, nor mouth, nor beak. How it therefore uttered such a voluble and incessant din, they were at a loss to wonder.

The donkey attempted several times to hail the winged creature as they approached, but it must not have heard, for it paid no notice until suddenly and with a tremendous start of surprise it broke off mid-crow.

As mouthless and faceless as it was, that it was eyeless also came as no shock, yet somehow it seemed to fix them with a piercing stare. Upon closer inspection, its aspect was that which might result had a chicken been mated with a night-gaunt. A reddish coxcomb on its head suggested it was male.

"Good evening," the donkey said. "How do you fare this day, Brother...?"

"Rooster," came the answer provided. "Or, near enough, for such have I lived as. And this day, Brother Donkey, I do not fare well at all, thank you for your polite inquiry."

"Why do you crow so full-lunged at this hour?" asked the dog. "The sun has all but gone down."

The rooster's leathery wings hitched in a helpless shrug. "What else can I do? What else have I known? I crow because I can, because I can do nothing else, and because it is only by purest good fortune I am still able to crow! Another day might have seen me silenced once and for all!"

They of course asked him how so, and what he meant by that, and why. To this, the rooster gladly responded.

"Until yesterday," he said, "I belonged to a chicken-farmer who lived in the hollow. Such a brute he was, in-bred, degenerate of nature and intelligence! He, not realizing my true nature, mistook me for a common cock and put me in with his hens. My presence alone so terrified them that, from thenceforth, they would lay far more than the usual number of rare double-yolked eggs."

No one chose to reply further to his remark as to his true nature, only musing to themselves that their initial supposition must in fact be not far from the case.

"Such eggs, of course, fetch a fine price at market," the rooster went on. "As for myself, it was no unpleasant living... I had, of course, as many fresh-laid eggs to eat as I wanted, and the occasional pullet or cockerel when I fancied warm blood and tender meat. I was required to do nothing more than crow with the dawn, and drive off any intruding foxes to the hen-yard—which, believe me, was no difficulty at all."

"No, it would not be," said the dog. "Foxes are slink-thieves and cowards. You must have scared them stark-white."

"Then, yesterday, the farmer's brother came visiting. A brute no less ill- and in-bred, though possessed of a slightly craftier cunning. When the oddity of the double-yolked eggs was mentioned at supper, boasted of at supper, this brother devised a notion to increase their profits even more. They resolved to rent their prize rooster around to other farms, sure that their neighbors would pay handsomely to share in the bounty."

"Ah," said the cat with an air of understanding. "The other farmers, however, might have recognized your night-gaunt lineage."

"Precisely so, Sister Cat. My neck would have been wrung in a trice. I made my escape this morning, before sunrise and without crowing, while the farmer and his brother slept. I only paused here to rest my wings, when the thought came to me that I had no other prospects and would likely not survive the night. I commenced, therefore, crowing for all I was worth, so as to get some final use from my voice."

"Your voice would have much use if you joined our company!" the donkey said. "We three are musicians, going to Arkham-Town to seek our fortunes. With such a practiced throat and lungs as yours, I have every confidence you will be a great success!"

Without hesitation, the rooster gave his most ready and enthu-
siastic assent. Because his wings were still tired, he rode perched
upon the donkey's broad back.

The trio now a quartet, they resumed their travels, a jolly party
in the highest of spirits. But such high spirits, it is sad to say, could
not last long. The heavy clouds that had been building over the
hills soon spread dark over the valley. Rain pattered down. The road
went muddy.

The four quickly became miserable, the cat most of all. They
trudged with heads down, squishing in mud, splashing in puddles.
The donkey tried to keep them in cheer with glowing accounts of
the fame and prosperity they would find in Arkham-Town.

"We will have a fine house," he said. "A fine brick house with a
slate-shingled roof. Rich cream for you, Sister Cat, instead of milk.
Rich cream in a silver bowl, with a cushion by the fire! For you,
Brother Dog, prime cuts of red beef, and all the ham-bones you can
gnaw. I will have oat-mash with honey for breakfast, and a bed of
softest new-mown alfalfa!"

"What of me?" asked the rooster, who, being able to fold his
leathery wings over his head and ward off the rain, fared somewhat
better—though no less miserably—than his other companions.

"Oh, whatever you should like!" said the donkey. "More eggs and
hens, if that is your will. Sleeping until well past noon rather than
having to wake to crow the dawn."

In this manner, they went on a while further, until the dog with
his keen hunting eyes spotted a glimmer as of light from a window,
off in the distance. It appeared to come from within a stand of tall
trees, and a narrow track led that way from the main road.

"Let us seek shelter," said the cat, her proud fur coat soaked and
bedraggled.

"Yes, perhaps it is an inn," the dog said. "We might find lodging
there."

"We'll sing for our supper," said the rooster.

Since the rain was growing steadier, and no other options presented themselves, the donkey wasted no time in agreeing. Single-file along the narrow track they proceeded, wending through the woods, catching yet more tantalizing glimpses of warmly lit and beckoning windows.

Upon reaching the building nestled amid the trees, they discovered it to be not an inn but a quaint little farmhouse, old-fashioned, neglected, and in some need of repair. Its barn had collapsed, its garden was weedy and overgrown. The roof sagged, cracks ran up and down the wall-plaster, and the lights that had guided them hither shone through missing shutter-slats over windows lacking glass panes. But, to the wet and weary travelers, it might as well have been a king's palace.

Low sounds as of chanting came from within. Moving shadows sometimes passed in front of the windows, blotting out the light... which, by its flicker and hue they judged to be candle-glow.

"Sister Cat, you are stealthy, and Brother Rooster, you can fly," said the donkey. "Go see what's what, then come back to us."

They did as he directed, returning shortly with the news. Instead of the elderly farmer and his wife that might have been expected in such a place, several people—a dozen or more—crowded the house's single main room.

"They wear robes," reported the rooster.

"And carry candles and chalices," said the cat.

"Their leader is a bald man with a wispy grey beard like that of a goat."

"He holds a book with a Greater Sigil branded into the leather."

"And stands at a round stone altar."

"Lined with chalk, and sprinkled with ashes and salt," the cat concluded.

The donkey's wither-tentacles twined about each other with a bristly rasp. "Aha!" he cried. "Cultists! They've remade this old farmhouse into their church! How splendid! Do they have a church-choir?"

"None. Only the chanting." A fat raindrop struck the cat on the nose and she flinched. "We must do something!"

"Indeed we must, and indeed we shall!" The donkey started for the nearest window, from which one shutter hung by a hinge and the other was missing altogether. "You stand upon my back, Brother Dog," he instructed. "Let Sister Cat stand upon yours, and our winged brother perch upon hers. Then we shall give them a taste of our choir, and they will be bound to welcome us!"

The others deemed this a good plan and readily took their places. With his fingerlike fore-paws, the dog clutched the donkey's thick hide. The cat stepped up daintily and hooked her fine needle-claws in the dog's fur. Lastly, the night-gaunt fluttered to perch on the cat's shoulders, head bobbing this way and that, wings spread.

"On three," whispered the donkey, then stamped time softly with his front hoof.

And, on his count of three, the company of musicians burst into song.

"Eee-yaw, eee-yaw, fthagn!" brayed the donkey.

"Yog! Yog-Soth! Yog-Soth-Oth!" barked the dog.

"Ia! Ia!" cried the cat, in her high and piercing meow.

"Cthu-hu-hu-hu-lu!" crowed the rooster at the top of his lungs.

All their voices together raised such a harmony the likes of which the cultists—or indeed any other living soul on this earth!—had never heard. They spun from their altar. They dropped their candles and chalices. Their leader squealed like a girl, letting the book with the Greater Sigil on its cover fall with a hefty thump onto the pattern of chalk, salt and ashes. With a flapping of robes, bumping and stumbling over each other, they all dashed for the door and fled through it, scattering into the rainy night.

"I think they did not care for our music," the dog said, after a startled moment of some disappointment.

"Their loss, then," declared the cat, "for they obviously must lack any proper sense of refinement, culture or appreciation."

"Even so, and good riddance," the rooster said.

"Ah well," said the donkey. "As we are here and the hour is late, let us make ourselves comfortable. We may pass the night here nicely enough, I daresay."

It was so decided, and the four musicians went inside. They found the place small but cozy. They feasted on the remains of the cultists' supper, laid out on a table, and made merry drinking each other's health from a jug of good wine.

Though the candles had gone extinguished, embers glowed warm in the hearth, and the cat settled herself quite happily there to groom. The donkey found hay strewn in a side-chamber, and while it was not new-mown alfalfa, he made a good bed of it. The dog, finding the bone of a leg-of-mutton still thick with meat-scraps, stretched out long and gnawing contentedly in front of the door. The rooster flew up into the rafters to perch on a roof-beam, holding fast with his talons and folding his leathery wings around his body.

Now, it happened that the cultists had run for some considerable distance in their fright, before they stopped and re-gathered themselves, and were greatly chagrined.

After all, they said to one another, had not they been gathered there for the very purpose of effecting a summoning of some eldritch creature? Was that not the entire sole aim of their ceremony? How foolish of them, then—and how shameful besides!—to scream and flee when the object of their ritual itself should appear to them in answer!

They must, they decided, return. They'd left in such a state of panicked rapidity that they had even left behind their book, an ancient tome acquired at considerable risk and cost from the library of Miskatonic University. Gaining access there again would be next to impossible, particularly since the events of the preceding August, when one Wilbur Whateley was said to have met his messy and unfortunate end within those hallowed halls.

Yes, they must return. Of that, there could be neither doubt nor dispute.

However, when they again approached the farmhouse, there arose doubt and dispute aplenty over whose task it should be to go in first and investigate. The windows were dark, the structure itself seemingly silent and unoccupied.

Of the creature that had manifested at the window—such a sight, even half-glimpsed! Conical and misshapen in outline, tapering to a height taller than that of a man! Many-headed, many-limbed and many-eyed! Worst of all, of many gaping mouths from which had issued those hideous, screeching ululations!—there was no current and obvious sign.

It must have, the cultists assured themselves, gone back to whichever realm from whence it had come. They should, should they not, be pleased by this development? Surely it was a sign of the Old Ones' favor!

Indeed! And indeed! And indeed thrice more!

Yet none were eager to volunteer, regardless of the threats or inducements offered by their leader—who could not, he explained, of course, himself go… the precise reasons for which he somehow neglected to fully articulate. In the end, they set to draw lots, with whosoever drew the short one being the first to enter.

The man who drew short was reluctant but had no other choice. He went on tip-toe to the farmhouse, peered into the darkness, listened to the silence, and finally climbed in through a window.

By then, of course, the four musicians, exhausted from their day's adventures, had gone to sleep. They did not waken as the cultist, oblivious of their presence, groped about until he found one of the dropped candles. He then crept toward the fireplace, thinking he might kindle a flame to its wick from the embers.

That was when the cat, curled there with her fur nicely dry and groomed, woke and opened her eyes. The cultist, seeing them shining there in the gloom, mistook them for coals and poked the unlit candle at the cat's face.

She, anything but amused by this indignity of treatment, sprang with a fury of spitting and hissing onto the man. Her needle-claws sliced his cheeks to ribbons and a darting bite of her ivory fangs nearly tore off his nose.

The cultist, screaming, stumbled backward and trod on the dog stretched in front of the door. The dog, likewise, sprang up in a fury. His powerful jaws took a swath of robes, and a chunk of buttock with it.

Shrieking now, in agony and terror, the man crashed into the table. The rooster, who'd been perched on the roof-beam just above it, dropped down to seize him by the collar. The rooster's whip-thin tail coiled, tickling, around the man's neck and stung him with itching welts.

Well into a panic, beset on all sides, the unlucky cultist ran for what he only guessed might be safety… the side-chamber where the hay had been strewn on the floor. Instead of safety, he was met with a strong kick from the donkey's hind legs. The force of that kick propelled him clear through a wall, leaving a great ragged gap in the plaster. He ran for his life—or hobbled—as fast as he could.

The other cultists, who'd been waiting, heard the sudden terrible commotion with great apprehension. Their comrade staggered into their midst, so much plaster-dust caked in his hair that they first thought it had gone white from fright. His face was furrowed with gashes, his backside bleeding profusely. Welts rose up red and inflamed on his skin, and several ribs had been broken.

He babbled at them from a frantic state of madness, babbled of devils and monsters, witches with knives for hands, beasts that bit like bear-traps, snakes that had vicious crab-pinchers at one end and scorpion-tails at the other, hulking indescribable horrors with hard hooves.

The cultists decided as one that they wanted no more of this. Casting off their robes, beating themselves about the heads in repentance, they ran every step of the way to the next town and its church without stopping, pleading for God's forgiveness with all of their might.

But, as for the donkey, the dog, the cat and the rooster…

Well, the four musicians decided the little farmhouse suited them quite satisfactorily, so that there was no more need to finish the long journey to Arkham-Town. They settled in, singing whenever they pleased, until the place got the reputation for being most dreadfully haunted so that the nearby folk stayed well away.

This made the quartet happy, for they had discovered they did not need fame and fortune after all. A roof, a well-stocked larder, and good company were more than enough.

And if no one has yet killed or banished them, then they must live there still.

PIPPA'S CRAYONS

"What are you drawing, honey?"

"Pictures."

"Can I see? Oh, how nice. Is this your house?"

"Nuh-unh. Is a farmhouse."

"A farmhouse, yes, I see that… this must be the barn… and what kind of crops are these?"

"Corns."

"Such tall corn, too. As high as the roof. Do you like corn, Pippa?"

"Not that kind."

"No? What kind do you like? Corn on the cob? Popcorn? Cornbread?"

"Not *that* corns! *That* corns is ucky."

"Ucky? It's so green—"

"No! It's ucky. It's sick-making corns."

"What about these things with the… wiggly bits?"

"Them's carrots."

"Let's look at your next picture, shall we? Oh… how… pretty… is this a garden? What kind of flowers are these?"

"I dunno."

"Have you seen flowers like that, honey? Flowers that… color?"

"I dunno."

"I didn't know we had glow-in-the-dark crayons here in the art room."

"*My* crayons. My grampy sended them."

"Your grampy... your grandfather, Mr. Pierce? Is this his farm?"

"Nuh-unh. Look, see, I drawed some cows, and some sheeps, and a horsie."

"...which ones are the cows?"

"These ones!"

"And this picture is the house again, but what happened to the corn and carrots? They're all grey."

"They's turning into dirt."

"Dirt?"

"Rock-dirt, all dusty."

"Whose face is this in the window?"

"The farmer lady."

"She looks happy, smiling like that."

"She's screaming. The farmer man made her go stay in the attic."

"That doesn't sound very nice of the farmer man."

"She was crazy-crazy. And look, I drawed another one, now there's a crazy boy in the attic too. But this other one, this boy, he falled down the well."

"Was he hurt when he fell down the well?"

"He died."

"He drowned?"

"The water was ucky. He died. His little brother died too. See, I drawed their bones in the well. Aminal bones too."

"Animal bones?"

"Aminals. Here's a bunny-bunny. Here's a bird."

"And what happened to the animals in this next picture? They're grey like the corn. Are they also turning into dust?"

"Uh-huh."

"This one... are they having a barbecue?"

"They was gonna eat the pig but it was ucky too. That's why they gots yuck faces with their tongues stuck out, yuck."

"I see them making yuck faces. Oh, and you've got some more pictures here... what... Pippa, honey, what's this one?"

"It's the farmer lady again!"

"She's…"

"She's all the *colors!*"

"Yes… the colors… Pippa, I've never seen colors like that."

"My grampy did."

"Your grampy saw colors like that?"

"They comed out of a rock."

"A rock?"

"A rock falled down from the sky and there was stuff in it and the stuff comed out and it was all the colors."

"Then what did your grampy do?"

"He killed the farmer lady, and the house fell down on the farmer man."

"What do you mean, your grampy killed the farmer-lady?"

"He did. Then he bringed the doctor and other mens, and *allllll* the colors comed out of the well and went waaaaay high back up in the sky."

"Is that… is that what this picture is? The colors… coming out of the well… going up into the sky, into space?"

"Except a little bit falled back down."

"Fell back down like the rock did?"

"Uh-huh! And that's what my grampy made my crayons from."

THE HOUNDS OF TINTAGEL

"**N**ever in all my days," said Tiberius Tempus to himself, peering past the woolen tent-flap to the wet morass beyond, "did I think to be so far from home."

Far, indeed. Far from the dry and dusty land where his family farmed hardscrabble for whatever harvest Ceres might allow them. His brothers farmed there still, while Tiberius had been sent instead to join the Legion. To serve with spear and shield and gladius rather than bucket, rake, and hoe. To cross strange channels to wild countries, savage, green, and grey.

And rainy. Their encampment, structured in neat order around the central command tent, looked far less grand and far more dreary. Banners hung in limp red rags from poles. Even the great golden Eagle seemed sullen and dull.

This place. This far, foreign, rain-soaked place. So primitive as to make Gaul's untamed frontier civilized by comparison. These Britons were every bit as brutal if not more so than the ruthless Gallic tribes. They ran in packs, as beasts, their bodies hairy and often naked, daubed with paint and clay. Their language was beastlike as well, a speech of grunts and gurgles. They dwelt in sod-dug hovels, sleeping side-by-side with goats and pigs. They made frequent, gory sacrifice... not to orderly gods such as Jove or Phoebus, but to dark-barked trees and fissured standing stones.

Tiberius suppressed a shudder. Why anyone should venture here was a mystery he could not fathom. But, such decisions were not for him to question. Such were for him to follow and obey.

All this way, they'd come, expanding the Empire's borders, bringing conquest and trade. Huts and hovels, savagery. Naked paint-daubed brutes who probably ate of their own dead, and rutted with their goats and pigs as much as with their filthy women, who probably *also* rutted with the goats and pigs.

Then, to their immense surprise…

Leaning a bit from the tent-flap's shelter, he peered through the deluge toward the fortification upon its rocky hill. Its high walls, slick with moss and moisture, came together in many angles. Towers rose to strange points, battlements jutted with sharp edges. From its narrow windows flickered occasional blue-tinged firelight.

That here, in this remote corner far past nowhere, should exist such a structure…

Not built by wild Britons, to be sure. Not built by Romans, either; it was too old, for one thing, and too disturbing, for another. Merely to gaze too long upon it was to invite an aching of the eyes, a twisting of the mind.

At the base of the hill the peculiar multi-angled structure stood upon, there clustered a sizable village, defended by a palisade of earthworks topped with brambles and sharp branches. The houses were made of logs and plaster, the roofs of thatch. It was no Rome, that was certain. Yet, after all else they'd seen and passed thus far, it might as well have been a mighty city.

Its inhabitants, too, were more like proper men than beasts. They even had a king—a peaceful king, a gentle man by all accounts, as opposed to the strongest and most vicious chieftains of the wild tribes. A king with whom their war-commander, by way of a translator, could converse. With whom an alliance could be forged. Better to bring them under the rule of Rome by peace, and then together bring the rest of the Britons… at spearpoint if necessary.

This, Tiberius knew, was the plan. A plan his fellow soldiers welcomed; they had marched far and fought hard, and were glad of a reprieve. They preferred to earn their pay, and their daily rations of bread and salt, by practicing their phalanx formations and establishing a stronghold—even in the rain—than by trudging through the wilderness never knowing when hairy, naked, painted savages would leap from hiding.

Besides, there were women in the village, and at the surrounding farmsteads. Women who, also, brewed potent drink. If they were not the elegant beauties of Rome, nor the drink a good grape-wine, both were still vast improvements on what else Briton so far had shown to offer.

One of the women, however…

Tiberius shook his head, knowing full well this too was not for him to question. He held private his concerns, just as he held private all misgivings. If something about the indifferent and diffident manner of this king, their new ally, made the nape of his neck prickle… if the silent warriors in their snarling hound-headed cloaks caused unease within his bowels… if the translator, some wandering white-bearded hermit who claimed to be a wizard and who'd fast become the war-commander's trusted advisor, possessed a slyness of aspect… if the tall strange angles of the hill-fort's walls cast uncanny shapes even into Tiberius's dreams… well, what of it?

***

"He is the one," the child whispered.

Around her, blue-tinged flames danced, tallow lamps in shallow bowls. Their shifting glow played over her small, pallid face and reflected in her wide, but unfocused, eyes. She sat on a pelt at once shaggy and leathery and scaled, bare legs folded beneath her, palms upturned on her knees. A simple tunic draped her slight frame, but jeweled pins held her hair.

Shadows moved in the strange corners where so many stone walls met… and within those shadows, other shadows moved of their own restless volition.

Their eyes were neither wide, nor unfocused. Their eyes were narrow, and saw all. Their ears pricked. Their claws ticked. Lean flanks twitched, between lanky bones and dusky hides. Nostrils flared and slitted, exhaling azurous steam. Thin lips leered back from spine-sharp teeth.

She spoke on, voice soft and older than her apparent youthful years. "It must be done by trickery and deception."

The shadows paced and passed, passed each other, through each other, in and out of the walls, in and out of existence. They were there and then not, gone and then back, pacing and passing. They had been and they were and they would be again, forever changing, forever the same.

Only the largest, the leader, remained steady. Remained solid, upright and alert across from the child. Its gaze fixed unwavering upon the wide blue-glimmered pools of her eyes. A low, rumbling growl rose from its gaunt and bony chest.

An observer might have described them as hounds, if only in so far as it was the closest word language would afford, the closest concept a mortal mind could have grasped. An observer might also have fallen dead at first sight, dead or fright-stricken unto madness... and counted such fate a mercy. Better that than to fall before the claws and jaws. Better that than to feel the coldly loathsome, unnatural touch. Or to breathe of their breath, take their scent, taste their air.

Better death. Better madness.

Yet, here, in this innermost chamber, this hidden heart, the young girl blinked and smiled sweetly. She extended a delicate hand.

The leader of the Hounds snuffled at the hand with its ferocious muzzle, the growl becoming a wistful whine. Its long hollow tongue licked her fingers, making her giggle. She patted its head.

"He is the one, dear sister," she repeated. "Utharius Draconis. He is the one."

***

Ygran.

He had to have her.

From the very instant his gaze first fell upon her, he could think of little else. As a goddess, she'd been… Juno herself made flesh, tall and proud and queenly. Her breasts ripe, her skin fair, her hips full, the promise of her lips a plum's juicy sweetness.

Even in the highest houses of Rome itself, such a woman would be desired above all others, renowned for her beauty. To find her *here*, of all places, here at the ragged unkempt edges of the world…

Oh, he had to have her. He must. He would.

He would have already, if not for this alliance. If not for the potential value and opportunity it offered, he could've had her husband cut down where he stood, taken Ygran then and there.

If not for the alliance… and a caution. Not apprehension, caution. His soldiers, he was certain, were more than a match for the silent hound-hooded warriors, but there was no sense in needlessly losing men. Until he knew them better, until he saw them fight, he was not about to risk it.

Not over a woman.

Ah, but what a woman!

How had Gyrloy of all people come by such a prize? How did he keep her? For all he called himself a king, he seemed oddly lacking of ambition, of passion and power. Witness their children! A true man should have sired strong sons upon Ygran, securing his name and legacy. Instead, soft-handed Gyrloy had managed only daughters, three of them, sickly, fey, and strange.

"I would get a son upon her so as to become legend," Utharius muttered, swirling wine-dregs in his bronze cup. He stretched his legs toward the nearest fire, braziers burning bright and hot within his spacious command tent. Outside, the night rain splashed and pattered, but in here was good comfort.

Comfort not lost on his advisor, who—with gratitude—baked the aches and chills from his old bones. At the war-commander's words, he glanced over, this bedraggled wandering wizard who'd shown up out of nowhere and offered to be their guide. He knew the country, he said. He knew the woods and moors and highlands, and more dangerous places. He spoke many languages, and practiced weirding ways, and, thus far, his counsels had been wise and sound.

"My pardon, lord of dragons?" Myrwyn inquired.

"Hmm?"

"You are troubled?"

"Merely musing aloud. What could trouble me?" Utharius swung an arm, encompassing the tent's interior. It was finely-appointed, furnished with couches and hangings and map-tables, a desk where his slave-scribe composed reports to send by courier, chests laden with tribute and treasure, a bathing area, a traveling household shrine. Dishes of food and urns of drink covered the low central table, hardly a lavish feast but far better fare than the local diet of boiled roots and barley.

"Perhaps matters of the heart?" Myrwyn suggested, a sly twinkle in his eye as he helped himself to a choice piece of tender pork loin cooked in oil.

"The heart?" Utharius chuckled. "It is not my *heart* foremost so speaking. But, what more can you tell me of this ally of ours? This King Gyrloy and his folk?"

Myrwyn shrugged. "They have lived here long and long, in the shadows of Tintagel. Some say it was built by spirits, or by giants, in times before time began, the great walls hewn from slabs of stone and set at angles—"

"What of the warriors with the black cloaks, and the hound's-head hoods?"

"They are guardians." He shrugged again. "They keep their secrets well."

"And they let no one enter the fortification?"

"No outsiders, lord, no."

"Not even honored guests and allies?"

"I have never heard of it so done."

"Yet, he sends his queen there."

Sagely, Myrwyn nodded. "For her safety, I believe, lord."

"From...?" Utharius prompted.

"Well, lord, it may be to protect her when your allied armies march together to conquer the surrounding wild tribes..." He let his words trail off, the twinkle still in his eye.

An eloquent gesture of his sword hand, perhaps surprisingly eloquent given the scarred and callused nature of said appendage, invited more. Myrwyn grinned.

"Or, were I to speak plainly, it may be because King Gyrloy was not blind to the way you looked at her."

"I far prefer it when you speak plainly."

"Queen Ygran is indeed a striking creature. Do you know, I have heard it prophesied—it's said one of her daughters has the Sight—that her son will be a mighty king, favored and gifted by the gods, to rule this land in its entirety and become immortal?"

Utharius paused with the nearly-empty vessel at his lips. "I thought Gyrloy had no sons."

"He does not, lord, no, not yet. Only the girls. But, is it any wonder he holds his wife with such possessiveness?"

"Has she ever given him cause to doubt her fidelity?"

Myrwyn shook his head. "She is devoted to him. They are loath to be apart. I'm sure it will pain and try her greatly when he goes off on war-campaign."

"A good woman. A good wife."

"Of that, lord of dragons, there can be no doubt."

"And future mother of mighty kings."

"Ah, well, but, you know, prophecies," said Myrwyn, with a scoffing laugh. "Uttered by a girl-child, no less."

"True enough, true enough." He held out his bronze cup and a slave rushed to refill it.

An idle wave dismissed the conversation, the wizard needing no further urging to return his attention to the fire and the food-laden table. Outside, the rain fell, and the men stood their watches or sheltered in their tents.

Utharius settled back upon his couch, sipping wine, and thinking.

***

Their *contubernium* went two-by-two, the path barely wide enough to keep jutting twigs like bony fingers from scratching at the edges of their shields. The crests had been removed from their helms to prevent entangling in the lower-hanging boughs. They held their spears low, angled forward, rather than straight and tall.

Nor was their procession a neat and proper march. The ground would not allow it. Each step was its own struggle with squelching mud and spongy soil, with loam and slippery moss, with thickly twisting hidden roots.

Honored though he was to have had his *contubernium* selected to accompany this scouting mission, Tiberius would have rather stayed at the encampment. It wasn't out of laziness. It wasn't cowardice; he had seen his share of battles, he fought stalwart and bravely, he was a soldier of Rome.

It was this furtive creeping, this dark and dripping forest encroaching from all sides. Should some threat come at them, they had scant room to maneuver. Even in full daylight, the shadowed gloom seemed more like dusk. The very air felt thick as cold oil within his lungs.

The scent… dank and green and earthy, with undertones of rot and decay. The sounds… creaking tree limbs, rustlings and scufflings, the slog and squish of their slow tread.

He did not like this place. Would not have liked it had it not been known hostile territory. Death, in the form of hairy, painted savages, might spring upon them at any moment. Several of the most brutish tribes called these dense woods their home, and were hated enemies of King Gyrloy and his folk.

"They make worship to great old gods," Ylan had told them. The girl, not yet to the cusp of womanhood, was one of Gyrloy's daughters. Like the wandering wizard Myrwyn, she had learned many languages, enough to serve as translator. "Great old gods with heads of snakes," she'd elaborated, lifting her hands beside her braided temples and weirdly wiggling her fingers.

When she did this, it drew from the king's silent hound-hooded warriors the first real reaction Tiberius had thus far seen—they tensed and seemed to cast disapproving glowers at the girl.

Her father, however, had merely nodded, unperturbed. As he ever appeared to be; the gloomy woods caused him no discomfort, the eerie behavior of his own elite guards gave him no pause, the visible apprehension of his other men—ordinary villagers, not soldiers; craftsmen and farmer's sons, just as Tiberius once had been himself—was, to Gyrloy, of no evident concern.

What manner of man would bring his daughter on an expedition such as this? Tiberius wondered. A scouting mission into deadly country, peopled by fearful foes? Yes, as a translator, Ylan proved useful, but…

Then again, what manner of king would come on such an expedition as this himself?

An odd man. An odd king.

Gyrloy had four of the hound-hooded warriors, a dozen men, and some servants. Hardly a royal entourage. Plus, of course, the *contubernium* from Utharius's command, eight soldiers and two *auxilii* to tend the gear and mule—though the mule had, in this instance, been left behind.

Under normal circumstances, their *contubernium* could have easily overpowered Gyrloy and his dozen. But they were under no such orders of treachery, and for that Tiberius was glad. For these circumstances were *not* normal, were indeed far from it. This place… and there were more than the village men to consider, weren't there?

Although his fellow Romans hadn't discussed it, he doubted he was alone in his unease as regarded the hound-hooded warriors.

Did they speak? Did they *sleep?* Did they eat and drink and void their bladders as did any other men? *Were* they, in fact, men?

Their steps never faltered or fumbled on the uneven ground. *Their* cloaks never caught upon poking branches. Only the smoky, bluish plumes of breath issuing through their hoods' snarling muzzle-jaws lent indication they were alive at all.

Should, for whatever reason, a confrontation come… a *contubernium* of the Legion, armed and armored and prepared, by numbers and training alone, by any rights… against only four…

Tiberius thrust the thought from his mind, maintaining his gladness they were under no such orders. Let Utharius lust after Gyrloy's queen all he liked—few among them had missed the hunger in their war-commander's gaze—but at least he had not dispatched them with treacherous instruction. The alliance was too important. No one woman, however lovely, was worth the risk.

***

"You are certain this will work?"

"But of course, lord of dragons."

"If it doesn't…"

"Yes, yes, if it doesn't, you can kill me."

"If it doesn't," Utharius repeated, *"I'll* be dead. Rest assured, however, wizard, my men will kill you for me."

"Fair enough, I suppose." Myrwyn brought him a brimming, steaming bowl from which arose vile wisps of vapor. The stench of it was horrendous, the taste would no doubt prove to be even more so.

They were alone in the command tent, Utharius stripped naked and standing amid lines of salt and sand and ashes, connecting oddly-colored crystals in a mind-twisting design.

It would be worth it. *She* would be worth it.

With a resolute sigh, he braced himself and swilled down the noxious potion in a series of convulsive gulps. A searing like molten iron flooded his gullet. His innards roiled and boiled, churned and clenched. The urge to vomit heaved his gorge, but by then it was too late. Pain seized him, seized every part of his body as if in vicious eagle's claws. He did not know if he was screaming. He did not know if he voided himself, or wailed, or wept.

When the wrenching, wracking agonies subsided, he lay curled and quaking on the floor. The design around him remained somehow undisturbed, though he must have flailed and thrashed in terrible paroxysms. Running with sweat, gasping for breath, he sat up.

The hands he held before him were not scarred and callused. Not a soldier's hands, meant for spear and shield and gladius. They were softer, and plumper, the skin pinkish, the nails unkempt. He brought them to his face, which itched and bristled, and as he touched it he learned why—a full brush of fleecy beard sprouted from the cheeks and chin. Instead of hair neatly cropped in the proper Roman style, a loose mane fell disheveled to his shoulders.

Utharius slowly rose on unfamiliar limbs. He moved, and stretched, gaining an acquaintance. He turned to Myrwyn, who had retrieved the empty potion-bowl.

"Well?" The old man grinned his sly, eye-twinkle grin. "Do you feel... kingly?"

"Yes," said Utharius in a voice that was not his own. "As it happens, wizard, yes, indeed, I do."

***

Having traveled a full day with no sign of the enemy, they found a clearing where a spring gurgled from a split stone and many deadfalls provided ample firewood, and there they set their camp. Tiberius and his fellows went about it with practiced military precision, while Gyrloy's men made bedrolls of blankets and goatskins. The servants constructed a quick shelter, hung with hides, for Gyrloy and his daughter.

The hound-hooded warriors, without a word exchanged, took up

sentinel positions. A Roman soldier joined each of them, at a re-
spectful distance, planning to trade watches throughout the night.
Tiberius and those whose watch was set for later went to the fire
where the *auxilii* had begun chopping salted fish and vegetables
into a stew to be eaten with their rations of bread.

After the meal, they sat on lengths of log and flattish stones.
Skins of drink were passed around. Desultory talk made, but the
prevailing mood was somber and wary. There was little joking, and
less laughter. No gambling. No singing. It was as if a great oppressive weight had fallen heavy over them all.

Tiberius held his gladius across his knees, cleaning and oiling the
blade, until he became aware quite keenly of the sensation of being
watched. Looking around, his grip shifting on the weapon, he saw
it was only Ylan, studying them curiously from a few paces away.

Their eyes met briefly before he averted his gaze, yet to her it
must have been invitation enough. She approached, and settled
onto the log beside him.

"What is your name, soldier of Rome?" she asked.

He glanced at Gaius Vorro, their *Decanus*. The last he needed
was to somehow offend their allied king, but whether speaking
to the girl or ignoring her was the worse offense, he didn't know.
Vorro gave a nod, but signaled caution, not that Tiberius needed
the warning.

"Tiberius," he replied. "Tiberius Tempus."

Leaning conspiratorially closer, the girl dropped her voice to a
whisper. *"They* do not like you, Tiberius Tempus."

The dip of her chin indicated the nearest of the hound-hooded
warriors, standing sentinel. Though the cloaked back was to him,
the guard's attention on the surrounding woods, a shiver ran the
length of Tiberius's spine. He wished no special notice from them,
good or bad, and found this news unsettling. Another glance to
Vorro showed the *Decanus* shared his sentiment.

He resisted the urge to grasp the gladius by its hilt. "What *are*
they?" Tiberius quickly corrected. *"Who* are they, I mean?"

"The Hounds," she said, as if it were a foolish question.

"And they serve your father?"

A strange expression crossed her face. "They serve their purpose, as he does his."

Tiberius frowned. He opened his mouth to ask another foolish question—why they should dislike *him* in particular—but it went unvoiced, because just then the silent hound-hooded warriors threw back their heads and howled, silent no longer.

***

The weird walls loomed above him, their angles slicing sharp wedges from the clouded night sky. Here and there, in narrow windows, unseen sources cast eerie blue-tinged glows. No sounds of normal activity came from beyond its gate.

A damp chill hung in the air. Utharius bundled the stolen cloak more closely around his stolen form. Myrwyn had by some trickery fetched the cloak, as well as other clothes, from the king's long low-roofed hall within the village. The garments were not, therefore, ill-fitting… yet, to Utharius, they felt awkward and strange.

Then again, so did this body.

Ahead of him, at the gate, Tintagel's sentinels watched him from deep within their hound-headed hoods. He almost faltered, then drew a breath and continued forward.

"I have come to see Ygran," he announced, in a voice as stolen as everything else he wore.

They regarded him for the span of several heartbeats, long enough for Utharius to swallow a qualm of fear. Had the second of Myrwyn's potions not worked?

"Drink this one down as well," the wizard had said. "It will let you speak and understand the local tongue. Would hardly do to have the king turn up with a translator at his elbow, would it?"

"If you could do this all along—"

"Ah, but then you wouldn't have as much need of me, oh lord of dragons. Even an old man has his livelihood to think of."

And so he had drunk it down.

Several more heartbeats passed—his heart, perhaps, beating at a faster pace for a variety of reasons—before the hound-hooded warriors slid deferentially aside. The gate opened. Utharius strode into the many-angled courtyard of Tintagel.

***

They howled, the Hounds, and as they did, the soldiers on watch also shouted sudden warning. Attack! Ambush! Surrounded! Sling-hurled stones and crude-made spears whistled through the gloom. Other voices cried out, bestial war-cries from all sides.

Two of Gyrloy's men dropped instantly, one with a spear-point through his throat, the other stone-struck to the temple. The rest rushed about in mad confusion.

Not so the soldiers of Rome. "Shields!" the *Decanus* bellowed. Shields, yes, and together as one came the *contubernium*, falling into tight formation, the best the camp-cluttered clearing would allow, but enough to deflect a second volley of stones and spears.

Nor had the Hounds given in to the confusion; they threw back their cloaks and drew strange hook-bladed weapons shining eldritch-blue. A glowing, smoky mist seethed from the eyes and muzzle-jaws of their hoods... which seemed, Tiberius saw with a thrill of horror, to no longer be hoods after all.

He could not pause to consider this; the dark woods disgorged a horde of their attackers. The firelight revealed them, brutish and naked, bodies daubed with painted clay in wavy, scale-like, serpentine patterns. Some wore headdresses of snakeskins knotted into tangles, lashing and flying about as if living snakes sprouted from their heads. Tiberius remembered what Ylan had said about their god, but could not pause to consider that, either.

They came screaming, bearing clubs and frenzied fury, and the battle was joined. The Roman phalanx held strong, Vorro calling orders, spears thrusting between overlapped shields. Flesh ripped, and blood spilled in hot, gory floods. For Tiberius, the world narrowed to the press of his fellow soldiers at his back and side, the slam and thud of impact as foes battered against them, glimpses of savage faces twisting in rage or in pain.

And, the Hounds...

Somehow, through it all, through the chaos of death, he saw the Hounds. How they moved. How they shifted. How they vanished one instant and reappeared elsewhere the next, cloaks flaring in dark whirlwinds of death. Their hooked blades slashed like silver-blue fire, opening throats and bellies, severing limbs, there for the moment to strike and to kill, then gone again.

***

News of his arrival had somehow preceded him; before he'd crossed more than halfway to the doors, they opened in a spill of misty bluish firelight. The figure this light outlined was tall and proud and shapely, and rushed toward him with a delighted cry.

Then she was in his arms, the wonderful curvaceousness of her, the press of high breasts against his chest and rounded hips to his loins. He held her tightly as he claimed her plum-sweet lips in a ravenous kiss. When she broke from it, she was gasping, her eyes shining like stars.

"Husband!" she exclaimed. "What *is* this impassioned greeting? I thought you away for many more days!"

"Can a man not miss his wife?" Utharius caressed her cheek, and trailed his fingers down the whiteness of her throat. "Can he not need her so, crave her so, as to find being gone from her unbearable, no matter the distance?"

"You came back all this way for me?"

"And would again, a thousand times!" He went for another kiss, feeling her eager response. "Now, wife, let us to your bedchamber. I must depart by dawn and do not plan to waste a single moment."

***

If their progress through the dense and dripping woods had been slow before, it would be all the slower now, burdened as they were.

With the wounded.

And the dead.

Those of Gyrloy's folk who'd been slain in the battle were, of necessity, left behind. Stony cairns covered their bodies, in the clearing that had gone from camp to slaughter-ground.

The enemy could rot, unburied, where they fell, unless more of their brutish, filthy tribes slunk back later to retrieve them. Trophies, however, were taken. A weapon here, a knotted snakeskin headdress there, severed hands and genitals, scraps of painted skin.

Although some sustained minor injuries, no Roman lives had been lost. The Hounds, of course, were entirely unscathed. Nor did they appear in the least wearied. Slung between the four of them was a makeshift litter, the laden weight of which they bore with ease.

Upon that litter, cloak-covered, lay the corpse of the king.

***

In the pre-dawn, Utharius rose from the bed without waking Ygran. She slept the sleep of well-earned exhaustion, a sleep he could have done with more of himself—Venus and Juno, what a woman!—but he knew Myrwyn's transformative potion would not last much longer.

He dressed, much more aware than before of the chamber's peculiar aspects, the angles of its walls, the multitude of its deep-shadowed corners. The night before, his mind had been on other matters. Now, with lust sated and clarity of thought returned, he marveled at the ancient strangeness of the place. Who had built it? When? And why?

After gazing once more at the beautiful Ygran, he stepped out and quietly eased shut the door. The labyrinthine halls of Tintagel stood silent around him, but he set out with confidence to retrace his steps.

He'd nearly reached the courtyard when—

—when he sensed eyes upon him. He was being watched.

***

"If any failed him," Vorro said to Tiberius, aside, in confidence, "it was his own men, untrained and undisciplined as they were. He should have brought more of the Hounds. *They*, now, they can *fight!*"

"Did you *see* them?"

"Did I see them? Do you think me blind? I'd not mind learning a few of their tricks."

"But, the mist and the blue fire… their heads, their faces… the way they… changed…" Tiberius trailed off then, finding only bafflement in the eyes of his *Decanus*.

"I thought you were unhurt. Some goat-sucking Briton bounce a stone off your skull after all?" Beneath Vorro's jesting tone was genuine concern.

Tiberius managed a wan chuckle. "It must have been the shadows. I am fine and well."

"Good. See that you stay that way. And look after the girl. However calm she seems, she has just lost her father."

***

Utharius stopped mid-stride, turning. He beheld a child, a slight and scrawny thing, barefoot and bare-legged in a simple tunic, but with jeweled pins in her hair. One of Gyrloy's daughters, not that he'd bothered to learn which was which, not that he remembered any of their names in the first place.

An uncomfortable smile creased his bearded, stolen visage. What to do? What to say? Address her by some sort of endearment?

She was looking at him, her eyes dark and steady. No, more than looking. Scrutinizing. Evaluating.

A dusky hound, disheveled and lanky, sat at her side, her hand resting atop its ungainly long-muzzled head. It, too, regarded him with a dark and steady scrutiny.

What had the old wizard said? Something about one of the girls being rumored to have the Sight? Was she, even now, seeing through the potion's magic? Would she tell?

If he struck quick, if he snapped her thin neck and smuggled the small body out beneath the stolen cloak—

The hound beside her snarled as if he'd uttered his thoughts aloud, as if it had understood them.

The girl-child merely went on looking at him, petting the hound between its tufted ears. "Mother is still sleeping," she said.

He hesitated. "Yes. Yes, she is."

"And have you made for us this night a brother? Have you made our future king?"

***

"You saw them, Tiberius Tempus. You saw them as they truly are."

It was the first Ylan had spoken in some time, otherwise walking quietly beside him as the tireless Hounds strode on ahead.

"Is that why they dislike me?" he asked, keeping his voice to a murmur.

"They know. They fear you'll interfere."

"Interfere with what?"

"What was, what is, what will yet be. What is meant to be."

A memory recurred to him, a memory from the thickest furor of the battle… King Gyrloy, beset by savage Britons, their crude spears stabbing… barely making even token effort to defend himself… indifferent and diffident as ever, as the sharp points plunged into his flesh…

Their phalanx had been by then broken, the soldiers engaged in furious melee. Tiberius rushed toward Gyrloy, meaning to take up the defense, but…

But then, out of nowhere, in a dark whirlwind of bluish smoke, a Hound. His mind refused to recall in full detail that inhuman visage, snarling so close into his face he felt and smelt its cold breath.

"They could have saved him," he said now. "Instead, they let him die."

"He had served his purpose," Ylan said. "As do they, as do I, as do my mother and my sisters, as do we all."

***

Some months later, in the village below Tintagel, bright bonfires burned. Folk sang and danced and feasted, Roman and Briton alike, in celebration.

How noble, the war-commander! To marry his ally's widowed queen, and swear to raise her unborn babe as if it were his own!

At the high table, swirling his bronze wine-cup in his hand, Utharius Draconis made no effort to hide his smug self-satisfaction as he watched his belly-rounded bride moving through the crowd of well-wishers.

The wait had been interminable, what with funeral and mourning, and obtaining permission by courier from Rome. Yet, tonight, he would have her again, his beautiful Ygran. Have her as himself.

All had gone far better than even he had planned!

***

Meanwhile, in Tintagel's hidden innermost heart, blue-tinged firelight shed a misty glow, and deep shadows moved in the strange corners of sharply-angled walls.

"It is done," intoned the girl-child, her dark eyes mirroring the shifting flames.

Around her, the Hounds ceased their restless pacing. They sat alert, tufted ears pricked, cold breath smoking. The largest settled into a relaxed posture, resting the chin of its long muzzle upon the child's knee.

"What of the Romans?" asked Ylan, their eldest sister.

"Some will stay, some will go. Their empire's reach exceeds its grasp. Already, it rots with poisons from within."

"And Tiberius? What of him?"

At the mention of the name, the lead Hound's eyes narrowed, and a disdainful puff snorted from slitted nostrils.

Myrgn's little mouth twisted as if tasting something bitter. "You know I cannot see his fate. What becomes of him is his own doing, so long as he does not interfere."

"But if he *does?*"

"You do not need *my* answer to that. Does she, Myrgos?"

The lead Hound chuffed and bared a maw of spine-sharp teeth. The sinuous dark length of a hollow tongue curled through them.

"And what of me?" inquired another voice, as Myrwyn stepped into the chamber. He'd abandoned his guise of ragged wandering wizard... indeed, he'd abandoned his guise of mortal man altogether.

"You played your part very well, Grandfather," Ylan said. "You and Mother both."

Or perhaps the guise was not entirely abandoned; a familiar sly twinkle shone in his eye. "The war-commander still believes it was his own cleverness and deception."

"And, soon," said Myrgn, patting their other sister on the head, "soon we will have our brother-king again."

"Once and future," Myrwyn said.

Ylan sighed and bowed her head. "Once and future, and eternal."

MAN OF THE HOUSE

"You're old enough, now," Meg said. "He'll be visiting you soon."

Thomasina looked up from her book. "Pardon? Who will?"

"Father."

"Visiting me?" She frowned. "We live in the same house."

Meg shook her head. "Visiting you... in your room... late at night."

For a moment, the only sound in the parlor was a clock's sedate ticking. Sunbeams slanted lazily through sheer window-curtains. Fresh-cut flowers, arranged in dainty vases, shed a sweet scent to counter the smoke from Meg's cigarettes. She stubbed one out in a full ashtray, promptly lighting up another.

"What a horrible joke," Thomasina finally said. "Whatever you're playing at, I don't find it at all funny."

"I'm not joking, you ninny. I'm warning you. Which is at least more than the others ever did for me." Meg drew a deep drag and exhaled a forceful, grey plume.

She'd been standing by the mantel but turned to face Thomasina, and it struck Thomasina how thin her sister was. Thinner even than was the current boyish-slim fashion, maintained by a diet of vitamins, celery, jazz, and bootleg gin. The sleek bob of Meg's auburn hair curved around cheekbones sharper than protractor angles. Her chin was a point, her collarbones prominent ridges. Her stylish sheath-dress might as well have been hung on a rack.

Nothing in her tone or expression suggested mischief. But, what she was saying... Thomasina must have misheard.

"Sorry, *what?*" she asked. "You can't be serious."

"Can't I?" A harsh laugh became a cough. "You mean, you've never noticed? I knew you were flighty, Toms, but I didn't think you were stupid."

"I'm not!"

Flighty, yes, all right, perhaps; Meg did have her there. She enjoyed fanciful fiction and stories, reading voraciously and occasionally trying her hand at writing her own, with a dream of someday being published in *Weird Tales* or another such magazine; at fourteen, she still wasn't *so* far gone from the days she'd held tea parties with her dollies or pretended fairies dwelt by the willow-pond below Aunt Clara's cherished garden. Flighty, fine. Stupid, however? A most unfair charge!

"Then open your eyes," Meg said. "Look at us. Look at our family. Is this normal to you? All of us living under one roof, under his thumb and sway? Not allowed to get married? Not allowed to have jobs, or travel, or have our own lives at all? What about Anna? What about Sarah; do you really believe that was an accident? Or Gertrude?"

"I... what are you saying?"

She scoffed roughly. "It's him, Toms. It's always been him. Long before Mother so conveniently died. Ask our aunts. Consider Lilah, and tell me she's *only* our cousin. Or, maybe you're too young to remember when Mina was born, but what about Eliza and little Kate?"

"Stop it!" Thomasina was on her feet without realizing she'd intended to move, book falling from her lap to the rose-patterned parlor rug. "Listen to yourself, Meg! Have you been drinking?"

"I wish! And I will be, soon enough. You might, too. You could start now."

"Why are you doing this?"

"I told you, you ninny, I'm trying to warn you! It's worse when it comes as a shock."

"That Father... our own *father*..." Bewildered, Thomasina passed a hand across her brow. "He couldn't... he wouldn't... it's just... are you insane? How can you make such ugly accusations?"

"Insane? No, that's Anna, in the asylum, remember? As for ugliness, you'll see for yourself. Remember, though. I warned you. I at least did that much."

Not merely stubbing out her cigarette this time, but grinding it into a broken corkscrew of ash, Meg barked one more harsh laugh and stalked from the parlor. Her low heels clacked as she crossed from rug to polished parquet. The door whisked shut behind her without a fittingly dramatic slam, but the effect was sufficient.

Thomasina stared after her, mind reeling. She'd simply been sitting there, sitting and reading, bothering no one, and then...

What in the world had possessed Meg? They weren't particularly close—a span of almost ten years separated their ages—but there'd never been particular enmity either! To say such things! About their *father*, wealthy and respected Eustace Abraham! About their aunts, and cousin, and sisters! Referring to their mother's tragic, untimely death as *convenient*?

She had to sit down again.

The clock on the mantelpiece ticked and ticked.

***

Around her, Hastenford House carried on its daily routine. It was not a castle, though might as well have been, certainly the closest to a castle in this part of the midwest, modeled after sprawling English country estates. Eustace Abraham owned land, quite a lot of it, purchased at a bargain during the expansion following the war... the War Between the States, that was, not the recent and terrible Great War overseas.

Land, and investments. Business. Factories. Railroads. Power.

Politics. She'd heard terms such as 'baron' and 'tycoon' tossed around in reference to her father and his associates, and they liked it. The old men, the rich men, who'd gather in the wood-paneled study for whiskey and cigars before descending to the cellar for their meetings. Who'd talk greedily about progress and opportunity even as they decried these changing modern times. Rights for workers, and colored folk... unions... women wanting the vote, wanting jobs and careers.

"Doesn't it worry you, Eustace, living with a houseful of women?" such a crony had once asked. "Got you outnumbered, my friend. Out*voted,* if you like."

"Outvoted, bah!" came the snorting reply. "Think on it. A single man has but *one* vote. A married man, two, so long as he's not henpecked like some I could name, eh Reginald?—" Here, there'd been a general mocking laugh, and a sputter of indignation from the butt of the joke. "While *my* vote now counts at least as *ten!* More, if you include the servants, so long as they know what's good for them."

With his considerable fortune and connections, including those obtained by having married wealthy heiress Charlotte Hastenford, Eustace Abraham had built up quite an empire. A proper dynasty in the making, except for having no sons to carry on the family name.

No sons, but many daughters to provide for. And spinster sisters, one of whom had a daughter of her own following a hush-hush youthful 'incident.'

Meg's words haunted Thomasina again... *Consider Lilah, and tell me she's* only *our cousin...*

She couldn't possibly have meant...

And Mina? What did poor simple-minded Mina have to do with anything? Or Eliza and little Kate, as if Toms were missing something obvious? Eliza had been sick the year Kate was born, staying mostly shuttered away in her room for months, but...

"No," she murmured into the quiet clock-ticking parlor. "No, now you truly *are* being a ninny. The very idea!"

Like something out of a torrid novel or sordid magazine! Meg and her nasty talk! Meg, who *did* drink too much, as much as Aunt Lucy if not more, despite her denials. Mean Meg, causing trouble, no doubt bitter because Father wouldn't let her move to Chicago, bitter and spreading poison within his very house!

As for Anna… and Gertrude… and Sarah…

Awful speculations ran around in her head, sending shudders of revulsion twisting through her entire body,

Whatever cruel mischief Meg was up to, it just would not do!

Thomasina sprang up again. She was no tattler, was not about to run to her aunts with such wild venom and spite, but she had to talk to someone. Alice might be the eldest, but Alice had lately gotten into spiritualism and the occult, attending seances, trying to reach people on the Other Side. Mary, though, Mary was capable and level-headed. Mary helped manage the household accounts, supervised the staff, and sometimes served as Father's secretary. Mary also had no patience for frivolous nonsense, and would set Meg to rights!

She hurried through the halls, and it occurred to her how empty Hastenford often seemed, especially for a house where so many people lived. According to the romances and farcical comedies she liked to read, a place such as this should be downright teeming with social activity. Dinners, and dances! Garden parties! Hopeful suitors and eligible ladies engaging in lively flirtations! Yet, there hadn't been an occasion in… well… forever.

The staff consisted of a housekeeper, a groundskeeper, two maids, a cook, and a driver, all of whom kept largely to themselves and their own attic rooms when not occupied by their duties. A tutor came in twice a week for the younger girls, though most of their schooling was seen to by their aunts and elder sisters.

The house rarely saw guests, not counting when Eustace Abraham hosted his cronies for their monthly gathering, some fraternal-order secret-society sort of thing. Which was hardly the same, those stout well-to-do gentlemen with their robes and their rings and their hoods and their chanting. Hardly the same at all!

Meg's words, again... *you've never noticed?... open your eyes... is this normal to you?*

From the music room came desultory piano-plinking, Eliza giving Caroline her afternoon lesson while little Kate sat on the floor with a puzzle-board. Thomasina paused, looking from Eliza to Kate with growing disquiet.

Her sisters... her many sisters.

Of course the Abraham girls all resembled one another to varying degrees; they were sisters, weren't they? She'd just never really seen before how very *much* Kate took after Eliza. Almost a perfect copy in miniature, down to identical moles by the same corner of the mouth.

Cousin Lilah, though... hadn't it been said she and Alice looked so alike as girls that they used to swap clothes and pull pranks on their teachers?

Or Mina... what *was* it about Mina? There'd always been some odd, unspoken tension around her, as if her simplemindedness were more a source of shame than cause of pity.

And Gertrude... who'd reportedly died of a sudden stomach ailment... but Thomasina recalled vague memories of blood, so much blood, and Aunt Lucy slapping a sick-faced maid and telling her to speak of this never, *never,* not if she valued her position here and her life...

Her hurried pace had increased almost to a flat-out run toward the octagonal tower at the house's northeast corner, which featured a two-storey glass-walled conservatory at the bottom—where Aunt Clara grew her exotics, oddities, and rare specimens—and a balcony-ringed turret at the very top, with its seven stained-glass oculi peering in different directions.

Not that anyone went up there, not anymore. Not since Sarah. It was a long drop from that balcony to the driveway below. A long drop, and a hard landing.

On the third floor, though, was the many-windowed room Mary used as an office. Thomasina bolted up the stairs and burst through the door with such abruptness that Mary, behind the desk, jerked in her seat. Her pen skidded a black slash across a page.

"Good God, Thomasina!" Mary clapped a palm to the base of her throat. "Is there a fire?"

Winded, Thomasina flapped her hands and shook her head and tried to catch her breath.

Unlike stylish Meg, Mary dressed primly, almost dowdily. She kept her coppery hair pinned up in a severe bun and eschewed both cosmetics and jewelry. Her fingers were ink-stained, her nails sensibly short. A typewriter and an adding-machine took up half the desk. Tinny-sounding opera spilled from the wireless. A telephone held place-of-pride on its own smaller table. Everything was papers and ledgers, invoices, correspondence, receipts.

"Sorry," gasped Thomasina. "Sorry, I... sorry."

Mary tutted, inspecting the black-slashed page. "What's got you tearing around like a maniac? Hardly ladylike or proper."

"Well... it was something Meg said..."

"Meg. Of course." She pinched the bridge of her nose. "It would be, wouldn't it? Politics again? Chicago? Unfair treatment of the servants?"

"No, it, uhm, it was about Father."

At that, Mary's gaze fixed sharply upon Thomasina's. "What about Father?"

"He... she said he might... visit me, in my room—"

"She what?!" Paper crumpled, clenched in Mary's fist. "Oh, thank you, Meg, thank you ever so much, ever so helpful, damnable mouthy meddlesome bitch!"

Whatever else Thomasina might have said went scattered, dashed by shock. She stood there gaping, dumbstruck, but Mary was far from finished.

"I suppose we should have expected it. She always did harbor a grudge. Blamed us for Sarah, too, don't you know? As if it would've made a bit of difference! What, she might have jumped sooner? Before instead of after? Sarah was weak either way, weak like Anna, and—"

Then Mary stopped herself, letting fall the crumpled paper, and with a visible effort regained her composure.

"I... I'll just go..." Thomasina slid a backward step toward the door.

"No, you will sit yourself down," Mary said. "The cat's out the bag. She shouldn't have interfered, but since when has that mattered to Meg? Sit *down*, Toms, I said!"

She pointed at a clerk's stool, and Thomasina dropped onto it as if the tendons of her legs had been cut. Her head was a clamor of confusion and protest, desperately seeking some explanation— were they in on it together, this horrid spiteful unfunny joke?

Mary shut the office door, locking it with a click.

"All right." She returned to her seat behind the desk and steepled her fingers. "What's done is done. Rest assured, I'll deal with Meg later—meddlesome bitch! For now, though, Thomasina, how am I to deal with you?"

"Deal with me?" Her voice was a meek mouse-squeak.

"Well, are you going to be a problem?"

"A... wait... Mary... you can't mean any of it's *true.*"

"What else would I mean?"

"But... *Father?* To my *room?* Late at night? For... not for... surely not for—"

"It'll probably be just the once," Mary said. "He's getting on in years and not as keen as he used to be. You've that much going for you, anyway; count yourself lucky."

"He's... you've... with the rest of you?"

"What of it? It's his due. We owe him. We'd be nothing without him, Toms. Nothing. He built our fortune, he maintains this house, he keeps us in livelihood. He asks only gratitude and obedience in return."

"Gratitude and... Mary, Mary, this is ghastly! We're his family, not his... property!"

"It doesn't matter. How far do you think any of us would get on our own? Penniless, destitute?"

"The world isn't like that now!" Thomasina said. "Since the War, and the workforces, and the vote—"

"You *are* as bad as Meg, aren't you? Workforces and voting, rights, independence... as if those don't come at their own costs! We have a good life here. We have money, and comfort. I won't let you, or Meg, or anyone else, ruin that for us."

"But you can't really mean—Mary, I don't want to! Can't I just not?"

"None of us wanted to; why should *you* be so special?"

Thomasina burst into baffled, frightened tears. "It's not right! It's not fair! I don't understand!"

"This is *why* we don't tell," Mary said, once again addressing the room as if Meg were there. "It's easier that way, easier for everyone. Get it over with, let it happen, take care of the rest later. Instead, now we have *this* mess. I hope you're happy."

***

Pleading a headache, Thomasina skipped dinner that evening. It was no pretend ruse; her head *did* ache. Her stomach felt sick. Her appetite had fled.

The prospect of the dining room with its long table—pristine white linen, formal place settings, crystal stemware—filled her with hollow dread. She could not imagine enduring the light chit-chat, minding her etiquette, carrying on as if everything were still the same.

How was she to sit there, surrounded by her family? Knowing what she did? How could she face them, look them in the eye? Her aunts, her sisters, Cousin Lilah? Her *father?*

How could she *ever* be near him again?

Not that theirs was a relationship exceptionally close; he'd always been the distant and aloof sort of patriarch. But she'd never feared him before, never outright *loathed* him the way she did now.

The rest of her conversation with Mary had been no less horrific, no less revelatory and revolting. In legal matters and financial, he held utter control. Absolute, utter control. He paid for their up-keep, their education… even their clothes weren't their own.

"Couldn't we leave?"

"And go where? With what money?"

"We could tell someone, then! The police—"

"Indeed, and why not go to the papers while we're at it?" Mary had suggested with frosty sarcasm. "I'm sure such shame and scandal would quickly blow over. Our reputations wouldn't be tarnished, our names not dragged through the mud."

Nor, Mary had gone on, did they need worry about Mother, or Gertrude, or Sarah. Could hardly hurt them, could it, being already dead? Caroline and little Kate were too young to understand. As for Anna, in the asylum… and poor simple-minded Mina—

"All right!" Thomasina had cried. "I take your meaning, Mary, really I do!"

"Do you? Father would end up in prison, lawyers and court fees would bankrupt us, his businesses would fail, all of this would be sold—"

"I do!" she'd repeated, nearly wailing the words.

She did. He had them. Absolute, utter control. Gratitude and obedience… or else. They couldn't afford, in any sense of the term, defiance or refusal.

Mary only presented the stark, cold reality.

And so, Toms pleaded a headache, and hid herself away in her room until those familiar surroundings began to seem unbearable. She'd always felt safe here, even when the walls thrummed low with the chanting of hooded men in the cellar, even when wafts of strange smoke unlike any cigar and music unlike anything from the wireless drifted up through the vents. This was her space, a room of her own without having to share. It was *hers,* private, inviolate, her own.

But it wasn't, though, was it?

It was Father's. Just as everything else was Father's. The land and house, the cars, the businesses, the money. All of it his.

Just as they were.

His to do with as he pleased.

She slipped from her room, listening for the discreet clinks and murmurs informing her the meal was well underway downstairs. The rest of the house remained quiet. Quiet, shaded, and somehow more secretive than ever.

The thought struck her to flee, to go, to simply run away.

To where? To do what?

Mary was right; there was no one she could tell, no one to help. The scandal would shatter all of them, ruin their futures. They might be split apart, the younger girls sent away, adopted out. Poor sweet simple Mina might be put in a home, or an asylum like Anna! They'd never see each other again!

No wonder he discouraged them from marrying. While it might have been a way, as in olden days, to increase the family wealth through alliances and legacies, he couldn't afford to let this news get out. Similarly for pursuing careers; he wouldn't want them to have access to freedom, and independence, and their own means.

How was it he could be such a monster? How was it, all this time, she'd never so much as suspected? Head too much in her fancies, nose too much in her books? Blind and oblivious?

She wandered the hallways, passing closed doors and trying not to wonder what had gone on behind them. Eventually, she came to the Lace Room, which had been one of her mother's favorite places. It was not locked, so Thomasina let herself in and switched on the lights.

Little-used since Charlotte Abraham-nee-Hastenford's death, the room was regularly cleaned but otherwise kept much as she'd left it. Lace curtains draped the windows, lace hangings graced the walls, lace antimacassars rested over chair-backs and couch-cushions. Lacy shades covered lamps. Atop lace doilies on small tables stood china vases and delicate porcelain figurines. The dusty potpourri scent of long-dried flowers hung in the still air.

A long antique sideboard, lined with a lace runner, stood against one wall. It held an array of framed photographs, moments of the past forever captured in time.

Thomasina went to them, trailing her fingers over the ornate carved swoops and swirls of her mother's bentwood rocker. Was that the ghost of old perfume she detected as well? She thought so. Perfume, and tea. Rosehip tea with honey.

She looked at the photos. Here were the grandparents she'd never known, stiffly posed and forbidding. Here were Alice and Mary in ruffles and bonnets, and a nanny-servant holding a baby that must've been Anna. Here was a six-year-old Eliza at the piano, so much like little Kate it truly was uncanny. Gertrude, in the garden, the grave far in her future. The entire family and staff gathered by a lavish Christmas tree.

Here, in a heavy silver frame, a wedding portrait taken on the front steps of Hastenford House… Mother, so very young, trying to smile despite grief-haunted eyes from the recent loss of her parents… and Father…

And Father, looking just as he always did, just as he always had. Thomasina could remember him no different. She could take this photograph—some three decades old—downstairs right now and compare them and find him essentially unchanged.

He'd been, what, fifty even then? A thickset man in a severe suit, stout of stature, ruddy of complexion, broad-faced and balding with bushy iron-grey muttonchops. No smile. No warmth. Eyes like small hard black stones. Abacus stones, cold and purely calculating. The only bright spots about him were the pin at his lapel and its matching ring, each seven cross-hatched angles around a polished gem. In the photograph, they looked pewter, but Toms knew them to be of a heavy, maroon-tinted gold. The gems were neither opaque nor clear but somehow murky and deep, like garnets partially dissolved in swamp water.

Fifty even then… at least eighty by now…

Mary's words this time, not Meg's: *He's getting on in years and not as keen as he used to be.*

It certainly didn't show. He seemed no different. Hale and hearty as ever. Unchanged.

Had she, in some hateful and evil corner of her mind, harbored the thought—the hope—that he was *too* old, that he might sicken or die?

Oh, wicked ungrateful child! What a wretched thing to think of!

To hope for!

To wish!

Yet, yes, she had.

If he did, if he died, not only would she be spared, and the younger girls yet after her, but they'd all of them be freed! They'd be better off!

Thomasina blinked back tears. How terrible she was, how terrible she must be, and the fact it was a useless, futile wish made it no less heinous.

He wasn't going to sicken, or die! Not any time soon.

Neither Mary's voice, nor Meg's, nor her own: *Unless…*

A whisper out of nowhere, a breath without breath, no more substantial than a forgotten sigh, but a roll of thunder or a cannon's blast couldn't have shaken her more.

She whirled, not sure who or what she expected to see behind her, and seeing only the otherwise-empty room, of course. Her mother's empty chair, long-dead flowers and porcelain figurines, and lace over everything, lace like layers of intricate spider's web.

Again, in sighing whisper, in breathless breath:

Unless…

***

Mary found him in the morning.

Of course it would be Mary. She was the one who always brought him his coffee and the paper, then sat at the escritoire at the foot of his bed to go over any daily business.

She did not shriek or wail or lose her head. She did not rouse the entire household.

But, oh, she was furious.

That much came clear the moment those she'd discreetly summoned stepped into her office above the conservatory. The youngest girls—Mina, Caroline, and little Kate—were not present, ensconced with the housekeeper and maids down in the kitchen. That left Alice, Meg, Eliza, Thomasina, Aunt Clara and Aunt Lucy, and Cousin Lilah.

And Mary herself. Furious Mary, face at once both livid and stricken with dismay.

Her office, cluttered as it was, lacked chairs and left scant room, so they perched on stools or stood or leaned wherever they could each find space. Meg and Aunt Lucy took spots by the window to blow their smoke outside. Toms, who suspected what was coming, lurked nearest the door.

Mary broke the news, and there followed no small uproar. The expected gasps and exclamations, the shock, the disbelief. No grief, though. No tears or bemoaning. Aunt Clara may have breathed a tremulous at-long-last sigh. Meg may have flashed a quick and savage grin.

Next came an overlapping flurry of speaking-at-once:

"Have you yet called anyone?"

"Not yet, I haven't."

"Not the doctor?"

"Or the police?"

"Was it his heart, do you think?"

"As if he had one."

"The *police?* What? *Why?*"

"About damn time, if you ask me."

"He's never been sick a day in his life!"

"Well, we have to call someone, don't we?"

"Why would we need the police?"

"Surely nobody's implying there was…"

"Good God!"

A sharp smack split the room as Mary slapped both hands palms-flat on her desktop. "Will all of you just *hush?*"

They did, shifting, exchanging uneasy glances.

"I think," Mary then went on, glaring icy daggers from one to the next, "none of you realize how much trouble we are in."

"Trouble?" echoed Cousin Lilah, arm around her mother. "I'll say it if no one else will… *what* trouble? We're *free!* Finally free!"

"It's not like he was murdered or something," Eliza said.

A long moment passed.

"Well, *this* is an awkward silence," Meg remarked, and Aunt Lucy coughed a smoky laugh.

"…*was* he?" Eliza added, timidly, her eyes as round as saucers.

Mary's icy daggers fixed on Thomasina, who alone among them had not spoken. "Toms? Anything to say?"

Then they all were staring at her, mouths agape, agog.

"Toms?" said Aunt Clara, clutching at Lilah. "Thomasina?"

Thomasina twisted fistfuls of her skirt, head down, looking at the floor.

"Evidently," Mary went on when it became clear Toms wasn't going to reply, "*some* meddlesome bitch-bird put it in her head that he'd be visiting her in her room late at night." Her dagger-glare flashed at Meg, who flicked it aside with a cigarette-sweeping gesture.

"She deserved to know," Meg said. "It's what Mother would have wanted."

"Mother did want to tell Eliza," Alice said.

Eliza's chin quivered. "But she never—"

"—Had the chance," Meg finished. "Because she so suddenly and conveniently *died.* "

"Meg!" snapped Mary.

"Leave it, leave it," said Aunt Lucy. "One mess at a time. Make it snappy, though. I need a drink."

"It's nine in the morning," her sister Clara pointed out.

"I'll put gin in my orange juice. Had no idea we'd start off with murder before breakfast."

Alice turned to Toms. "Thomasina… did you?"

Still looking at the floor, still twisting fistfuls of her skirt, she nodded.

"Mary, say you *didn't* call the police!" Eliza cried out, rushing to Thomasina's side. "They'll put her in prison!"

"I told you," replied Mary with a distinct lack of patience, "I've not yet called anyone. Not the doctor, not the police, not anyone. But we'll have to—"

"Wait," said Meg. "Toms, what did you do?"

"She *killed* him!" Mary slapped the desk again.

"Yes, I got that," Meg retorted crisply. "What I want to know is, how? Could it seem like natural causes? Or an accident? Or did she stab him with a butcher knife a dozen times?"

Cousin Lilah made a small, vicious sound, as if rooting for the latter.

"I…" Toms steadied herself, the memories a fevered chill. *"I went to his room, late at night. After his meeting. After the others left."*

***

It felt like forever, the waiting. Hearing their strange chants thrumming up through the walls, men's voices low and guttural, some language of gargles and strange ululations. Smelling that faint, acrid smoke-scent wafting from the vents… not tobacco, not incense, not candles, not woodsmoke… was it opium? Hashish? Another exotic drug from the Far East?

The waiting, in her room, fully dressed and awake, unwilling to rest in her bed even for a minute because she might succumb to sleep. Miss this chance. Lose her nerve.

Or, worse, suppose he decided tonight was *the* night? Suppose his tread fell outside her door, his hand came grasping at the knob?

She might never sleep again, with such thoughts.

Finally, though, finally, the sounds of departure. Engines growling to life, motorcars rumbling away. Departure, then silence. And silence. And silence. No tread outside her door. No hand at the knob.

She'd slipped from her room in the stillness of the clock's smallest hours, Hastenford House at its quietest. She'd made her way through the silent halls, soft-footed so he would hear no tread at *his* door.

How pale and tiny, *her* hand grasping at the knob. But it turned easily, the door opening easily, without creak or click. And, in she went, guided by window-filtered moonlight and the dim glow of a lamp left on in the adjoining bath.

No framed family photographs or graceful porcelain figurines stood upon these well-polished furniture surfaces. Instead, an assortment of items and odd memorabilia: chunks of rock with fossils or crystals peeking through rough stone, squat primitive jade idols, heavy brass cups, ornate boxes carved from exotic wood, a glass dome over what appeared to be a desiccated paw or claw, other things she couldn't—and didn't want to—identify.

In his bed, phlegmatically snoring, lay Eustace Abraham. Thomasina had worried the sight of him would test her resolve, had worried he'd look innocent and harmless in slumber.

Instead, if anything, it was the opposite. He slept with a smug, cruel-lipped sneer. Like a gloating dragon. Like a god-emperor, secure in his invulnerability. He slept with his arms crossed on his chest, like an Egyptian pharaoh, like Stoker's dreaded vampire. His pin was set aside in a nightstand valet-case, but its companion ring, upon his left forefinger, shone balefully.

She moved the coverlet over him, covering the ring, covering him to the shoulders. She tucked everything in tight on both sides, until he was swaddled snug as a babe.

Then she took up a spare pillow, and pressed it down over his face.

***

No one said anything for a while, and then Eliza asked, "Didn't he struggle?"

"A little," Toms said, shuddering at the recollection. The fitful jerking of his legs as if to kick, the desperate heaving of his chest trying to draw breath... and the noises he'd made, the gruff and ragged awful noises... even muffled by the pillow, they'd been terrible.

Toward the end, he'd worked one arm free. The febrile grasping reach of that leathery hand would haunt her nightmares. Had it touched her, she surely would have screamed. But it hadn't. It had twitched and clawed the air, then dropped. Dropped like a dead thing, a dead vulture-bird or crusty old toad. Then, he was still.

She'd kept pressing down hard upon the pillow, though, half-certain that as soon as she lifted it away he would suck in a great gasp of air and lunge upright at her, eyes blazing in murderous rage. As she pushed, leaning with her entire weight, shaking with fear and fatigue, it seemed other presences joined her in the room, adding unseen strength, whispering encouragement.

This last part, she did not mention to her raptly-listening aunts and sisters. They would have thought she'd lost her senses. Well, maybe not Alice, with her fortune-cards and spirit-boards, but Mary of a certain, and Mary was already furious enough.

Finally, after what must've been most of an hour but felt like forever, she had released her hold and stepped back, watching warily. The only movement was the pillow itself, slowly relaxing from the deep impressions of her finger-marks, reassuming its normal shape. Father did not stir. He did not stir even when she made herself remove it from his face.

Seeing him, she knew instantly—just as Mary would see and know, some hours later. He was dead. His skin had gone grey and sallow, the texture of cheesecloth. Sunken bruise-hollows ringed his eyes. One was shut, as if still in peaceful sleep; its partner had rolled up beneath an askew lid to show only an arc of bloodshot white. His jaw hung slack, chin and jowls sagging against his neck. His wrinkled lips were tinged towards blue.

"I loosened the coverlet, and replaced the pillow where it belonged," Toms continued. "Nothing else had been disturbed. So, I left. That's it. That's all."

"That's it?" echoed Mary. "That's all? You killed him, Thomasina. You committed patricide, and doomed us all."

"Oh, hey," Meg said, intervening. "Waxing melodramatic much, Mar? Doomed us all, my foot. Lilah's right. We're free! She freed us!"

A ripple of relieved excitement and dawning hope passed among them, bringing more overlapping conversation:

"He *was* old."

"Eighty, at least!"

"Given the way he ate and drank and smoked…"

"Would it be all that surprising?"

"Natural causes, Meg, didn't you say?"

"… reason to suspect otherwise…"

"It'll be fine, Toms, you'll see!"

"No one else need ever know."

"Not like we can't keep secrets in this house!"

"We just have to—"

"Oh, *stop!*" cried Mary, smacking the desk a third time. It had to have hurt, to have stung her palms, but she showed no signs of noticing. "Listen to yourselves! Do you honestly believe he'd let it be that easy?"

Aunt Lucy took the forefront. "If this is about the money, I think it's safe to say we'd look out for each other."

"Damn right," chorused Lilah and Meg.

"We're all in this together," said Aunt Clara.

Eliza nodded. "Share and share alike."

"Very fine," Mary said. "Very noble. All in this together, look out for each other, share and share alike." She uttered a shrill, mirthless laugh. "We'll all have equal shares, then, of absolutely *nothing!*"

***

How often had he boasted of his dominance? His utter control? He had them under his roof, under his thumb, did he not? Wife, daughters, sisters... and yes, they might outnumber him, but he was far from powerless.

Let them have the vote, and why not? They'd vote just as he told them, his vote counting as ten. They'd *do* just as he told them. Gratitude and obedience. Or else.

As for what happened when he was no longer with them? Well, few men ever had any intention of dying. Rich and powerful old men least of all.

Besides, he'd taken *steps*.

"Do any of you know," Mary said, after this brief preamble, "how old he actually was?"

All eyes shifted to Aunt Clara, the elder of Eustace Abraham's two sisters. She shot a troubled frown in return at Aunt Lucy, who merely shrugged and blew a smoke ring toward the ceiling. Lilah gave her mother an encouraging squeeze.

"He was... our half-brother, really," Aunt Clara said.

"Or so they told us," added Lucy. "For all we know, he was our uncle as well, or—"

"Don't," Clara pleaded. "Just don't. None of that will help. The point is, Eustace was a grown man even when I was a small girl. His hair was already grey by the time I was Thomasina's age."

"So, what you're saying is," said Meg to Mary, after they all ran quiet mental calculations, "he could have been a hundred years old, or more?"

Eliza shivered. "That's impossible."

"He had no intention of dying," Mary said. "And why not, after so long a life? He never fell sick, was never in ill health, despite the way he ate and drank and smoked. He thought, planned, and fully expected to live much longer."

"He didn't have a will?" asked Aunt Lucy. "Is that what you're telling us? The crafty, cocksure old bastard was so confident of his immortality that he didn't bother to make a proper will?"

To quell the ensuing uproar, Mary waved her hands. "Oh, no, no, he had a will, all right. A full and proper one."

"Then what are we all fussing for?" Lilah tossed her head in exasperation. "Whatever it says, we'll make do, one way or another. If he played favorites, well, fine; I've always accepted my lot."

"He believed," said Mary, "the family could not go on without him. It was in everyone's best interests. We'd be lost without his guidance, his stern captaincy at the helm."

"We'll see about—" Meg started.

Mary raised her voice. "I told you he'd taken *steps,* didn't you hear me? Maybe he did worry some day something like this might happen, and wanted to make sure we'd suffer for it if it did. His will, my dearest aunts and sisters, leaves us *nothing.*"

This time, the uproar could not be quelled, not for several frantic outraged minutes.

"None of us," Mary went on. "Not an inch, a scrap, a cent. In the event of his demise, all his properties are to be sold, his businesses dissolved. The entire resulting fortune—which *is* a fortune, take my word! far more than you might guess!—goes to various political and charitable organizations."

Yet another overlapping babble followed:

"He can't do that!"

"He can, and did. I've seen the will myself."

"But *why?*"

"To make sure we didn't smother him in his sleep?"

"Don't be catty."

"What? It's true."

"To what end, though? If he meant it as insurance, a threat held over our heads, what good if none of us—?"

"This house and land belonged to our *mother!*"

"Never sick or in ill health or not, accidents still happen!"

"Yes, if he'd been in a car smash, what of us then?"

"He didn't care. He's never cared."

"Everything? The entire fortune?"

"—said without him we'd be destitute, but—"

"What will we do? What will become of us?"

"What political and charitable organizations?"

Once again, with effort, Mary brought them to a caesura. "It doesn't matter. What matters is that he is dead, and we are ruined, and it's Thomasina's fault."

"What?" Toms blurted.

"You did kill him."

"Yes, but…"

"You can't kill our father and say 'yes but,'" Mary scolded. "As soon as his lawyers learn of his death, however it happened, we're done for. We'll be out on our ears, lucky if they let us keep the clothes we stand up in."

"Can't we fight it, then, damn it?" asked Meg. "Contest it as unjust?"

"These *are* new times," Lilah said. "Things have changed."

"Not that much," said Mary. "Not for women. See how he's held us hostage all these years? Remember what happened to Gertrude? She didn't have to die that way. Do you think I wanted to keep Mina? I had no choice. None of us do!"

"Violet made her choice," Aunt Clara said to Aunt Lucy, who winced.

"Violet?" asked Alice. "Who's that?"

"Our other sister," Lucy said. "She did what Sarah did. Only, laudanum, not jumping." Her eyes narrowed at Clara. "We'd agreed never to speak of it."

"We agreed, but we were wrong." Clara buried her face in Lilah's shoulder and began to sob.

"No one escapes," Mary said. "No one. Gratitude and obedience.

It's his due. It's what he demands."

"Well, what about Anna?" Meg demanded. "She escaped—"

"To an asylum! And the only reason he let her be sent there was because no one would believe her ravings."

"Dark, inhuman things with claws, and skin like leather…"

"Shut up, Eliza!" three or four of them cried at once.

"Did he kill Mother?" Thomasina asked. "Did she know, and did he kill her?"

"It doesn't *matter!*" Mary flailed her arms. "None of it! Not then, and certainly not now! He's dead, the will stands, and we're *ruined!*"

Her last word echoed, and brought them all to silence.

Then, very quietly, a soft voice spoke.

"Unless…"

***

Six months later—

"Meg!" Thomasina had heard the car pull up, and all but flew downstairs to embrace her sister in the foyer before Meg even had a chance to slip out of her coat.

From various corners of Hastenford House, the other Abraham women quickly appeared, equally delighted and excited. Aunt Clara, in her gardening gloves, came out of the conservatory. Alice, who'd taken to wearing the loose garb and veils of a medium, drifted down from the library. Little Kate's new nanny and Mina's live-in tutor brought the younger girls to join them. Caroline, accompanied by a rambunctious pack of spaniels, dashed in from playing on the lawn.

"How was Chicago? Was it wonderful?"

"Is it as windy as they say?"

"Your letters were too short!"

"Have you met many gangsters?"

"Tell us everything!"

"You should have called more often!"

The staff—more than a dozen of them now, most of recent well-paid employ—paused in their duties to look on, smiling. With preparations underway for a spring dance and music recital, the ballroom shone expectantly. The kitchen bustled with activity. Refurbished guest rooms awaited, at long last, use. Deliveries and workmen came and went via the side doors.

The cheerful reunion went on for a good while. There were many hugs, and compliments all around—although still fashionably slim, Meg's sharp angles had softened into appealing jazz-club curves; Eliza's perpetual fretful expression had been replaced by rosy cheeks and sparkling eyes; Aunt Lucy looked ten years younger; even stern Mary had become more relaxed.

More relaxed, perhaps, but it was Mary who, as usual, called them all to order. "All right, all right, let her at least catch her breath. It's been a long trip. I'm sure she wants to freshen up, and say hello to Father. We'll have plenty of time for news of Chicago later on."

"Oh, I've so much to tell you!" Meg said. "And, I've brought presents—"

"Presents!" squealed Caroline, Mina, and little Kate, setting the spaniels off again into flurries of giddy yips and yaps and capers.

"—but," she went on, "yes, how *is* our dear father?"

"As well as could be expected," Mary said. "He keeps to his room more often these days."

"Luckily," Aunt Lucy said, "our Mary's more than capable of running things on his behalf."

"No doubt," said Meg. "Our capable Mary."

"Toms," their capable Mary said, not without a wry twist of her mouth, "why don't you help Meg get settled, then take her in to see Father? We'll have your bags brought from the car."

"No peeking at the presents!" Meg teased, making the girls giggle. She stretched, and followed Thomasina upstairs. "It will be nice to have these shoes off. They're the kippiest, but they pinch my feet like you wouldn't believe."

"They *are* very kippy," Toms said, half in admiration and half in envy. "Were they expensive?"

"You know it." Meg winked. "But *I* didn't pay for them." Once in her room, she kicked them off, undid her garters, rolled off her stockings, and rubbed her bare toes into the rug. "Ahh. Better. So, how is the old bastard? Cold and stiff as ever?"

"Meg!"

"What? Can't we joke?"

"Someone might hear!"

"Who, the servants? As if they'd give a gimlet. For what they're getting paid, they wouldn't say a word if we had him stuffed and mounted over the parlor mantel."

"That's horrid."

Meg considered, and nodded. "True. Imagine having him up there." She struck a ghastly rigor-mortis pose. "Speaking of which, though, he's still not rotting?"

Toms shook her head. "Aunt Clara really has worked marvels. Nothing like the preservative powers of exotic plants! I'd no idea. I wouldn't say it's perfect, but, you can hardly tell without getting in close."

"Which no one wants to do." Meg fixed her hair and did some touch-ups in the mirror. "No trouble from his lawyers, or business associates?"

"As long as the checks and paperwork are signed, they don't much seem to care."

"Our capable Mary, an expert forger, who knew?"

"I think," added Toms, leaning in to whisper, "one of the lawyers is sweet on her."

"Stop the trolley!"

"No, I do!"

"On Mary? Well there's a blue-eyed wonder! But, good. If she can snare him, so much the better. We could use a lawyer on our side. What about the phone?"

"He never liked the phone in the first place, so everyone believes he just has her making and taking his calls."

"Brilliant. Let's go have a peepsie."

Unlike most of the rest of the house, Eustace Abraham's room was largely unchanged. The only striking addition was the wheelchair, into which he was secured. It had been rolled over by the window. With hands folded atop a plaid lap-blanket, and his head drooped to the side, he merely seemed to be dozing in the slanted sunbeams. Only upon very close inspection was his lack of actual breathing evident.

"Hey, he doesn't look half-bad," Meg said. "Good thing he never trusted doctors, either. The less of them nosing around, the better."

"As long as we push him around the garden now and then, no one's the wiser."

"And if somebody *does* start playing nosy, I may know people." She grinned. "*Chicago* people."

"You haven't *really* met gangsters, have you?"

"I'll tell you all about it later." Meg prodded the back of their father's slack hand with a nicely-manicured nail. "Where's his ring?"

"Alice has it. She keeps it, and his pin, for, you know, *those* nights."

"I cannot *wait* to see how that works. When you and Alice first suggested it, I thought you'd both gone petticoats to Peoria. Never would have guessed there was actually any truth to that spiritualist hokum."

"It's… spooky. When she puts the ring on him, and pierces her palm with the pin, and her eyes go all foggy…"

"With the, what do they call it again?"

"Ectoplasm. Then he starts to move, copying whatever she does. Only, slow, and kind of clumsy. Like he *did* have a brain-stroke or something, which is what we've been saying when anybody asks. She hasn't been able to get him to walk yet. But, when she whispers, he'll repeat her words. Slow and clumsy, same as when he moves, but it's his voice, sure enough."

Meg let out a low whistle. "Alice, Alice, Alice. I owe her an apology. The way I'd make fun of her hobbies, and here she is saving our bacon."

"It's fooling them so far." Thomasina shrugged. "Not sure about the chanting and whatever else they do down there. Alice won't talk about it. She goes over all pale and strange if you ask."

"It'll do, though, won't it? At least until Mary gets the will sorted?"

"That's the plan."

They regarded him for a moment, slumped in the wheelchair, hands folded, head down, eyes shut.

"Well, it might not be the gratitude and obedience he wanted," Meg finally said, "but, one way or another, he's still the man of the house."

BRICKWALK MOLLIES

*O*h *Molly, my Molly, sweet Molly Malloy*
Where have you gone to, my Molly?
The girl who passes her days in the areaway below my window sings this, incessantly, almost as if she does not know she does so aloud.

Her voice is sweet, a high, youthful lilt. Perhaps the only true sweetness to be found amid these squalored alleys and avenues.

And yet, like all things sweet, too much can soon 'come cloying. Sugar to arsenic, honey to poison.

I wonder, also, if she knows the origin of what she sings. I remember the song from my boyhood; the Molly Malloy so referenced was a woman famed for her infamy and lucky escapes. Back then, we even called others who plied such a trade "mollies." Does this girl know of that, or does she simply sing unawares, just as children dance and chant Ring-A-Rosey without realizing it hearkens to the world's most murderous plague, worse by far even than the recent years' flu?

I could venture down there and ask her to stop, but I wish to draw no undue attention to myself. My errand is far from finished. Nor, for similar reason, is the option of closing the window-casement against the noise… I must needs keep a listen to the passing chatter and clamor. Not to mention, without what small breath of ventilation the breeze affords, this room would be yet more a stifling hell-hole.

It is in part because of the girl, singing below, I have taken up this journal, the better to pass my idle hours and occupy my ever-more-troubled thoughts. May it help to distract me from her voice, that treacle-sweet Irish lilt, seeping syrup-like into my ears.

Such an odd counterpoint it makes. The other talk that I hear—both in languages understandable to me and languages perhaps understandable to no sane man—is coarse, rough and gruff, often peppered with obscenity, salted with profanity, spiced with vulgarity, seasoned by anger or cruel laughter.

This prevailing speech is an audible equivalent of the cooking-smells wafting thick in the air as evening meals draw near. A pungent melange, heavily foreign and strange, watering the eyes with curry and onion, garlic, smoky oils, dried chilies of evil disposition. I find at times my appetite oddly whetted, my stomach set growling... yet at other times the very prospect of eating even a crust of toast sends me reeling with nausea to the chipped and cracked wash-basin in the corner of my room.

However, just as there is the little Irish girl, she of the lilting song—

Oh Molly, my Molly, sweet Molly Malloy
Where have you gone to, my Molly?

—there are also the aromas of stewed cabbage, potatoes, dark beer, soda-bread... on occasion corned beef. Fair skin and ruddy flushes can be seen amid the mingling swarthier crowds. Red-headed mollies, if mollies they still are called, ply their trade alongside their duskier sisters of the street. Gangly freckle-faced lads lurk and loiter with gangs of stocky tar-complected and wiry slanted-eyed specimens. Their fathers, workingmen at the wharves and warehouses, are met with jovial Pat-and-Mike jokes, or asked how many potatoes does it take to kill an Irishman? (the answer being, of course: none).

My landlady—if the wretched creature deserves to be elevated by the title, corpulent mahogany toad-faced thing that she is—disdains these paler folk with sneers. Shanty-Irish, she calls them,

shirttail Irish, shit-can Irish. I have witnessed her spit in the direction of the aforementioned, and even fork hand-signs of warning.
Once, when a priest by name of O'Flynn paid a call on an ailing
parishioner next door, this landlady retreated to her filthy basement
kitchen, shaking a beaded gourd and muttering cryptic swampish
spells as she went, and later that evening I found the freshly-killed
corpse of an enormous harbor rat nailed upside-down to a board.

This, yes, is Red Hook. How much, and how little, it has changed
since my own long-ago and largely forgotten boyhood here. Just as
I, myself, must have changed both much and little. I may be, now,
a learned and educated man, but my education began here in this
polyglot hodge-podge. The unfortunate circumstances of my mon-
grel heritage, which casts me as something of an exotic or curiosity
among Arkham society, makes me by no means an unusual figure
to these neighborhoods of casual intermixing.

My current place of habitation is a miserable third-floor flat, ad-
vertised, by a liberal stretch of exaggeration, as two rooms. The
lodging-house is set some blocks back and some hills up from the
waterfront, along what the locals have taken to calling The Brickwalk. My window overlooks it, affording a view of an old church—
not that of the good Father O'Flynn, I am told, though I have yet
to determine to which congregation it does belong. Its bells, I have
noticed, toll at odd hours, and their resonance is of a quality most
unsettling to the nerves.

I did not choose this lodging-house or room for the view of the
church, but for that of the Brickwalk entire, and several other structures of particular interest. Somewhere, along its stretch, the reason
for my purpose here had by all accounts last been seen. Somewhere
in the Brickwalk, before his disappearance. A disappearance so
complete, were it not for the fact of his uncle who'd hired me, he
may never have existed to begin with.

This... street, for want of a better word... is named on no city
maps, and would appear to be a glorified alley but for its well-
trafficked usage. Well-trafficked, that is, by foot alone. No motor

or cart, nor even a bicycle, could readily navigate its steep, narrow, crooked progression.

Further, it is paved not in cobblestone or macadam but all of brick, though by no means uniformly. The bricks themselves come from an irregular variety of colors and sizes, often not fitting flush together, adding to the impression of overall unevenness. It strikes the eye and mind as if some great constructor patched together the leftover materials of untold other works into a single winding thoroughfare.

Other and yet-smaller avenues twist off from it, some connecting, some to ominous dead ends. There are numerous doorways, alcoves, porticos, and nooks... cellarholds and coal chutes... downspouts gurgling trickles of grimy, sooty water—and when it rains heavily, filthy cataracts rush downhill toward the docks.

Packed to either side of the Brickwalk stand decrepit buildings, crowded shoulder to shoulder or leaning askew. Window-gables jut at angles like skeptical, bony eyebrows; the windows themselves squint with murky, unwashed panes. Now and then a furtive hand might twitch at ragged curtains, or a dark face appear, briefly pressed to the glass.

And below me, below my window, the Irish girl sings.

Oh Molly, my Molly, sweet Molly Malloy
Where have you gone to, my Molly?
From the chapel in white to the hook all of red
Gone not to workhouse or to marriage bed
Gone not to play shopgirl or to become a nun
Where are you, my Molly, dear, where have you run?

She sells—not seashells, as the tongue-twister says—but cigarets, or a shoddy semblance thereof. Hand-rolled, hardly the crisp and neat machine-mades so much the rage these days, with their flashy packaging and clever advertisements. As I understand it, her family had once been respected tobacconists—Delaney and Sons—before the companies ran so many small shops out of business.

To add insult to injury, the once-proud Delaney sons now do the sweeping-up at one such factory. It is from these sweepings, which they smuggle home, the girl's mother and aunts make the product in her basket. I daresay they are as much dust and sawdust, rat droppings and hair, as they are shreds of tobacco. They burn fast and flare-furious, the smoke reminiscent of tires and despair.

Though she appears to move with a limp, and suffer some slight deformity of her right hand, the girl is nonetheless a pretty thing. Thin and waifish, upturned of nose, apricot of hair, with enormous eyes I can see even from here are the very Kelly-green of Irish clover. Despite her flaws, I suspect she'll be a head-turner when she's a year or two older, a head-turner and heart-breaker. If, that is, life on the Brickwalk doesn't wear her down.

Indeed, if I'm any judge, she already has at least one admirer; I've noticed the same young chap lingering at a wistful distance on several occasions. To my knowledge, he has not yet mustered the nerve to approach, but will stand casting his shy glances toward the girl. With so little else to do while I wait and watch, I must take what entertainment in observing such miniature dramas as I can.

Oh, but I could do without her incessant singing, however honey-lilting her voice might be. Some nights, long after she's taken her basket back to wherever she goes, I lie wakeful in bed with the sound of it still in my ears.

Oh Molly, my Molly, sweet Molly Malloy
Where have you gone to, my Molly?
Have you sailed on a steamship, or taken a train
Traveled the wide world or come home again?
Oh Molly, sweet Molly Malloy

The cigaret girl seems to do a steady enough trade despite the poor quality of her product. And why not? Many men came home from the War with a taste for the habit but without the wherewithal to support the store-bought form. Many women have taken it up as well... not just the younger generation, those free-spirits with a fondness for jazz and for gin... but housewives and grandmothers and elegant society ladies.

Not that the lattermost would ever be found on the Brickwalk. From here at my window-vantage, I occasionally see well-dressed gentlemen go by—fine hats and coats, gloved hands gripping canes—but, no, never ladies. Any lady of quality, such as those with whom I've brushed elbows at faculty affairs in Arkham, would be far too scandalized, shocked, and aghast by the affronts to senses and morals were they to venture to set dainty foot here.

There is, however, Kitty.

Although this is my own journal, which no eyes but mine shall read, I hesitate and feel the heat in my face to so much as commit her name to its pages.

Kitty. Kitty O'Shea.

It is a wrongness, I know. An unhealthy interest. A base fascination.

I am not some shy chap in tweed cap and knickerbockers, sending wistful glances at the object of his romantic fancy.

And she is no suitable such object.

Yet, whenever evening draws nigh, as it does now, my pulse quickens. My ears keen for the brash boldness of her laugh, the lilt of her voice not syrup-sweet like the girl's but as potent as Irish whisky. My eyes sharpen for the first glimpse of her sleek foxbrush-red hair, the powdered-cream of her cheek, the carmine pout of her lips. I wonder what scent she might wear—lilac? rose?—dabbed at wrist and neck. I wonder what curves are concealed beneath her straight slip-fitted dress.

This is my own journal; where else may a man be honest with his thoughts?

The worst of it is, I *could* have her.

No. The worst of it is, *anyone* could.

Haven't I seen her, often enough, going off with whichever dock-worker, sailor, or factory-Johnny who's flush with his wages or had a run of luck at the dogfights? Race, creed, or color, it's of no mind; a dollar's a dollar all the same. If I went up to her…

Again, this is my journal; I will not scratch out that last. But neither will I follow it further. What would there be for it, any-way? I could not bring her here, not without drawing the ire of my landlady—and perhaps a heathen hoodoo curse on my head into the bargain. I certainly cannot let myself be led to a backroom mattress-flat or grimy Brickwalk alcove of standing-room-only.

Would that my purpose here involved more direct investigation, requiring me to go out among the local denizens and make discreet inquiries… which would still, of course, under the particular cir-cumstances of the case, offer little excuse to speak to the likes of Kitty O'Shea. The man I seek on behest of his rich uncle is not a man who would keep her kind of company. His proclivities, one might say, tend rather elsewhere.

The sun sinks but is not yet set. The buildings' strange shadows stretch long. The pungent cooking-smells and street-clamor inten-sify. Up the way, at the brownstone with the concrete cornices of Egyptian design, lights have switched on behind drawn drapes.

I hear a ship's whistle like the dying cry of a bird. I hear the girl singing below my window and catch myself humming along.

Oh Molly, my Molly, sweet Molly Malloy
Where have you gone to, my Molly?

***

"This," hissed the whisper. "This is what you wanted."

Breath hot in his ear. Skin hot against skin.

Hands on his body, gripping, caressing.

"This is what you sought, what you asked for."

Senses heightened to the most exquisite pleasures.

The most exquisite pains.

"To suffer, and surrender, and succumb."

Helpless and writhing, lost in sensation.

The drugs seething through his system, every nerve sharply alive, every touch, sound, and taste.

Ether and opium, gin and cocaine, others for which the world has no name.

"To give yourself to us. Give yourself to our secrets, to the sacred service of our eternal masters."

His breath the endless wind over salt sea and sand desert.

The stars in the sight of his sightless eyes spinning.

His mind its own captive universe, twisted in cosmic knots, witnessing immense entities dance on the head of a pin.

"They see, and they know, and they take what you offer."

Touching him. Touching him in all the ways he had so long desired, desired and never dared speak of.

Starving him, shaving him, slaving him, sinister punishment, sinister lust, the assault upon self until self stripped away.

"One last step. One last sacrifice. Will you accept?"

Such exquisite suffering, pleasure and pain.

His answer, his answer, a sighing susurration.

Yesssss.

***

It was the kind of day, Deenie thought, her Gran would say meant the Devil's wife must have hung out her washing.

Not rainy, but dampish, sometimes with drips. The sky yellow-grey, the air heavy and hazy and warm. On the buildings, a dull glisten, as if the bricks themselves sweated. For the people, there was no 'as if' about it. Men mopped their brows and the backs of their necks with dirty rags. Women fanned their faces with folded newspapers as they gossiped and shopped.

The talk seemed to be of an upcoming prize-fight, another mutilated body found by the canal bridge, the rumored theft of a strange carven sculpture, the police raiding a jazz-joint, and whether two missing neighborhood girls had run off or met trouble.

Downstreet, where a few wider alleys intersected the 'Walk, a pump-spout pipe had been busted. Tepid water gurgled from it. Children played in the spray and splashed in a broad muddy puddle.

She wouldn't have minded to join them, older though she was, but she worried how clumsy she'd look, with her limp. And her mam would scold for wet clothes... and, of course, she had her cigarets to sell.

"Oh Molly, my Molly, sweet Molly Malloy... where have you gone to, my Molly?"

She sang to help pass the time, and to distract her mind from the grumbling of her belly as the afternoon drew long. No food-carts could traverse the Brickwalk, but all along were vendors with temptations: boiled eggs for sale, pickles, greasy corn-fritters, hot dogs sold through a half-door, penny-lick ice cream, apples, curried meat served in hollowed-out hard rolls.

"Beef and lamb, so they *claim,*" one of her aunts had said. "With all that onion and spice, who can guess? All I know for a fact is there's far less rats and stray cats 'round the 'Walk than when *I* was your age."

Deenie's brother had favored a different theory, one he'd heard from his pack of street-tough friends. "Ah, sure as there's less cats and rats about; the Globbers come up from the canals at night, in the dead of the night when the moon's hidden dark." Bryce would tell this to the younger Delaneys, as they huddled wide-eyed in their thin-blanketed cots. "Up from the canals, up from sewer drains, oozing wet and stinking of fish, and if they catch you out of doors after bedtime, if they catch you, they'll gulp you right down whole!"

As a littler girl, Deenie had believed him without question, and why not? Even now, who would *she* be to say whether Globbers were real? There were *things* in the night, dangerous things, everybody knew that. Things roosting and rustling in attics and belfries, things lurking in deep basements and cellarholds. Evil things. Deadly things.

Some of them men, yes; evil men, deadly men, men with knives and needles and vile intentions. Some, though... some couldn't be so readily explained. If there were saints and angels, as Sister Mary said, then mustn't there also be devils, witches, and worse?

Why not Globbers? Why not gaunts and haunts, shadowed tendrils, pale-segmented worms with human faces? Why not goats on two legs, beast-headed gods, lumpy masses of sucker-mouths and lidless eyes?

Who knew? Who could say?

Certainly not her brother, not now. Not now, and perhaps, not ever again.

Despite the humid weight of heat, Deenie shivered as if ice had run melting down her spine. She shook herself. The Globbers had *not* gotten Bryce. If he'd met a bad end, it was by more normal means, a run-in between his gang and another, or hit trolley-dodging on the uptown tracks. Or he'd been crimped by a ship-master; crime or not, it still happened. Maybe he'd come home from o'erseas one day, taller and tanner, a traveled-man with new tales to tell.

Or he wouldn't, and they'd never know.

It did no good to wonder. With Bryce gone, it was a mouth less to feed at the table, but it was also the loss of the money he'd brought in by his various means. Leaving the rest of them, Deenie included, to try and make up the lack.

She returned her attention to the streams of people going by. This late in the afternoon, workhouse whistles had blown, the crowd-bustle thicker as shifts changed and so-called 'tea houses' and 'social clubs' were opening their doors. A few early molly-girls strolled around, chattering and laughing, hoping for someone to buy them a drink.

Soon, she had done a good bit of business, several more cigarets sold, grubby coins jingling in her basket. A man went by hawking peanut-chews wrapped in wax paper, and her stomach muttered.

"Where are you, my Molly, dear, where have you run?" she sang to silence it. "Who was it you fled from, was it Doctor Jack? With his bag of sharp silver and long coat of black?"

Then she saw the lad standing watching her from across the way, and caught her breath, forgetting all about peanut-chews and singing and rumbling stomachs.

She'd seen him before, many times now. Hard not to notice; he simply was *the* most beautiful boy. Oh, and with *such* hair, tousled curls yellow as butter, looking plusher and softer than a rich lady's mink stole…

He rarely crossed over to her side of the 'Walk, and had never spoken so much as a simple hello. But, once, a little sprig of garden-flowers had been left by her spot, on another occasion a packet of gum; could she dare to think that maybe, just maybe…?

Their gazes met, and Deenie felt a blush bloom in her cheeks. She glanced away, then glanced back, just as he did the same. Feeling flustered as well as blushing and clumsy, she almost knocked over her basket.

He smiled. Oh, too, *such* a smile, shy but perfect, perfect with the straightest and whitest of teeth, a movie-picture smile if ever there was one. And smiled at *her,* smiled *for* her!

Faith an' begorrah, as Gran might have said, but didn't her heart just go a'leap and a'flutter in her chest!

As she answered with her own smile—equally shy, but less perfect—a spate of shouts and commotion erupted upstreet. Men swore. Women screamed. Punches flew; so did vegetables and bricks. In a half-dozen languages, people urged the fight on or called for a stop. Glass broke with a crash. Someone's shopping-parcels scattered and dogs shot from nowhere to tear at the sausages and bread.

Deenie strained on tip-toe to see through the thronging onlookers, gripping her basket tightly in case the disturbance surged her way. At the top edge of her vision, a figure leaned out from a window, dark hands braced on the sill.

A dull, dragging clang cut through the din, the toll of a bell echoing flat and atonal from the overcast Devil's-wife skies. It seemed Deenie *felt* it, felt the sound press against her like a wave, thrumming her bones, crushing the air from her lungs. She thought of iron, and anchors, and vast deep hollow drums.

Another sound followed, as if in challenge or reply. A piercing sound, shrill and shrieking, brazen-brass, like the screech of an enormous fierce bird. Heat-lightning sheeted behind the sooty haze. Everyone on the street had stopped short. They flinched, shoulders hunching against thunder that didn't come.

"The eye," someone said. "The falcon's eye opens. It searches. It seeks."

The iron bell tolled a second time, a low and wavering note that set the spire of the old stone church to quivering. As it faded, as if down some bottomless well, it drew all other noises after it.

The Brickwalk, for a moment, stood in utter and absolute silence.

No one moved. No one spoke.

"Well, then," called a girl's voice, strong and strident. "Get on with yourselves, why don't you? The day's fair to wasting!"

It was as if a spell had been broken, or an unseen switch thrown. Suddenly the normal activities resumed, the normal levels of talking and walking and folk going about their business. The combatants upstreet—rival gangs, by the look of it—hastily dispersed, both sides bloodied, both sides wagging fingers and waving fists, promising payback, each trying to have the last word.

Deenie turned in hopes of catching glimpse again of the lad with butter-blond tousled hair, but he was gone. Had slipped away, again without a word. Her heart sank... until she saw, resting atop the cloth covering her basket, a length of waxed paper twisted at the ends. A peanut-chew, left there, like the flowers and the packet of gum.

She reached for it.

"Careful with that, if I were you, little sister."

The voice was the same as had called out, a girl's voice, strong and strident, if pitched now at a conversational tone. Deenie's eyes widened as she recognized its owner. Not that they were acquainted, no—*God and heaven forbid!* as her mam and Sister Mary would have it—but she surely knew Kitty O'Shea right enough.

Oh, and *such* clothes, such a figure of fashion, as if she'd stepped straight from the pages of a magazine! Her chemise-dress creamy lace over periwinkle chiffon, the hem high enough to show stocking-tops rolled to the knee! Her button-up shoes, half-unbuttoned, flapped loose. A long strand of pearl-tone beads hung 'round her neck, a beaded bag swung on a silvery chain at her elbow, and a smart cloche hat perched rakishly atop the neat finger-wave auburn bob of her hair.

How could Deenie help but stare, both in scandal and a kind of envious fascination? Yet she recovered her wits and found the dignity to protest.

"I'm not your little sister!"

"Maybe not, but you're still one of us."

"I'm no molly-girl, either!"

Kitty laughed. Her face-powder was smooth and dry despite the late-afternoon's mugginess, her eyes thick-lashed with mascara. Her lipstick was the reddest of reds, the reddest red Deenie had ever seen. She drew a drag from a cigaret in a stylish holder, and blew out a ribbon of smoke.

"I've heard you, though," she said. "Singing. Singing our song."

***

"This is what you wanted."

The knife. The knife, gleaming.

Smooth flesh laid naked and bare.

"This is what you promised."

The altar. The lamps blazing oil.

Men. Boys. Priests.

The stern and surrounding visages of gods.

"This is what we need, what they demand."

Ether and opium. Gin and cocaine.

Vulnerable. Helpless. Bound and waiting.

"Take the knife."

He took it, fingers curling around the jeweled handle. He lifted it, feeling its hunger, feeling its eagerness, its power.

The blade, a razor-edged mirror, showed him a quick reflection of himself. His own changed appearance, head shaved even of eyebrows, skin intricately etched with symbols, brilliant inkings and sacred scarifications.

"A steady hand, and sure."

She blinked heavy, drugged lids. Her struggles tugged feebly at the knots holding her wrists and ankles. "No," she mumbled. "No, please, no. Let me go."

Breasts and belly, hips and thighs, the vile whore's cradle of her loins.

"Here. Begin here."

A single welling drop, ruby-dark, bulged. Bulged and grew. Then broke, and ran dribbling, as she strained more strongly against the bonds in a surge of fear and pain.

"Make the incision."

***

Now they are both of them singing. And yet, curiously—or perhaps not—I cannot find it in myself to complain.

The cigaret girl, who introduced herself as Deenie when asked, and Kitty O'Shea. Their voices together are whisky tempered with honey, not a hot toddy but a cooled one for this sweltering dusk. To young Deenie's scandalized intrigue, Kitty knows the rest of the verses. The ones beyond that brief mention of Doctor Jack. The ones few mothers would want their daughters to sing or to hear.

Oh Molly, my Molly, sweet Molly Malloy
Where have you gone to, my Molly?
Who was it you fled from, was it Doctor Jack
With his bag of sharp silver and long coat of black?
When he came for the ladies those dark foggy nights
Opened to the cold air their sins and delights

The pieces, cut from them, the pieces he took
Has he followed you, Moll, from chapel to hook?
Oh Molly, my Molly Malloy

As I stand here at my window above them to watch and listen.

The occurrence of earlier, the atonal tollings of the churchbell in conflict or conversation with that shrill and brassy shriek (accompanied by the lightning? I should like to call it coincidence, but I fear I know better)... the effect upon everyone within the Brickwalk, myself included...

Something, I am certain, will happen tonight.

Whether it will be something pertaining to my particular purpose here, I cannot yet say, though my suspicions tend strongly toward such a conclusion.

The brownstone with its cornices of Egyptian design once again shows signs of activity in the lit rooms behind its drapes. Moreso than on previous evenings. Already, I have noticed a larger than usual number of well-dressed gentlemen making use of its discreet side entrance.

What was it someone said? The falcon's eye opens?

The falcon's eye.

Deenie says something about how much trouble she'll be in, coming home so late, not to mention that her 'mam' would 'fair to have fits' if she knew she was so much as talking to the likes of Kitty O'Shea... whose reply is along the lines of how everyone's 'mam' says that, until it's one of their own gone missing.

As, she suggests, Deenie might if she falls into the habit of accepting gifts from 'pretty lads.'

It seems an unlikely sentiment for someone in her line of work. Going by Deenie's dubious expression, she and I are in agreement on that.

But then Kitty goes on to not merely caution the girl but outright warn her, and I realize with chagrin my earlier mistake. Did I think there was no need to make inquiries among the mollies regarding my errand here?

After all, cults conduct rituals... rituals require sacrifices... and has it not often been from among the population's most indigent or disreputable that such victims are chosen? With few to care or notice, to make outcry?

Well-dressed gentlemen. The falcon's eye. Doctor Jack. Piercing brass pipe-notes and stonework of Egyptian design. Pretty lads.

Pretty lads to charm and disarm, as Kitty tells Deenie. So shy and polite, clean and well-kept, clothes not shabby, manners not rough, must be of good breeding, have some wherewithal... and that is the trick, the bait for the trap.

"We call them the Quiet Boys," she says. "But they're not same as us. I don't think they're human."

Never a word, not so much as a peep... poor things, might think they're mute, such a pity, so handsome and all... mystery, appeal, curiosity, captivation... how they get you... trick and catch you... lead you on, lure you on... not just don't speak but *can't* speak... nor eat or drink... not like us, not human... under their clothes... no more 'down there' than a child's toy doll... not human but alive, or at least can bleed, can be killed...

"We've done it. We've had to. They, or rather, their masters, would do the same to us. Would do and have done. Not *every* girl, molly- or otherwise, who goes missing from the 'Walk does so at their hands, not every girl... but enough."

This last, I took great care to write down word-for-word. The previous, mere notes and snippets jotted in haste as she spoke.

She claims she has seen it happen before, too often. That the smiles and little gifts left for Deenie—by the selfsame lad I have already remarked upon—indicate he has selected her, not for courting but as a next victim. To be eventually coaxed or persuaded into going off somewhere with him, perhaps under the impression it's to meet his family, but instead it's to be delivered to his masters, never to be seen again.

Deenie's skepticism makes it clear she believes herself on the end of some elaborate joke, and is only playing along in the spirit of being a good sport. Whyever on earth would *she* of all people—?

—because she is herself young and pretty... because with the mollies aware of their schemes and fighting back, they've had to turn elsewhere for prey... because she caught their eye for any number of reasons. The why, Kitty says, doesn't matter.

Caught their eye; the falcon's eye?

And these masters she speaks of, what masters?

I must know more.

***

"Do it. We command it. They command it. *He* commands it."

Stern-visaged gods, crowned with suns and horns. Lapis, malachite, carnelian, copper, topaz, white-metal silver.

The boys, such beautiful boys, quiet and beautiful, supple blond angels garbed in sheer linen. The men, some young and lusty, some greying and distinguished. The priests, smooth-shaven hairless and covered with hieroglyphs.

"Evil lurks within her. Evil and corruption. Slice her open, cut it from her womb, cut it out and destroy it."

On the altar, she sobbed and begged. "I'm not, I swear! I'm not! Don't hurt me!"

But they commanded it. *He* commanded it.

He desired it, and for *Him,* anything. Anything for *His* approval and pleasure.

The knife seemed to guide itself, to pull itself in a single, swift, sure stroke.

She screamed.

And there it was, just as they'd said. Nestled among her organs. Slick and wetly pulsating. A squirming, seething, loathsome mass.

Holding the knife with one hand, he reached with the other into the warm, slippery cavity of her body. He felt, with the most vivid and crawling horror of his life, the living monstrosity inside her try to clutch at him even as he seized it, even as he severed its fleshy, sinewy moorings.

"Bring it to *Him*. Present it to *Him,* and become one with *Us.* "

It writhed in his grip and made thin, pitiable mewling cries. He let fall the knife, let it clatter to the bloodied altar beside the woman's head. The others parted, stepping back, opening a path through their ranks to the raised dais.

Where *He* stood waiting, tall, robed, and regal. Headdress framing a face of chiseled perfection. Eyes outlined and outswept toward the temples not in kohl but in gold, painted liquid gold upon skin like onyx, like obsidian.

In *His* noble, elegant, long-fingered hands was an ancient vessel, not of alabaster or faience but simple and humble red Nile clay. Similar vessels, stoppered and sealed, filled the shelves of a vault behind the dais. From them came myriad tiny noises, pitiful keenings and wails identical to those emitted by what was being carried forward through the chant-murmuring crowd.

Trembling with dread, exultation, and desire, he let the clinging thing slip from his palms, and into the hollow clay belly of the jar. A lid was placed upon it, the seam sealed with wax, and it was added to the vault's shelves.

Then *He* spoke, with a voice unearthly, a voice of dark wind and water.

"With each so taken," *He* intoned, "let *Her* strength here be weakened, let *Ours* be gained."

"As it was," said the worshipers. "As it is. As it forever shall be."

***

"—as far back as London they were hunting our kind, you see," Kitty O'Shea said, the ember at the end of her cigaret tracing idle streak-glow sigils in the air as she gestured. "The Molly you sing of, Molly Malloy? It was true, all of it, true, but she escaped Whitechapel to hop a ship to New York. They would have killed her just as they killed the rest, cut her open to see what she had inside her."

"A bairn, do you mean? A baby?" Deenie asked. Oh, and she'd be in for it right enough when she got home, staying out so late. It was well past dusk now, well past supper, but she couldn't tear herself away from the daring and fashionable Kitty, or her story.

"Well, she *was* pregnant, that also was true. With the child of a rich man, so they say. A high-born rich man, a lord, maybe even a prince of the realm."

"What happened?"

"She came here to Red Hook, and used the money he'd given her to start up her own business." Kitty tilted her head, winking one mascara-lashed eye. "If you take my meaning."

"And that's why they call you molly-girls?"

"That's why, though there was more to it than that. She taught us her trade, and she taught us her secrets, and how to look after ourselves."

"But what about the baby? Did she keep it?"

"Gave it over to the Church." She paused, regarding Deenie, and smiled. "A girl, it was, I think, and I seem to recall hearing that girl grew up to marry a tobacconist's son."

Deenie's jaw slowly dropped. "Sure as you're not saying—"

Kitty shrugged. "Ah, you'd have to ask old Sister Mary about that. The point is, little sister, like it or not, you're one of us... and if they've now got their eye on you, you'll need to be careful and you'll need to be ready."

"Who *are* they, though? And... Doctor Jack... *did* he follow her? Did he come here, too?" She hugged herself, peering around the Brickwalk's weird looming shadows, as if fog might suddenly swirl up and disgorge a menacing black-coated figure, the bogeyman of bogeymen, stalker of a hundred nightmares. "Well, but that was, what, thirty-and-more years ago; he wouldn't *still* be—"

"I'd not be so hasty," said Kitty, blowing another ribbon of smoke. "They have ways. They have magic. I told you the Quiet Boys aren't even human. Who knows for their masters? Or their masters' Master?"

Just then, a door banged somewhere nearby, the sound startling Deenie so that she half jumped out of her skin. She sucked in a breath as a shape rushed around the rooming-house corner.

It was a man, moving fast, coming straight at them.

Fast as he was, Kitty O'Shea was faster. In a flash, she'd snatched out from her bag a gilt-handled clutch gun; she pointed it, unwavering. Everything in her manner declared she both could and would pull the trigger, and had done so before.

That brought him up short, right enough. He skidded to a stop, hands raised and empty. "Wait," he said. "I'm on your side."

He wore not a black coat but dark trousers and rolled-up shirt-sleeves, his collar part undone, his braces looped dangling from his belt. Hatless, his hair was cropped close and woolly. With his burnished-bronze skin, and broad, striking features, he looked like an Araby genie from a storybook picture.

"What do you know about anyone's side?" Kitty demanded.

"He has the room just up there," Deenie said, recognizing him. "Just at that window. Some sort of writer or artist or such, sitting with his papers and pens. He's been listening to us!"

"Oh, have you?" Kitty did not lower the gun. "Who are you, Mister Writer-or-Artist-or-Such?"

Still with his hands raised, he said, "My name is Elijah Aarush. I'm a scholar, an investigator from Arkham. I was hired to look for a young man who may have some connections with a cult operating in this vicinity, and I believe we may be able to help each other."

***

The drugs... the drugs from before...

Ether and opium, gin and cocaine, others for which the world has no name.

The drugs with their heightened sensations, their euphoria, their transcendent otherworldly rapture...

The drugs were nothing compared to *Him.*

To a god.

To the touch, and kiss, and embrace of a god.

He had earned this reward. He had proved himself. Done what they commanded. Joined them. Made sacrifice. He had cut the hideous larval spawn from another of Yhagni's foul witches, and won favor.

Such favor! Such great, glorious, joyous favor!

The god, pushing into him, penetrating. Their sighs of ecstasy— his and *His*—mingling. Exquisite pleasure beyond pleasure, exquisite pain beyond pain.

All around them, the others in orgy, men and priests and boys like angels... so like angels... so like angels, but still, nothing like a god!

But then, interruptions, alarms.

Infiltration? Invasion? Attack?

Shouts and confusion. Gunfire. A sudden, scrambling panic. The voices of women, feminine fury, a madness of maenads, shrieking for rage and revenge. Glass shattering, bludgeons swinging, more gunfire, shots fired! Blood and bone! A man staggering with his torn scalp flapping over his ear... a boy, silent ever and forever, his throat blown wide open... priests with terror writ larger than the hieroglyphs on their faces...

And *Him,* the tightening crush of *His* arms, the urgent hiss-whisper of *His* words... "You wanted this, you wanted *Me,* will you promise yet more? Sacrifice yet more? Take *My* essence, take all of *Me,* into yourself?"

"Yes," he said, instantly, without hesitation. "Yes!"

He had been penetrated, he had been filled.

Now he was *entered,* and felt himself die.

***

Although this is my own journal, meant for no eyes but mine to read... although I have already committed here many shameful truths and admissions…

Although I intended only honesty within these pages…

I find I cannot record in their entirety the events of that final night. I have already done in some detail a report to my employer, regarding his nephew.

Suffice to say, the young man in question was indeed located.

He had indeed fallen in among a cult, and it was in their temple—situated within the brownstone previously mentioned—we found him. Drugged nearly senseless, and… violated… in some incomprehensible manner I cannot begin to describe.

As I understand it, his uncle will be consulting with surgeons of cosmetic medicine to restore to the best of their abilities his appearance. Once, of course, his physical condition has been stabilized. His mental condition may well be another matter altogether. When not lapsed into catatonia, he laughs in a manner such as to distress anyone within earshot, and occasionally makes nonsensical utterances in what appears to be a very ancient Egyptian dialect, as well as other and unfamiliar languages that to me sounded far older.

I do not believe he would have left willingly, nor do I believe I could have recovered him on my own. It is largely to the credit of Kitty O'Shea and her mustered troops of fellow mollies that we were able to gain admittance to the building… and fight our way back out again.

There had been in progress an orgiastic rite of the most depraved sort, involving drugs and carnal congress of varieties such that the mind shudders to comprehend. The mollies are women who have known men at their most base and vulgar; nonetheless, they were nearly as aghast as I myself was.

What we found… what we saw… what they had done…

The woman on the altar, what was left of her, gutted, eviscerated.

The boys, the Quiet Boys as Kitty called them… they were not human.

Those jars, those clay vessels, shelves and shelves of clay vessels…

The things they contained were still alive.

Alive.

And not human either.

Not human.

I thought the mollies would smash the jars, destroy the contents, kill and crush the horrors within.

Instead, they took them. Held them, fussed over them like lost children, cooed and cuddled and cradled them to their breasts.

Kitty...

I will never see her again, and I am glad.

I leave Red Hook tonight. I leave the Brickwalk, its conglomeration of strangeness, sights, smells, and sounds. I go back to Arkham, alone. Alone but for questions, unanswered questions for which there may be no answers, and for that I am glad as well.

But, for now, I must be done with this journal. I must be done with this room, with my landlady, with the view from my window and the girl who sits in the areaway under it.

Who sits there, selling—not seashells, as the tongue-twister says—but cigarets. And singing.

Oh Molly, sweet Molly Malloy.

PROFESSOR PATRIOT AND THE DOOM THAT CAME TO NICEVILLE

I n dark-shadowed dimness, a pallid light flickered and tinny voices spoke.

The hush was classroom-quiet, a surface listening attentiveness underlain by the swinging of feet and shifting of bodies, the soft scritch of a pencil, the rustle of paper as notes were passed or comic book pages surreptitiously turned, the occasional whisper.

The projector continued its rattling hum. The educational film played on, showing a cartoon family in a cartoon dining room.

Dad sits at the head of the table, Big Sister Susie to his left, Little Brother Jimmy to his right. Mom, smiling, carries in a steaming pot roast from the kitchen.

Ding-bong!

"What's that?" says the narrator. "Someone at the door?"

Susie hops up, all poodle skirt and ponytail. She goes to answer it. "Hi, Uncle Bud!"

"It's Uncle Bud," the narrator says. "And he's brought someone with him. Who could it be? Why, it's his new fiancée!"

Cartoon introductions and small-talk follow, during which only Jimmy seems uneasy, frowning and suspicious.

With a *pthoo!* sound, a spitwad flew through the air and pasted itself to the blackboard beside the pull-down screen. Muffled snickers and giggles erupted around the room.

"Eddie," Miss Chambers said, using one of her milder but serious warning tones.

He immediately adopted perfect posture and an expression of angelic innocence. The other children followed suit.

By then, of course, they'd missed the dramatic moment in which cartoon Jimmy exposed Uncle Bud's new fiancée for the batrachian monstrosity she truly was.

"Golly, Jim, thanks!" Uncle Bud ruffles Jimmy's cartoon cowlick hair. "Good thing for me you knew what to do!"

"Aw, shucks," says Jimmy, freckled and grinning a wide gap-toothed grin. "I just pay attention in school, is all."

The rest of the family crowds around them, lavishing congratulations on Jimmy before Dad suggests they go out for ice cream sodas.

"Looks like it worked out all right..." The narrator trails off into an ominous pause. "... this time. But would *you* know what to do? Would *you* recognize the signs? Let's go over them again. Read along with me."

Bold lettering appears on the screen.

THE INNSMOUTH 'LOOK':
1. BULGING EYES
2. CLAMMY SKIN
3. WEBBED FINGERS
4. MUSHY VOICE
5. SEA-SMELL
6. GILL FLAPS

"Now that you know what to watch for," the narrator says, "it's up to you to stay alert. If you notice anyone with some of these telltale signs, report it at once. Remember, the safety of your family, friends, and fellow Americans could be depending on *you.*"

The closing-credits came up—"This has been a civil defense production from the Department of Eldritch Emergency Preparedness." Then the 3-2-1, and then a blank white square filled the screen. The loose end of the film strip made its familiar whap-flutter-whap noise.

Mikey, puffed with self-importance at being one of this week's Class Helpers, switched off the projector and began the process of re-threading the reel to rewind it. Georgina turned the overhead lights on and raised the blinds, letting spring sunshine spill through the windows.

Miss Chambers glanced at the clock above the door and saw that they still had time to go over some fractions before the readiness drill. The students groaned when she instructed them to open their math workbooks, but complied.

They did eight problems before a click and a chime issued from the PA speaker on the wall. Principal Ross read the noon announcements—Open House next week, 6th grade field trip permission slips due, Arkham Care Brigade was collecting letters for injured servicemen, cast list for the school play would be posted after lunch.

There followed a pause, another click, and a brief scratchy hiss. Then the speakers jingled out a bouncy tune and a chorus of perky singers:

What do you do when the sirens sound?
And the sky goes strange for miles around?
Well the first thing you do is to hit the ground!
You DUCK (do-dee-do) and COVER
Just DUCK (do-dee-do) and COVER
What if there's a color from out of space?
And cyclopean horrors all over the place?
Well better make sure that you hide your face!
Just DUCK (do-dee-do) and COVER
Yes DUCK (do-dee-do) and COVER
(do-dah!)

The song finished with a brassy flourish and cymbal clash. The alarm whooped a shrill triple-blast.

The children, on cue, in a flurry of motion, pushed back their chairs, scooted beneath their desks, squeezed their eyes shut, tucked their foreheads down by their knees, and laced their fingers at the napes of their necks.

Miss Chambers walked among the rows, checking, nodding, and making occasional corrections. "Head lower, Marcie. Billy, your left foot's sticking out. Mary-Lou, are you chewing gum? That had better not be a comic book, Charlie."

Mary-Lou was able to get rid of the evidence with a guilty gulp, but Charlie did not have that option.

"It's Professor Patriot, though!"

She tapped her foot, snapped her fingers, and reached down.

"Awwww..." He snaked up his arm to hand over the comic.

"Thank you," said Miss Chambers crisply. She rolled it into a tube and proceeded toward the rear of the classroom, smacking the cylindrical roll of colored newsprint into her palm.

When the all-clear and then the lunch bell sounded, the orderliness broke into a genial chaos. Students scrambled out from under their desks, girls fussing at their clothes, boys jostling each other. They raced for the row of lunchboxes and brown bags on the shelf beside the door.

Moments later, the last echoing footsteps faded from the hall, and the room was quiet again.

Miss Chambers smiled, shook her head, put down the confiscated comic, and went about tidying up in preparation for the afternoon lessons. She straightened askew desks, pushed in chairs, erased the fractions from the blackboard, and listed a dozen new vocabulary words:

Squamous
Rugose
Cyclopean
Amorphous

Stygian

Unutterable

Loathsome

Tenebrous

Foetid

Ichor

Monolithic

Lambent

Satisfied with the state of the classroom, she sat down and slid open the drawer where she kept her own sack lunch. As she arranged the sandwich, carrot sticks, hard-boiled egg and oatmeal-raisin cookies, she noticed that Charlie's comic book had relaxed into a mostly-unrolled curl.

Professor Patriot...

She smiled and shook her head again.

There he was on the cover, in a dramatic action pose, wielding a glowing yellow-white stick of chalk that reflected in the lenses of his hornrim glasses. Professor Patriot always managed to look both respectable and rumpled in his tweed jacket with the elbow patches, slacks, flag pin, and sneakers. His brown hair was short enough to not alarm anybody's parents, but tousled and unruly enough that the kids found it 'cool' as well as vaguely rock-and-roll. Young but not too young, old but not too old, he gave every impression of the dedicated teacher... but quirky, the kind that made learning fun.

Also on the cover were hideous half-reptilian/half-canine creatures, fanged and gaunt, boiling out of an unearthly rift in reality, raging as they came up short against a brilliant flare of light issuing from the equations Professor Patriot had etched in mid-air.

Bold comic-book lettering splashed jagged and excited across the page: WILL THE POWER OF EUCLIDIAN GEOMETRY DRIVE BACK THE HOUNDS OF TINDALOS???

She'd brought a paperback to read while she ate her lunch, but found herself leafing through the comic instead. It was silly, without a doubt. It made light of the everpresent threats under which they all now lived, turning horror into mockery. It was absurd and over-the-top in its heroics.

And yet...

Reading it somehow made her feel better. More hopeful, more in control, more confident that the world they knew and loved would survive this, would emerge stronger than ever.

That was the entire purpose. Like the daily drills, and the civil defense films put out by the Department of Eldritch Emergency Preparedness. Yesterday, it had been Big Sister Susie who had the problem... her best friend Ronette had fallen in with a Bad Crowd.

"Aw, come on, Susie, don't be a square! We're just going down to the lake to drink some beer and do the Dance of Dagon. *All* the cool kids will be there!"

Or like the jingles, which yesterday had been about what to do if you found a suspicious tome of ancient evil sitting around:

Just don't LOOK
(do-dee-do, do-dee-do)
In the BOOK
(do-dee-do, do-dee-do)
JUUUUUUSSSSST
DOOOOONNNNN'T
LOOK!!!
(dah-dah!)

So, they had their Fungus-Free Victory Gardens, and the Arkham Care Brigade delivering letters to the hospitals and asylums. They had cartoons in which various Warner Brothers characters carried out wacky hijinks against the Mythos Menace, and the MovieReel clips celebrating the brave scholars and scientists of this great nation's military fighting the good fight to protect the American way of life. They had comedy sketch shows like *MIskatonic 6-5000* on television, and radio serial dramas like *The Rats in the Walls.*

And they had Professor Patriot. There was even a stage show that toured the country, with puppets, comedians, and an actor in a tweed jacket and hornrims. The chorus girls were the Patriettes, leggy beauties in short pleated skirts and tight tweed vests. The highlight of the performance was said to involve the Professor punching Cthulhu in the face.

The comic's last page was an advertisement in which the Professor rescued an innocent family, closed the 13 Gates, and saved the day, all because:

"Even evil cultists can't resist the wholesome fruity goodness of Mostest Snack Pies! Mmm, they're the Mmmostest!"

The back cover sported a mail-in offer to sign up for the Professor Patriot Fan Club, complete with certificate, flag-pin badge, Patrioteer membership card, and Omniglot Decoder Ring. The ring in the picture—an antiquarian sort of relic, corroded with verdigris—bore little resemblance to the plastic baubles she'd seen several students wearing to school.

Done with her lunch, Miss Chambers stepped outside for a breath of fresh air before venturing over to the teachers' lounge to get a cup of coffee.

She'd walked to school through another perfect Niceville morning of clear blue skies, warm sunshine, butterflies dancing above the flowerbeds, birds twittering in the trees. Now, the day had warmed and gone slightly muggy. The breeze had stilled. The cars motoring up and down Main Street, chrome glinting, fins gleaming, looked dreamlike and faraway in the haze.

In the lounge, the talk was of Senator McCarthy's latest committee findings, the relative merits of Oldsmobiles versus Buicks, the unfortunate Ladies' Garden Club incident regarding Mrs. Mallory's debut of her "Sweet Yuggoth" orchid, Mr. Jenkins's new color television, and the subversive musical and literary influences of juvenile delinquents possibly creeping toward their very own town.

"Here?" Mr. Benson scoffed as he filled his pipe. "In Niceville?"

"Preposterous," said Mrs. Andrews, with the imperious declaratory tones worthy of the seniormost member of Ashton-Smith Elementary's faculty.

"I did hear that they caught a group of teenagers over in Fairview,"

Nurse Harper said. "Reading... reading *The King in Yellow.*"

Gasps arose, but Mrs. Andrews withered them all with her gaze. "Well, that *is* Fairview for you. Ever since they put in that roller-rink, what do you expect?"

Mr. Evans, the vice-principal, nodded. "Heard they were talking about having one of those drive-in movie theaters put in, too."

More gasps, and a round of tutting disapproval, greeted this. They moved on to a discussion of Niceville's own movie theater, the Paradise, which normally showed decent, family films like *Singin' in the Rain* and *Cinderella*. The latest poster in the 'Coming Soon' display case, however, was for Marlon Brando and James Dean in *The Thousand Young.*

Jill Chambers, sipping her coffee, listened and said nothing. Her status in the school hierarchy—newest, youngest, unmarried, pretty, a hometown girl who'd been in many of these very teachers' own classes not so long ago—didn't lend itself well to speaking out.

Besides, she'd been on dates to roller-rinks and drive-ins... she'd read part of *The King in Yellow* herself in college, though it had frightened her so badly she'd thrown the book away long before reaching Act II... and she might go see *The Thousand Young*, despite the leather jackets and sullen pouts that made both stars look like Bad Boys of the worst sort.

It wasn't as if she had her family's reputation to worry about, either. She was the only Chambers left in Niceville now. When her parents were mentioned, it was usually in tones of sidelong sympathy flavored with delicious hints of gossip, tragedy and scandal.

"You heard about Frank Chambers, of course," they'd say. "Poor Vera. It's no wonder she..." This would be accompanied by a significant, knowing lift of the eyebrows and a pantomime gesture of tilting a glass.

"All because of what happened to their son, you know."

"Surprising the daughter stayed, don't you think? Oh, she's a nice enough girl and all, but..."

Danny Chambers had been the ideal clean-cut all-American

boy—good-looking, popular, athletic, class president as well as captain of the football team. Everyone adored and admired him. When he'd enlisted, it seemed like the whole town turned out to see him off at the train station, waving from the platform as he waved back from the window, on his way to San Diego.

Jill, who'd adored and admired him more than anyone, had even planned to join the Army Nurse Corps when she finished high school. She'd follow in his footsteps, do her part, serve her country, make them proud.

But then, Danny died in the South Pacific, along with all of his shipmates aboard the *USS Derleth* at the Battle of R'lyeh. Their father... well, they'd found him in the garage, the military notification telegram still in his hand, as if he'd figured no further note was needed.

After the funerals, their grief-stricken mother had gone to Des Moines to live with Aunt Rose, leaving Jill on her own.

She did have to admit it was lonely sometimes. The house, small though it was, often felt too big with just her in it. She'd given up on the nursing idea, becoming a teacher instead... and though she liked it, and was good at it, she still had the occasional pang of wondering what might have been, of feeling as if she'd taken the safe path rather than the right one.

From out on the playground came the distant trill of the recess monitor's whistle, signaling the students to gather up their jacks, jump ropes, basketballs and bubblegum cards. The faculty performed their own variation on this, rinsing cups, finishing crosswords, and stubbing out cigarettes.

The change in the weather sapped the sass out of even the most rambunctious of her students. They went through the Presidential Health-and-Fitness regime with limp dispiritedness, barely complained at all when Miss Chambers sprang a math quiz on them, and wrote listlessly in their journals without the usual giggling and whispering.

The afternoon dragged by, each tick of the clock more and more sluggish as the hands crept endlessly around.

The alarm whooped.

Miss Chambers, who'd been fanning herself—with what turned out to be Charlie's comic—nearly sprang out of her skin.

The familiar triple-blast was followed by a series of shriek-pause-shriek-pause siren wails that went on and on.

The students, startled but well-trained, obediently shoved back their chairs and ducked under their desks.

"We already *had* the drill," said one of the girls in an indignant fussbudget *that's-so-unfair!* tone.

"Heads down," Miss Chambers said, recovering herself as she got to her feet.

In the pauses between the shrieks, she heard protests from neighboring classrooms and annoyed outbursts from her fellow faculty. She was sure there'd be a good deal of discussion in the lounge about *this.*

Her own training took over with the comfort of routine, despite the ongoing sirens. She moved down the aisle between two rows of desks.

Another more distant but ear-splitting screech joined the din.

"Is that the town whistle?" someone shouted.

"That's the town whistle!" shouted someone else.

Anxiety rose in Miss Chambers's throat like bitter acid.

"The fire bell, too!" a third someone cried, and yes, there was a persistent jangling clangor adding to the cacophony.

Several of her students chimed in:

"What's wrong?"

"What is it?"

"I want to go home!"

"Make it stop!"

"Miss Chaaaaaaambers!"

"Stay where you are!" she barked, in her most authoritarian teacher-voice. "Heads *down!*"

The classroom door burst open and Tommy stumbled in,

clutching the restroom pass. He lunged at her, tripped, fell to his knees, and grabbed her skirt.

"The sky!" he howled. Then he dove under his desk.

The other children screamed.

"Stay *put!*" Miss Chambers ordered.

She rushed to the nearest window, and immediately wished she hadn't.

The sky over Niceville was green.

A terrible, churning, bilious green... the western horizon choked with clouds that were not clouds but undulant, amorphous, spongelike masses... from which dropped a rain that was not rain but something else, some sort of writhing, dark specks...

Townspeople ran, frantic, in all directions. Cars sped down streets, tires screeching. They sideswiped mailboxes, hopped curbs, plowed headlong into storefronts or collided with each other in snarls of chrome and gleaming metal.

"The bunker! The basement! Hurry!" It sounded like Mr. Evans, the vice-principal, his voice a hectic urgency mixed with the maniacal laughter of impending insanity. "Get the students to the bunker!"

The school hall filled with a mad stampede of footsteps, voices raised in cries of fear, cries of pain.

Some of Miss Chambers's class began sliding out from under their desks but she knew if they went out there it'd be a packed mob of bodies, a throng, pushing and jostling. They'd be trampling each other in their panic. She raced to the door and banged it shut.

"Stay *put!*" she ordered again.

It halted their surge toward the exit, but they did not all return to their duck-and-cover positions. They gathered in the aisles, the girls clutching hands, the boys trying to act brave.

They'd propped the windows open in vain hopes of catching a sluggish breeze. Now a hard wind gusted. It stank of mold and spoiled coleslaw. The half-lowered blinds snapped and flapped, whipping about, some rattle-rolling back up. Papers blew everywhere.

The hideous green sky filtered the daylight to a swamp-sickly hue. The black, spongelike masses dipped lower, toward the buildings, shedding their weird rain of writhing specks. Closer now, they resembled burrs or jellyfish, something both prickly and tendriled. There was purpose in their descent, as if targeting in on anyone or anything that moved.

As Miss Chambers and her students stared in horror, one of the writhing things divebombed a fleeing man. Its myriad whip-thin tentacles lashed around his head and neck. He tried to yank it off, went into flailing, jerking spasms, and landed in a flowerbed amid a flurry of tattered petals... but, mercifully, blocked from view.

"Class Helpers, shut the windows!"

She hadn't known she was going to speak, but Mikey and Georgina were on it like a flash. They slammed and latched all the windows.

Aircraft swooped in from the northeast, fighter jets with engines roaring and machine guns firing in peppering staccato. All the boys cheered and some of the girls did too as the jets engaged the clouds-that-weren't-clouds in an aerial battle. The enemy fired back with some kind of organic javelins, long and twisted, glistening, tipped with barbed points.

The machine guns riddled the not-clouds, pierced and perforated them, blew off large irregular chunks that hailed down in a grisly shower of ichor and dark, spongy matter.

A helicopter appeared next, buzzing in low and heavy like a bumblebee. It was apparently heading for the Niceville Town Hall when the plummeting shredded mass of one of the not-clouds struck it with a wet, indescribable noise of rotors chugging and chopping and clogging. The helicopter veered out of control. A man either jumped or was hurled from it as it wobbled, wallowed, and plunged drunkenly toward the school.

"Get down!" Miss Chambers cried, seizing as many students as were within reach and pulling them to the floor.

DUCK (do-dee-do) and COVER jingled in her mind, perky and

inane. It was drowned out seconds later by an enormous thudding crunch, the shrill shearing of metal, and the fiery thunder of an explosion. The building shook. A window broke, showering them with fragments.

Half-deafened, shaking glass from her hair, Miss Chambers raised her head and did a frantic count-check. Some of the children had sustained scratches, bumps and scrapes, but none of them were seriously hurt and she almost sobbed with relief.

The stink of mold and spoiled coleslaw was not improved by the smoke from burning fuel. They picked themselves up, coughing, waving at the thick and foetid air.

Foetid... amorphous... ichor... Miss Chambers wondered how many more of this week's vocabulary words they were going to need before this was done.

The helicopter had missed the school, leaving a scorched crater and a smoldering track as its mangled wreckage skidded to a stop just outside the front doors. Burning debris and bubbling clots of sludge littered the lawn. If anybody had still been in it when it hit, the fireball blaze was too bright to see.

"Hey, look!" Mikey pointed. "There, in Home-Safe Tree!"

Miss Chambers looked where he pointed. The name had been bestowed on the grand old oak long before her parents' time here; it was a landmark in its own right as well as being the centerpiece of many recess games, and a shady place to sit on sunny days when the teachers decided to take some of the lessons outside.

Now, a figure struggled amid the leafy branches. It was the man who'd jumped or been flung from the stricken helicopter. He seemed to be trying to clamber the rest of the way down, making a precarious job of it. Whether this was due to him being injured or just dazed was impossible to tell, but, even as they watched, he lost his grip, tumbled to the ground and collapsed.

Several of the children spoke:

"I see him!"

"Is it the pilot?"

"Is he dead?"

"He's not moving."

"He's dead."

"Maybe not!"

Charlie, who'd been staring out with a stunned expression, said, "It's Professor Patriot."

Eddie elbowed him. "Don't be a dumbo."

"It *is!* See the jacket?"

"Professor Patriot's not real," sneered Eddie. "He's a made-up thing for babies, like Superman, Mickey Mouse and Santa."

"You take that back, Eddie Parker!" Marcie faced him with imperious foreboding, arms crossed, jaw set, glowering with such wrath that Eddie, class bully and troublemaker though he was, cowed.

"Whoever he is," said Miss Chambers, "he needs help."

"I'll go!" Charlie said at once, starting for the broken window.

She caught him by the collar before he could climb out. "No. I'll get…"

… the principal, she'd been about to say, or one of the other male teachers, or Mr. Savinsky the janitor.

But the hall, previously packed, was empty when she opened the door.

The rest of them must have reached the basement survival bunker. They'd be huddled in there, adults doing their best to keep everyone calm, waiting for the all-clear, for the government radio announcement, or for rescue to arrive.

Another glance outside told her those might be a while. The aerial battle had shifted north, over Mr. Prescott's fields instead of the town, but Niceville remained awash under that turbulent green sky, downtown swarming with the monstrous burr-jellyfish creatures that writhed and flailed over Main Street's tidy shops.

Her mind wavered.

This wasn't supposed to be happening.

The final bell should have rung by now. She should have been walking home, skirt swishing demurely around her shins, looking forward to a quiet evening grading papers while *I Love Lucy* and *The Dark Door* were on.

An urge seized her to just go, just run for it, get to her little house—

But she couldn't abandon her students. And she couldn't just leave that man out there by Home-Safe Tree, whoever he was.

Danny wouldn't have done it.

"Wait here," she said.

She used a science workbook to brush away the glass, scrambled through the windowframe with no regard for teacherly dignity, and ran with both arms waving above her head like someone trying to fend off bats. It would do no good if one of those things dive-bombed her, she knew, but she did it anyway.

He certainly *dressed* like Professor Patriot, she noticed as she neared the groaning, stirring man. Charlie had been right about that.

Tweed jacket, slacks, sneakers... respectable but rumpled— though he *had* also just fallen from a crashing helicopter into a tree, which would rumple a person.

Closer yet, she had to admit the resemblance to the comic-book character was striking, even as battered as he was from the fall. All he lacked were the hornrims.

Miss Chambers knelt beside him. "Sir?"

He groaned again, mumbling something incomprehensible.

"Sir?" She grasped his shoulder, shook it, hesitated, and said, feeling not un-foolish, "Professor?"

His eyelids twitched open. The eyes beneath were brown. He squinted up at her, clearly confused, if not stunned or concussed. "Hello?"

"Are you all right?"

"Ahhh... where am I?"

"Niceville—"

"Niceville!" He bolted to a sitting position, winced, and doubled over with a hiss of breath through his teeth, cradling his left arm to his ribs. "And you are... Miss—?"

"Chambers. Jill Chambers."

He touched his face, then groped about in the grass. "Miss Chambers, I don't suppose you see a pair of glasses anywhere?"

She found them. Hornrims. Of course. She saw that he even had a flag-pin in his lapel. Suddenly it made partial sense. The stage show, the stage show was playing up in State City.

"Thank you," he said when she gave them to him. He settled them into place and looked around. "That's better." When he looked again at her, the corner of his mouth tilted up in a half-smile and he added, *"Much* better."

Miss Chambers, caught off-guard, blushed and hoped her curls hadn't gone too frizzy from the humidity.

Yells from the direction of the school made her glance back, almost glad of the distraction. Her students were crammed against the windows, Charlie and Eddie both trying to lean out of the broken one. When she shifted her glance in the direction of their urgent gestures, a chill of horror, like some loathsome trickle of cold, gelid fluid, shivered the length of her spine. It was very effective in quashing her flustered reaction.

A cluster of the burr-things, floating somehow, propelling themselves by whipping their tendrils, advanced from downtown. Though they diverted and paused to examine various objects, their meandering course brought them slowly but steadily toward Home-Safe Tree.

The man, following her gaze, uttered something that sounded like, "Nyeeth," and shuddered. It summed up her own opinion of the creatures fairly well.

"We have to get indoors," Miss Chambers said. "Can you walk?"

"I…" He got most of the way to his feet, swayed, and grimaced.

"Here, let me help you." She put her arm around his waist.

"Miss Chambers—"

"I know, we've only just met, this is highly irregular…" She swept her free hand to encompass the scene. "But then, what of this isn't?"

"Good point." He leaned on her and together they made their awkward way at a quick hobble back to the building.

They detoured around the places where helicopter-chopped lumps of the spongy matter appeared to be slowly sinking in on themselves, deflating like ruined souffles.

Youthful voices clamored:

"Hurry up, Miss Chambers, hurry!"

"The monsters are coming!"

"It's okay, everybody, Professor Patriot's here now! He'll save us!"

Miss Chambers cast an anxious look at the man. "Please play along. For the children's sake?"

"Play along?"

"They need something to believe in. They need hope. Please."

"Miss—"

Squeals in terrified unison came from most of the girls and some of the boys.

"Look out! Eeeeeee! Look out!"

One of the creatures swept toward them. Miss Chambers saw it all too well—the round body nothing but a cluster of chitinous pincers, flexing around tiny tooth-ringed orifices... the dozens of thin, scaled, pustule-covered tendrils lashing... the nightmarish noises it made, a sharp clicking and slithery rustling...

"Move, dumbo!" At the window, Eddie elbowed Charlie aside. He held a slingshot, and regardless of everything else, Miss Chambers noticed it was not the same one she'd confiscated from him only last week. That one's handle had been yellow; this one's was black.

He drew back, took aim, and let fly. Something whizzed through the air, passing not a foot over their heads. It scored a bullseye on the creature with a sharp crack that sounded strangely like the break-shot in a game of pool.

"Gotcha!" crowed Eddie. "Take that!"

Then they were at the window. Again, regularity and teacherly dignity were cast aside; she gave the man a boost by the seat of his pants as Mikey and Charlie pulled on his jacket, then hoisted herself up and through with such fear-inspired strength that they all ended up on the floor in a heap.

"Cover the window!" Miss Chambers said, panting for breath. "Desks... pile them on the art shelf... barricade..."

Four of the boys did as instructed, while Georgina and Peggy pulled down all the blinds. Gloom filled the classroom, tinged swampy-green at the edges.

"Will it hold?" Billy asked.

Mary-Lou shushed him.

Everyone waited, tense.

...click...

...scrape...

...rustle...

...click-scraaaaaaaape...

Silence.

"Is it gone?" Katie whispered.

"I think it went away," Charlie said.

"Yeah." Eddie lowered his slingshot. "Did you see? I beaned that ugly bastard with my aggie!"

Betty raised her hand. "Miss Chambers, Eddie said—"

"Never mind," said Miss Chambers, deciding that if teacherly dignity could go on hiatus, so could teacherly discipline. "That was a very good shot, Eddie. Thank you."

"Saved our lives, sport." The man in the hornrims heaved himself into a chair, favoring his left side. "Well done."

"What are they, Professor?" asked Charlie.

Miss Chambers cast him another anxious, pleading look.

"Nyeeth," he said again, in reply to Charlie. "They're called the Nyeeth. And you, son, you must be one of my loyal Patrioteers, am I right?"

"Yes, sir!" He proudly showed off his plastic Omniglot Decoder Ring.

"That's swell!" The man clapped Charlie on the back, making the boy beam, and raised his eyebrows at the others. "Anyone else?"

Several eager hands went up. The children pressed around him, all chattering at once, bombarding him with questions. Tommy, shyly, offered up a Mostest Snack Pie he'd traded for at lunch but had been saving for later. At that, the Professor laughed and told them he'd put them in for commendations.

"Patrioteers First Class, how does that sound?"

Their delighted smiles said it sounded great. Miss Chambers even found herself smiling at their excitement. How the day had gone from normal to horrific to *this...*

He really was good, this 'Professor.'

Not to mention handsome...

"I am very glad to meet you all," he said. "Right now, though, I think we need to get to someplace a little safer, don't you?"

Heads nodded in vigorous agreement.

"Miss Chambers? The school must have a bunker."

"In the basement," she said. "Though they'll have locked it, and closed the Seal, by now. They won't just open it until the all-clear, not without notification from the government, the Office of Civil Defense or the Department of—"

"Oh, absolutely," he said, brown eyes twinkling. "Nor would I expect them to, under normal circumstances. But, as you mentioned earlier, these aren't. Shall we?"

She studied him a moment, lips pursed. There *was* such a thing as *too* good, when it came to acting.

On the other hand, if they couldn't get into the bunker proper, the basement would be better shelter than a classroom with a broken window.

Miss Chambers clapped twice. "Line up, assembly order, please."

The students scurried into place, two lines, boys and girls, the Class Helpers at the front.

"One more thing, Miss Chambers?"

"Yes... Professor?"

He grinned disarmingly. "May I borrow a fresh stick of chalk?"

"I'll get it!" Charlie bounded to the supply cupboard.

"Are we ready?" Miss Chambers asked, standing by the door. "Good. Calmly, patiently, staying together."

Their little procession made its way into the hall, Miss Chambers at the lead and Professor Patriot bringing up the rear. Evidence of the earlier stampede was everywhere—posters half torn from the walls, wastepaper baskets overturned, the Academic Excellence trophy case cracked, dropped pencils, someone's lost shoe—and the only light came from the EMERGENCY EXIT signs. Here and there on the tiles were spots and smears of what she thought might be blood, hopefully nothing more serious than a bloody nose or scraped knee.

The south stairwell had never seemed creepier. Their steps were loud on the industrial-grey metal stairs, echoing hollowly back from painted cinderblock walls. A yellowish bulb in a wire cage sputtered high overhead.

At the bunker door, she stopped.

"It's locked," she said. "The Seal is closed."

As she'd known it would be... so, why did she feel such a crushing weight of disappointment?

She stood there with her palm laid flat on the thick steel, letting her head slump forward. A ragged sigh escaped her. They would have to make do in the basement storage area after all.

"Pardon me, Patrioteers. Excuse me, Miss Chambers, may I?"

Shrugging indifferently, she moved aside.

He took out a stick of the chalk and began swiftly etching numbers and symbols on the door. Equations. Algebraic and geometric equations... which weren't *on* the door, she realized, but suspended in the air before it... as the chalk-stick took on a strange lambent glow.

Lambent, another of this week's vocabulary words...

The Seal released, the lock unlocked, and he pulled the bunker door open on its immense hinge-pins.

Miss Chambers stared at the man in the tweed jacket and

hornrims. "I thought you were an actor," she said.

He flashed her a quick grin and a wink as he tucked the chalk into his pocket and ushered the children inside. The next few minutes were something of an uproar of exclamations, outbursts, demands for explanations, and assorted confusion. He ignored it all, his attention on her students.

"You'll be safe here," he said. "Re-lock the door, re-close the Seal, and keep everyone calm until rescue arrives. I'm counting on you, Patrioteers."

"Yes, sir," they chorused. Even Eddie, who'd scoffed before, was convinced.

Charlie added, "But aren't you staying, Professor?"

"I can't right now." He gripped Charlie's shoulder and gave it a firm squeeze. "The Nyeeth are still out there, and I have work to do."

"Will we see you again?"

"Of course you will," he said. "And, Miss Chambers, it's been a privilege. You are a very brave, cool-headed and capable young woman. Your brother would be proud."

"How do you know about Danny?"

"I was at R'lyeh, too," he said, and a haunted look shadowed his eyes. "Oh, yes. I was at R'lyeh."

"I…" she began, but did not know what to say.

"They were heroes," he said, shaking off the haunted look. "They all were. So are you." The corner of his mouth slanted up again in that half-smile. "If you ever want a job as an Assistant Professor, look me up."

With that, he stepped out of the bunker. He saluted. The children saluted in return. The huge, heavy door began to swing shut.

The safe path… the right path…

"Professor!" Miss Chambers darted through the narrowing gap. "Wait! I'm going with you!"

And, together, off they went to save the town and their fellow Americans from the doom that had come to Niceville.

INCENSE AND INSENSIBILITY

M rs. Aylesbury, being a widow with two daughters, had fallen rather into dire straits since the death of her husband. When, therefore, a cottage at Star-Winds became available by the graces of a distant cousin, she was gladly obliged to accept.

That cousin, although born John Yaddith, had taken to going by the name of Brother Zoar. A large man, caftaned and sandaled, possessed of a leonine white mane, he welcomed them with immense affection.

The cottage proved both humble and cozy, smallish but adequate to the needs of the Aylesbury ladies. They found the environs most agreeable, set as it was in a cool, pearly-dawned coastal forest of fog-drenched ferns and redwoods.

Within a matter of days, they felt very much at home. During the daylight hours, they busied themselves with the activities of the community. They helped in the garden and kitchen, learned to macrame, wrote poetry, practiced the arts of tie-dye and beading.

Evenings, when they gathered cozily together, they would touch flame to some scent of incense or other—sandalwood, cinnamon, strawberry, less identifiable fragrances. These fragrant concoctions, along with blends of tea, potpourri, natural remedies, soaps and candles, were made and sold to augment the community's modest income. Some had an invigorating effect that went well with card games or chatter; others, more calming, lent themselves to the enjoyment of quieter pursuits.

The elder of the sisters, Eleanor, had a particular interest in the botanical and found herself fascinated by the various processes. She struck up particular friendships with a girl called Hesperia and a striking youth known as Chaos. They, for their part, were more than glad to show her around and instruct her.

Dried and ground substances—tree bark, seeds, leaves, fruit rinds, flower petals, moss—all went into the making. Men and women perched upon stools, working the mixtures together with soft resins, gum arabics and pine saps. The resulting material, they formed into cones or pellets, or molded around thin sticks, or packaged into small round tins for use in incense-burners.

Eleanor noted the predominance of patchouli, lemongrass, sandalwood, cloves, charcoal and essential oils. Each breath brought minglings of aroma: floral and spice, sweet and bitter, fragrant and pungent.

Some, she almost knew but could not name. They danced enticingly, evocatively, at the very edges of her memory. Others, she did not know at all, and the merest whiff of them stirred a strange and vague expectancy of something almost akin to dread or revulsion so deep it was almost subconscious.

"I don't recognize the..." she said, faltering. "I can't quite identify..."

Chaos's dark eyes glinted. "We know all the places where the most rare and secret things grow."

"Rare and secret?" Eleanor echoed. She took up a pinch of the gritty, sticky stuff and rolled it between her fingertips and thumb. It felt like grainy clay, like wet salt dough, like wads of damp cornmeal. She sniffed it and sensed again that strange, vague expectancy... that something-akin-to-dread... and wasn't sure if she wanted to recoil, or inhale more of its weird perfume.

"Like, so rare and secret, you won't find them anyplace else," Hesperia said.

"This blend," said Chaos, savoring it, "is among the rarest of them all."

Again, Eleanor sniffed at the incense, crushing it against the pad of her thumb to release more of its aroma.

Its predominance was a strong, damp earthiness... not quite like mildew, nor mold, but similar. Loam? Peat? The moss that grew thick and furry in crevices of redwood bark? Yet... fleshy, somehow... slightly sour, even acrid... or was it?

And there was some undercurrent of... spice... carnation? Marigold? Anise? Was that a hint of anise she detected? Or possibly fennel; it lacked the sweetness particular to licorice root...

"When it burns," said Chaos, leaning close, so close that his cheek almost brushed against hers as he spoke, and his breath tickled warm and soft in her ear, "when it burns, you'll see the colors in its smolder, glowing spires like faint suns in skies of flame, and red-gold thrones where gods no longer sit."

She trembled, though with what precise emotions, she couldn't quite define. His words seemed both profound and utterly without meaning, imbued with passion and promise. She felt poised at a threshold to some greater knowledge, some epiphany. A step further, and she might find her way to the enlightenment that would open new worlds of understanding.

Hesperia leaned in just as close on Eleanor's other side, long hair falling in a shimmering drape. She held out a cupped hand, in the palm of which were strewn several loose petals.

Eleanor caught her breath at the sight of them. They were unlike anything she'd ever seen before. The nearest resemblance she could think of was less botanical than entomological, putting her in mind of the veined, glassy-clear wings of dragonflies.

The fragrance wafting up from them was that of fading, unearthly, dying starlight.

The very thought struck her as strangely poetic to have come from her own usually more prosaic consciousness.

Fading, unearthly, dying starlight?

The petals showed only a slight wilting that suggested they'd been recently plucked from the bloom… petal by petal, in the loves-me/loves-me-not manner with which a romantic might pluck the petals of a daisy.

When she picked one up, she found it—though delicate-seeming—strong and supple, somehow silken to the touch, yet also oddly… membranous. She held it beneath her nose and inhaled deeply of that strangely poetic fragrance.

Yes… fading, dying, unearthly starlight.

Images that were not images, but more akin to half-remembered visions from someone else's dream, drifted through her inner darkness.

"What is that?" she asked.

"We call it *nithon,*" Chaos said.

"We'll need to gather more soon; this is the last handful left." Hesperia dropped the petals into a mortar and took up a pestle to begin grinding them into a thick, clearish jelly.

"Gather it where?"

"Oh, past the sphinxes," said Chaos, in a casual, off-hand manner.

"Past the garden gate," Hesperia added.

"What garden gate?" Eleanor asked, the words sounding faint and far even to her own ears.

"The sphinx-guarded one," Chaos replied. "The labyrinth of wonder."

This made no sense to her, yet she found herself nodding as if in comprehension of some deep and abiding truth.

"Can you imagine," murmured Hesperia, "what else might grow there?"

"Yes…" she sighed.

They smiled the way indulgent adults might smile at some whimsy from a child.

"Oh, but you can't," Chaos told her. "You can't imagine. No one can."

"Then show me. I want to see."

"When you're ready," he said.

She wanted to protest that she was ready there and then, but something in the glinting darkness of his eyes convinced her she would do better not to push yet for more answers.

Instead, she settled onto a vacant stool. The men and women at the table were glad enough to make room for her as they demonstrated their techniques. Soon, Eleanor had the knack of it. Her palms and fingers became discolored, stained from the damp, granular residue.

Had she thought the mixture smelled vaguely unpleasant before? Mildewy and sour? It still did, a bit, but... she did not mind it so much now. Perhaps it was an acquired taste, improving with familiarity and exposure? Or had the thick, clearish jelly of the *nithon*-petals tempered its scent?

Her nose tingled. She thought of what Chaos had said, the colors in its smolder when it burned, and wondered anew what he had meant.

But when she looked up from her work to ask him, she saw that while she'd been occupied, he and Hesperia had drifted away. Resolving to seek them out later, she remained making incense the rest of the afternoon.

It rained that night, a heavy, steady rain, a grey and sodden dreariness that hung a dense pall over everything. A shifting in the weather carried murky tidal smells inland from the sea. The eaves did not so much drip as flow with miniature rivulets. Mud and puddles replaced the paths.

A general irritation built despite the cottage's coziness. Before long, the Aylesbury sisters had taken to bickering over phantom trifles. They found even their dear mother's attempts at kindly cheer to be grating, while she began to find them irksome in a way she never had before. Opening the shutters to let in the air let in only wet chill and brine. They lit candles and incense in hopes of chasing out the lingering disagreeable atmosphere... both figurative and literal, as it were.

Eleanor watched the granular cone smolder in a ceramic dish. Threads of fragrant smoke curled up from the deep red fire-ruby of the ember. It issued forth the very scent she remembered from earlier.

"Where did that come from?" she asked.

"Your friend Hesperia brought it by," her mother said. "She told me we should try it tonight, that it's more potent when it rains. Something about how the moisture intensifies the scent. I saw her taking some to everyone."

"I don't much care for it," said her sister. "It smells of gone-off mushroom soup."

They sat quietly for a few moments, watching the smoke spiral up, spreading and drifting, diffusing, effusing. Eleanor found her gaze drawn to the ember, to the deep red ruby ring smoldering into grey ash.

What had Chaos said? *"…glowing spires like faint suns in skies of flame, and red-gold thrones where gods no longer sit."*

And the strange perfume of it… loam and spice, a fleshy acrid sourness… that hint of something not-quite-anise… but tempered by the scent of fading, unearthly, dying starlight.

They conversed in desultory fashion for a while, then fell silent again, each lost in her own thoughts.

Eleanor's dwelt upon the glassy and somehow membranous petals Hesperia had shown her. *Nithon,* but who had ever heard of such a thing? She wished she'd had a better chance to examine them. Or, better yet, see the blossoming plant itself—

"… past the garden gate," Hesperia had said, and asked her if she could imagine what else might grow there.

After a while, the younger Miss Aylesbury opened up her page-worn notebook and began to write, the scratching of pen on paper an oddly eerie counterpoint to the drumming of the rain. After a while longer, hardly seeming aware of it, she began murmuring as she wrote, her words gradually becoming audible.

"From Leng comes Death to strip us of Life's mask… silken folds of skin torn free to bone and entropy beneath—"

"Goodness," Mrs. Aylesbury said, rousing as if from a torpor. "How morbid."

"I'll read another instead." She turned a page. "Old when Babylon was new, sleeping beneath its mound, vast pavements and foundation-walls, stone steps leading down, to eternal night's black haven where the primal secrets frown—"

"That's still rather grim, dear, don't you think?"

"We found the lamp, the brazen bowl." Her eyes gleamed strangely in the reflected candle flames. "The oil, how it blazed! In its mad flash, the shapes we saw, vast shapes! The maze-wall, and the gate sphinx-guarded!"

"I think," said Eleanor diplomatically, herself feeling rather as if she'd emerged from some half-dream, "that we've had enough poetry for now, don't you?"

One by one they sank again into their private musings. They lit another cone of the same incense when the first was spent. The irritations and annoyances with each other did seem far and silly. It was better to sit here. So peaceful, so relaxing. Watching the fire-ruby ember shift and change as it burned its slow way down, releasing the musty, mossy, mildewy scent.

The younger Miss Aylesbury swayed in her seat. "Through what sphinx-paths winding in the night, pointed to by far blue rays! Where vine-choked gates of graven dolomite open to the stone-lanterned maze!"

"What was that, dear?" queried their mother, again like one stirring from a doze.

"It is the hour... the hour when the moonstruck... moonstruck..." Then she settled her cheek onto her notebook, yawned once, and fell asleep.

Mrs. Aylesbury blinked drowsily. "Oh, how odd. She must be very... very..." Her head lolled onto her shoulder and she exhaled a slow, sighing breath as she, too, succumbed.

Eleanor stirred herself from her chair, and from her own attendant

lethargy, with considerable effort. The uppermost third of the incense cone had become an ashen mound, the widening ring of the
ember a strange twist of gold. As she reached for the dish, her hand
struck it, knocking it askew. For an instant she suffered an image
of scattering sparks on the braided-rag rug, igniting myriad hungry
tongues of fire. But the incense merely wobbled, shedding flecks of
ash, and did not spill.

She picked it up and carried it outside, holding her breath as she
did so. Raindrops splashed on ceramic, hissing when they met the
smoldering cone, forming a sooty puddle around it.

Soon, neither smoke nor steam arose from the sodden lump. Eleanor decided this was still an insufficient measure, and tipped the
dish entire into a ditch of muddy water, where it sank with a gurgle.

As it vanished into the murk, she let herself breathe again. The
distant low-tide miasma of the sea crept into her nose and throat
and lungs. Her mind, however, felt more clear.

Had the incense been... drugged?

She almost could not believe it. Did not want to believe it, that
much was certain. True, certain illicit substances were far from unknown at Star-Winds, but those who partook did so of their own
knowing, willing accord.

Didn't they?

Or did they?

The incense... the tea... the potpourri and soaps and candles...
all the things they made... and sold... local farmer's markets, street
fairs... mail order... herbal remedies and traditional medicines...

The rain fell. Her wet hair hung limp along her cheeks, her wet
clothes clung to her skin. Water trickled down her neck and back.

It seemed so quiet. She heard no voices, no laughter, no crying
babies or barking dogs. Not even any music. No one else was out
and about. Everything looked bedraggled, shabby and run-down,
dispirited in the sodden, dreary weather. But for a few lights flickering through curtains and shutters, the neighboring cabins might
have been deserted.

She went to the largest, a redwood lodge that served as home to Brother Zoar and his innermost circle. When her knocks brought no reply, she peered through a window. Sheets and swags decorated the walls and hung from the rafters, giving the effect of the interior of a nomadic tent. Bean-bags and oversized cushions heaped the floor, serving as beds for partially-clad people. Amid a clutter of water-pipes and wine jugs was a large incense-holder in the shape of a beaming, chubby Buddha. Several spent cones made gritty mounds of ashes in the burning-dish.

Her taps at the windowpane, then more knocking and calling, elicited no response. They merely slept on. If not for the steady rising and falling of their chests, she might have presumed the worst.

Hesperia had given it to everyone; did she know of its potent effects? Was this result her deliberate intention? If so, then *why?* And if not... if not, then...

It occurred to her that Hesperia was not among those slumbering figures. Neither were Chaos, nor Brother Zoar himself.

Despite the openness of the community, she nonetheless felt a qualm of manners as she let herself into the lodge. None of the three were to be found within. She passed through and came to the back deck, pausing briefly to glance out at its rain-sluiced redwood planks. A gleam out in the forest beyond, some shining amber beacon, caught and held her eye.

Why anyone would be in the woods at night, in this miserable weather...

"We know all the places where the most rare and secret things grow," Chaos had said.

And Hesperia... *"We'll need to gather more soon; this is the last handful left."*

How they had whispered, soft, conspiratorial.

"Past the sphinxes."

"Past the garden gate."

"The labyrinth of wonder."

How they had leaned so close and intimate, breath tickling silkily in her ears… the tantalizing allure of the *nithon* petals, like nothing she'd ever seen…

As she stepped closer to the sliding doors, her hip bumped the edge of a table. Something heavy and rounded wobbled atop it. Eleanor caught the item before it fell, and gasped at how warm it was to the touch.

It was made of bronze, and she initially took it for some sort of lidless little teapot—short and stout, as the rhyme went; there was its handle and there was its spout—but it held no liquid, no dregs of leaves. She thought next that it might be an incense-burner and cautiously sniffed at it, anticipating that same dank, mossy, fleshy scent.

What she smelled instead made her think of hot oil left too long on the stove, not quite to smoking but very nearly to the point of bursting into flame.

Fine lettering embossed the object's curving metal side. She ran a fingertip along it as she puzzled out the archaic-looking script.

The Nameless One For Whom We Raise A Thousand Smokes.

The voice that recurred to Eleanor then was that of her own sister. *"We found the lamp, the brazen bowl,"* and something about a mad flash, great shapes, gates and mazes.

The residue coating the inside of the brass—

"… lamp, the brazen bowl…"

—container looked greasy, like streaks of paraffin or petroleum jelly.

Acting on an impulse—even a compulsion—she could neither understand nor resist, Eleanor found and lit a match. The match-head flared, then guttered in the breeze. Before it could blow out, she dropped it through the lidless opening.

With a flash—*"a mad flash!"*—the oily substance ignited. It burned glassy-clear flames etched and shot with lightning-blue. Thin beams sprang from the lamp's spout, a dancing, dazzling intricacy of—

"…far blue rays…"

They pointed in the direction of the light, the amber beacon. There, the rays touched upon and illuminated—

"...*great shapes... the gate, sphinx-guarded... gates of graven dolomite... the stone-lanterned maze...*"

She set a hand to her head, which seemed filled with voices, all speaking at once.

"...*the hour when the moonstruck poets know...*"

The rays *did* touch upon and illuminate shapes she swore had not been there before. Statues, two hulking granite statues, of winged lionesses with the heads and breasts of women. Sphinxes. They stood moss-encrusted and climbing with ivy, flanking a gateway topped with a carved arch of some pale-hued, crystalline-glittering mineral.

Through the archway was a narrow path, a high-walled maze, marked by lampposts also made from granite and set with golden lozenges of glass. She caught a glimpse of someone just turning a corner—fleeting though it was, she was sure she recognized the long white hair of Brother Zoar.

Without pause for concern or consideration, Eleanor slid open the doors and stepped outside. Heedless of the rain, she dashed across the deck and down the steps toward the forest.

The far blue rays and amber beacons vanished as she left the brazen bowl behind, but she did not need their guidance. Within moments, slipping on wet grass, she reached the place where she had seen the sphinxes.

They were not there.

She blinked and wiped raindrops from her face.

They *were* there.

Looming above her, stern-visaged, terrible and strange, the sphinxes *were* there. And between them, the gate with its carved arch... but the gate held only nothingness.

Not blackness, not blankness, not emptiness.

Nothingness.

Eleanor hesitated, then stepped through.

The rain stopped as decisively as if she'd gone indoors, but no ceiling stretched above her. The maze's high, vine-choked walls were open to the sky. Open to the pink sky, a sky not rose-pink with dawn or blushed with sunset's fires but pink nonetheless, a pink sky where the stark outlines of birds like herons flew.

She stood, dripping, on a path of dry bricks, porous-seeming as if cut from thirsty pumice. The air felt balmy. It smelled not of cold fog and wet brine but of a more stinging alkaline; she thought of salt-flats and deserts.

When she looked back the way she'd come, she saw the silent sphinxes continuing to loom there. She saw the backside of the arched gateway, and the nothingness it held.

Spindly insects buzzed faintly as they ticked and batted against the lozenge-shaped panes set into the stone lampposts. She recognized them no more than she recognized the vines that grew up the high walls, or the kinds of trees whose boughs interlaced above the decorative stonework at their tops.

This was not the world as she had always known it. This was someplace else altogether. Someplace strange, unreal and unfamiliar.

To call out, to raise her voice, seemed a terrible transgression. Eleanor hastened on instead. The path was indeed a maze, bending and switching, splitting off in every direction, filled with hidden alcoves, intersections and dead-ends.

"The labyrinth of wonder," Chaos had said.

And, indeed, so it was. Within moments, she'd all but forgotten in her fascination her true purpose for coming here.

Or *was* this her true purpose in coming here?

Were they not, perhaps, one and the same?

Each pace she took brought new angles of view. Apertures in the walls, slanting from width to narrowness like castle windows, offered peeks at tantalizing features—terraced gardens, crumbling slabs and statues, puzzling shrubs laden with shiny clusters of fruit, low bridges spanning pools where what resembled monstrous lily-pads and lotus-blossoms floated against the reflected pink-hued sky.

These always seemed but a turn or two ahead, yet when she reached where they should have been, she found only more of the winding maze itself. She saw broken towers, decaying spires twisting upward to weathered white turrets, and a gaping hole where stairs descended into a blackness darker than eternal night—

Or had that been something her sister said, reciting from her poems?

"...*stone steps leading down, to eternal night's black haven where the primal secrets frown...*"

The vines rustled against the walls. A bird cried somewhere on high, its screech that of a madman. Thin, brittle leaves whirled around Eleanor in a frenetic blowing dance. The insects buzzed and ticked against the amber glass of the stone lampposts.

Somewhere, it seemed, a cracked flute played, the music splintered and atonal, the sort of music to which lunatic throngs might caper.

Another turn in the maze brought her to a gate, this one not flanked by sphinxes or topped with an arch but a simple gate of corroded metal bars. It hung askew on a hinge, wedged partway open and weedily entangled as if it had not moved in centuries. The pumice-brick path she walked on continued a ways past this gate, but more and more weeds straggled through cracks, and it was swiftly overgrown and lost.

The scene beyond it was one of fetid greens and greys. Mossy hills humped up from marshy moors. Ground-mist seeped in steamy vapors. Ancient stumps and fallen logs lay half-buried by layers of mold. Pallid, fleshy growths of fungus sprouted from their decomposing crevices... not mushrooms in any sense that Eleanor could comprehend, but horrid rugose stalks topped by caps somehow both bulbous and pendulous... and the ground-mist, she realized, was not *ground*-mist at all but issuing from the sporulating folds and gills forming the undersides of those caps.

The prevailing odor was both mildewy and acrid, slightly sour, with the barest hint of something almost spicy, something not-quite-anise. She felt again that sense of expectancy and dread, vague but overwhelming.

"We knew you'd come," Chaos said from behind her.

Eleanor spun to see him emerging from an alcove concealed in the stonework of the maze walls. He smiled, his dark eyes glinting. Behind him, Hesperia and Brother Zoar also appeared.

"We knew you couldn't resist," Hesperia added. "Now you can help us gather what we need."

"You... you make incense from... *these?*" She shuddered as she indicated the clumps of sighing fungal growths.

"Not only those." Chaos held up a jagged, spiky stem tipped with a single glassy-clear flower. The petals—veined and membranous like dragonfly wings—blossomed out in a radiating spiral from its vile heart.

She caught its scent of fading, dying, unearthly starlight. This time, it repelled her and she drew back.

"Child." Brother Zoar raised empty, upturned palms. "My dear Eleanor, you do not understand. Our search for enlightenment is the Nameless One's poison dream. It lures us into the idiot vortices, and loses us amid the cosmic spheres."

"Looking for awareness," Hesperia said, "looking to expand the consciousness and open the inner eye."

"They don't know," Chaos continued. "They're making themselves more vulnerable."

"Vulnerable to what?" cried Eleanor.

"The madness of the Outer Gods," said Brother Zoar. "The streams of Time, the voids of Space."

She gazed at him in incomprehension.

"There is no harmony," Chaos said. "There is no purpose, only visions in the muttering dark. We are nothing."

Hesperia nodded. "We have seen into the gulfs, and retained our minds. We've seen ourselves upon the altar. We've stood alone before eternity, and nothing since has looked the same."

"Think of it as an inoculation," Brother Zoar said. "To save us from ourselves."

They showed it to her then, the truth beyond the truth. They showed her where unknowable things flopped and fluttered—formless things, shapeless, perhaps once human but no more—to the shrill piping of insane flutes.

She beheld with her own living eyes the dead eyes of blind Azathoth, and ceased to hope... because she understood.

THE MINDHOUSE

What do they tell you about me, I wonder?

The truth, now that you're old enough to hear it? The truth, because families are about honesty, about trust?

Or do they tell you the same lies they told the rest of the world? The lies they wish they themselves could believe, the lies they wish were true?

Maybe it was with what they considered the best of intentions. To protect you. To spare your feelings. Why should *you* have to grow up with so much hanging over your head? Besides, it was easier for them. Preferable. Less painful. Safer.

At least I can be sure they've had to tell you *something*. You may not have been old enough to remember when I went away, but they can't deny I ever existed. No, you must know you have a sister.

Or... had one, at least.

They could claim I'd died, I suppose. Who would have doubted it? And if so, how far did they go with the ruse? Was there a funeral? A faked death certificate? Would I see my own name on a headstone, or engraved on some urn, if I ever went home?

Not that I can leave Evergate.

Well, I *could*. Maybe. I've made great progress.

I *am* all right.

Now. I'm all right *now*.

That's the catch.

131

Well, that and the rest of it. What we do in the mindhouse helps *us,* but what about the long run, the big picture, the grand scale? The fate of humanity? The fate of the world?

It'll happen anyway, though. Why fight it? It'll be far in the future, long after we'll still be around. We can't change things. We can't stop it. We have to look out for ourselves and our own best interests. Is that so wrong?

My friend Nathan agrees with me. Of course, he also knows what would be waiting for him outside of Evergate. It's one thing to admit the guilt and feel the remorse. Having to be held accountable, to take responsibility... it's daunting. It's daunting for people who've done lesser wrongs than his.

We can't help wanting to take the easier way. The less painful or less shameful way. It's just instinct, preservation, simple human nature.

Like our parents did all those years.

I was never sick.

Not that way. Not in the way they wanted everyone to think.

There was no cancer. Chemotherapy and radiation treatments didn't make me the way I was. That's just how they explained it away. It looked better, you see. It made *them* look better. How *brave* they had to be. How brave and noble and strong. To be pitied, and admired, for bearing up so heroically.

And did they make the most of it! Basking in the sympathy, milking the attention for all it was worth. If not quite to a Munchausen's-by-proxy level, that is. They didn't try to *exacerbate* my condition. They didn't want to *keep* me like that. When it finally really got to be too much, they relented and sent me to Doctor Hasturn.

What I did to them was beyond unforgivable.

Worse than if I *had* gotten cancer.

Worse than drug habits, sex scandals, pregnancy or a criminal record. Any of those could be written off as a phase, the wild waywardness of youth.

Or joining a cult... which would have been ironic enough, the way things turned out...

These days, some things once deemed shameful carry a certain cachet; our parents would have earned bonus points among their social circle if I'd been a lesbian, and they could be just *so* very tolerant, so open-minded and progressive and trendy about it.

But, no. No such luck. Nothing that dramatic, exciting or politically correct. I couldn't even be something controversial like a vegan, a liberal, an atheist.

All right, at least I wasn't *fat,* but still!

Insanity is never going to be a cool stigma.

I don't mean eccentricity, oh, no. That's for the quirky, temperamental artistes. I don't mean ordinary mood swings or picky people calling themselves OCD. I certainly don't mean edgy but endearing sociopaths as depicted on television.

I mean mental illness. I mean schizophrenia. In the *real* sense of the word, not the usual stupid Sybil-joke misconception. Paranoia. Delusions. Hearing voices. Hallucinations, by no means limited to the visual.

Did they tell you your sister went crazy?

Somehow, I doubt it.

Oh, denial, that river in Egypt. Our father was the pharaoh, and our mother had her own personal Cleopatra barge.

They didn't want to admit it, acknowledge it. Of course not. It'd reflect badly on them. Cancer was one thing, but madness? Imagine the talk, the whispers, the gossip. Imagine the disastrous effect on the family's reputation! Business! Political ambitions! The country club!

And so on.

Yes, I was insane.

Either way, sick or insane, I suppose you're surprised to hear from me. At all, let alone after all these years of silence. I'm surprised, too. I expected it'd be discouraged from both sides. Our parents wouldn't have been in favor of it, and Doctor Hasturn says that contact with anyone from our former lives tends to be less than therapeutic.

An exception was made for us, though.

I'm better now. It won't seem that way once I explain, but you never saw me the way I was before. How bad things got, there toward the end. In the hospital. The psych ward. The locked unit. The restraints.

It was terrible. The suffering, the torment. I don't mean the way I was treated, or the drugs they pumped into me... the way they never let me have a moment's privacy, a moment's freedom. I don't even mean the food.

The worst of the torment was in my own head.

You have no idea.

Or... do you? Sometimes there are hereditary components. Sometimes these things run in families. And you are now about the age I was when I had my first major psychotic break.

But, no, if you did, you wouldn't be so accomplished already, so successful. There'd be signs. Early indicators I'm sure they would have been watching for. Watching closely.

Then again...

Well, someday you might have children of your own. You should know the risks, what kind of legacy you might be handing down to them. You've seen what it can do to a family. Whether you understood or not, you grew up surrounded by it.

I'm sure you'd handle it better than our parents did. I'm sure you wouldn't let any child of yours go through what I did. You'd do whatever you could to help, wouldn't you? To spare them the torment I suffered?

If not for Doctor Hasturn, if not for Evergate, I'd still be there, in the hospital. Doped to the gills, on meds for the symptoms, and on meds for the side effects caused by the meds for the symptoms.

Or I'd be out on the streets somewhere, me and the other homeless crazies, camping under overpasses, panhandling, scrounging through the trash, doing what's called 'self-medicating' on cigarettes and cheap booze.

Or I'd be dead.

Instead, I'm much better now. I'm cured. Thanks to Doctor Hasturn. Thanks to the mindhouse.

My hair's grown back, by the way. You've probably seen the old pictures; they must keep them around to shore up the sympathetic image. Awful ones where I look like a skeleton in pajamas, all pallid and bony, dry skin, scabby lips, burning-mad eyes sunk in bruise-purple sockets. Ready for the debutante ball, right?

We kept her at home as long as we could, they'd say... but she needed the kind of care not even a live-in nurse could provide... see how thin she is, she could hardly keep anything down, they had her on those nutrition shakes... and her hair, her poor hair, it got so wispy, falling out in patches, so they shaved it...

That wasn't how it happened.

Look closer at those pictures next time. If they're the ones I'm thinking of, my hands will be wrapped up. Bandaged, or in these padded glove-mitten things.

Trichotillomania. How's that for a word? I pulled it, you see. My hair. Pulled it, twisted it, plucked it out by the roots, one by one, strand by strand. Eyebrows, too. And eyelashes. Even with my head shaved and the mittens.

Some people eat it, too, chew on their hair, swallow it, risking it clumping up in their intestines and causing a blockage. Not me. That isn't why I lost so much weight. I wouldn't have eaten it. I wanted to get *rid* of it. To yank it out of my scalp, out of my face, and get rid of it. Burn it, if I could. Flush it down the toilet, if I couldn't burn it.

It's grown back now anyway, as I was saying. My hair. It's past my shoulders. I know I used to pull it, I remember doing it, and I remember it made sense to me at the time. It seemed like the only thing I could do. The smart thing.

I thought—don't laugh; I know how crazy it sounds—that it wasn't *my* hair. That it wasn't *hair* at all. That it was something else. Cilia, maybe. That it was alive, that these alien spores had burrowed into my head and were extruding themselves in these fine wiry filaments, threads that looked like hair, that fooled everyone but me. The longer they got, or the more of them there were, the stronger they'd become. Until they took me over. Replaced me, or kept me trapped inside while they used my body to do things. So I had to pull them out.

Crazy, I know. But that's why I didn't chew my hair, the way so many other trichotillomaniacs do. Mine wasn't a compulsion. I didn't do it without thinking about it, as an unconscious habit. I did it deliberately, because I had to, in order to save myself from the cilia spore aliens. And the last thing I'd want to do was ingest those filaments, take them back inside myself, like tapeworms. Bad enough they sprouted from my scalp and face and eyelids, where I could see them, where I could reach them to pluck out. I couldn't stand the idea of having hairy tangled knots collecting in my guts.

Would you? Would anyone?

But try explaining that. Try explaining that the reason you won't eat is because that only feeds the cilia spores and maybe if you can't pluck them out you can starve them instead. Try explaining that you can't sleep because the moon sings and the sun groans and the stars scream terrible words into your mind, words that would kill people or drive them insane if you said them aloud... day or night, it doesn't matter, because the stars are always there.

It was terrible. Imagine not being able to trust your own senses, your own thoughts. Imagine watching someone waste away, tortured like that. Someone you care about. Wouldn't you want to help? Wouldn't you want to do anything in your power to make it better?

Luckily, like I said, I'm fine, now.

Since coming here. Since Doctor Hasturn.

Since the mindhouse.

I want you to understand that. I want *someone* to understand that.

Someone who isn't also here at Evergate. Obviously, *we* understand. It just doesn't necessarily mean much, given our situation.

What's that they say? Consider the source? Take it with a grain of salt? Maybe the lunatics aren't running the asylum outright, but, the rest of the world isn't very inclined to believe us when we try to tell them we're not crazy anymore.

We're not.

We're fine now. We're better. We're cured.

As long as we continue our treatments. That's why we can't leave. If we do, we'll revert. We'll go back to the way we were before. Nothing else will work for us. Nothing else has. Medication, ECT, behavioral modification plans, everything short of old-school lobotomies… been there, done that, no use.

Others have tried. They've decided that, hey, since they're cured, there's no need to stay. No need to continue treatment. Certainly no need to stay locked in the loony bin. You see that all the time, even with people who aren't suffering psychiatric disorders. They don't follow the full course of antibiotics, they stop taking pills as soon as the symptoms go away, they treat the dosage instructions as optional. They sign themselves out of the hospital against medical advice. We all think we know best.

We're wrong.

Some choice, huh? Between madness and seclusion. Between a sane life in Evergate and a real life in the real world.

Here, we can be normal. We have clarity of thought. Focus. Freedom from the voices and hallucinations, the delusions. We can function. We can have valid interpersonal relationships.

We also contribute to the slow but inexorable downfall of humanity.

What kind of argument is that, in making a case for not being crazy?

Oh, we're not crazy anymore, because our doctor is a warlock cult-leader who's guiding us in rituals to siphon off our madness and funnel it through a psychic vortex…

Why, yes, that seems perfectly sane and reasonable, doesn't it?

But it's true.

So much for credibility, right? So much for proving I'm *not* delusional.

Doctor Hasturn doesn't *claim* to be a warlock. Or a cult-leader, for that matter. We don't wear robes. We don't shave our heads—ha, wouldn't that be fittingly absurd?

When we go to the mindhouse for our sessions, it's cognitive meditation and structured group glossolalic therapy.

Otherwise known as: we sit in a circle and chant.

Not in any actual language. They're just nonsense syllables, made-up words. Like mantras. They don't mean anything.

Except they do.

They have power.

Did I tell you earlier about hearing the stars scream terrible words that would kill people or drive them insane if uttered aloud?

It's kind of like that.

Power. Those sounds have power.

Yagth amur fthagn yagthos rullos orann'ti.

See?

Thig'alla haroun, haroun ob ik'shmai.

Do you feel it?

The shiver?

The power?

But the words… they aren't words. That's what glossolalia is. Sometimes known as 'speaking in tongues.' Though it isn't the kind of holy-roller frenzy you might be imagining. We aren't transported into states of euphoria or manic religious ecstasy. No angels, no sobbing, no wild hallelujah choirs, no stigmata.

We just… chant.

Doctor Hasturn doesn't preach, doesn't sermonize. The mindhouse isn't a church, strictly speaking. We don't have the usual trappings associated with ceremonies—candles, chalices, idols, relics. We don't drink wine. We don't perform blood-sacrifices or burn incense or have orgies.

There are books, sure. Books, but not Bibles. Not hymnals or tracts. An entire shelf of books, with worn leather bindings and gilt-edged pages gone yellowed and brittle from age. The covers are embossed, stamped with symbols and sigils. A few have titles in what appears to be some sort of crude, bastardized Latin. *Librios Turpis Atroxi,* for instance. And *Valde Vetus Res.* Others... others I can only guess at the pronunciation, let alone the meaning. *Zsossonoggos U'trys Deighrn,* and *Cthlotha Fthagnd.*

I suppose it *has* been a church, at times, in its fashion, the mindhouse. It was originally constructed as a private family chapel. You know how it is with these places. Starts off as a mansion built by a land baron or railroad tycoon, gets converted to a hotel, maybe repurposed as a military academy, turned into a hospital, used as a relocation center during World War II, remodeled into a boarding school, rented out for writers' and artists' retreats, and so on.

Yes, Evergate's gone through a lot of incarnations over the years. Additions, outbuildings, updates to the plumbing and wiring, periodic redecoration. But, always, at the heart of it, at the core of it, the mindhouse. Unchanged.

Nathan has read up on it. The house, the history. The Evergates themselves and the mysteries surrounding what happened to them, back in the 1900s or whenever it was. He's been here quite a bit longer than I have. You'd recognize his full name if I told you. They still hold memorials on the anniversary, you know.

He's not proud of it, his notoriety, what he did, the people he hurt that day, the lives he ruined. He hates to think about it. Like with me and the hair-pulling, what he believed seemed real to him at the time. He was certain that he was doing the right thing. Now, he knows how insane he was.

If anyone from outside saw Nathan now, they'd evaluate him and determine him fit to stand trial. He'd be sent to prison... where the effects of the mindhouse would gradually wear off. They'd be punishing a madman for deeds beyond his control.

It's one of the hardest parts about the therapy sessions... cringing at the now-clear recollections of your worst moments, your most painful choices and shameful actions. Having to confront and live with your own inescapable past.

Our illnesses, Doctor Hasturn says, can only *explain* our behaviors. Not *excuse* them. We can't look to others for forgiveness or absolution. We can't look to a benevolent God. There is no moral order to the world, and society's efforts to establish laws and justice are only feeble, crumbling bulwarks against the capricious entropy of chaos.

We are agents of it, that chaos. The very prevalence of insanity is a sign that we are on its path, a steepening speeding downward spiral into the abyss. As a species, we are mad. We always have been. In some of us, the madness is to an extent and of an excess that it can be tapped. It can be drawn off and channeled.

That's why we hold our sessions in the mindhouse. Something about the design of it serves as a prism, an amplifier. I've no idea why, or how; I don't understand the architecture of it, but it's curiously fascinating.

It's an odd-shaped space, situated where several of the mansion's other walls come together at angles that somehow don't add up. The roof tilts in uneven wedges toward an off-center peak; if you gaze up at it too long, the lines of the ceiling panels start to look like the strands of a web spun by a psychotic spider. I often wonder how they did that, whoever designed the room, whoever built it.

Of course, that might just be my own ignorance speaking. Someone who's studied such things might look at it and find it simplicity itself. Then again, I could be wrong; maybe it would perplex even an expert. Maybe it'd pose a real challenge, a real puzzle. I guess that's far much more your department than mine. You are the educated one, after all. You'd probably take one look and be able to explain the mindhouse's peculiar geometric effects in the same way you could those of the House-of-Mystery varieties of tourist trap.

But I honestly believe there's more to it than that, than mere tricks of vertigo-inducing perspective and proportion. More than optical illusions and subliminal suggestions in the décor.

The floor's done in tiny mosaic tiles, worn and faded along the paths where people walk, but at the edges it's still as vibrant as the day it was installed. As with the ceiling, the longer you look at the random design, the more it seems to form patterns... indiscernible patterns with meanings that can't quite be grasped.

There are windows, but they don't admit daylight. None of the frames are the same size, and none of the panes have straight edges. Some of the glass is clear and some clouded, or frosted nearly opaque. The stained glass portions are jewel-toned, marbled, and swirled. They glow, as if from within, as if by their own eerie, eldritch illumination.

The mindhouse's acoustics are as peculiar as the rest of it. Sometimes a whisper will resonate like a gunshot; sometimes the loudest shout vanishes into thin air. It might be silent as a tomb at midnight in that room, or the very space itself might hum with a sourceless vibration, a deep bass-note from everywhere and nowhere. Footsteps echo as if the space beneath is a hollow chasm... or they thud as if on solid ground... or they are swallowed up as if absorbed.

Occasionally, we hear chimes. Silvery, horrible, musical yet atonal chimes. A few times, it's seemed like distant voices answer back, murmuring in multitudes. Once—thankfully, just that once—we heard a wet, heavy grunt and a slithery shifting I could have done without.

You might think that it's a weird, creepy place for asylum inmates to be brought for groups, and you'd be absolutely right. As crazy as I was my first time there, I wasn't so crazy as to realize that it very much was *not* the typical setting of durable stain-resistant carpet, fluorescent lighting, and folding chairs. No. I'd seen plenty of rooms of *that* kind before. The mindhouse was different, very different, right from the first.

Similarly, Doctor Hasturn is *not* the kind of psychiatrist I'd typically encountered before arriving at Evergate. Tall and slender, pinch-faced... jaundiced of aspect and bloodshot of eye, as the poets might put it… nothing of the caring, kindly counselor or the wise, nodding sage here. We never talk about our mothers, or our unresolved issues with potty-training and fears of abandonment. We don't discuss our anxieties or neuroses; lines like "mm-hmm and how does that make you *feel?*" are never said.

Dreams, though, we do discuss. Dreams, according to Doctor Hasturn, are the secret speech of the universe. They aren't to be analyzed with trite symbolism, nothing so new age or Jungian as that. They are deeper messages, far deeper than the sub- or unconscious. They are from beyond, from outside, from the primal currents of the underpsyche.

In the dreams, sometimes, the nonsense syllables of our glossolalic therapy chants aren't such nonsense after all. They begin to seem like words, like a language just beyond our comprehension. I've asked the others and we all agree… they're almost within grasp. Almost.

And sometimes—when Doctor Hasturn has cots brought into the mindhouse, to conduct sleep-studies on us there—sometimes the dreams become much more than dreams. Much *other* than dreams.

Once…

I won't say it was a vision, because that *would* be insane. But it *was* very vivid, the most vivid dream I've ever experienced. Tangible. Tactile. Each sensation true to my senses, so real in its unreality, so unreal in its reality.

I heard the chimes, ringing and clinking, pure as glass, dull as bones. Papery reeds, thin as spider-legs, hissed a susurration in a hot and airless breeze. I felt the dry, pebbled ground beneath my bare feet, my steps kicking up gritty puffs of yellow dust. It smelled sour. Sour and yellow and old. Tickling my nose. The taste of it settling, dry, so dry, on my tongue. The screaming stars wheeled above me, unfamiliar and hideous constellations viewed through a murky-green veil of sky like dead sea-water. What passed for a sun hung bloated and pustulant above an endless horizon, silhouetting the corroded ruins of some ancient city.

Or palace.

Or temple.

Or tomb.

Doctor Hasturn questioned me extensively when I awoke. Had I seen anyone? Spoken to anyone? Were there landmarks I could name? Had there been any living thing besides the papery reeds? Could I plot a star-chart of those strange constellations?

I later learned from Nathan that I was not the first to have such a dream. In his, there'd been a road, cart-tracks having worn ruts in the dirt, and a pile of stacked stones like a mile-marker. Some of the others had glimpsed sticklike figures moving in the distance, wearing tattered garments of coarse brown cloth.

It doesn't *mean* anything, of course. They weren't actual visions of an actual, real place. Let's not go nuts, here. Subliminal suggestion, mass hallucination, any of that's unsettling enough without…

Though, now that I think about it, Doctor Hasturn did start questioning me even before I'd really begun describing my dream. Pressing for specific details about things I don't remember mentioning. Asking if I'd noticed marks on my skin, for instance, painted symbols, or designs like henna tattoos.

If dreams *are* messages…

And messages have to come from *somewhere*…

If the mindhouse is the focal channeling point of a psychic vortex, as Doctor Hasturn says, then what is on the other side?

On the *outside?*

Outside of ourselves, outside of everything?

What else might be there?

What… entities?

What feeds upon our mental chaos?

Nothing good, I can tell you that much.

Dark forces? Evil powers? Otherworldly elder beings who will one day shatter the dimensional barriers, enslaving or destroying us all?

Whatever happens, it'll take far longer than our meager human lifetimes to reach the tipping point. Therefore it isn't *our* problem, right? Because we're such small and insignificant portions of the greater scheme of things. From the big-picture perspective, I mean.

From our individual, personal perspectives…

It takes away our madness. We have our own minds again, our own thoughts and lives and souls and selves.

Yet we're helping to empower and strengthen something. Something dangerous. Destructive. Something *other*. Something *Outside*. Each contribution, however slight, pushes this world toward the brink. The clearer we get, the closer we all come… the closer to crossing that threshold.

Save our sanity, doom humanity.

Kind of catchy.

If horrible.

I know how this sounds. How crazy it all sounds. But I'm not crazy. Not now. Not anymore. My symptoms haven't just been managed with medication or suppressed by behavioral tricks. They're gone. *Gone.*

I'm not expecting you to believe me. I'm not asking for your forgiveness.

I just want someone to know. To understand why we do this.

Why we want, and *need,* the mindhouse.

Besides, it's not like there aren't others. Other mindhouses, situated at key points around the globe. A dozen more, at least.

It's still not enough, though. When I think of all the people out there, suffering like I did… when I think of the families torn apart like ours was… when I think of all that pain, all that torment…

Wouldn't it be wonderful to be able to help them?

To restore their sanity? To heal them? To spare anyone else from having to go through what I've endured? I know *I'd* want to do what I could. I'm sure you would, too.

The thing is, *you* could. If you wanted to.

Doctor Hasturn showed me the articles you've written, the papers you've had published in the leading journals. You're about to embark upon a brilliant international career, sure to make a lasting and memorable mark.

They're calling you a prodigy, you know. The most innovative, intuitive and accomplished young architect of our time.

You should definitely come to Evergate for a visit. I'd love to see you again. I'm so proud.

And, who knows? Maybe you'll pick up a few new ideas.

NINESIGHT

"They're doing it again," Mel said.

Her sister, flopped on the bed with her phone, didn't answer. Courtney was practically almost a teenager, and she made no secret of how she was way too grown up and mature to pay attention to a little baby bratty-brat like Mel.

Courtney made no secret of lots of things. Like how annoyed she was that Mom and Dad had sent them to spend the week with Aunt Vera and Uncle Joe, instead of letting them stay home by themselves. Or, better yet, just sending *Mel,* and letting *Courtney* stay home by *her*self.

"You don't even *trust* me, *gah!*" she had said during the Big Family Discussion, then done the drama-queen huffy hurt flounce to slam her door and sulk.

She was annoyed that Mom and Dad were going on vacation without them. But, of course, she would have been just as annoyed to be dragged along, complaining about the plane ride and the hotel and the beach and there not being any cool kids her age to hang with or whatever.

Most of all, she was extra-special-double-bonus annoyed because, at their aunt's house, she and Mel had to share a room. It was, like, worse than *prison* or something, the way she went on about it.

They had to share a *room,* there was nothing to *do,* she couldn't hang out with her *friends,* the house was old and weird, she didn't like Uncle Joe's cooking, there was hardly even decent *internet,* and she was totes going to die of *boredom* already!

And she hated Aunt Vera's cats. The cats were mean. The cats were creepy. The cats did that thing, that thing they were doing now, and it freaked her out, and she hated it, and she hated them, and she hated everything.

"Courtney," Mel said, knowing it was teasy-needling bratty-brat stuff, but so what? "Courtney, *looooook,* they're *doooing* it again."

Mel thought the old house was neat, full of creaky steps and dusty nooks and explory-corners. It was great for pretending she was a detective, spy, or secret agent. It would have been even better for hide-and-seek if she had anybody else to hide from or seek for. The room she and Courtney had to share was still bigger than both their rooms at home put together, the beds with carved wooden posts, and a windowseat where the windows angled out on three sides. She enjoyed helping Aunt Vera in the garden, enjoyed what Uncle Joe called his crazy kitchen experiments, and enjoyed the old-timey card and board games they brought out after dinner, instead of just watching TV until bedtime like normal people.

The cats...

Well, okay, maybe she didn't *hate* the cats like Courtney did—she *wanted* to like them, and have them like her, too—but they really *were* kinda mean. They wouldn't cuddle or play. They hissed if anybody tried to pick them up. Sometimes, they'd let her pet them a little bit, and they might even lean into it, but then just as suddenly they'd whirl and claw and bite her hand.

They also really were kinda creepy, like when they did the thing they were doing now. Mel tried not to let her own goosebumps-feelings show, though, because it was more fun to see how much it bugged Courtney.

Aunt Vera had asked them to leave the door always propped open a little, so that the cats could come and go as they pleased. Otherwise, she said, they'd scratch at it and yowl, and it was their house too and they were used to having the run of it, and were stubborn and set in their ways. It gave Courtney something else to complain about—"We don't even get any *privacy, gah!*"—but she would have complained more if the cats did go scratching and yowling all night.

The biggest cat, Ulthar, was what Aunt Vera called a gingerstripe. His short fur was a few different colors of orange, his body was thick and heavy but not fat, and the yellow-green color of his eyes made Mel think of sour pickles. He had been all sprawled on the windowseat cushions as if inviting someone to come give him a tummy-rub, though Mel had found out the hard way that was an arm-shredding trap.

Now, he'd gotten up and sat straight like a tiger on a throne, those sour-pickle eyes fixed in an unblinking glare on the part of the wall where it met the ceiling. His nose and mouth were wrinkled in the kind of face cats made when they smelled a yucky-gross smell.

Ishtar, sleek-slim and blacker than black, was no longer prowling around the edges of the room but had stopped, hunkered low in the space between the dresser and the tall floor lamp. Her eyes, which were bright gold, stared up at the same spot that had Ulthar's interest, and the white points of teeth against pink gums showed that she was also making the yuck-face. Though no other part of her moved, the hair along her back rose up into a fuzzy line like a Mohawk, and her long thin tail bushed to twice again its normal size.

Fluffy grey-and-white Queenie stood in the doorway with her front paws just over the threshold. Thanks to her flat, squashy, pushed-in nose, it was hard to tell if she made the yuck-face or not, but her wide sky-blue gaze exactly followed those of the other two.

"*Cooooouuuuurtney—*" Mel began, drawing her sister's name out in a sing-song.

"I *see* them, okay? *Gah!*" Courtney lowered her phone long enough to glance at the cats. "Why do they *do* that? It's, like, *so* creepy!"

"Maybe they see something."

"There's nothing *there!*"

"Well, maybe there is, and they can see it, but we can't."

"Shut. Up."

"What? I'm just saying—"

"I said, shut up, Muh-*liss*-sa!"

"Look," said Mel, dropping her voice to a whisper. "It must be moving, whatever it is."

True enough, all three kitty heads silently turned, as if their three sets of eyes—still unblinking in blue, gold, and sour-pickle green—followed a slow, tracking course across the ceiling. Not in a straight line, but in a sort of meandering lazy-curvy one.

Queenie slinked the rest of the way into the room, ears laid so flat they almost disappeared in her poofy fur ruff. Ishtar made a kind of "eh-eh-eh" noise through her bared teeth. The tip of Ulthar's tail snapped twitching back and forth.

Courtney shivered. "Gah… make them stop."

"What do you think they see?"

"I don't care. Stupid cats. I hate them." In a sudden lunge, Courtney seized her pillow and flung it. "Go on! Pssst!"

She missed any of the cats by so much that Mel couldn't even guess if she'd been aiming at one in particular, but the whirling thump of it into their midst made them all jump half out of their skins. Ulthar hissed and leaped over Queenie, who tried to whirl and bolt for the door but got a claw hooked in the rug and stumbled. Ishtar streaked past them both in a fast black blur.

Then the cats were gone, and Mel looked accusingly at Courtney.

"I'll tell Aunt Vera."

"Go ahead, tell her, so what?"

"They weren't hurting anybody."

"They were creeping me out!"

"Why are you so scared?"

"I'm not! I told you, it creeps me out when they *do* that! They're always *doing* that, staring at *nothing*, getting all *weird!*"

Mel snickered. "Maybe the house is haunted. Maybe they're chasing ghosts."

"That's not funny, and there's no such things."

"You believe in Slenderman."

Courtney scowled. "Well, *you* believe in *Santa.*"

"Wait, what? Santa's real."

"Huh-unh." Her lip curled in a bitter kind of triumphant sneer.

"Yeah-huh!" said Mel. "He left me my deluxe junior investigator kit for Christmas!" She pointed at the playset, which was her favorite toy ever and the main one she'd chosen to bring along on this visit.

"How dumb can you *be?* Gah!" With that, Courtney hopped off the bed, grabbed her phone, and stepped into her shoes. "I'm going out on the porch so I can text and stuff without stupid *cats* and *sisters* everywhere."

"But it's cold and rainy."

"So? You're not *Mom!*"

"Okay, jeez, sor-*ry!*"

"Hnf!" went Courtney, all huffy-like. She did, though, stop long enough to get her hoodie. Then she was gone, clomping down the hall.

Mel rolled her eyes. Some people just couldn't be happy. If that was what it meant to be almost-a-teenager, she'd rather stay a kid. Lying about Santa that way, too, wow...

She slid from her own bed, leaving behind a scatter of crayons and an activity book with a picture half-colored-in. Why *did* the kitties do their staring-at-nothing thing?

Then sometimes get all weird and go racing-chasing around?

Aunt Vera, when asked, had only shrugged and said it was because they were cats and all cats were a little bit crazypants. Mel figured she was probably right, but, it was more fun to treat it like a real mystery.

Cats could see super-good, way better than people, especially in the dark. Maybe nine whole times better; ninesight to go with nine-lives. What if they could see *more,* not just *better?* What if they really *could* see things that the rest of them didn't even know were there?

Skipping over to her jumbled pile of luggage and toys, she popped the clasp on the sturdy black plastic case with the FBI and CSI stickers on the lid. Soon, she was geared up and ready to go, a vest with official lettering on the back and utility belt worn over a lab coat, nightvision goggles hanging around her neck, and a headlamp blacklight strapped to her forehead just under the bill of a cap to match the vest. She slid a pair of mirrored sunglasses into place, checked the mirror on the closet door, and flashed herself a double thumbs-up.

"Detective Investigator Special Agent Mel is on the job!"

She paused in the hallway, looking around, sweeping a penlight in slow, cautious arcs. Musty-dusty dust motes danced in the thin beam. Her sunglasses made normal rainy-day indoor shadows into even darker darkness, turning the already-kinda-spooky old house into what really *did* seem like it could be a crime scene.

Or haunted.

A skinny, crooked flight of stairs at one end of the hall vanished up into third-floor total blackness, and it was way too easy to imagine someone hiding there, watching her.

Someone... or some*thing*...

Mel shivered a little, partly enjoying the thrill and partly wishing she hadn't teased Courtney about Slenderman after all.

From downstairs, she heard music, the big-bandy old-timey music her aunt and uncle liked. They were probably in the kitchen, Uncle Joe reading the paper and Aunt Vera doing one of her puzzles.

Up here, it was quiet except for the tick-tock of a tall clock. Its pendulum, swinging back and forth, made a streaky-brassy glimmer in the gloom.

Another glimmer shined at her, two glimmers really, two eerie rounded glowing glimmers. She realized they were eyes, cat eyes, peering out from under a table that held some music boxes and a vase of flowers.

"Here, kitty-kitty," Mel said. "Want to be my detective helper?"

The eye-glimmers narrowed. Mel figured that was a nope. She caught a quick flick of movement at the edge of her vision and turned to see another cat, a fluffy pale puffball that could only be Queenie, darting along the carpet-runner and going *whoosh* fast up the crooked, skinny stairs.

"Let's find out what you're after." Removing the sunglasses, Mel folded them shut and tucked them into her lab coat pocket.

Then she settled the heavy battery-laden nightvision goggles into place on her face and flipped the switch on the side. The lenses lit up video-game-green. The eyepieces hummed with a faint tingling sensation she felt in her cheekbones and temples.

Under the table—Aunt Vera called it an occasional table, which made Mel wonder if it was occasionally not a table at all but became something else—the rounded glowing cat's-eye glimmers now looked bright as the headlights of an oncoming car. She saw the greenish-white flash of teeth, too, and heard a low, warning yowl.

"Ishtar?"

Whoosh and up the crooked stairs Ishtar went, too, following Queenie. Her black coat was almost invisible even with the nightvision. Mel made her way after them, trying not to bump into or knock anything over. The reflection of her penlight flowed like silvery water across the glass of picture frames, the tall clock's front, and a collection of snowglobes on a shelf.

These steps weren't carpeted, but were wooden and creaky. Mel climbed with her free hand trailing along the old carved banister. She'd been up there before, of course, during some of her previous explorings.

One room had been the art studio for Uncle Joe's younger brother, who went crazy or died—or went crazy *and* died; she wasn't quite sure on the details—long before Mel had been born. All sorts of his paintings and sketches and stuff were still in there. They were, *she* thought so at least, pretty good… if also kind of freaky and gross.

Another room, the round room at the corner of the house where it rose in a towery-turrety thing, had belonged to Uncle Joe's sister, the one who'd run away from home when she wasn't much older than Courtney was now. A teenager, and probably just like Courtney, too; sure that she knew everything and was all grown up and could take care of *herself*, she wasn't a child, *gah!*

The rest of the family didn't talk about it much, but when they did—usually at gatherings after the grown-ups thought the kids had gone to bed or were otherwise occupied—the stuff they said made it sound like there was more to it even than just running away from home in a snit.

Like maybe drugs were involved. Or stealing. Or a bad boyfriend.

"Or *murrrrr-derrrr,*" Mel whispered.

But that was a mystery she didn't think anybody would let Detective Investigator Special Agent Mel look into. They'd just say it could wait until she was older.

The doors to both of those rooms and the smaller linen closets and storerooms had been left slightly open so the cats could go in and out. In the dim video-game-green haze of her nightvision goggles, Mel recognized the unmistakable thickset body of Ulthar sitting in the doorway of the turret room. His back was towards her, and his striped tail swish-whished behind him on the floor.

Queenie, whose white-and-grey fur made her show up almost too well, was doing the same exact thing in front of the art studio. Ishtar, Mel couldn't spot anywhere now; the black cat must have gone into a room.

"What do you guys *see?*" she murmured. "What's *in* there?"

Obviously, neither of them answered, or even looked at her. Mel crept closer, wishing she had the good real kind of nightvision goggles like spies or the army might use... with infrared spectro-thermo-whatever... so she could see in the dark as well as the cats did. Or X-ray specs; X-ray specs would be cool.

Remembering her blacklight headlamp, she switched it on too. It shed an even eerier radiance, a strange misty thunderstorm purple that lit up electric-brilliant on various spots, splotches and speckles of what she figured must be old paint or something, because it probably wasn't really, like, *blood*.

She edged up to Queenie, ready to jump aside at a hiss or snarl. When none came—Queenie only kept staring, making the nose-wrinkled yuck-face again—Mel nudged the studio door open a few more inches with the toe of her sneaker.

Some light came in from outside, around the sides of the curtains and shades. Cloth-draped easels and blank canvases loomed pale like strange ghosts. An uncovered, half-finished painting, one of the freaky-gross ones, showed what looked like an extreme close-up of an eyeball with different color gummy-worms curling across its glistening surface. In the combined nightvision/blacklight, it looked way majorly seriously *weird*.

"There's nothing," Mel whispered to Queenie. "Except the wormy eyeball picture, which, okay, yuck-face, I get it. But there's nothing else in here."

Still, and still obviously, Queenie didn't answer. But, when Mel made to go into the room, the fluffy cat swiped with claws out. They snagged into Mel's sock and jabbed sharp pinpricks into her ankle. She sprang back with a yip just as Queenie tried to dash underfoot. Mel did a crazy little hop-skip dance not to step on her, succeeded in that much, then tripped over her own feet and went bellyflop onto the floor.

The fall didn't hurt, but her head whiplashed forward with a whack-crunch so hard she saw sparks and stars, and that *did* hurt. For a second, she thought she must've cracked her skull open, like her parents always warned would happen if she rode her bike without a helmet.

She only didn't howl or start crying because the landing had knocked her breath out in a big *oof*-cough. Pinwheel spiral fireworks whirled and spun, seeming both in front of her watering eyes and behind them. She wouldn't have been surprised to see a ring of cartoon tweety cuckoo birds going around, too.

Her forehead trickled wet—*oh jeez am I bleeding?* As she pushed herself to a sitting position, the weight of her goggles and head-lamp shifted, making a tinkly clatter of falling tiny plasticy bits—*oh jeez worse, did I break them?* Her hands flew up quick to check, grope-patting, and she winced and yipped again because the grope-patting hurt too, pain-darts needling into her face.

Whimpering some, starting to sniffle, Mel rocked back and forth on her butt. She blinked, tried to wipe her eyes but couldn't be-cause of the goggles, tried to take off the goggles and set off more stabby-needly pain-darts. She squinched her eyes tight-shut, which at least made some of the colorful fireworks go away.

There was a hum in her ears, too, a faint, ringing buzz that she could more feel than hear. It reminded her of being at the dentist, when they polished her teeth with the spinny thing.

What if she really *was* hurt, really *bad?* What if she was going to pass out or something? How long would it take anybody to notice and come looking for her? How long would it take them to find her? Maybe the cats would go and get help—

Or was that only dogs? She remembered stories on the news about dogs that called 9-1-1, and once even a parrot… but not so much cats. Cats, one of the bigger kids at school liked to say, would be the pets that ate the lips off old ladies in the commercials who fell down and couldn't get up.

"Don't eat my lips off, you guys," she said in a woozy-sounding mutter. "Queenie, okay? I know you don't like me but I didn't step on you, did I? Ulthar? Ishtar?"

She peeked one eye open to look for the cats, and thought at first somebody had turned the lights on up here. Then she thought she must have busted her nightvision goggles after all, because instead of shades of video-game green, the hallway was awash in a weird prickly-white glow. The white was speckled with staticky flecks of grey and black, an ancient-TV-set kind of effect.

When she opened her other eye, the view didn't change, except that now she could see more, and better. If better was the right word for it; it hardly looked like the ordinary third floor anymore. The hall was still there, sure… and the doors to the various rooms… but…

But, actually, the longer she peered at her surroundings, the less it seemed like she was even in the same *house*. The faded wallpaper and wood paneling were etched with moving lines—long, skinny squiggles in neon shades of pink, yellow, and blue. The floorboards, upon which she still sat, looked totally solid and normal, but something like liquid smoke or thick rainbow-sheened oil rippled up from underneath them, the way waves might rise and subside through gaps in a half-submerged and falling-apart footbridge.

Ahead of her, in the doorway to the turret room, Ulthar either hadn't even moved when she fell down, or had gone back to what he was doing before she'd noticed. He was still sitting there, still with his tail swish-whishing, still making the yuck-face at nothing. Now, though, she saw the ginger-stripe tabby outlined in brilliant orange, and twin glowstick-colored rays of light shot from his eyes like laser-beams.

"Ulthar?"

His ear flicked, but he didn't turn. His whole attention stayed riveted on the turret room. Queenie, meanwhile, was back in her same spot by the studio door, just as if Mel had never nearly stepped all over her… and Queenie, too, had a shining outline, though it was fuzz-blurred by her fluffy fur. She looked like she was in front of a bright-white full moon.

And Ishtar… a black cat in the blacklight with an ultra-black halo, moving lean and low and swift down the hall… leaving a streaky trail in the air behind her as she went… if Nyan Cat had Peter Pan's shadow…

Ishtar was following something, stalking it, and Mel recoiled with a shudder as she suddenly saw what it was.

Blob-spider-jellyfish was the best she could come up with.

She touched the side of her head, just under the edge of the goggles, and wondered again how badly she'd bonked it.

Words kept trying to push themselves into her mind, words she didn't know and didn't like the sound of.

Undulant, amoeboid, mucilaginous, quaggy, geloid, viscous, protuberant, effusion.

It... oozed.

Oozed and squished.

Reached out with gooey string-feelers and rolled the—

—globular mass—

—gross wet snot-bubble of its body along them... pushing with a cluster of spindly leg-things that stuck out the back... and inside the—

—translucent glutinence—

—kinda see-through jelly were these dozens of—

—tumorous ocular nodules wavering with fine hairlike cilia—

—lumpy, knotted, hairy twists of gristle she realized might be its eyes.

Mel sucked in a breath, ready to scream. If it was a nightmare, so what? Let her wake everybody up, let Courtney laugh at her and tease her from now until forever!

If it wasn't a nightmare... if she was seeing things because she'd cracked her skull open, so what? Scream anyway, and they'd come for her, find her, take her to the doctor, make her better.

Except, before she could scream, Ishtar's luminous bluer-than-blue gaze found hers. The black cat meowed once, a sort of musical but urgent warbling chirp. Then Mel felt cloud-soft fur brush her arm, felt the nudge of a whiskery nose, both felt and heard the busy rumble of a purr as Queenie twined and rubbed against her side.

None of the cats had ever wanted to cuddle or nuzzle. Mel was so surprised she almost forgot about needing to scream, though she sure as heck did not forget about the—

—semi-fluid quivering monstrosity—

—yucky awful blob oozing toward the stairs.

Where several more of them squished and flowed, overlapping, mushing together, bulging, squeezing, stretching. Some were

smaller than a cupcake, others were too big to fit in the staircase…
but that didn't matter because they passed right through the walls
like the walls weren't there… they drooped through the ceiling and
wallowed up out of the steps themselves the way whales did, only
without the spouting and tails…

Queenie climbed onto her lap and started doing the pushy-
paws kneading that cats did. Her purrs rumbled louder. Her claws
pricked at Mel's lab coat and jeans. She bumped her head against
Mel's chin.

Startled by, and not quite trusting, this unexpected display of
affection, Mel hardly dared move for a minute. Then she hesitantly
raised a hand and ran her palm along Queenie's back, making the
cat arch and push harder and purr even more.

The cats saw them, the blobby things in all their—

—*multihued slickness of mucoid tissues*—

—horrible, horrible jellyslime colors.

This was what the cats had been seeing all along. This was what
their ninesight showed them.

This was what crawled sluglike all through the whole house. All
through the whole world! And people didn't know.

People didn't *know!*

Those oozy blobs might be *any*where. Might be right by a person,
under them, over them, *on* them! Creeping *through* them the way
they crept through solid walls!

Ulthar strolled toward her, did a *biiiiig* stretch and yawn, and
sprawled flop at her feet. Between her and the stairs. Between her
and the mounds of wobbly goop squelching silently—or *were* they
squelching silently? just because *she* couldn't hear them…

They knew, the cats. The cats knew. They understood now that
she was seeing what they did, what most people couldn't or didn't.

A deep-body shudder started way down deep in Mel's bones and
guts.

Both Ulthar and Queenie purred and acted all super lovey and
cute. Like they wanted to distract her from the—

—amorphous coagulant loathsome protrusions of extradimensional abominations—

Meanwhile, Ishtar paced the hall, long and sleek as a panther, sparing only a slitted glowing-blue glance of warning Mel's way. As if to tell her to not say anything, not react in any way, not let on that she could see what the cats saw.

But, why? Didn't they want people to know? What if those blob-jelly things were dangerous? Or was it *because* they were dangerous? Crazy-killy dangerous, for people if maybe not so much for cats?

Because something bad might happen, if the blob-things sensed or realized Mel saw them, too?

Because then they might… be able to… what?

Reach her? Touch her? Get to her somehow?

She thought suddenly of the wormy eyeball painting in the studio, and the other freaky-gross artwork Uncle Joe's brother did before he died. She thought of Uncle Joe's missing sister, the one who'd supposedly run away from home.

What if they'd been able to see…?

And the jellyslime blobs had found out, and did something to them?

That was silly, though. The only reason *she* could see any of this was because of her nightvision and blacklight. Which somehow—after she whacked her head with them on and maybe broke something in there—gave her ninesight like the cats.

It occurred to her, as she petted Queenie and Ulthar curled around her feet and Ishtar reared up on her hind legs to swat at something dangling down the wall—

—elongating in supple and pendulous pseudopodic tendrils—

—in long gluey, goopy strings, that all she had to do was take off the goggles and headlamp. Then she wouldn't have to see these ucky things anymore. They'd go away.

She grabbed the goggles by the sides again and felt another needling zap-shocker of pain, as if part of the electronics inside had jabbed into her skull, wires stuck like splinters. It stung and sizzled.

More wetness trickled down her forehead. But the pain and the bleeding couldn't be as bad as what she was having to see, and deal with, and *think*.

With a terrific wrenching yank, she ripped the goggles from her face and dropped the headlamp on the floor in a brittle crunch of glass. It hurt even more than when she fell and whacked her head in the first place. Tears gushed from her eyes and blood dripped on her cheeks and nose.

Sniffling, she used the collar of her lab coat to mop at the mess. She blinked. She wiped her eyes. She didn't want to play anymore. Detective Investigator Special Agent Mel wanted to be *off* the case.

The hallway was all dark and empty, except for her and the cats.

It had worked.

The oozy blob-spider-jellyfish things and wormy dangling strings were gone—

Except, then, with a rising cold terror, she realized she was wrong.

The cats with their ninesight were still watching the stairs.

Just because *she* couldn't *see* them anymore... didn't mean they weren't... *there*.

They might even be moving toward her *right now*.

But no one else would see them either. No one would know. And nobody would believe her, because she was only a kid.

Sitting on the floor, hugging Queenie, Mel started to cry.

WAXEN

Another package on the stoop.

The old bitch and her scented goddamn candles... the whole house smelled like a fruit truck, a florist's stand, a bakery, and a candy shop simultaneously exploded and then burnt down.

Sighing, he picked up the box. It got everywhere, that smell. Permeated everything. He kept his bedroom door shut but it still got in there. Into his clothes and hair. Coating his skin with waxy-feeling residue. People remarked on it.

But what was he supposed to do? The old bitch owned the place. The old bitch's disability checks paid the bills and then some. As long as they kept rolling in, he didn't have to get a real job. All he had to do was take care of things here.

Besides, the candles did help cover the sickroom stench.

He let himself in and yep, there it was, a faceful of citrus and spice, vanilla and roses, something that was supposed to be clean linens, something else that was supposed to be spring rain, a mingling melange of dozens more. Plus those whiffs of wax and smoke.

Clocks ticked, the ancient refrigerator hummed, and a stand-fan whirred as it stirred the musty-dusty perfumed waxy air. He went through to the kitchen and set the box on the counter. An idle glance at the label didn't tell him much.

C&C Candles, Lake Hali, The Hyades.

Never heard of them. She must've belonged to like six different candle-of-the-month clubs, not to mention guilt-gifts from distant relatives too busy to bother with actual visits.

He snagged a beer, popped the top, and took a long swig. A cheap brand, but he wasn't about to shell out for the good stuff when whatever he ate or drank ended up tasting like scented wax anyway.

Once he'd finished the beer, he held off on opening a second and decided to at least act as if he was doing his job. He picked up the box again—the logo on the label was creepy, though he couldn't quite pinpoint why—and carried it down the hall.

"Yo, Edith, you got another candle."

The sickroom scents grew stronger the closer he got to her room. Not urine; he kept her catheterized for that. Not shit either; the old bitch probably hadn't had a true bowel movement for years. Stale and sour sweat... chemicals, medication, ointment... the tang of alcohol wipes... and...

"Whew," he said, waving a hand in front of his nose.

And that, friends and neighbors, was *eau de cancer,* a body rotting from the inside out. Strong today. Very strong.

In her room, the air seemed thick with waxy particles. The wall-paper was more waxpaper by now. Fussy antique sideboards or hutches or who-the-hell-knew stood around, covered with candles. Most were in little glass jars, white wicks rising, flames flickering above molten puddles.

"Edith? Still with us?"

The old bitch didn't respond. She was a mummified bundle of sticks and wrinkles, one eyelid sunken shut, the other half-lidded over a filmy, faded orb. Her mouth drooped slack. If not for the shallow hitches of her chest, he would've thought she'd gone and died on him.

How long and how well, he wondered, would the candles mask full-on decay? When she did die, nobody had to know, did they? The checks would keep coming until it was reported, and who else but him would be reporting it? Quitting the agency and claiming he'd been hired as her live-in was the smartest thing he'd ever done.

In the meantime, though, might as well go through the minimum motions.

"Let's see what this one is," he said when he'd dealt with the IV. He slit the tape—that logo, that weird symbol, what *was* that?—and opened the box.

Packing material… plastic wrappings… and aha, finally, the candle itself.

He hesitated, nose wrinkling. "Eugh."

Not in a jar. A squat, stout cylinder. Yellow, but not citrus-yellow, not lemon-meringue-pie yellow, not honeycomb yellow. A darker, nasty-somehow yellow. Earwax yellow. *Diseased* earwax yellow. Greasy. Greasy to the look and to the touch. Like poorly-rendered tallow.

And its scent…

Not floral. Not fruity. Not candy-bakery-sweet.

Acrid sprang to mind. Alkaline. The bitter mineral salt flats by a strange lake. A warm lake. *Lake Hali? In the dry shadows of the Hyades where black stars shine sharp?*

No wick protruded from its top. It was just a cylindrical blob, greasy and unpleasant, and why was he holding it, turning it around and around? Leaving impressions of his fingers in its soft, luridly organic substance…

Was it a candle?

It felt like butter. Bad butter. A bad, rancid lump of butter. Churned from the yellow milk of some… *thing*…

He squeezed and met a gooey resistance, a squirming undulant sort of movement. He thought of insectile larvae in wet cocoons… unborn malformed embryos slippery in congealed fluid… boneless and gelatinous…

As myriad inhuman eyes peeled open, as the first slick tentacles oozed to curl around his fingers, he heard a low and chuffing rattle-sound, and realized the old bitch was laughing.

LET ME TALK TO SARAH

"You say one of them is a child?"

"Lulu. A little girl. She cries a lot. She thinks it's her fault Mommy and Daddy fight so much."

"Is it?"

"No, but how can you explain that to a child? She blames herself for everything. Of them all, she's the only one I feel sorry for. The others are horrible. I hate them all."

"I understand—"

"Do you? Do you, really? I feel like I've gone crazy, like I've been torn apart. I have all these strangers inside me. And they never shut up! Why can't they go *away?*"

"If they did go away, what would happen next?"

"… to… to me, you mean? I… I wouldn't have to listen to them anymore. Wouldn't have to put up with them or the things they do. They're ruining everything I ever had, everything important to me."

"Which must be very upsetting. However, you must also realize, your situation *has* changed."

"I'm fractured! I'm not whole anymore. There are walls inside me now that never used to be there, locked doors, parts of me closed off! I'd rather be alone. At least, alone, it'd be peaceful. I'd be myself again."

"Perhaps we should discuss Sarah—"

"I asked you not to mention her. Please don't."

"All right. Why don't you tell me about some of these others you're having troubles with, then? You said a few of them are men?"

"Well, there's Rick. So clean-cut, so ultra-conservative on the outside. He's on the computer and it's nonstop hatespeech. But at the same time, he's watching gay porn, hardcore stuff, some of it violent. Visiting chatrooms, exchanging graphic messages, while he's... well, you know. He thinks nobody will ever find out, but *I* know; worse, it's as if *I'm* the one right there *doing* it!"

"Are you disturbed by the idea of homosexuality?"

"What should I care about something like that?"

"And Sarah? Did Sarah—"

"We're not talking about her. We're talking about these others, these strangers. I want them out of me. I don't want to be like this. Sometimes it seems like it's getting worse. Like I don't have any control. Like I *never* had any. They're taking over, and I can't stop them; there's nothing I can do! Julie went out again the other night—"

"Julie is the one you told me about during our last session? The, how did you put it, party girl?"

"I only said 'party girl' because I thought 'slut' might be too harsh. The drinking was bad enough, but she's started doing drugs... sleeping around with men she's only just met, 'hooking up' as she says... sometimes she's not home until four in the morning, sometimes she doesn't come home at all... sometimes she brings these guys home *with* her!"

"Making consistently poor choices."

"You call unsafe sex, illegal drugs, the bad part of town, bringing her hookups *home* 'poor choices'? What if she gets arrested? Beat up? Raped or even killed? What then? Police everywhere, what a disaster! And she just doesn't care. YOLO, she says, whatever *that* means."

"You Only Live Once, as I understand it. A popular catch-phrase among younger people."

"It's ridiculous. One of those losers who stayed over left drug paraphernalia in the bathroom. Drug paraphernalia! In *my* bathroom! Another vomited all over the porch, *my* porch, and of course *Julie* wasn't going to clean the mess. *Julie* thought it was funny! The whole thing makes me wish I could set myself on fire."

"That's a rather specific phrasing."

"... I didn't mean... I'm not... I wouldn't..."

"If you ever do start having serious—"

"I won't! I'd never! Like I told you earlier, I'd be fine with being left alone, ignored and neglected. I mean, sure, I'd prefer to be beautiful and famous forever; wouldn't we all? But..."

"Fame isn't always what it's cracked up to be. It can easily cross over into notoriety. And you'd still be sacrificing the privacy, peace, and quiet you claim to crave."

"I suppose you're right. I mean, I enjoyed having visitors, even guests sometimes. Parties—not Julie's kind of parties, but *real* parties, dinner parties, dances. And holidays! How I loved the holidays! The decorations, the lights and the snow... everything's magical then, everything glows. I even liked Halloween, isn't that silly? Not the parts where they egg houses or leave bags of doggie-doo on the stoop, but those decorations too, and the children coming to the door, trick-or-treaters in their costumes, sometimes scared, but always excited."

"Maybe you'll still be able to enjoy all those things."

"It won't be the same. Not with *them* around. I miss the way things used to be. I... I miss her. I miss... Sarah."

***

"You seem agitated today. More troubles with Julie? Or with Rick?"

"Neither... well, both, but nothing new. It's just Albert. He's really beginning to annoy me."

"Albert, ah yes, the older gentleman. The, banker, was it?"

"Some kind of business executive or another; I don't remember. I don't care. He's retired now, has nothing better to do than try to micro-manage everything. Thinks *he* should be in charge because of his years of corporate experience or whatever. He's driving me bonkers!"

"I see."

"Is it all right to use that term? Or is it, I don't know, offensive? These days, with political correctness and trigger warnings…"

"You may use any terms with which you feel comfortable. We have complete privacy. Complete confidentiality. To borrow another of those 'these days' terms, consider this a 'safe space,' as they say."

"Thank you. I apologize, though, for my temper."

"No apology needed. It's quite understandable. You've been under a great deal of stress. Remember, my role isn't to judge. My role is to listen, consult, counsel, and support."

"And keep the lunatics locked up."

"Only the dangerous ones."

"Am I dangerous?"

"You tell me."

"What could *I* do to hurt anybody? Even if I wanted to?"

"Do you want to?"

"I… well, sometimes… the guys Julie brings home, the addicts, puking, trashing the place…"

"What about Julie herself?"

"Oh, you know, I'd love to be able to grab her, shake some *sense* into her, the stupid YOLO slut. Or Rick, with the horrible hateful things he posts online. He could use a smack upside the head, for sure. But I wouldn't *hurt* them. I mean, we're kind of stuck with each other."

"It sounds as though you're coming to accept these, ah, people as more than simply intrusive strangers."

"I still want them gone. I want them to shut up, I want them out, I don't want to have to deal with them anymore. If I *am* insane, it's *their* fault. I was never this way before. I was whole, and peaceful, and happy. Not… not fragmented… tortured and torn apart!"

"Do you need a moment?"

"Yes, please."

"Very well."

"Thank you."

"Better?"

"Much."

"Ready to go on? You were telling me about Albert, I believe. Who feels that he should be in charge because of his managerial experience... how, exactly, does he propose to do that? Call a meeting?"

"Ugh, I really would go bonkers then. All of them together, all talking at once, arguing? It's bad enough the way he goes sticking his little notes everywhere... reminders about sorting recyclables, keeping the thermostat at such-and-such temperature, turning off lights, locking the front door... his latest favorite trick is to photocopy dictionary pages, highlight words like 'consideration' and 'responsibility,' and then tack them up on the bulletin board."

"Rather passive-aggressive of him."

"On the plus side, he does make sure the trash is taken out and utility bills get paid on time. Which *is* helpful; I guess someone has to take care of those details."

"How do the others respond to his notes?"

"Ignore them, laugh and roll their eyes, sigh and shake their heads. There's been the occasional snarky scribble, and once a rude drawing. Nothing *too* nasty or confrontational... so far."

"Let's hope it stays that way. Your situation is difficult enough without additional internal strife."

"I just... I just wish I could go back to the way things used to be."

"Which is only natural. Nostalgia is a powerful force."

"But I know it's impossible. I know memory is subjective, there's no turning the clock, what's done is done and what's gone is gone. I need to get past this and move forward. End of story."

"Except it isn't the end of the story, is it? You still haven't come to terms with what happened to Sarah."

"I've told you I don't want to talk about that. I'm not ready."

"Are you angry at her?"

"What? No! That's silly. Why would I be angry at Sarah?"

"Maybe you feel as if she betrayed you. Broke your trust."

"No… no, she didn't… she wouldn't… she was never like that."

"Or do you feel as if *you* betrayed *her?* Failed her, somehow? Do you blame yourself?"

"What could *I* have done? I couldn't save her. I couldn't help."

"What about Tommy? Are you angry at him? Afraid of him?"

"Angry, yes. Afraid? No. What else can he do? He's already destroyed me. He's already turned me into… into… into *this,* into whatever I am. This thing… this fractured, divided, insane *thing.*"

"Do you consider yourself insane?"

"You're the expert. But, what's the quote? The famous one, from literature?"

"Jackson, or Poe?"

"The one about the house."

"Again… Jackson, or Poe?"

"Very funny. Can a person be haunted? Can a place be possessed? Where's the line? What's the difference?"

"Those are interesting, significant questions. However, in terms of your relationship with Tommy—"

"I don't have a relationship with Tommy. He never cared about me, always thought I was too old and too ugly. Do you think *he* gives a damn about nostalgia? About history, and memory? No. He only cares about money. He'd desecrate his own mother's corpse for a profit, let alone mine."

***

"I thought we were supposed to be getting *rid* of them! Instead, now, there's a new one!"

"Situations such as yours are very complicated, and handling them requires a certain delicacy. We mustn't move too fast. It could prove dangerous."

"I know... but she... this new girl... she's up to something. I think she's a witch."

"A witch?"

"Don't tell me you don't believe in witches. In *this* town? In *Arkham?*"

"My reaction was more of surprise than of skepticism, I assure you."

"Things go on here. Weird, unnatural things."

"I'm not disagreeing."

"It's the architecture, isn't it? The way the streets are laid out, the lines and angles. The way certain places, certain sites, are like a locus... or a focus... where forces converge... where they overlap, and cross."

"What does this have to do with the new girl you mentioned?"

"She *knows* things. She has maps, old maps. City plans. Blueprints. Books that must have come from the university library, though I don't think she's a student. Which must, by the way—the whole Miskatonic campus, I mean—just be a *hotbed* of borders and gateways, pivot-points in dimensions."

"You are correct."

"And...?"

"The Asylum? Oh, very much so."

"You knew?"

"I've always known."

"What about me? What about Whateley House? Were you going to tell me, or were you going to leave me ignorant, in the dark?"

"I was waiting for you to reach your own conclusions. But, tell me about this new girl. What's her name?"

"... now, don't go making a big thing out of this..."

"I beg your pardon?"

"It's coincidence, pure coincidence. Doesn't mean anything."

"Very well."

"Her name's Sarah."

"Interesting."

"Coincidence, I told you. It's a very common name."

"Of course. You say this new Sarah is an occultist... on what do you base this suspicion?"

"The books, the candles, the designs she chalks onto the walls. The way she dresses, like one of those... what do they call them? Goths? All in black, with pale makeup, dyed hair, freaky contact lenses. Silver jewelry. Pentacles and lopsided stars. That kind of thing."

"I see."

"She's looking for the room. The secret room. I'm afraid what will happen if she finds it."

"How likely is that?"

"It's well-hidden. None of the others know about it. But, the new girl, she's got old maps from somewhere, maps of the neighborhood, with floorplans. She's measured and seen how the numbers don't quite add up. She figures there must be a space unaccounted for, where the angles all come together. She thinks it's a source of power, or something."

"Which, of course, it is, isn't it?"

"She can't go in there! No one can! No one should! No one has, not since..."

"Sarah? The original Sarah, as it were?"

"It wasn't her fault. She didn't know. She was only meaning to clear out the furniture and boxes of junk that had been stored in there forever. She never would have hurt anyone. They *made* her do it, the things that came up from the floor. *Through* the floor."

"You've told me again and again that it wasn't Sarah's fault. It wasn't yours, either."

"I should have stopped her! Should have warned her!"

"Tell me what happened."

"She... she'd moved a bunch of the larger items into the hall before she noticed the pattern on the floor, the mosaic. Between that and the stained glass mock-skylights—they can't be seen from outside; the regular roof covers them over—she wondered if it was some sort of private chapel. I guess she wasn't far wrong, was she?"

"Perhaps not."

"She thought she might turn it into a conservatory, grow orchids. Or a studio, take up painting or pottery, something like that. She loved gardening, you know. And she was very artistic. A good person. Good, and kind. She didn't deserve to end up locked away!"

"Few people do. It is often tragic."

"On her own, in her right mind, you have to believe she never would have done what she did. It was the things that came up through the floor. Maybe, when she cut herself—it was a broken vase, that's all; she bumped a stack of boxes, and it fell, and it broke, and when she went to pick up the pieces, a shard sliced her thumb. That's what it was. That's all it was. Some blood dripped onto the floor. Onto the tiles. It... woke them up, summoned them, the things from the floor."

"What were they?"

"I don't know. Like worms made of ice and oil and smoke. Like snakes without heads, wires without plugs. They moved, but they didn't seem sentient, or alive. Not... the way people are. And nothing like us."

"No, they aren't, are they? They're nothing like us."

"So, you believe me."

"Of course I believe you."

"And you knew about this, too. You knew about these things. You knew they were real, but you didn't tell me. Didn't warn me! I thought I was going insane even then, too! Even before the others showed up and took over! Now I'm full of noise and strangers, I can't have a moment's peace, while all along *you knew!*"

"I understand you're upset—"

"Upset?! What else are you hiding from me, 'Doctor'? How am I supposed to trust you when you're keeping secrets? Were you hoping something like this would happen? Hoping Sarah would find that room and… and activate it, or whatever that was? Or hoping she *wouldn't?*"

"Why would I—?"

"Then, an innocent woman gets carted off in a straitjacket! From one crazyroom to another, from the one with worms in the floor to the one with padding on the walls! More business for you!"

"I assure you, I have all the business I can handle."

"No shortage of lunatics in Arkham Asylum."

"Tragically, no."

"Tragically, bah… you asked me once what would happen to me if I got rid of all these strangers living inside me… what would happen to *you* if all the crazies got cured?"

"Given the state of the world these days, that's unlikely. However, speaking of which, I'm afraid our session is almost up, and I think you could use some time to settle yourself."

"Calm down, you mean. I'm sorry."

"Not at all. We've made some excellent progress. We may even be close to a breakthrough."

***

"I wanted to apologize—again—for my behavior last time. I got very emotional. I know it isn't conducive to a forward-moving therapeutic relationship."

"It's quite all right. In fact, I welcome it. Detachment and avoidance are far less conducive."

"Well, I guess. If you say so."

"Now, I'd like you to tell me more about these entities, the ones that emerged from the floor tiles. You described them, I believe, as 'like worms made of ice and oil and smoke,' correct?"

"Yes, though they didn't emerge, exactly. They had no tails, no other end. They just kept… extruding. Rising upward. Swaying. And there was… I don't know if it was a *sound* so much as a vibration, a low thrumming buzz. Nothing window-rattling or wall-shaking. In the beams, in the foundation."

"Were you frightened?"

"More shocked, at least at first. To think these... *things*... had been there all along, just waiting for a touch of blood to bring them seething up out of nowhere! It felt so invasive, a violation of sanity and reality. And Sarah... poor Sarah... it was the end for her. She just... her mind, her psyche... just shattered."

"Go on."

"Do I have to?"

"It will help for you to talk through it, to process what happened."

"She... she shattered. Started screaming, or trying to; she was gasping, couldn't get her breath. Before she could even try to run, they snared her. Twined around her arms and legs. She shook like someone being electrocuted. And light... light came shining in through the stained glass mock-skylights. The ones covered from the outside by the roof, so no sunlight can reach them, but it wasn't sunlight. I don't know what it was. But its source seemed to be moving behind the panes, because the tinted rays shifted, tracing patterns on the walls."

"Can you describe these patterns?"

"Some were like the ones set into the floor mosaics, but most... they... no. There aren't words."

"That's fine. Please, continue."

"Then, Sarah... her screams turned into something else. Something like chanting... in a language I don't think belongs on this world."

"Do you remember any of it?"

"Even if I did, I wouldn't want to repeat it. Names, maybe. Unearthly, horrible names. Phrases of... power... invitation and invocation. They were trying to use her to open a way between here and... somewhere else. Because of her blood. Her bloodline. Her heritage."

"Except that it didn't work."

"It didn't work because she fought them. She was too strong for them. She got away. But it broke her. Broke her mind into a million pieces, broke it like a mirror, edges jagged, reflections uneven."

"So I've noticed."

"She hid the room, though. After... the other stuff."

"The criminal assaults."

"I told you, she didn't mean to hurt anyone. She didn't know what she was doing. When they knocked at the door, she thought they were... something else. Monsters wearing human disguises. That they had those worm-things inside them, controlling them like puppets."

"When, in reality..."

"... they were the postman and the Avon lady."

"And by 'hid the room,' you mean...?"

"Put up paneling and wallpaper over the door, made it look normal. When people came in later, they never noticed. Even workmen, contractors. Of course, they were always the cheapest ones available for hire, slipshod and lazy, doing shoddy work, cutting corners right and left."

"And no one's found it, no one's visited it since?"

"No one's even suspected. Until... until this new girl, the other Sarah. With her books and blueprints, floorplans. I'm worried that she'd know what those patterns meant. I don't want her snooping around. I don't want any of them. I want... I want Sarah again, *my* Sarah, home again and happy, the way things used to be. I miss that. So much!"

"As I've told you—"

"I know it's impossible, you keep telling me, you don't have to tell me again. But, to be locked up, tied down, medicated, treated like an animal... it's no kind of life. If I could just talk to her somehow! But you won't let me, will you?"

"It's hardly a matter of letting you or not. Believe me, I wish I could talk to her myself. But that's really neither here nor there, now, is it?"

***

"I'd like to discuss Thomas today, if you don't mind."

"Tommy? Oh, I am so glad he's not around all the time. I couldn't stand it. I really couldn't The others are more than bad enough, but, him? So horrid, so disrespectful. Even when he was a little boy, he'd be coloring on the walls, or trying to slide down the front stairs on a sheet of cardboard or something. He never cared about me. All he cares about is money."

"I meant Thomas Whateley, Senior. You cannot tell me *he* didn't care about you."

"Oh, him? Well, yes, he did… I know he did… in his way."

"How do you think he would react to your current situation?"

"He'd be furious. Thomas always did have a temper. He hid it pretty well, the way he hid lots of things, but it was there. Behind closed doors, it would come out."

"Was he ever abusive? Physically or otherwise?"

"No. No, of course not. He saw enough of that in his own family. His response was to turn it inward. He drank. A lot. Sometimes he'd… how would your psychiatrists put it? Engage in self-harm."

"Cutting?"

"Not usually. I think he had a phobia about blood, particularly his own. He didn't trust it. Said there was a toxic strain, an evil taint to the Whateley bloodline."

"If not cutting, what manner of self-harm did he display?"

"He'd… pinch himself, his flesh, with clothespins or hard metal clamps—not in any sort of sick, sexual way; don't get that idea! But he'd be all-over bruises. Or burns, putting out cigarettes on his skin, holding his hand to a flame."

"Which does shed some interesting light on the manner of his death."

"Why he hanged himself, you mean? Instead of slashing his wrists or using a gun?"

"Yes. He also did it outdoors, from a tree in the back garden, if I recall correctly."

"I don't think he believed in ghosts, not exactly, but he didn't want to die too close to that room. Something about energies and transference, his essence becoming trapped."

"A valid concern, under the circumstances."

"Can you imagine, having him still hanging around, too?... oh, that was an awful way to put it, I'm sorry. But, it's bad enough with all the others already, and Thomas, like I said, wouldn't take to it at all."

"As I understand it, he was a learned, well-educated occultist, if not much of an actual practitioner."

"No need to sugarcoat it. He was awful. A total failure. He had the white hair and pink eyes, the weak chin, but he could barely read Latin, let alone anything more complex. That's why he ended up only using the room for storage. He could close it up and forget about it, especially once his parents were no longer around to harangue him."

"Strong choice of words."

"They did, though. About that, about his reluctance to have children… they wanted to see their line, their legacy, continue. A trueborn heir to Whateley House, you see. Given the familial connection on Sarah's mother's side, as well? Distant cousins, but not *so* distant—this *is* New England; if you go back far enough, everyone's related to everyone else. Why, the results might even have been a successor to rival the Old Man of Dunwich himself! But, instead, they had to settle for *him.*"

"Tommy. Thomas Junior."

"Adopted, of course. There are a lot of orphans, abandoned babies, and foster kids in Arkham, have you noticed?"

"I am in frequent contact with the various orphanages, hospitals, churches, and care-homes around town, yes. But, tell me, might the adoption be why you never bonded with Tommy?"

"He never liked me anyway, I told you. All he ever cared about was what he could get out of me. Room and board, free rent, a place to stay; if I needed anything, he'd begrudge the expense, he'd piss and moan and complain like it was the end of the world! I was so glad when he finally moved out."

"Would you have felt differently if he'd been a Whateley by blood?"

"I'd have felt differently if he hadn't been such a brat! And now, look. Look what he's done, look what he's doing. He'd get rid of me once and for all if he could. He looks at me and sees a burden, responsibilities he doesn't want. If not for Thomas's will, he'd sell me in a snap. Or, better yet, burn me down for the insurance money and put up pricey condos."

***

"I used to be so beautiful, you know. Whateley House, a manor, a real showplace. Sarah took such good care of me, both before and after Thomas died. My woodwork... my windows... I could have become a museum, or an inn, a lovely historic bed-and-breakfast."

"You still would have been plagued by strangers inside you, an even more constant coming and going."

"Yes, but people who admired and appreciated me for what I was! Who respected me! Who didn't defile me with cheap, flimsy wallboard... staple down ugly carpets over my polished hardwood floors... add substandard plumbing, drill holes to run wiring. My elegant rooms and suites, all hacked up, sub-divided! Rooms for rent, turning me into a shared-kitchen boarding house. Boarding house? Barely a step above a *flop*house!"

"What about your original furnishings?"

"Again, if not for the will, I'm sure Tommy would have wasted no time selling off as much as he could. As it is, not even the will stopped him from having most of it hauled to the attic or basement so these people could bring in their own hideous furniture. Garage sale thrift store free-on-the-curb rubbish, probably infested with bedbugs and woodlice."

"Before anyone is admitted here, all of their clothing and other belongings are thoroughly treated against such infestations."

"Yes, well, good for *you*, but, I have no say on who moves in or how. It's all up to Tommy, and as long as they pony up the cash, he doesn't care. No background checks or anything."

"You'd think it would be in his best interest all around to provide adequate upkeep and maintenance regardless, if he does hope for an eventual sale."

"Which is why he'll probably just want me knocked down. He figures the land, the location, would be worth far more. He doesn't live here himself, of course, so it's nothing to him how they carry on... how much damage they do, or how much noise they make. It used to be so *quiet*, so nice and serene. Sarah, *my* Sarah, would watch her programs and listen to the radio sometimes, but these ones? It's nonstop with music and televisions, doors slamming, faucets running, footsteps clomping on the stairs."

"How many tenants currently?"

"Eleven, eleven now... twelve if you count Julie's latest drug-head boyfriend who sleeps over more often than not... thirteen including the dog, the damn *dog!*"

"You hadn't mentioned a dog."

"The newlyweds who moved in a few days ago; they agreed to pay fifty a month extra. But they both work all day, so they leave it cooped up, and it yips and it howls and it scratches at the door, and I'm sure it's only a matter of time before it's doing its business inside instead of waiting until one of them comes home to walk it. So of course Albert has already left them a few of his annoying little notes, and he also got into it with Lulu's father over the recycling..."

"That all sounds very stressful."

"Not even the half of it! Lulu's *mother* made some remark to Julie about her drug-head boyfriend, so now they're sneering and sniping when they pass in the hall... meanwhile, it seems the *boyfriend* knows *Rick* from some best-not-thought-about encounter in a bar bathroom and is blackmailing him, which has Rick in a panic..."

"Your very own soap opera. I know how that is. Between the staff and the patients, sometimes I can barely keep track."

"I don't *want* to know how that is! I've started to think the best possible outcome would be for them all just to kill each other. Strangling, stabbing, shooting, pushing down the stairs... I don't care anymore. If Albert wants to turn the master bath into an ab-attoir, dismembering bodies in the tub so the blood runs down the drain... if Rick midnight-buries Julie's boyfriend in the back yard... murders and suicides and murder-suicides, bring it on! I'd rather be known as a death-house than go on like this!"

***

"You seem much calmer today."

"Yes. Yes, thank you. I am."

"Matters with your inhabitants have improved?"

"Very much so."

"...are they all right? In our last session, you'd expressed some fairly violent impulses toward them."

"Well, but that'd be just silly. I'm only a house. It isn't as if I could *do* anything."

"Have they harmed each other?"

"Not yet, not that I know of. However, the night is still young. We can hope."

"Previously, you'd also evinced concern of what more in-depth police or forensic investigations might discover—"

"The secret room? The nexus, or mindhouse, or whatever it's called?"

"Yes... but... where did you come by that particular term?"

"Mindhouse? Oh, I've been learning things lately. I've been learning a lot. What I wonder, though... what I can't quite figure out, is whether you want it to stay hidden and inert, or whether you want it restored and activated."

"Now, why would I—"

"You, the hospital, the university, whatever's left of the old Dun-wich place. How many of you are in on it?"

"I'm not quite following what you're getting at here."

"All this time, I had it like a cancer inside me, that room, that damned room, needing a true Whateley to bring it fully to life. But, since Thomas turned out to be no good as a practitioner, and Sarah went mad, there was no one to do it. Is that what you want-ed? Did you drive her mad on purpose so you could take her away, lock her up with the rest of your loonies?"

"When did you begin experiencing these paranoid ideations?"

"Tell me, 'Doctor'! Tell me the truth!"

"There's no truth to tell. No occult conspiracies—"

"Don't give me that, not in this town. What happened at Dun-wich—at the original Whateley House—brought, or let, some-thing powerful through. Is that what the room in me is for? If so, are you hoping to awaken it, or keep it… keep *me!*… quiescent?"

"Do you need a moment?"

"What I need is an answer."

"I cannot give you one. Even if I could, well, the point would be moot. The room is hidden. Thomas Whateley is dead, Sarah will never leave my care, and Tommy was adopted."

"Right. No shortage of orphanages and abandoned babies in Arkham, as we said. Good thing, too. Made it much easier for Sarah, all those years ago, when she became pregnant."

"… I beg your pardon?"

"Don't be shocked. Even *I* didn't suspect. She couldn't tell her husband, obviously; who knows what he might have done? Hid-ing her condition was the most difficult part, until she devised the pretext of staying a few months with an invalid friend to help out."

"You cannot possibly believe Sarah Whateley bore a child."

"Of course, she had to leave the baby as an anonymous foundling, one of those safe-care drop boxes at a hospital or church. Couldn't very well bring it home, claiming it to be another adoption, could she? Thomas would have taken one look and just known. Blood calls to blood, after all. Power calls to power. Particularly Whateley blood, and Whateley power."

"This is insane."

"Well, you *are* the expert."

"Someone would have suspected. Someone would have guessed."

"I think someone did. The albinism and weak chin must have been a giveaway. They spirited the baby out of town, out of New England."

"I suppose I may as well play along with your delusional fancy. Why would they have done that?"

"Maybe Sarah left a note, not wanting her husband to find out. Maybe whoever did it was afraid of the elder Whateleys; the family reputation twenty-odd years ago wasn't at its best, to say the least. Better than it was in Dunwich a hundred years ago, sure, but still, not great. A conscientious nun or nurse might've been reluctant to turn an infant over into their influence."

"A simple medical examination by one of the staff physicians would verify whether or not she'd ever given birth."

"What are you waiting for? Nudge them. Have one of your psychiatrists put in an order. I'm sure you have that much control."

"I will, if only to show you how far-fetched this new defense mechanism of yours is."

"Why would I make up such a story?"

"Because you are unwilling to let go. Instead of accepting reality, you've dreamt up a fantasy, an escapism, a possible rescuer to sweep in, depose Tommy, and restore your world to the way it used to be."

"Would that be so terrible?"

"I understand its comforting appeal. But, let's address it logically. If we are in fact to believe there's a trueborn Whateley out there somewhere, raised under another name, what makes you think—"

"I told you! Blood calls to blood, and power calls to power. Especially Whateley blood and Whateley power. Sooner or later, curious about where they came from, they'd make their way home."

"And go unnoticed? Here? In Arkham?"

"That's the thing about those Goths, though… having pale skin and avoiding sunlight… the contact lenses, hair dyed jet black… for them, it's just part of the image, it's totally normal and expected."

"Do you… you don't mean…"

"The names, well, it turns out that wasn't a coincidence at all. Sarah and Sarah. Like mother, like daughter."

"The new tenant, the one you worried was a witch?"

"Oh, 'Doctor,' I don't have to worry about that anymore. I won't have to worry about anything. Once she finds the secret room, she'll take care of everything. The others… Tommy… everything."

"Where is she now?!"

"Pulling down the last of the paneling over the hidden door. It's almost over. It won't be long now. I just thought you ought to know."

WHEN LAVENDER IS IN BLOOM

"It is a bad place for a stranger," the old man told me. "You'd better take a guide."

I turned to look at him. He sat frail and wizened in a wheelchair, wearing a soft heather-colored sweater. A crocheted blanket lay over his lap, suede slippers protruding from beneath its edge. How he had gotten up here to this cliffside viewpoint was, at first, beyond me. Then I saw, not far away, one of the many care-complexes clustered along the outskirts of the town, and supposed he must have wheeled his way over from there.

"I shall not lose myself," I replied, or hoped I did, in my careful guidebook French. The local dialect was different from the Rosetta Stone crash-course I'd undertaken before this trip, and I went about in perpetual fear of inadvertently insulting someone.

His smile was the saddest I'd ever seen, the sigh accompanying it a wistful breath of eternities. "That's what I said, so long ago. That's what I said. And of course I did lose myself. I lost myself and it was wonderful. I would have stayed lost there forever. You're American, aren't you?"

"Yes." I knew of fellow travelers who preferred pretending otherwise, claiming to be from Canada to escape the not-altogether-undeserved reputation, but I sensed no accusation in his query.

He nodded. "So was I, once."

A moment passed, a waiting pause that seemed to hang like a held breath between us.

"Once?" I asked, when it seemed an encouraging nudge was somehow expected.

"When I was young," he said. "Young, like you. American, like you. Though, when I set out for my day's ramble through the moors, I went with a gun upon my shoulder, thinking perhaps to hunt."

I held up my botanical collection kit. "I only hunt with this."

"Good. That's good. Quieter. More peaceful. Though there is something to be said for the older ways, as well. When hunting was as much art as sport."

Below us, where the steep switchbacked path I meant soon to descend met the sprawling denseness of hilly green grass and bracken I also meant soon to traverse, a brown hare bounded from the underbrush in long leaps as if to prove his point. A breeze wafted up to us, cool and sweetly fragrant, laden with the clean scents of nature. It stirred wisps of hair against my neck, long strands escaped from both braid and hiker's cap.

The old man looked me over, and I braced for the usual admonitions, as if every woman traveling abroad alone was sure to end up in some Eli Roth torture dungeon. Instead, he smiled again with his sad smile, and said, "Beautiful, and cruel."

"I beg your pardon?"

"The moors. Beautiful and cruel, like a woman. They are enchanted, you know. I used to go back often. As often as I could. Always searching... always hoping... that *this* would be the time, each time, and I would find my way again... my heart bade me try and try, even as my mind already accepted the truth. Had I not seen the stone? The shrine? Had I not read the words inscribed upon it? Oh, but fate is also beautiful and cruel, and history inexorable."

"I don't understand," I said.

He went on as if I hadn't spoken. "The past was set; I had been and gone and played my part. I left her. I did not wish to. I would have stayed. But fate, so cruel, so beautiful, had other plans. No matter how I retraced my steps, how long I wandered, how far I explored… no matter how many nights I spent sleeping there beneath the sky… and sometimes I would hear the whirr of wings, the cry of a hawk or hound, and such joy would leap within me…"

His voice trailed off into a quaver, even as tears trailed from the creased corners of his eyes.

"Monsieur…" I'd taken a half-step toward him, reaching out as if to place a hand upon his shoulder, moved by his evident grief despite my lack of understanding. Before I could complete the gesture, his own hand shot up and seized mine. His grip was tremulous, but surprisingly strong.

"I had seen the stone, the shrine," he repeated. "She died for love of me. She pined, she languished. Perhaps she believed I had abandoned her. I was torn from her, cruelly torn, and there would be no returning. I could not change the past."

Uncomfortable, if not quite alarmed, I tried gently to free myself. He held firm. His eyes met mine, and through their veil of tears they were sharp and bright.

"After a while," he said, "I stopped. I stopped trying. After years had gone by. So many years. She loved a *young* man, you see. A healthy one, and handsome. Not some ancient relic in a chair. What use would I be to her now, even if I did find my way?"

Someone came hurrying toward us, a bustling gingerish fellow with a broad and freckled face. He wore the kind of smock-top and pants I associated with hospital scrubs, in a shade somewhere between mint and moss. Various antiseptic smells—liquid sanitizer, bleach, iodine—hung around him in a cloud, and the fact he'd attempted to counter these with liberal applications of body spray and aftershave did not help the situation.

"Philip, Philip!" he chided in the sort of tone one would use with a wayward child. "Whatever are you doing out here? My apologies, mam'selle! Did he frighten you?"

"Of course not," I said. "We were merely talking."

The old man, Philip, had released my hand. His momentary vigor, the strength of his grip and the bright sharpness of his eyes, dulled. He sagged in his wheelchair, looking even frailer and more diminished. His gaze drifted off forlornly across the vast expanse of moors.

I was struck by a sudden, unfamiliar, almost overpowering urge to kneel and embrace him. To tell him that, yes, I knew what it was to yearn for what was lost, for history and bittersweet nostalgia.

Was that not why I'd come on this trip? To attempt, in my own fashion, to recapture bygone eras? To return to simpler times, reclaim the cleaner and purer essences of an earlier age? For personal reasons as well as for business, though my personal reasons might have been deemed less than acceptable in other than these tolerant, enlightened, more modern days.

The fellow in moss-mint scrubs came closer, further assailing me with an intensifying melange of chemicals. No doubt, he thought his grooming regimen would make a favorable impression on the ladies, be they nurses or doctors or visiting relatives of patients. Or, as was the current case, a chance-met vacationer such as myself. His grin broadened. Little did he know, of course, that such particular pursuit was an effort in futility to begin with, and his pungent choice of product only made matters worse. My nose wrinkled.

I noted, by contrast and in passing, that his charge smelled mainly of unscented soap and a pleasant blend of breakfast teas, underlain with a faint hint of some medicinal ointment.

"It was a snake," Philip said. "A serpent, a venomous viper. It struck me. It would have bitten her as well, but I flung her away."

"Don't mind him." The orderly fussed around, adjusting the crocheted lap-blanket draped over the old man's legs. "He's no harm at all. Just wandered off, as they do sometimes. You see how it is."

Oh, I saw how it was, and found it disturbing, even offensive. The patronizing manner, the tut-tutting, the talking over and around, the conspiratorial tone almost like a wink. How tragic, the elderly, how pitiable in their decaying bodies, with their eroding mental states. While we, we two, *we* possessed vigor and vitality. *We* counted. *We* mattered.

"Jeanne," Philip sighed, still gazing as if into a distance of years as well as miles. "My dear Jeanne."

"It has been nice meeting you," I said to him directly. "But I must be on my way, if I'm to be back before dark."

He blinked, drew a breath, met my eyes. "If you meet her, tell her I never meant to leave. I never meant to hurt her or cause her any distress."

"Philip," chided the orderly. "Enough of that. You'll upset this pretty—"

I leveled him a cool look, then bent and touched the old man's bony wrist. "I will. If I meet her, I will tell her."

His other hand covered mine, warm, and patted. "Thank you."

"Mam'selle, you should not encourage him." The orderly's tone had changed, become huffy and brusque. Disapproving. How dare I. "Come along, Philip. Let's get you home."

Lingering a moment, I watched him wheel the chair away. He pushed it with purposeful strides toward the care-complex. Philip sat placidly, letting himself be rolled, head hanging. It still seemed I felt the warmth of his hand on mine, and my heart went out to him.

Then I adjusted the straps of my small day-pack, slung my botanical kit over my shoulder, snapped my folding titanium hiking stick to full extension, and faced the switchbacked cliff-path. I inhaled deeply of the fragrance-laden air. Earthy. Natural and clean.

I smelled wildflowers and budding blossoms, and… lavender? It seemed too early for lavender; my itinerary included Provence in July, when it would be at the height of the season.

Yet, I did catch whiffs of it now, lovely and teasing on the breeze.

The moors spread and stretched and sprawled toward the horizon. From here, they appeared to be low green hills and shadowed valleys, dotted with boulders. A deception, I knew; once down among them, those hills and valleys would be ridges and ravines, the boulders great rearing granite outcrops. The grass would be not parklike lawn but deep and untamed meadow. Bracken and brambles would knot among the yellow gorse and supple reeds. Springs would well from damp earth or trickle from cleft stones, feeding into streams and meandering creeklets just as likely to vanish as to lead toward the sea.

Beautiful and cruel, Philip had said. Beautiful and cruel, like a woman.

Like his Jeanne?

He had not sounded, when he spoke of her, as if she'd been the cruel one. Nor had he. Only fate, also cruel and beautiful, bringing lovers together only to tear them apart.

I could not see, from this high vantage point, the soft blue-purple dustings of lavender in profusion, but as I drew another deep breath, I took in the scent stronger than ever. An early-blooming variety, perhaps. Something classic, but fresh and new.

It might be just what I needed. To my family, this trip was an indulgence, a graduation gift, a chance for me to sate my youthful wanderlust before settling in as a productive member of our business empire. They would have me in board rooms and executive offices, wearing smart designer skirt-suits and take-no-prisoners heels.

Whereas I, I had other plans. I wanted to create. To launch my own line, my own brand. To take the company in a different, back-to-basics direction.

We were perfumers. We had been perfumers as long as our genealogy could be traced, through Colonial times and the Renaissance. Possibly as far as the Black Death; my ancestors could have been selling pockets full of posies to ward off the stench of plague.

Posies... rosewater and rosehips... dried citrus peel... cedar shavings... cloves... lavender and mint and lemongrass... myrrh and cassia... pine... herbs, oils, extracts, and spices... violet and jasmine... ambergris and musk.

The way it used to be done. When someone's choice of perfume

might be highly individualized, even custom-crafted to comple-
ment and enhance their own pheromones. Before chemistry took
over, synthetics, mass production.

Nowadays, it was less about the actual scent and more about
price, prestige, packaging. The more expensive, the better. Perfumes with names meant to evoke sex and wealth and power, without giving any indication what they might smell like... because
that didn't matter. What mattered was cut crystal bottles and gold
inlay, celebrity endorsements, exclusive boutiques.

Elements like cedar, rosehips, orange peel and lavender were
widely considered elderly hallmarks these days, old-fashioned stuff.
Potpourri dishes and sachets for the underwear drawer. Musty-
dusty floral phantoms, the ghosts of corsages pressed and forgotten for decades between diary pages. Associated with antimacassars, delicate collections of teacups and saucers, spinsters, widows,
grandmothers and great-aunts.

Well, not *my* grandmothers and great-aunts, that much was for
certain. *My* grandmothers and great-aunts were jet-setters, society
queens, fashion plates. Impeccable and perfect. Devout disciples of
Our Lady of Perpetual Botox. Birthdays were marked with poison-
sweet passive-aggressive gift certificates to salons or spas or clinics.
They had been cougars before 'cougar' was a thing, *femmes fatale,*
man-eaters.

And here I was, in sturdy boots and trousers, setting off across
the trackless moors. Not touring Paris or Monte Carlo or Venice.
Staying at village inns instead of posh hotels.

"You'd better take a guide," Philip had told me.

"I shall not lose myself," I'd said.

I certainly did not intend to. I had GPS on my phone, but was
sensible enough to realize cell reception couldn't be guaranteed, so
I also had a proper compass and maps tucked into my day-pack.
I had water bottles, energy bars, a lightweight space-age thermal
tarpaulin, matches. I was prepared.

As I'd surmised, the terrain did prove far more rugged than it had appeared from above. What I'd taken for low shrubs turned out to be stands of brush and bramble sometimes as high as my head. Birds flitted here and there. More hares bounded away at my approach. Once, a hawk dived, stunning in its deadly majesty.

The elusive scent of lavender continued to tease and tantalize, leading me onward. I glimpsed many varieties of wildflower, some unfamiliar to me. I took pictures with my phone and gathered samples with my collection kit. The sun hung as if in timeless suspension in a silvery-clear arching span of sky.

"You'd better take a guide," he'd said.

To which I, with all the confidence of youth, had replied I would not lose myself.

Imagine therefore my chagrin when I paused for a rest and a snack, and looked around to realize I had no idea where I was. A not-unpleasant ache of exertion in my legs suggested I'd been hiking quite some time indeed, though that hardly seemed possible when the sun had barely...

Wait.

When had the sun dropped so close to setting? When had the sky gone from silver-clear to a soft and dusky purple-blue, the very shade of lavender in bloom?

I checked my phone. It confirmed the lateness of the hour, as well as my suspicions about reliable cell reception.

Had I really gone and lost myself after all?

A warm flush having nothing to do with exercise suffused my cheeks. I clambered to the highest vantage point I could find, peering for landmarks. The cliffs I'd descended were no longer in view. I saw no lights, no houses, no signs of habitation whatsoever.

Consulting my maps and compass, I made what I determined to be the most likely guess and struck out at a purposeful pace. I already knew the chances of reaching my snug room at the inn before dark were remote, and was both bracing for and resigning myself to a night spent roughing it.

The lavender twilight glowed vibrant, shedding a strange

iridescence over a fine evening mist now rising from the moor. Pools and creeklets glimmered. It was beautiful...

"Beautiful, and cruel," Philip's voice seemed to whisper. "Like a woman."

The lovely scent of lavender seemed more prevalent as well. I wondered if it was an illusion in my mind, brought on by the sky's dramatic hue, or if I were about to stumble into full fields of it after all. With a farmstead where I might shelter for the night, the guest of humble country folk who would offer to share homemade bread and rustic stew, and provide me a cot where I'd sleep bundled safe under a quilt.

Instead, I found tumbled blocks of masonry and crumbling curves of wall. It was some sort of structure, a ruin overgrown with moss and ivy. A little church, perhaps, or the remains of an old keep.

Or *un petit chateau.*

The words came unbidden to my mind. I shrugged them away, thinking at the very least the ruins would be a place to make my camp. By the fading purple light, with hawks observing keenly from the treetops, I set about collecting fallen branches. A patch of bare flagstone in what must have been a courtyard would do as a place to build a fire, if I decided I needed one.

As I went about this task, I glimpsed another piece of stonework some distance from the outer wall. I used the flashlight app on my phone to make my way over to it, curious, and found it to be a monument.

Again, I seemed to more hear than simply recall the anguished voice of Philip. "I had seen the stone, the shrine... she died for love of me... Jeanne, my dear Jeanne..."

I read the inscription. I brushed my fingertips over the carved letters and numbers. My skin prickled with gooseflesh for a moment, and then I thought I understood.

He had come here, as a young man, to the moors. He'd found this very spot, this very stone with a name the same as his own upon it. But, rather than recognize it as mere uncanny coincidence, he had fabricated a tragic fancy, dreamed up a romance of doomed love. It had taken hold of him and held tight ever since.

The poor man. My heart went out to him again. Old and frail, wheelchair-bound, locked in his dementia, forever in love with his imagination of someone who'd died centuries ago.

How beautiful… and, yes, how cruel.

Like a woman.

Like the sculpture of a woman also marking this monument. Perhaps she was meant to be an angel or a saint, or perhaps the Virgin Mary. But there was little angelic or saintly, little holy or beatific, in her timeworn expression.

Beautiful, and cruel. Avaricious. Cold.

Other letters, done by some later and far less skilled hand, had been crudely chipped into the stone below her visage.

Y-D-H-R, they appeared to be.

They troubled me for no good reason. I thought of the I-N-R-I often seen on images of Christ, and supposed it must mean something similar, but had never encountered this particular example before.

With my phone, I took a picture of the monument with its carvings and inscriptions. The quick bright pop from the flash made the cruel-beautiful features seem to twitch, seem to twist for a brief instant into a malevolent leer.

Gooseflesh raced across my skin again. I shivered.

Don't blink, I thought, and wished I hadn't.

Suddenly, I no longer wanted to camp here for the night. It felt wrong. A trespass, a transgression, a mistake. I did not belong in the shadowed ruins of this *Chateau d'Ys*. I could make camp elsewhere.

Away from this desolate, sorrowing place. Away from that stone shrine with its merciless goddess.

I went with little regard for direction, simply hiked at a good clip until the encroaching dusk made my footsteps too precarious.

Then, aided again by the flashlight app, I found a dry-looking hollow. I did without a fire, just wrapping myself in the crinkly silver space-age tarpaulin.

My sleep, when it came, was thin and fitful. Every rustle startled me wide-eyed in the darkness. Instead of the dense fog I expected, stars pierced white as diamonds in a dome of crystalline black.

At some point, I must have fallen into a deeper doze, because I woke from it to find dew dampening my clothes. The sky was lavender again, but this time in pale pastel, like a swath of fine silk edged with cloudy lace and gold filigree.

I sat up, feeling more refreshed and rested than I had any right to. I wasn't even stiff from a full day of hiking followed by a night curled on the ground. Tiny birds flitted from twig to twig, bees bumbled among the flowers, and the morning air smelled sweet.

As I stretched and rubbed my eyes, I heard an excited yipping. Next I knew, I had a lapful of dog, all cornsilk fluff and exuberance, whole-hindquarters wagging, with a determination to lick every inch of my face.

"Hello!" I sputtered, helpless not to laugh. "Hello there, aren't you a friendly one?"

The dog yipped again, presumably in agreement. I found that silly, because I'd unthinkingly spoken in English... and then found it sillier I should worry, when this was a dog. As I raised my hands to fend off its furiously diligent pink tongue, I noticed that my new friend sported a fancy velvet collar, from which hung some sort of engraved tag. But, with all the energetic wiggling, I only caught a glimpse of a peculiar symbol.

Then a melodic, girlish voice called out. "Hastur! Hastur, my little pup, where have you gone?" She, however, *did* speak French, with a quaintly pretty accent.

Hastur barked, cavorting around me as I got to my feet. The owner of the melodic voice and I saw each other at the same moment, and we both gasped. She, no doubt, because she had not expected to find some stranger in the moors... and me, because...

well, because 'quaintly pretty' described far more than just her accent. It described everything about her, from the style of her dress to her smooth-as-cream complexion, even the beribboned bonnet and gauzy parasol.

My age or a little younger, she looked as if she'd stepped entire from the pages of a Jane Austen novel. And here I was, rumpled and dew-dampened, having slept in my clothes, my braid a fraying rope-twist of wisps and straggles.

"Oh!" she said, pressing a hand to her bosom. "How you have surprised me!"

"I'm sorry." My guidebook French sounded clumsier than ever. "I became lost. I spent the night."

"How dreadful! You must come to the house. We will see you fed and cared for."

"I'd hate to be a bother—"

"Pff." She dismissed my demurral with a flick of the same hand she'd pressed to her bosom. "It would be no bother. It would be a pleasure. We do not often have guests. Please. Do come to the house."

As if I could refuse? "Thank you," I said.

I gathered my belongings as she summoned Hastur to her side. The dog went with prompt obedience. I noticed her glancing quizzically at various items—my cell phone, the thermal tarpaulin, the folding titanium hiking stick—but she said nothing about them.

We introduced ourselves as we set out walking, Hastur running through the grass ahead of us, stirring up and chasing butterflies.

"American," said the young lady, tilting her pretty head to one side. "I have never before met an American."

I half-expected her to tell me her name was Jeanne, but it proved instead to be Renaea.

"Renaea," I repeated.

"Yes." She ducked her face with a shy smile, but not before I saw charming dimples and a delicate blush. "Renaea de Lavande."

"Lavender? As in the plant, or the color?"

Her laugh was music. "Oh, both; they are the same. And the scent. Lavender is in all three things the definition of itself. What else could make such claim?"

"Orange?" I suggested.

"The fruit, yes, and the color... but orange itself is not a scent."

"Rose, then," I said.

Again came the musical laugh. "Ah, but think, if you say the color, it means a shade of pink, while if you say the flower, well, are not roses found in a variety of colors? At the house, we have them in red and white and yellow besides."

"You have gardens?"

"Many gardens. And many gardeners to tend them. My family have been, for long years, growers of exquisite blooms."

"So I see," I said, the words spilling from my lips before I could recall them, my tone far too warm, far too intimate.

The dimples and delicate blush made a reappearance. Had I been lost already, here upon the moors? That was nothing compared to how lost my heart was now, and all the more so when she folded her slim fingers through mine.

"Gardens," she went on, "in the French and the English style. And hot-houses for rare orchids brought from afar."

We walked, hands linked as if it was the most natural thing in all the world. It *felt* like the most natural thing in all the world. I knew it likely meant nothing, was likely a simple gesture of innocent affection on her part, yet felt like so very much more.

We walked, and she talked, and I listened and nodded. The sky cleared to blue, and the sun shone pale gold. A grey hare sprang from the underbrush and Hastur gave chase, but was no hound to the hunt, and came trotting back to us as the hare escaped.

"... but, most of all, most prized, are our lavender fields."

And the breeze brought the strengthening fragrance, sweet and lovely, so that when we topped a rise and a valley opened welcoming before us, I thought I'd be ready for the sight I beheld.

I was not ready.

It was breathtaking, a lush and luxurious expanse, sure to put even the vaunted fields of Provence to shame. Low hills rolled light green and purple, the plants not laid out in tidy rows but permitted their unfettered freedom. They were fluffy puffballs at this distance, cloudy fragrant powder puffs, feathery and soft, rippling in the breeze like the fronds of anemones swaying to an unseen oceanic current.

Rising from the middle of it, an island in this lavender sea, was the house Renaea had mentioned. And, again, I was not ready. I'd been thinking cottage, something fairytale and Disney-esque, or a little Tudor-style construction of dark beams and whitewashed walls.

But, no, it was a proper country house, a modest manor in the old tradition, with carriage house and outbuildings, a round crushed-gravel drive with fishpond at the center... and the gardens.

Oh, the gardens! Also as Renaea had mentioned, in the French and English style, but far grander than my imagination had led me to expect. On one side of the manor, the grounds were Versailles in miniature, manicured hedges and trees trimmed to careful shapes, flawless lawns, geometric designs, pools and fountains, marble benches. On the other, it was Stratford-on-Avon, tall grasses brimming with aster and sweet verbena, lilies, columbine, daisies, peonies, and primrose in a full rainbow of colors.

"This is where you live?" I asked, my senses drinking it all in.

"I was born here, as was my mother, and her mother before her," said Renaea.

"How large is your family?"

"Not so very large these days. My parents are often away, touring some court or other. They are very in demand, you see, as floral arrangers for events. You do know, I'm sure, there is a language in flowers, a secret language. Each has its meaning. Each sends its message. A bouquet is a poem; I have seen sonnets in vases. What they present, my parents, are symphonies fit for queens and princes."

"You don't mean you're here alone."

"Oh, no, not alone. There is Pelagie, the housekeeper, who was my nurse when I was a child. There are the gardeners, of course, and a groom and cook, and servants."

"How very *Downton Abbey,*" I remarked, observing the absence of any power lines, telephone poles, satellite dishes, or similar indications of modern conveniences.

"I plead pardon?"

"Nothing. It's magnificent."

"It is true, though, that although not alone, it can at times be lonely. I am so very glad to have met you. You must stay a while."

"I'd like that," I said with earnestness. "But I'm not really dressed for a visit. I only went out for a day-hike."

"For which trouble you spent a night cold upon the moors!" Renaea squeezed my hand. "Come and refresh yourself. We will find you something suitable to wear. You must be faint with thirst and hunger as well."

She led me through the meandering fields of lavender. The scent was blissful heaven. Each plant seemed the picture of perfect health, in full bloom despite the earliness of the season. So, too, were all the flowers in the gardens. All in bloom, all at their peak and in their prime, all at this same time of the year.

Which shouldn't have been the case. Which was, really, quite botanically impossible.

I started to say as much to Renaea, but thought better of it.

The same proved true, I soon saw, for the fruit trees. Here were plump cherries rich and ripe as garnets, and pale pink cherry blossoms, sharing the same boughs... plums and apricots likewise...

We reached a willow-shaded lane that brought us to the gravel drive. From here, the hills of lavender went on as if forever. Gardeners worked among them, men wearing homespun and suspenders, silent men who nodded deference to us as we passed by.

Many more questions clamored in my mind. But, again, I thought better of voicing them. I let myself be ushered into the stately house. I let myself be turned over to the housekeeper,

Pelagie, a stout and efficient woman with a cap of neat grey curls. Maids were summoned. Clothes were sent for. I was shown to a guest room that surpassed in every way the quaint little inn where I'd booked lodging.

Fortunately, the lack of modern conveniences did not extend to running water. A hot bath later— infused with lavender, of course— I felt my night outdoors melting away. I donned the clothes that had been left for me, similarly old-fashioned to what Renaea wore, unfamiliar yet surprisingly comfortable. The dress was goldenrod overlain with ivory lace, the shoes were genuine kidskin, and I was able with some effort to twist my hair up into a loose and vaguely Regency-looking bun.

Now I, too, looked as if I'd stepped from the pages of a Jane Austen novel. My grandmothers and great-aunts would have, one and all, pinched the facelifted bridges of their noses to ward off a despairing tension headache at the very idea. But I liked it.

So did Renaea, when I joined her in the morning room where a late breakfast had been set out. She sprang up with a delighted cry, rushed to me, and clasped both my hands in hers.

"How lovely you are!" she exclaimed. "That color suits you so!"

Hastur sniffed and wagged approval, then sat pertly at our feet plying us with cute head-tilts and soulful doggy eyes as we ate. Neither of us could resist sharing with him morsels of buttered croissant, thin-sliced ham, and cheese. We sipped tea with lavender honey, nibbled berries with clotted cream, and talked.

She told me more of the secret language of flowers and floral arranging. Romances, even entire courtships, could be carried out with barely an uttered word, clandestine messages of passion exchanged with the untutored oblivious left none the wiser. I told her about my travels, my family, our business as perfumers. I told her how I'd come on this trip with the hopes of rediscovering the old ways, the lost arts.

After our meal, we strolled the gardens. We went once again hand-in-hand, still as if this were the most natural thing in the world. Renaea pointed out to me various buds and blossoms and their meanings. I wondered if it was just my wishful imaginings that she should particularly indicate those she said were for desperate passion, and forbidden desire.

Some ways from the house, we reached a white gazebo that had until then somehow missed my notice. Yet, here it was, quaint and charming amid the lavender, overlooking a duckpond where lilypads floated. We sat side by side upon a wicker lounge, hands clasped, while Hastur gamboled in the grass.

Then I asked her, perhaps foolishly, about the Chateau d'Ys.

"Oh, *that* place," she said. "Have you been there? Was it haunted?"

"I was there, yes," I said. "As for haunted, I can't say... *is* it?"

"If anywhere is, it should be. Such a sad story. Pelagie told me. She once claimed she worked there, in her youth. Jokingly, of course. Not even Pelagie is so ancient!"

She laughed, and I laughed with her, recalling the date inscribed upon the weathered stone marker I'd seen, there at the ruins. A date centuries removed from my own time...

Quickly, I banished that line of thought.

"Besides," Renaea continued, "she has also told me of the Green Wolf, and the Black Goat, the Widow of the Woods, and the Maskless King, and I know such tales cannot be true. Still, truth or fancy, d'Ys is indeed sorrowful."

"A sad story," I echoed. "How so?"

"Jeanne d'Ys was the last lady of the castle," said Renaea. "Well, a girl, like us; she was barely twenty when she died. They say she... they say she met a stranger upon the moors, and... and fell in love. He was from very far away. Very, very far. But they had only a day or two together, before he disappeared."

"What happened to him?"

"No one knows for certain. One version of the story has it that he gave his life saving hers, another that her relatives had him murdered. Or that he seduced and abandoned her, and broke her heart.

I do not like to believe the last one. I believe he loved her, too, but fate was cruel."

"Beautiful and cruel," I said.

"Pardon?"

I shook my head. "So, he just vanished? Without a trace, no body left behind, never seen or heard from again?"

"Such is the story." Renaea paused, her gaze shifting away from me to watch Hastur capering at the duckpond's bank. When she spoke again, her tone was hushed and faltering. "Do... do you think it's possible?"

"For someone to disappear?"

"No... to... to meet someone upon the moors, a stranger... and fall in love?"

My breath caught. My pulse fluttered. Did she mean... could she...

There was nothing else to do but turn to her, gently lift her chin, and kiss her. For a frightening instant, she seemed frozen, rigid with shock. She would draw back, horrified. She would slap me. With eyes and voice gone cold, she would demand I go, and never venture here again. Unnatural, she'd call me. Sick, even depraved.

Renaea gave no such dreaded, dreadful reaction. After that initial startled instant, she swayed toward me as if melting. Her lips parted with tender sweetness. We kissed, there on the wicker lounge. We embraced and held each other in the gazebo's shade. Lavender's cool fragrance wafted all around us. Words were no longer needed. We said them anyway, in wondering sighs and murmurs.

Somehow, the afternoon went by almost before we knew it. We kissed once more, and Renaea touched her soft palm to my cheek.

"But will it end the same for us?" she asked. "Will you disappear, and leave me?"

"No!" I cried, covering her hand with mine to hold it there. "No, I want to stay. I never want to leave you, not for a single day, not even for an hour. I want to be here with you, always."

Hadn't Philip said much the same, to his dear Jeanne?

I believed him now. Not dementia, not some madness of the moors, a chance coincidence of names carved into stone. It was true. It was real.

This place *was* enchanted; it had me in its spell. My former life was meaningless. Everything I'd searched for was to be found here. Here among the lavender, among the gardens. I would learn the language of flowers, the art of their arranging. I would craft sonnets and symphonies for my beloved Renaea, and I would make perfumes such as the world had never seen, and we would be happy here, happy here forever.

Together, no longer hand-in-hand but fondly arm-in-arm, we made our way back to the stately country house. Hastur ran ahead of us, yipping, the gold-inlaid ornament on his collar twinkling in the late day's sun.

"We must wash and dress for dinner," Renaea told me as we stepped through the great front door and ascended the curving stair. "After, I will show you the conservatory."

"I look forward to it," I said. A quick glance around preceded a quicker kiss, and then we parted ways for our separate rooms.

When I reached mine, I found other garments laid out and waiting. A silk dress like shimmering twilight, a shoulder-wrap of silvery lace, dainty slippers. They fit as if tailored to my measure. I brushed out my hair and fashioned it into an elegant chignon. The vanity table had been supplied with a small selection of cosmetics, which I also made use of.

There also, in the room, were my old clothes. Cleaned and folded, piled neatly on a chair. How ugly they seemed! How awful, coarse, and crude! I never wanted to wear them again. Never wanted to *see* them, would have been just as glad to watch them burn. My boots were there as well, the clumsy clunky things, set on a mat below the chair. My day-pack hung on the chair's back, and even that looked foreign, almost alien, to my eyes.

My folding titanium hiking stick... my cell phone, its screen a blank and glassy strangeness... the maps and compass... water bottles, energy bars... they did not belong here. They should not be here. Why would I need energy bars when I'd be going down to dinner? As for the cell phone...

Force of habit nonetheless made me pick it up and switch it on. The battery still had life—I had the charger in a side pocket of the day-pack, for all the use it'd be—but no bars, no service. The icons might as well have been hieroglyphs. I barely cared or remembered what most of them meant. On a whim, though, I snapped a selfie.

The bright pop of the flash reminded me anew of the previous picture I'd taken, at the monument shrine near the ruined Chateau d'Ys. That cruel and beautiful graven image, goddess or angel or saint, the fleeting impression of stone features twitching, the cold and malevolent leer.

I put the phone away, feeling oddly guilty for my technological transgression. I daubed attar of lavender at the pulse-points of throat and wrist, and went downstairs.

Renaea met me, a vision in softest chiffon. Her hair had been upswept and adorned with flowers. A corsage graced her breast. I knew, even from the few lessons she'd already taught me, that they had been chosen to speak, in their silent language, of love.

We dined. On precisely what, I barely attended. Each course was delicious, exquisite; that much was undeniable. Some light broth flavored with herbs and crumbled petals... some sort of small fowl, Cornish hen perhaps, roasted stuffed with rosehips and served in a sweet rose-wine sauce... crisp salads, seasoned vegetables... an array of fruit pastries... but what I feasted on most, what both sated and stirred my appetites, was the company of my dearest Renaea.

After, as promised, she did show me the conservatory. How I had missed seeing it from outside of the house, I couldn't guess. It was a large round room of latticework and glass panes, sloped ceiling rising to a point high overhead. By day, in the sunshine, I'm sure it dazzled with color and light. Here, now, at this hour, it was whisper and shadow, a velvety hush of darkness faintly illuminated by filtered moon-rays and stars.

All around us were potted plants and raised planters, trellises embroidered with climbing vines, feathery fronds, sleeping buds tucked tight, night-blooms unfurling to release their heady fragrances. I recognized several as exotic species and rare varieties, imported from Africa and South America, the tropics, the Orient—however politically incorrect the term might be in my own day and age.

As we moved among them, again arm-in-arm, Renaea in her own hushed whispers identified those unfamiliar to me. Here were the twinned *camilla* and *cassilda,* here in a mosaic basin of water a cluster of lilies from Lake Hali, and here—

I stopped. We had come nearly to the center of the conservatory, where a pedestal rose from sprays of leafy greenery. Atop it, where a sundial might have been, was the sculpture of a feminine figure, a robed woman.

The style and artistry were different, the stone neither timeworn nor weathered, but her face... her features...

"What is it?" inquired Renaea, stopping as well. She followed my glance, and smiled. "Ah, you've found *La Perennielle.* "

"Who?"

"Our lavender lady, patroness saint to my family."

The figure's arms were crossed at her chest in the manner of Egyptian statues, though in her hands she held not ankhs or staves but bundles of flowering stalks. Even depicted in stone, I could tell that, yes, they were sprigs of lavender.

But her face was, I was sure of it, the same as I'd seen on the monument at d'Ys. Beautiful, and cruel. Regal, but avaricious and cold. Ready to twitch at a flash into a malevolent leer.

"Pelagie says she represents the eternal renewal," Renaea went on, "reinventing herself in incarnation after incarnation, constantly reborn."

I leaned closer, pushing aside the dry, brittle curls of dead leaves collected at the statue's base. The flat disk of the pedestal upon which it stood was worked into floral patterns and spirals, but directly at the robed woman's feet was a scroll like something from medieval heraldry, bearing the letters Y-D-H-R in ornate calligraphy.

"...that rebirth demands sacrifi—," Renaea was saying, when the tiniest flicker of movement just above her head caught my eye.

A teardrop-shape darker than the conservatory's whispering shadows... a fine pearly-pale filament extending up from it. Even as I realized with a chill what it was—a spider, a glossy black spider, descending its line—it alit upon one of the flowers Renaea wore in her hair.

She must have seen my look of horror, pausing in mid-word to ask what was the matter.

"Do not move!" I told her.

The spider scurried down the side of her neck, a loathsome black inkblot against her smooth, pale, perfect skin. It bore a mark on its back; not a scarlet hourglass or white fiddle, it was blue-purple in color, like a budding lavender bract.

Its legs must have tickled, because she reached involuntarily as if to brush it away despite my warning. I seized her wrist, staying her, while my other hand shot out. I snatched up the spider in my fist, felt it writhing and squirming, felt a sharp sting of pain before I crushed it.

The venom's effects were immediate.

I staggered, gasping for breath, a terrible icy numbness rushing through my body. Renaea clutched at me. I heard her calling my name... calling for help... screaming for Pelagie and the servants... I heard her sobbing, begging me not to leave her, telling me I'd promised to stay, that she would surely die without me.

My fingertips caressed her cheek. She was weeping. I wanted to reassure her, wanted to say so very much.

But I fell, and it seemed I kept falling, falling and falling away into an eternity of forever.

When I returned to myself, it was as if from a tremendous distance.

And to a tremendous despair.

Without even opening my eyes, I knew.

I knew from the astringent, antiseptic, chemical smells. I knew from the squeak of soft-soled shoes on tile and the metallic rattle-roll of carts. From the tight stickiness of tape holding an IV needle in place, the machine-laundered texture of the thin cotton gown, the upper part of the bed tilted up... oh yes, I knew.

The bed would have rails, and a curtain on a track. Perhaps there'd be cards propped on a windowsill, perhaps shop-bought flower arrangements shouting gibberish. A television would be on but muted, tuned to news or soccer, closed-captioning scrolling in French. The walls would be painted some shade meant to be soothing.

Tears beaded my lashes, spilled from beneath closed lids to trickle freely down my face.

How had it played out? Missing tourist, search parties? A chance discovery by fellow hikers? Had I been unconscious when they found me? Had I been raving, a madwoman on the moors? What might I have told them? What might I have said?

Not that it mattered. Not that I cared.

So what if everyone thought me insane? So what if my family pressed for competency hearings and committal?

Let them medicate me. Let them lock me up in some room with soft walls. Let them talk to me in that *tone,* that patronizing doctor-nurse-orderly tone, as if to a dim-witted child. Let them hook me up with electroshock, if they wanted.

So what?

I had lost my beloved Renaea. I'd never be able to get back to her again, not if I spent a lifetime looking. Even if I found the same place, the country house would be long gone by now, its gardens and lavender fields overgrown, its dear young mistress...

The tears spilled faster. My chest ached. My body shook from the effort of holding in a tempest of shrieking, wailing grief.

Y-D-R-H. *La Perennielle.* Rebirth demanded sacrifice.

If the door to my room had been left discreetly ajar, the faint creak of hinges and a draft of moving air informed me it had been pushed wider, someone coming in. With tears streaming, body shaking, fists clenched, there'd be no way to feign having been asleep.

I braced myself for squeaky-sole nurse-shoes footsteps, and for that *tone*... some chirpy-sweet variation on "well, look who's awake" or condescending "and how are we feeling today?"

Instead, I heard a slow trundling as of rubber-fitted wheels. And someone said, "I believe you."

I opened my eyes to see exactly the sort of room I'd expected, the paint a green somewhere between moss and mint... the same color as the scrubs the staff would wear... and the window looked out on a view of well-tended grounds, beyond which the cliffs dropped away to the moors.

Philip, in a different sweater but the same chair, with the same crocheted blanket spread over his lap, wheeled to my bedside. He offered me a box of tissues, then patted my arm.

"I believe you," he said again.

"I... I believe you, too," I managed, through sniffles and breathy hitching hiccups. I mopped my face, blew my nose. "Not that anyone else will ever believe either of us."

He smiled, not without sadness and sympathy. We sat a while together, in a silence of our shared despair. This, for all these years, had been his life. A suffering prison, torn between truth and insanity. Both equally without comfort, because, in the end, it did not matter.

I let my head fall against the pillow. My disconsolate gaze roved the room, half-unseeing, still blurred by tears. The muted television, the expected senseless cacophony in some deliver-florist's vase upon a table, a little wardrobe-closet where—

Where my day-pack hung on a hook. My day-pack, with my cell phone snugged securely in its usual side pocket.

My cell phone, with which I'd snapped a selfie after dressing for dinner.

With such a picture… with actual proof…

Why, then, should I suddenly feel so cold? So breathless with apprehension? So suddenly terrified?

If there *was*…

Oh, but if there *wasn't*…

And it seemed I heard a goddess laughing, beautiful and cruel.

MARY IN THE MIRROR

"…three times, then you see her behind you!"

"Nuh-unh!"

"Yeah-huh! And her face is real grody, all bloody and gross, with big long teeth and these holes where her eyes are supposed to be—"

"No way!"

"Yeah way! My cousin told me; she went to a party with her friends and they tried it and this one girl totally freaked out, like, so bad they put her in the looneybin—"

"Did not!"

"Did so!"

"Okay, all right, okay," said Tanya, before Steffi and Brooke could go from *did not* / *did so* to *I know you are but what am I?*, or something. "So, let's try it and see."

"What? You mean, like, now?" Steffi asked. "We can't—"

"Ha!" Brooke jabbed an accusing finger. "Because you *know* it's a bunch of bullpuckey!"

"Is *not!*"

"Is—"

"Come on, hey, come on." Tanya stepped between them and made a T-for-time-out signal. "Steff, what's the problem? It was your suggestion."

"Well yeah, but—"

Brooke snorted, crossing her arms over her *Knight Rider* shirt. "She doesn't want to because she knows it's bullpuckey."

"Nuh-unh, we just can't do it right now!" Steffi waved at the window, filled with glowing sunset colors—gold, magenta, rose. "We have to wait 'til midnight, duh!"

"Oh," Tanya said. "I guess that makes sense."

"Makes *sense?*" echoed Brooke. "Why? Why midnight?"

Rolling her eyes, Steffi said, "Duh squared, the witching hour! My cousin Lisa told me, weren't you listening? That's when you *do* the spooky stuff, like with those boards to talk to ghosts."

"There's no such things as ghosts."

"Says you."

"Says my dad, *and* Mr. Holt from school."

"Mr. Holt's a poop. He says there's no such things as Bigfoots, either, but our neighbor saw one once."

"Would you both take a chill pill?" Tanya said. "We're here to have fun, not argue the whole time. When it gets to midnight, we can try Mary-in-the-Mirror and find out for ourselves. If we can stay awake that long."

"I can," said Brooke. "I can stay awake longer than anybody."

"Me, too!" Steffi bounced on the balls of her feet. "This will be so cool! Let's turn on MTV while we set up. There's lots of chips and soda pop, and my mom's gonna make these little mini-pizzas out of English muffins with whatever toppings we want, and ice cream for later—"

They trooped downstairs. Brooke and her dad lived in a dinky apartment behind the K-Mart, and Tanya's family shared a duplex with the Philipses next door, but Mr. and Mrs. Kepler had a nice big house, a split-level on a hill. The bottom floor was mostly a big wood-paneled family room with burnt orange shag carpeting, latch-hooks and macrame owls on the walls, a saggy brown couch, and a shelf of white-over-green encyclopedias. Rough avocado-colored curtains hung over sliding glass patio doors, through a gap in which could be seen the fenced back yard, a scatter of lights from town, and the fading dregs of crimson in the purple-indigo sky.

"I brought some magazines," Tanya said, fanning out a display of *Teen Beat, Tiger Beat,* and *Dynamite* like a poker hand of pretty boys, perfect hair, perfect teeth, perfect smiles. "Sonya said she was done with these, though she kept all the ones with Michael Jackson."

"I brought my Chinese jacks and jump ropes," Brooke added. "And you have Atari, right?"

"Jason does," Steffi said. "In his room. He's always up there exploding aliens, and never lets me have a turn. He says video games aren't for girls."

Soon, the coffee table was pushed clear back against the couch, their three sleeping bags unrolled in the open space in front of the TV.

Adam Ant wondered, don't drink don't smoke, what do you do? A cheerleader with pigtails cheered about oh Mickey, he's so fine, hey Mickey.

From somewhere outside came a rolling, rumbling noise.

"Thunder?" asked Tanya.

"Just airplanes, I bet," Brooke said.

They ate chips—regular *and* barbecue, though Brooke said barbecue chips were "Barf me with a spoon!" to which Steffi replied "It's *gag* me, like duh, omigod, and they are not!"—and drank soda pop.

Madonna sang about lucky stars, and Journey about open arms, though Brooke insisted it was broken arms. Lionel Richie was going to have a party all night long, all night.

They colored outfits with Steffi's Fashion Plates, then got silly and swapped in some from the old superhero/monster set Jason didn't play with anymore.

In the distance, sirens wailed and warbled. First one, then more and more, yodeling back and forth, weird wolfhowls from the dark.

The Wham! guys, in who-wears-short-shorts, said wake me up before you go-go. Then Quiet Riot said to bang your head, but nobody liked that heavy metal music so they muted it.

Flipping through magazines, they debated who was cuter, Matt

Dillon or Rob Lowe, or Johnny from the new movie about the killer who gets you in your dreams. Not that any of them had seen it. But Steffi's cousin Lisa had, and according to Steffi, according to Lisa, it was way scary and grody to the max.

"… this glove all with razors on it, and a whole upside-down waterfall of blood, and this girl's on the phone and a tongue comes out, comes out of the phone, and licks her on the mouth—"

"Guh-*ross!*" Tanya cried.

Right then, the phone rang. Upstairs, but there were extensions in other parts of the house including the family room, and the sudden burr-*ring!* made them all jump.

Steffi went, "Eek!" and started giggling.

"Lordy, I almost peed," said Tanya, settling a hand on her chest the way Gran did when she'd had a fright.

It rang again.

"Answer it," said Brooke. She waggle-slathered her tongue at Steffi like a KISS video.

"You answer it!"

"I don't live here."

A third ring.

"Mo-o-om!" Steffi hollered at the ceiling. "Pho-o-one!"

"I got it, I got it," Mrs. Kepler's voice came back, counterpointed by hurrying footsteps.

"She was probably out on the deck, smoking," Steffi confided in a stage-whisper. "She told Dad she quit, but she sneaks them at work and when he's not home."

"But she's a nurse," Tanya said. "Doesn't she know those give you cancer? My grampy died of cancer."

"My dad, he knew this guy who had it," said Brooke, "and they cut a hole in his neck and you could see right inside."

"Oh! Turn it up, turn it back up!" Steffi scrambled for the remote control. "I love this one! Wooh, wooh, they just wanna, they just wanna-ah-ah—"

All three of them were hop-skip-dancing and singing along, feet kicking, high-jabbing elbows everywhere, when they realized Steffi's mom was on the landing part where the split-level stairs switched back halfway down. And going, "Stephanie-*Ann!*" in a way that said she'd been calling for a while now and was getting annoyed.

They stopped, Brooke and Tanya exchanging an *oops* look while Steffi rapid-thumbed the volume to more tolerable-normal levels.

"Sorry, Mom—"

"Never mind that. I have to go out. The hospital just called, there's some kind of emergency downtown. Which means—"

"Aw, noooo, don't cancel the sleepover, you promised!"

"I also promised your friends' parents I'd be here to look after you."

"But Mo-o-o-o-om!"

"Start getting your things together, girls. I'll—"

"My dad's not home, though," Brooke said. "He dropped me off here on his way to go shoot pool and drink beer in Winston City."

"Can't we stay? We'll be good, we'll be fine, honest! Come on, Mom! *Pleeeeeeease?*"

"We really will," said Tanya. "I babysit sometimes for the Philipses next door. They say I'm real responsible and mature for my age." Her cheeks felt warm, given how they'd been dancing around like spazmoids a minute ago, but it *was* true, they *did* say it.

Mrs. Kepler shot a glance at her watch. Another yodeling wolf-howl siren rose and fell, sounding not too far away. It seemed to decide her. "All right. But you don't go anywhere, you stay in the house, you call me at the hospital if there's any problems."

Amid a chorus of *okay / sure thing / thanks Mom / cross our hearts,* she hurried back upstairs.

"I bet it was that rumbly noise we heard," Brooke said. "I bet it *was* an airplane, and it crashed or something. Maybe into the school, and we'll get the whole rest of the year off!"

Tanya went to the patio doors, parted the avocado-green curtains, and peered across the yard. The way it sloped to follow the hill, she had a pretty good view over the fence toward town. "I don't see any big fires. Lots of police lights though, the flashers… but they're going in all different directions."

"Weird," said Steffi.

"I'm leaving now," Mrs. Kepler called down the stairs. "If you want those mini-pizzas, you can either wait for me, or make them yourselves, but if you do, be *careful,* don't get cut or burned!"

"Okay, Mom!"

"And *don't* leave me a mess in the kitchen!"

"We won't!"

"Your brother's in his room. I told him he's in charge."

"Aww—" Steffi began, but the others vehemently shook their heads, so she managed to turn it into, "—ll right, Mom!"

Door open, door shut. Though the house had a garage attached on the lower level, it was mostly taken up with Steffi's dad's tools and model train set, so they parked out front in a gravel turn-around. A car door closed with a muffled whump. After a long-enough-to-light-a-cigarette delay, the engine grumbled to life, and gravel crunch-gritted under the tires as parental authority drove away.

"Turn it up again!" said Brooke. "Ess-ess-ess-ess Ay-ay-ay-ay Eff-eff-eff-eff Tee-tee-tee-tee—"

"You forgot the E, dumbnuts," Steffi said.

"It's not a spelling test!"

"No, but it's the song."

Brooke raspberried at her, then began trying to make the do-doop-DOOT-DOOT-do-doop-de-DOODLE-doop notes. Tanya flung herself backward on the couch, laughing. "I really *am* gonna pee!"

When the video was over, she ran down the short hall connecting family room to garage, to a bathroom not much bigger than a phone booth. No tub or shower, just potty and sink, seashell wallpaper, coral-and-blue tile, and a teensy window of that frosted-pebbled glass so nobody in the back yard could look in. The mirror, hanging over the sink basin, had a kind of wickery frame thing woven into kind of seahorse designs. Tanya studied it as she washed her hands.

Just a regular, ordinary mirror. Not even with a medicine cabinet. All it reflected, besides Tanya herself, was more seashell wallpaper, a towel rack—coral and blue to match, unlike the raggedy old striped or floral or whatever towels at her house—and a decorative art-thing of sand dollars and dried starfish glued to driftwood.

Nobody behind her.

Certainly no grody-faced witch with long teeth and no eyes, all bloody and gross.

Of course, it wasn't midnight yet, and Tanya hadn't said her name three times. Or even one time.

Steffi's cousin Lisa and her friends probably *were* full of bull-puckey. Mr. Holt from school probably *was* right about there being no such things as ghosts. Or witches. Or Bigfoots.

Then again…

Her own gran swore the place she'd grown up in had been haunted, that some little boy had fallen down the coal chute and died, and when you went in the basement, you might hear him crying, or feel his cold little fingers tugging your sleeve or grabbing at your ankle. Gran said that once, when *her* gran sent her down cellar for a jar of pickled tomatoes—t'maters, in Gran-talk—she had seen the dead boy's shadow "out the corner of m'eye."

Tanya stared into the mirror, trying not to focus on her reflection or the seashell wallpaper but on the space between, over her shoulder. The space where, according to Steffi by way of Lisa, Mary's haggard leering visage would appear.

Had a girl *really* ended up in the looneybin because of it?

Even if it *did* work, how scary could it be? It was just a face in the glass, just Mary-in-the-Mirror, it wasn't like Mary could actually *get—*

RAP!-a-tap-tap on the door.

Good thing she'd already peed. She managed not to shriek, either, though her grip on the sink clamped to a tight-knuckler.

"Did you fall in or what?" came Brooke's voice. "We're gonna make the pizzas."

"Okay, be right there!"

She washed her hands again, for no good reason, and avoided any further glimpses of the mirror. By the time she got upstairs, Steffi had English muffins and cheese on the counter, while Brooke rummaged in the cupboards for sauce.

"We got, um, pepperonis, mushrooms, olives," Steffi said.

"Should we make some for Jason?" Tanya asked.

"Cripes, no!" Brooke snorted. "Let him make his own. Or, maybe, if he lets us play Atari."

"You could ask him," suggested Steffi.

"You ask him, he's your brother."

"Nah, he's in his room, let him sit there, long as he leaves us alone."

They laid out baking sheets and started the messy work.

"There sure are a lot of sirens," Brooke said, piling a ton of pepperoni on hers. "And, do you hear that? That whup-whup-whupping sound? I bet that's helicopters."

"Your poor mom," Tanya said to Steffi. "If lots of people are hurt, she might be stuck at the hospital all night. When does your dad get home?"

"Not until like eight, but he also said since I was having a sleepover, he'd stop for donuts."

As Steffi slid their pizzas into the oven, Tanya went through the dining room to the deck. A half-moon shone pale in the black sky, against a spatter of stars. The trees rustled in a cool breeze.

"See? Helicopters, I told you!" Brooke stood beside her, pointing at buzzing bulbous shadow-swoops making orbits around downtown, beaming narrow spotlight-searchlight rays.

In places, whole blocks of buildings looked dark, illuminated in red and blue spinny flashes. Now and then, under the siren warbles, Tanya heard—or thought she did—popcorn noises that might've been gunshots, and…

"Are those screams?" Steffi asked, joining them." Is someone screaming?"

"I think so," Tanya said.

"Weird."

"Yeah."

"Wonder what's going on." Brooke went on tippy-toe, holding onto the rail, but as short as she was, it wasn't going to make much difference. "I bet it's *Red Dawn.*"

"You didn't see *Red Dawn!*" scoffed Steffi.

"My dad did, and he told me. Wolver-*eeeeenes!* I bet that's it, it's *Red Dawn* happening right here tonight."

"Who's talking bullpuckey now? C'mon, let's get the pizzas and go watch more MTV. We can clean up the kitchen later. I'm starved."

Some of the cheese had bubble-melted over the edges, and grease puddled everywhere from Brooke's piles of pepperoni, and the mushrooms had shriveled into slimy brown twists and curls, but the pizzas smelled great. And tasted better, once they'd cooled down enough to bite.

Meanwhile, Boy George rode an old-timey Mark Twain riverboat, and the Pointer Sisters went jump-jump for your love, and David Bowie said let's dance.

Then, a screen with words followed by what looked like the start of a scary movie came on, and they abandoned their plates to crowd as close as they could to the screen. Because, when this one came on, everything stopped, everybody dropped what they were doing, and that was just the way it was.

Until, just at the absolute scariest part, when the zombies were closing in, right before his girlfriend turned around to see—

The TV went *fzzt-zkortch!* and turned into a jagged zig-zag of broken spiky lines and weird colors. Tattered fragments of music fought with hissing static and hosts of garbled voices.

"Augh!"

"What?"

"The heck?"

"No!"

"What happened?"

"Fix it fix it!"

As they all clamored their anguish, Steffi leaped up and started thumping the cable box. Brooke smacked the side of the television. Tanya seized the remote and shook it, as if that would help.

Ksssssh-kznakk-nweeeeee... something sounding *el rapido excitamundo Espanol* like a Mexican game show... BECAUSE IT'S THRILLER, THRI-*vvvvvglik!...* part of the this-is-a-test-this-is-only-a-test... a shrill cartoon Woody Woodpecker laugh... a low, underground-echoey chanting: *Tsa'Glorthaa, Tsa'Glorthaa, ias ftheros Tsa'Glorthaa...* "interrupt this broadcast to"... NO MERE MORTAL CAN ESCAPE...

"Turn it down!" Brooke put her hands over her ears.

"I'm trying!" Tanya said, pressing at the controls.

...*Glorthaa damaan Glorthaa dolurr...* machine guns and bombs... the *bwong-chicka-bwong-bwong* of one of those scrambled boobies channels kids weren't allowed to watch... THE BEAST ABOUT TO STRIKE...

"Turn it *off!*" Steffi matched deed to word, jabbing the power button on the front of the set herself.

Sudden blank dark screen. Sudden quiet, except for their own relieved gulpings of breath.

"Jeez." Tanya dropped the remote on the carpet.

"What *was* that?" Brooke asked, lowering her hands.

"I don't know," said Steffi. "Stupid TV. Right in the middle of the best video, too."

They gave it a few minutes, then braced themselves and tried again. But, instead of the zig-zags and jumbled crazyloud barrage, they only got a slightly brighter dead grey, and a high-pitched whine.

"Your cable went screwy," Brooke said.

Steffi turned it off again. "Well, poop. You want to try the Mary thing?"

"Now?" asked Tanya. "It's only ten-thirty."

"Yeah, you said it had to be midnight."

"I know, but we could still try, and if it doesn't work, we try again later." Steffi grinned at them, eyes twinkling. "Besides, it'll be way spookier with my mom not home."

"Are you sure we should—" Tanya began.

"It'll be radical!"

"Bullpuckey; nothing's going to happen."

"Says you!"

"Okay, all right, okay." She gave up, not wanting to go through another round of *did so / did not / yes way / no way*. "The bathroom down here? What do we need?"

The bathroom could barely fit them all, packed around the sink like sardines. Steffi carefully lit one of Mrs. Kepler's holiday candles, setting it in the soap dish.

It was a dark red candle, supposedly cranberry-scented. To Tanya, once the initial burnt-match whiff faded, that it smelled more like... something vague but familiar... she couldn't quite identify... sort of fragrant, fruity-floral, but artificial too, like plastic or gasoline... like scented markers, scratch-n-sniff stickers, those Strawberry Shortcake dolls... sickly-sweet and kind of nasty.

This was dumb. This was a mistake.

Nothing was going to happen.

She wished Steffi's mom were home. Or Steffi's dad. Or any other grownup, instead of only Jason, upstairs exploding aliens in his room.

With no idea they were down here doing this. No idea at all.

Nobody knew what they were doing.

...ias ftheros Tsa'Glorthaa, she thought for no good reason. What did that mean, anyway? What language was it?

"Brooke, turn off the light," Steffi said.

No, don't, Tanya almost said, but didn't. Here she was, freaking herself out already, and they hadn't even started. It was only a silly party game, anyway. Bullpuckey, like Brooke said. There were no such things as ghosts.

Whatever her stance on ghosts and bullpuckey, though, Brooke cooperated readily enough. The tiny space, now illuminated only by the candle flame and the candle flame's reflection, managed to feel bigger and smaller at the same time. The seashell wallpaper came and went in shadow-flickers. The pebbled-frosted window held only milky black. The seahorses woven into the mirror's wicker frame almost appeared to twitch.

Gran's story about the dead boy in the basement…

Just a story.

"Who wants to go first?" Did Steffi sound nervous? Or was she playing it up, putting them on?

"You," Brooke said. "It was your idea."

"Well, yeah, but, it might be better if one of you—"

"Why?" asked Tanya. "So you can grab us or scream or something, and go 'gotcha!'?"

She gasped in hurt shock. "I would not!"

"You better not," Brooke told her. "I'll dunk your head in the toilet if you do. Give you a swirlie-whirlie the way those fifth-graders did to Mikey Nelson."

"Mikey Nelson deserved it," Tanya said. "Lordy, what a brat."

"I'm not gonna scream or grab anybody!" Steffi said. "Jeez omigod!"

Tanya nodded toward the mirror. "Then you go first."

"Fine! I will!" Steffi squared her shoulders, swept her hair back, and faced the mirror. "Ready?"

"Ready for a whole bunch of nothing," said Brooke.

"C'mon, get serious, or it won't work."

Which it wasn't going to anyway, but Brooke and Tanya both put on their soberest, most solemn, studious, attentive expressions. The ones they wore when everybody had to attend an assembly at school, about drugs or drunk driving or stranger-danger.

Steffi rested her palms on the porcelain basin. Her lips quirked as if undecided whether to smile or frown.

It was so quiet in here.

If there were still sirens and helicopters and whatever going on outside, they couldn't hear any of it.

Only the faint sizzle-sputter of the candle... their own quick shallow sips of air... a rustle as Brooke shifted from foot to foot... a gurgle that might've been someone's stomach or from down-deep in the pipes.

They should just forget it and go back to the family room. If the cable was still screwy, bring down Steffi's boombox and cassette tapes. Or play a card game or a board game. Uno, maybe, or Life. They could ask Jason to share his Atari.

"Ready?" asked Steffi again.

"Are you gonna do it or not?" asked Brooke.

"I am! I am! Can everybody see in the mirror?"

"Only ourselves," Tanya said. "And that piece of driftwood with dead stuff glued to it."

Steffi took a long, slow breath. "'Kay, here goes. I have to say her name three times, so, nobody else talk."

The candle and its twin flickered, flickered. Pinpricks of pale gold light glinted in Steffi's eyes, eyes with pupils wide-so-wide. Tanya felt pressure in her hands and realized she was twisting them, twining them, her flesh sweat-moist and clammy. Brooke's reflection, eyes also all-pupils wide-so-wide, chewed on her lip.

"Bloody Mary..." Steffi said, in a wavering rush, and looked surprised she'd actually done it.

They all flinched, wincing, in awful anticipation.

Of course, nothing happened.

Because that was only once. It had to be three times. It had to be twice more.

This was really stupid. Why were they doing this?

Goosebumps prickled Tanya's flesh.

What if another face really *did* appear in the mirror? Where would it be? Where would it fit? Would it overlay her or Brooke's reflection like those Haunted Mansion hitchhikers at Disneyland, luminescent green and leering?

Steffi's throat clicked wetly as she swallowed. "Bloody Mary," she whisper-squeaked.

That was two.

Tanya suddenly had to pee again *so* bad, and wished she'd done so before they all crowded in here.

Twice… one more. One more, and it would happen if it was going to. One more, and they would know.

Did the candleflames sputter just then?

Did the mirror look different, somehow? More… liquid? Less like glass, more like the jar of mercury Mr. Holt had passed around during science? Quicksilver, both dark and shiny, runny, unnatural, thick.

The urge to stop Steffi clamored along Tanya's nerves… to yell and grab or goose her, *gotcha!*… sure, the others would shriek, and be mad, but then they'd laugh like crazy. And *then* agree this was a big dumb waste of time. They'd return to their sleeping bags, their magazines, soda pop and chips.

Hadn't Steffi said something about ice cream? Ice cream would be good, better than being crammed into this dark little bathroom, breathing nasty candle fumes, psyching themselves out over nothing.

One more time.

Don't do it. Don't.

Brooke nudged Steffi, eyebrows raised: *well?* Steffi shot her a *keep your shirt on!* look. Brooke crinkled her nose and mouthed a deliberate, dramatic *bulllllll-puckey*.

"Bloody Mary!" Steffi's voice rang loud and firm, defiant, sure.

From overhead came a humongous crash. They jumped. They screamed. They jostled. The soap dish clattered into the sink and the candle went out. They screamed again. Tanya sprang backward, collided with the wall, the towel rod like a steel bar across her back. The driftwood sculpture glued with sand dollars and starfish fell from its hook and clonked her on the head. Brooke yelped, followed by a thump, a clunk, a splash, and another high-pitched cry.

Steffi shoved past Tanya—"The light turn on the light the light!" Tanya heard her slapping at the wall, heard the flip-click of the switch, but nothing happened.

"Turn it on already!"

"I am, it isn't working!"

"Open the dumb-damn-door!" yelled Brooke.

Somehow, Steffi did that without hitting any of them with its wooden edge, but no welcoming spill of light came in from the hallway, either. The laundry room, family room, and stairwell, all were pitch-black dark.

For a little while, it was panic, a crazy bumbling stampede. Steffi blundered into the hall, bawling for her brother at the top of her lungs. Brooke sounded like she was pinballing against the walls, saying words she must've learned from her dad, trying to find her way out of the bathroom. Tanya tripped over the driftwood thing, kicked something that skittered and rattled, recognized the noise as the box of matches, and crouched to try and find it. At that moment, Brooke tripped over *her*, and went sprawling with a grunted *oof.*

"Hang on, hang on!" Tanya called. "Let me get the matches!"

"Jaaaaayyson! Why won't he answer me, the booger? Jason! I think the power's out!"

"Yeah, you *think?"* Brooke scrambled the rest of the way off Tanya—one of Brooke's arms, brushing hers, felt cold and dripping. What the heck?

Tanya groped across the tile floor, touching a nubby weird dead starfish, a crumpled towel, and then finally a small cardboard box. Luckily, it had not come open and scattered its contents. Even more luckily, she had it right-side-up when she slid the drawer, so she didn't spill the matches herself either.

She struck one, and it snapped alight with a bright pop and puff of sulfur. Again, the shadows leaped and twitched around the puny flame. Before it could blow out or burn the stick down to her fingers, she reached into the sink and found the candle. The stout, greasy-smooth cylinder resisted, stuck to the porcelain by its own half-melted wax—unsettling cranberry, disturbing, red puddled like blood—but Tanya wrenched it loose and got the matchflame to the wick.

"There, okay, I got it." She picked up the soap dish from the sink and put it back to use as a makeshift candle holder. The fruity-flo-ral-artificial scent wafted sickly-strong into her nose. "Everybody all right?"

"No!" said Brooke. "My arm's all wet! My hand went in the toilet!"

"You mean, *you* fell in?"

"Shut up!"

"What?" Steffi snort-giggled. "Brooke fell in the toilet? Was that the big splash?"

"I didn't fall in! Just my hand!"

But it was no use, Tanya and Steffi both were laughing their heads off, Tanya so hard she had to hold on extra-careful to the soap dish. "I sure hope it was flushed!"

"Oh, grody-gross that's sick!"

"Who used it last?" asked Steffi. "It was you, Tanya, wasn't it? Did you flush?"

"Pretty sure."

Brooke said more of her dad's words—he had been in the army—and pushed her way to the sink. The knobs made haunted-house-hinges creaks as she twisted them, then spun like loose teeth, but no water came from the faucet. "Your sink's power's out too?"

"Does it even work that way?" Tanya tilted her head.

"We had the pipes freeze last winter," Steffi said. "And I remember they turned off the water to the whole block once when they were digging up the street. But it's never gone off when we had a blackout before."

Grumbling, Brooke grabbed one of the coral-colored towels from the floor. "This sucks," she said. "This bites the big kahuna. I want to go home."

"Hey, come on, don't be like that," Tanya said. "I really did flush, I'm positive."

"It's on my shirt."

"You can put on your pajamas, and we'll… uh… well, I guess we can't stick it in the dryer, but we can hang it up and wash it later."

"I can't believe the power went out right then," Steffi said. "Scared me half to death, you guys! Like totally!"

Tanya nodded vigorously. "Me too!"

They made their way by candlelight to the family room, which was a looming cavern without even silvery moonbeams coming in through the curtains. There hadn't been any thunderstorms or anything; Tanya wondered if the power outage was connected to the accident in town, if poles had been knocked over and lines brought down, if transformers had blown up or whatever they did.

As Brooke, still grumbling, changed from her Knight Rider tee shirt and jeans into Smurfs pajamas, Tanya went over to the sliding glass doors again. "Everything's dark," she said. "I don't even see the police flashers or helicopters anymore."

"It must be over," said Steffi. "Maybe my mom will be back soon. I'm gonna tell on Jason so much! We could've been being murdered to pieces down here, screaming and yelling and everything, but did he come and check?"

"Probably too busy exploding aliens," Brooke said.

"Not with no electricity for his Atari," Tanya pointed out.

"And what was that big crash we heard?" asked Brooke. "Just after Steffi went 'Bloody Mary' the last time? Which, still, bull-puckey, nothing happened, did you see her, I sure didn't, no face behind us in the mirror, your cousin's full of it!"

"Hey!"

"What was that crash, though?" Tanya frowned at the ceiling. "Maybe a tree fell on the roof? Maybe your brother's trapped up there, maybe hurt, and that's why he didn't come check on us.

Maybe we should go check on him."

"Yeah, maybe, I guess," said Steffi. "Or he's playing a joke on us... heard what we were doing, and his room's over the bathroom, so he made that noise... and when we go up, he'll bust his guts laughing."

"If he does," Brooke said, "I'll kick him where it counts. Bust his guts, bust his nuts, stupid butthead Jason."

Steffi found a bunch more holiday candles—evergreen, pumpkin pie, winter snow—though they all turned out to have the same nasty-plastic artificial scent-notes as the cranberry. Each girl took one and they left the rest grouped on the coffee table with their unfinished pizzas.

"There should be a flashlight in the kitchen junk drawer, too," Steffi said.

"Yeah, good, that'd be good," Tanya said, only halfway paying attention. She raised her candle and looked past Brooke, down the hall toward the garage and laundry room and bathroom.

"What?" Brooke also turned.

"I..."

...thought I saw someone, something, she almost said.

But what had she seen? Or thought she'd seen? Only darkness overlapping darkness, shadows moving against shadows, in the unsteady flamedance.

Thriller and Mary-in-the-Mirror and Gran's story about the ghost-boy in the basement... no grownups here, Jason not answering, the power out, the pipes not working... the voices and stuff from the TV, the creepy chanting...

...Glorthaa damaan Glorthaa dolurr...

Was it any wonder she was keyed up, on edge, imagination running wild?

"...nothing," she finished. "Never mind."

It wasn't as if there'd actually *been* a figure in the hallway. Angular and strange, with empty black hollows for eyes, blacker-than-black, emptier-than-empty, hollows like wells / like holes / like never and forever, vacant eternities spiraling…

She hadn't seen anything like that. Hadn't seen anything like that at all.

There was nobody else down here. Nobody could have come in through the garage; Steffi's dad kept it locked, both the exterior roll-up door and the interior one. He said it was for safety, since he had so many dangerous tools, drills and sharp saw-blades and nails. Probably it was to keep people from messing with his train set.

So, yeah, nobody could come in that way. Except Steffi's dad, of course, but he wouldn't lurk silently in the hall. Mr. Kepler wasn't scarecrow-thin with long arms all multi-jointed like a spider's, or matted cobweb strands of hair falling around him, part-shroud, part-cocoon. He didn't have a narrow, tapering jaw reaching half-way down his chest, packed with bristling needle-teeth and bony slivers. Or spindly, grasping three-fingered pinchers tipped with curved hook-claws, perfect for the deft, surgical scoop-slicing of tongues or eyeballs.

Hot cranberry wax splattered her wrist. Tanya gasped. Her hands were shaking. *She* was shaking, trembling head to toe, and her friends were looking at her in the cautious way reserved for potential crazies.

"What?" asked Brooke.

"Are you okay?" added Steffi.

"Fine. Just, you know…"

They nodded, like they knew, but they *didn't* know.

Or maybe she didn't know. She hadn't seen anything. Certainly hadn't seen it in such detail. Couldn't have, because there wasn't anything there. Nothing, nobody. Imagination running wild. Eyes playing tricks on her, shadow-tricks, candle-tricks.

Peeling cooled dollops of wax from her skin, she followed Steffi and Brooke up the stairs. It was just as dark up there, just as quiet.

"Jeez, who left the deck doors open?" Steffi complained.

"Not me," said Brooke.

"I could've sworn we closed them when we came in to get the

pizzas," Tanya said.

"Well, they're wide open now."

"Jason?" Tanya suggested.

Steffi poked her head out. "If it was, he's not here now, and... huh... come see, it's really weird."

Brooke hesitated. "Weird how?"

"Weird-weird, how else?"

They joined her on the deck again, and it was weird. Dark. Not just dark, but *dark*. No lights but their own, as far as they could see. No lights in town, no lights at the neighboring houses, no streetlights tracing the curves and grids of the roads. No helicopter spotlights, no police car or fire truck or ambulance flashers. Nobody with flashlights, or other candles.

Tanya scanned the sky, expecting the stars to be a vivid bright-white planetarium sprawl the way they were on a camping trip way far from civilization, but saw no stars either. Or the moon, which had been half-full when they were out here before, not very long ago. Had it clouded over that quick?

Only... the air didn't feel cloudy, didn't smell cloudy... it smelled thicker than ever of scented markers and Strawberry Shortcake dolls... and the sky had no sense of... of sky, of space. It felt... opaque, solid, enclosed. Like invisible walls painted matte-black. Like a heavy, muffling, oppressive curtain-tent.

"Do you guys hear anything?" Brooke asked, voice subdued, super-quiet.

"Hunh-unh," said Steffi. "What the heck's going on?"

"This is bad," said Tanya. "Whatever it is, it's bad."

"Call your mom," Brooke said to Steffi.

"Will the phones work?"

"I dunno, try!"

"Yeah. Yeah, okay."

As they went back in, Tanya made sure to close the deck doors, and thumbed the latches. Inside was better; the kitchen still smelled mostly like pizzas, but she had that nasty-fake fruity-floral miasma coating her nose, could almost taste it.

The phone didn't work. No dial tone, no out-of-service beeps, just another empty hollow tunnel of forever black nothing.

"We're the only ones here, right?" whispered Brooke.

"Us and Jason," Steffi said, also whispering. "Why?"

"Hundred percent?"

"Why? We better be!"

"I..." She glanced around, chewing her lip again. The Smurfs on her pajamas cavorted in the candlelight.

La, la, la-la-la-la, their theme song chimed inanely in Tanya's brain. *La, la, la-Tsa'Glorthaa.*

"We're the only ones here," Steffi said, at a more normal volume as if trying to reassure and convince herself as much as Brooke. "Us and Jason."

And whoever Tanya had seen downstairs.

Had *not* seen! Hadn't seen anyone, anything! No skeletal cocoon-shrouded figure of angles and joints and hook-claw-needle-teeth.

"So where is he?" Brooke asked.

"In his room. This way."

Steffi led them past a fussy yellow guest room and her own room, past a bathroom—this one had a lighthouse motif—and linen closet. At the end was the door to her parents' master suite, and the door to Jason's room. Both closed.

Hard to believe he'd still just be in there, in the dark, with no electricity... that he hadn't come to check on them... maybe he was asleep, or reading comic books in a bed-fort with a penlight...

...or gone...

Tanya shivered again, dribbling wax on the Keplers' upstairs hall carpet.

Gone, he'd be gone, disappeared into nowhere the way the whole rest of town seemed to have done, the way the whole rest of the world seemed to have done, the world and the moon and the stars and everything.

There'd be only them left. Only her, Steffi, and Brooke. Only them, in this house, where they couldn't leave and had nowhere to go if they did.

Only them and Mary-in-the-Mirror, Mary who wasn't in the mirror anymore, Mary-*from*-the-Mirror, who they'd called and who came through.

Steffi raised a curled hand to knock, didn't, reached for the door-knob but stopped before touching it, then cleared her throat and went, "Juh-Jason?"

No answer.

So maybe he really was asleep.

...or gone...

"Jason? It's me, Steffi, are you awake?"

...taken...

"Jason!" She did knock then. "Jason, c'mon, don't be a poop!"

"Yeah, don't be a butthead, Jason!" Brooke said. "It isn't funny!"

...gone, taken, consumed, devoured...

"I'll tell! I'll tell Mom and Dad! They'll ground you for a month and take your stupid Atari!" Steffi wrenched at the doorknob like she fully expected it to be locked, then blinked with surprise when it opened.

"Don't," Tanya said, catching her by the shoulder.

...damaan, dolurr...

Steffi paused. "What?"

"What what?"

"What'd you say?"

"I said don't. Don't go in."

"No, after that."

"I... just said don't."

"Weird. I thought I heard... eh, forget it." Shrugging off Tanya's grasp, Steffi pushed the door inward. It swung partway, then caught on a pile of dirty clothes, *MAD* magazines, school books, and can-dybar wrappers. She maneuver-stepped her way over the mess. "Jeez, what a slobbo. Boys are totally grody... hey! He isn't here!"

...ias ftheros Tsa'Glorthaa...

"Steffi, no—" Tanya began.

"Someone *is* here," said Brooke from behind them, in a thin whisper. "Someone's on the stairs!"

"Oh, don't even try to scare us—" Steffi said. The door to Jason's room slammed shut, with her on the inside. She screamed.

The gust from the slamming door blew Brooke's and Tanya's candles out, plunging the hallway into darkness. They screamed, too.

Then, it was quiet.

***

Lynda Kepler pulled into the gravel turnaround, a headache throbbing in her temples, and crushed out her cigarette butt in the car ashtray.

What a night. What a long, long night.

The eastern edge of sky was paling toward pearly grey tinged with rose and gold She desperately wanted a shower, but was so exhausted she'd probably fall asleep standing up before she could rinse her hair.

And, meanwhile, it looked like every goddamn light in the house was on.

She let herself in at the mid-stair landing. From below, MTV blasted at full volume—evidently Billy Joel couldn't handle pressure, and wanted to make sure nobody else could, either. Lynda considered hollering, but they probably wouldn't hear her and the prospect made her skull feel fit to split.

Instead, she trudged upstairs, through the living room, and into the kitchen. There, she stopped dead, mouth working in silent disbelief. Phrases like 'war zone' and 'crime scene' and 'disaster area' flitted through her mind. They'd left the deck doors wide open, and the oven on to boot.

Slinging her purse on a stool because there wasn't an inch of counter space not caked in crumbs and cheese and red sauce, she turned to march downstairs.

...we'll be good, we'll be fine, honest... responsible and mature... don't leave me a mess / we won't!

Uh-huh, and just see how well that had worked out.

Billy Joel had given way to some tough chick in black leather. There were soda cans and chip bags and teen magazines scattered to hell and back, three plates of half-eaten English muffin pizzas on the coffee table, three empty sleeping bags, an empty couch, and a basically empty family room.

Lynda turned off the television. The sudden silence fell like a weight.

"Steffi? Stephanie-Ann? Tanya? Brooke?"

They didn't answer. She checked the bathroom and laundry room, but those were also empty. Starting to feel uneasy now, her exhaustion pushed aside but her headache worsening with each step, she climbed the stairs again.

Maybe they'd gone to Steffi's room, and fallen asleep there—but, no. The bed was still made. Nobody was in the guest room. She tried Jason's door and found him sprawled snoring on the carpet in front of that video game thing.

"Jason!"

He snuffled, coughed, peeled open an eye, and squinted at her. "Mom?"

"Where's your sister? Where are the girls?"

"I dunno, downstairs?"

"They aren't."

"Well, I dunno."

"I left you in charge..." She held up a hand, palm toward him. "We'll talk about this later, once we find them."

***

But they never did.

SHE WALKS IN TATTERS

I first noticed her, really *noticed* her, at the Montague estate sale. Oh, I'd seen her before, sure. At other, similar events. At swap meets and library sales, used book stores, local literary fairs.

She was hard to miss, in her mismatched layers covered by that long too-big-for-her coat, a scarf always tied over her head and the shapeless floppy droop of an old hat atop that. With hunched posture and shuffling gait, burdened with satchels, she resembled a not-too-destitute bag lady, or some eccentric old widow or spinster with nineteen cats.

If I'd thought about her at all, it was only in passing. Only dismissing. Just another regular at these scenes, another shelf-and-stack haunter, another rummager of musty book-boxes, another picker-through of paperbacks. I saw them all, the housewives on the hunt for torrid bodice-rippers, the gothed-out teens homing in on black covers, the sci-fi geeks and eBay resellers. I saw them all, in passing, dismissing.

It's not like I spoke to them. It's not like they were on my level. I was Sebastian Drewe after all, highly respected in academic circles despite my relative youth.

Sometimes, I'd cross paths with antiquarians and rare-edition dealers, scholars, professors, fellow specialists. Them, I *would* speak to. We might each be seeking different things, but, connections were important. Word got around. You never knew. A friend of a friend of an associate of a cousin of a colleague, and so on.

A whisper here, a rumor there, any lead however tenuous, any link however obscure, could result in the *find* of a lifetime. Career-making. World-shaking. We craved it, that elusive moment of discovery. Of validation and vindication. Of truth. Of treasure!

Her, though…

I'd looked right past her, looked right through her. Dismissed her without a flicker of consideration. The old woman in her threadbare coat, its ragged hem dragging in the dust, her spidery-fingered gloved hands riffling yellowed pages.

Until the Montague estate sale, when I happened to be on the other side of a tome-laden table, and she *found* something.

A gasp, stifled though it was, caught my attention. I'd been poking without much hope through a pile of depressingly ordinary occultiana, having expected much better from the private collection of Aubrey Montague, only vaguely cognizant of nearby presences.

Then, the gasp. Then, I'd raised my gaze and saw her. More than saw her. Really, finally, and fully *noticed* her, and realized how wrong I had been.

She wasn't old, for one thing. She was my own age, or even younger. What I'd taken for skin like aged parchment was in fact skin like ivory silk. Her hair, what of it was visible beneath the floppy hat and tied scarf, wasn't straggles of nicotine-tinged grey I'd believed, but delicate wisps of platinum-blonde. Her features were fine and exquisite, her eyes—currently wide with the very thrill I myself forever coveted—were the color of twilight upon a dark lake.

They fixed, those remarkable eyes, on what she'd unearthed. Her gloved fingers were far from spidery, but slender, and delicate. Amid a packet of folded papers, very worn and very creased, had been tucked a thin volume like a journal of some sort.

I might have dismissed this as well, with an indifferent sniff. Love letters, a diary, all sentiment and yearning and poems. But my gaze, trained keen and sharp, fell on the journal's faded indigo cover. It, too, was very worn, scuffed, the corners blunted and rounded, the gilt-embossed design stamped into it all but rubbed away... and yet... and still...

The design. Something about it resonated, shivering, in my mind. I knew that design. Didn't I?

The journal's strap and clasps were broken. I watched as the woman's elegant fingers flicked swiftly through the pages. Captivated by her find, she was unaware of my scrutiny, unaware of my own stifled gasp and subsequent held breath.

Just from what fleeting glimpses I could make out, it was plain to me this was no sentimental diary. What, precisely, it *was*, I couldn't tell. I only knew that I had to see more.

The woman, this beautiful young woman so strangely attired in mismatched layers and that long, tattered coat, pressed the journal between her slim palms. Her remarkable eyes closed briefly as she gathered herself, steadied herself.

I almost spoke then. Almost inquired. Hesitation held me back, however, and I used the opportunity instead to gather and steady myself as well. I affected obliviousness, picking up a book at random, as if I remained unaware of her at all.

In truth, I remained very aware. I watched, surreptitiously but like a hawk, as she put on her own show of casual nonchalance. After selecting a few other books—chosen, I'm certain, as randomly as the one in which I pretended to be immersed—she made her way to the exit. The bored-looking man at the till barely gave her or her items a glance.

Then she was gone, and I was kicking myself for not having spoken up. Perhaps, if she hadn't been beautiful, and young... perhaps, if she had been the aged, shabby crone she'd seemed... I'd never been at my best with the fairer sex, not even when I'd been a lad. Give me a dowdy librarian to talk to, or a dowager aunt, and I'd be fine; put me in a room with a pretty girl, and all my wits flew right out the window.

The next time I saw her, I noticed at once and with no mistake.

It was at a flea market, one of those great sprawling affairs, where row after row of tents filled a gravel parking lot, selling everything from designer-knock-off sunglasses to pottery handcrafted by local 'artisans.' At one end were food trucks, filling the air with enticing aromas of smoke, salt, and grease. At the other were port-a-potties, the aroma far less enticing. The rest was a jumble of used furniture, second-hand clothes, bins of toys, cheap cosmetics, horrible paintings, farm tools and auto parts, and, of course, books.

Most of the books were garbage. Mass-market paperbacks, encyclopedia sets so old Hawaii was still listed as a territory, kids' books with ripped or colored-on pages, big-name book club hardbacks. Garbage, yet I still had to look. You never knew. I'd once found a nearly-complete *Et Ordinatio Stellae* in a milk crate full of 1970s cookbooks.

As I looked, I saw her again. Hunched and shuffling, burdened with satchels, her ragged coat dragging in the gravel, her shadow a haggard blotch on the ground in the sunlight brightness of the day. She moved up and down the rows, pausing, as I did, whenever even a few books might be on display.

I worked my way toward her, following as discreetly as I could. Her layers of clothes seemed the same: a mustard-yellow sweater unraveling into strings, a blouse the hue of newspapers left forgotten in an attic, a skirt like antique funeral lace over tea-colored leggings, heavy sensible shoes, and baggy argyle socks. The satchels, I felt certain, were the same ones I'd seen her carrying before. The shapeless hat, the ragged coat, the scarf... all the same. All the same, and surely too warm for this sunny weather.

Had I been wrong in my own up-close impression? Had I imagined the exquisite ivory-silk beauty and fine platinum-blonde hair?

My dubiousness took another large step when she approached a stall where the vendors could at best be charitably described as leftover hippies. Everything was tie-dye and macrame, caftans, incense, peace signs, and crystals. There was a small selection of books at the back, but I hadn't bothered. As the woman in the tattered coat made her way toward them, I again almost spoke up. No self-respecting occultist...

Perhaps I *had* been mistaken. Whatever she'd found at the Montague estate sale, whatever the design or sigil embossed on the cover of that journal, whatever the incantations and formulae inked onto its pages, clearly it must've been a mere fluke, a lucky chance on her part.

I sidled into the next stall over instead, enduring a heated discussion between two men about the quality of sports-watches for sale. By positioning myself just right, I could peer through the gaps of the tent-sides and see the woman crouching to examine the contents of a short bookshelf.

As I'd surmised, it was hippie-stuff, woo-woo new-age foolishness. Mixed in were a few college texts dating from decades before I was born. Disdain and disappointment filled me. I started to turn away, when I heard another of those stifled, excited gasps.

Wedged behind the textbooks was a slim indigo journal. I wouldn't say it was identical to the one I'd seen her with before, but it was surely a sibling if not a twin. Someone had, in the distant past, pasted a psychedelic flower sticker over the embossed sigil, its garish colors by now gone a weathered pastel, but the strap and the clasps were intact.

The clasps, I observed, were metal... some wan, tepid shade of patinaed bronze... and shaped in a way that made me think, oddly, of theater masks... comedy and tragedy, with their weirdly contorted faces...

She carefully undid them. A shout rose in my throat, a warning, a NO. I choked it back, turned it into a cough, wondering what was the matter with me.

Her delicate fingers—and yes, they *were* slender, elegant, not spidery at all in their pale gloves—opened the cover. I glimpsed pages of writing, a scratchy archaic script in thin indigo ink; though I could not read it at this angle and distance, the pattern resonated to my very bones.

Next were a few missing pages, torn out. And a few blank pages, unused. Then, toward the end, some other more modern hand with more modern implements had doodled in sketches of peace signs and marijuana leaves, partial nudes, and swirling starbursts.

Although never a violent person by nature, in that instant I wanted to punch a hippie all the way back to the Age of Aquarius. Instead, I continued spying as the woman rose from her crouch. In fleeting profile, before she turned, I saw again the fine features in their youthful flawlessness. How could I, how could anyone, mistake her for old? How could she go about in those rags and tatters, when she should be gowned, and crowned, like a queen?

"Hey, buddy, you wanna watch, or what?"

Wanna watch? I *was* watching... then my confusion cleared. *Want a watch?*, the man had said. I mumbled a vague apology to the stall vendor, bought a timepiece I didn't need, and made my hasty exit. But it was not hasty enough. She'd already disappeared into the bustling Saturday afternoon crowd, with her mysterious prize.

The next few times that I saw her—at a church rummage sale, a neighborhood arts fair, and the opening of a new used bookstore (oxymoron as it may sound; *new used*)—I paid more attention to her than to my own business. Both of our quests proved fruitless. She made no new discoveries, and I learned nothing further... except to reconfirm my impressions. The same or very similar layers of shabby garments. The same deceptive appearance concealing the same exquisite beauty. The same ever-present hat and too-large coat, even when summer's heat had others in tank tops and shorts.

Others, but not me, of course. To dispense with my suit-jacket was the extent of my concession; I'd no sooner venture out without a tie than I would venture out in my pajamas. I'd often felt I'd been born into the wrong era. It had earned me no small amount of teasing as a child, or at university.

It also made me, I suppose, in my own way, as conspicuous as her. Too conspicuous to do anything like trail her when she left each unsuccessful search. She'd shuffle toward the bus stop or the subway, where I could hardly follow. And what did I intend to do, anyway? Go to whatever hovel she called home? A dismal apartment, a shelter for the destitute, a tent or cobbled-together shack under some overpass? For what purpose? To what end?

The journals, though… their indigo covers, that disturbing sigil… the writing within, the diagrams and drawings and maps… she had *found* something. They *meant* something.

I wanted to know. *Needed* to. *Had* to!

All these years, and yes, I'd made the occasional modest discovery, but never the *big* one, the one to firmly establish my place among the most elite inner circles.

Weeks went by with no further developments. I pursued my studies with less than my normal vigor, and attended some society meetings in such distracted a manner that colleagues asked after my health. I thought about making inquiries about the woman in the tattered coat, but caution held me back. Caution, or ambition. Whoever she was, whatever she'd discovered, I didn't want to alert her to my interest, or tip my hand to anyone else that I might be on to a momentous find.

Then I learned, via roundabout whispered sources, of an upcoming auction, reputed to have acquired, by fair means or foul, the contents of several defunct archives and private collections. Such a temptation, I would not have ignored under any circumstances, but now I was all the more eager to attend.

So eager, in fact, that I arrived early. Days early. I rented a suite of rooms overlooking the hall—a Masonic lodge—where the auction was to be held, and conducted my version of an amateur stakeout. I observed the comings and goings of workers and deliveries. The sight of crates stamped with the logos of universities such as Atherton and Miskatonic set my pulse racing. Other shipments had clearly come from overseas, marked in French, Italian, or German. One, I'd swear on my life, bore the seal of the Knights Templar… another, an ancient symbol linked to the lost Library of Alexandria.

A cruder man might have salivated.

She would be here. I had no doubt. She would be here the preview day, waiting outside like a bargain-crazed Black Friday shopper, impatient to rush the doors the second they opened.

The last time I'd seen her was at a park, checking one of those 'little libraries' well-meaning people set up and kept stocked with random books. I wondered if she would show up at the auction in her same disheveled tatters... wondered if they'd let her in, or turn her away.

It occurred to me that I might have become somewhat obsessed. I shrugged it off.

She would be here. So would I.

I, however, wasn't planning to rush the doors. Or to wait outside.

Just as I had never been a violent person by nature, nor had I ever perceived myself as a man of intrigue or action. I was a scholar, a thinker, an academic.

I was also a Mason, by way of several generations before me. I'd never made much of it beyond attending a few meetings, enough to satisfy myself that their rituals were not the deep occult mysteries for which I'd hoped, but I knew their ways, and it proved an easy matter to gain access to the building the day before the preview.

It proved a trickier matter to hide until everyone else had left, but, this too I managed without much difficulty. A night watchman, elderly even by Masonic standards, made cursory rounds before settling in front of an equally elderly television. He put on an old war movie. The muted sounds of gunshots and artillery were soon joined by the less-muted sounds of his snoring.

The lodge was a silent, somnolent husk, appropriately weighty with shadows and secrets. The lack of windows helped as I made my way around with a penlight. Dark wood gleamed. Old draperies and upholstery musted quietly. Here and there glinted the Square and Compasses, and other symbols. The dead gazes of portraits and marble busts peered blankly past me. Velvet ropes on brass posts barred off the stairs leading to the upper floors, but the auction was to be held in the spacious basement, which did occasional extra duty hosting dances and bake sales.

Rows of folding chairs had been set up, facing a stage with a podium. Numbered auction paddles, programs, and the usual accouterments were on hand. Along the side walls stood sheet-shrouded bookshelves and tables, cordoned off not with velvet ropes and brass posts but those ordinary plastic-and-canvas-belt type seen at airports.

I paused for a moment to close my eyes and inhale the familiar scents of paper and parchment, binding glue, ink, gilding, and leather. The evocative aromas of lore and learning, knowledge and time. The elusive, tantalizing whiff of power.

A shiver went through me. It would have under any such circumstances; this was kid-in-a-candy-store time. Only, more so. This was being the first child at an Easter egg hunt when all the rest were still fetching their baskets. I wanted to bar the doors so no one else could get in, and just indulge, just wallow in it, just live here going through these treasures at my leisure with no other cares in the world. To hoard and to guard them as jealously as any dragon.

I got a grip, though, on my booklust. I reminded myself of my purpose.

With methodical care, I commenced my search. I disturbed the arrangements of items as little as possible. I donned thin white cloth gloves to protect the fragile materials from skin-oils—that this served also to mask fingerprints was merely a side bonus. A surgeon, or bomb-disposal expert, could not have had a lighter touch.

Oh, and there were treasures, all right. Treasures to be sure. The bidding would no doubt be ferocious. Even my coffers were not unlimited, and there was much here to be desired.

It pained me, almost physically *pained* me, to pass over the bulk of books, tomes, and grimoires. Then the beam of my penlight fell upon indigo. Cliché though it is, I'm certain my heart skipped a beat.

Feeling more like a surgeon or bomb-disposal expert than ever, I gingerly extracted the slim journal from its innocuous position between some Edwardian swain's handwritten volume of love poetry and a schoolmarm's manual dated 1873. The strap was snug, the clasps intact. I turned it over with a gloved, trembling hand.

My penlight's pale moon highlighted the embossed mark centered on the cover, at which I'd not yet before managed to get a good look. In the one instance, it had been worn and weathered to a ghost; in the other, that stupid psychedelic sticker had been pasted over it.

Now, though…

Here, though…

At last…

It shone as precise and pristine as if it had been stamped yesterday. Fine gold lines, forming a profoundly simple yet profoundly ornate design.

A design that… that meant nothing to me, that I did not recognize… and yet…

I stared at it for a long time, that design on the journal's cover. My nerves seemed to be singing. My blood coursed not like blood but like chilled champagne in my veins. Every inch of my skin had risen in gooseflesh. A thrill of triumph raced through my body. Another man might have loosed a victory whoop and pumped his fist in the air.

I'd done it, I'd found it, I'd gotten here first! I'd beaten *her* to the punch! Whatever mystery she pursued and possessed, my lady-of-tatters, she wouldn't keep it to herself anymore!

All I had to do was make note of the lot number and—

No. No, that was insane.

To have this journal right here in my hand, and then to risk letting it somehow slip away? To hold it, to touch it, and then be outbid? Cheated? Denied?

I would sooner gouge out my own eyes, sooner slit my own throat!

I *had* it. I *held* it. It was *mine*.

A part of me, a part highly shocked and affronted, clamored in outraged protest. What did I think I was doing? I was Sebastian Drewe! I came from family and history and wealth and prestige! Would I sully that legacy? Doom and damn my own reputation by becoming no better than a common thief?

The journal couldn't have fit more neatly into my inner suit-jacket pocket if my tailor had sewn it with this very outcome in mind. It rested flat and undetectable against my ribs.

Very well, then. This was indeed what I was doing.

But it did not make me a common thief! A thief would've had only profit in mind, and I knew full well then and there I'd never sell or part with this. Not for profit, not for love or money as the saying went, not for anything!

The distant, muffled toll of a church bell brought me back to alertness. I checked the time and realized, with a cold dash of horror, it was nearly dawn. Had I been standing here for hours, like one in a trance?

Hastily, but still with meticulous care, I arranged the school-marm's manual and the volume of poems so as to display no suspicious gap, and replaced the sheet. I cast my penlight—its weakened beam attesting to a waning battery, further proof the hours *had* gone by—around the room, confirming all appeared undisturbed, just as I'd found it.

There. Good. No one would ever know.

At the top of the stairs, I quite literally bumped into the watchman. We both jumped. We both cried out. He dropped a mug, porcelain shattering, coffee spraying. I dropped my penlight, still shedding its weak, waning glow.

"What the—who the—good *God*, you scared the—" was as far as he got.

Never a violent person by nature, not a man of action, I nonetheless struck at him with reflexive, panicked strength. It was a ridiculous maneuver, more a shove than any sort of blow, the heels of my hands smacking him in the chest.

Smacking him hard in the chest. So hard that I felt the creaky not-quite-give of ribs.

The breath coughed from his lungs. He staggered back, wheezing, pawing at his sternum.

I shoved him again. Off-balance, he fell over, landing with a thump. I was on him in an instant. Holding him down. Pressing him down, so that I felt again that creaky not-quite-give. Not enough to crack or break brittle old bone, but enough to prevent his inhaling.

In the pallid yellow light, I saw his eyes bulge and mouth gape. I saw his face darken, suffused by unhealthy colors. He shuddered beneath me, shuddered and twitched, pushing feebly at my arms.

Then he went limp and lay still. His head lolled. A blankness filled his gaze... like the portraits, like the marble busts... the blankness of a dead gaze.

I checked for a pulse and found none.

None.

I waited five more agonizing minutes to be sure. My own pulse raced. My mind did as well, but in crazed, senseless circles.

Thievery, and now this?

Now murder?

No. No, I hadn't *killed* him. He'd just... he'd just *died*. He must've been in his eighties, and the sudden shock of my appearance had been too much for him. A heart attack. It could have happened any time. Hardly a surprise, really. A man of his age, of his frail condition? Probably long overdue. Who would have reason to suspect anything else? It wasn't as if there were signs of injury.

My crazed, racing mind, which had been galloping those senseless circles like a horse beset by bees, found its course. I surveyed the scene with critical attention. Even the broken coffee cup fit the narrative. He'd been making his rounds, and then, just... boom. He drops the cup, he staggers about a bit, he collapses, he dies. It's relatively quick, relatively painless.

Yes, I'd struck him, but any bruising could be attributed to the throes of death; hadn't I even *seen* him pawing and thumping at his own chest? I hadn't strangled him, had only checked for a pulse. And—ha!—I was still wearing the thin white cloth gloves!

I left him to be found by whoever would find him. Someone was sure to arrive soon, to set up for the day. Thus far, I'd been lucky, and would not push it further. I let myself out by way of a side kitchen door, locking it behind me.

The sun had not yet done more than begin to brighten the east, but a few early risers were already up and about their business. Delivery trucks rumbled through quiet streets. A paperboy pedaled by on his bike—when was the last time I'd seen one of those? Women in pink smocks slid trays of donuts into a bakery window's display rack. An obnoxiously fit young man jogged past with his dog, neither so much as deigning to glance at me.

I walked a few blocks at random, purchased a newspaper and a donut and a coffee of my own, then took a circuitous route back to the hotel where I'd rented my suite of rooms. Across the street, the Masonic lodge looked just as it had. Somnolent. Silent. Keeping its secrets.

As I approached the front doors, the nape of my neck prickled. I caught furtive movement from the corner of my eye, as if someone had just ducked stealthily into the alleyway.

Probably nothing. Certainly not *her*, watching me, spying on me, knowing where I'd been and what I'd done and what I was up to.

Certainly not. I was just jumpy, and no wonder. It had been a long, stressful night.

The desk clerk nodded as I crossed the lobby. I'd been out for a morning paper and bite of breakfast, that was obvious, that was all, and he merely hadn't noticed my departure. Good. Fine and well.

I resisted the urge to sneak a furtive peek over my shoulder. I went up to my rooms, where I'd left the drapes drawn. Without turning the lights on, I peered through the merest sliver of a gap.

The lodge, somnolent and orderly, its latest secret as yet undiscovered.

The alleyway, trash bins and boxes, occupied only by a scavenging ragged yellow stray cat.

Secure behind locks, I finally permitted myself to relax. I wolfed the donut, guzzled the coffee, washed and dried my hands with operating-room diligence, donned a fresh pair of gloves, and then removed the slim indigo journal from my inner coat pocket.

At a small writing desk, in a small pool of lamplight, I undid the masklike clasps. Comedy and tragedy, I'd thought before, though now upon closer inspection, there was something altogether different about them. Less comedy, and more the maniacal laugh of madness. Less tragedy, and more a soul-wrenching shriek of ultimate terror.

I gently opened the sigil-embossed cover. The pages were creamy, like fine parchment, like ivory silk. The ink was somehow darker than black, yet oddly iridescent. I thought of jewels. I thought of the carapaces of strange beetles, midnight scarabs from some ancient desert.

The handwritten lines were in beautiful calligraphy... and in no language I recognized.

I frowned.

The letters *were* letters, not hieroglyphs or runes. But they didn't seem to fit any of the known alphabets or phonetic scripts.

It couldn't be. I should have at least been able to identify, or to *guess,* but...

A cipher? A code? That had to be it. The only possible explanation.

I turned more pages. The layout hinted in places of poems or a play-script, but there were also boxed diagrams, spell formulae, and what could only be incantations meant to be spoken aloud. But I couldn't for the life of me begin to surmise how to pronounce the words.

Exhaustion must have caught up to me at that point, coffee or no coffee. When my senses returned, I found myself on the floor. I sprang up with a burst of fear. Had I been robbed? Had I dreamed it? Was it real?

The journal rested upon the writing desk, cover neatly shut, sigil shining in the pool of lamplight. I regarded it with a mixture of covetous longing and ice-cold loathing. Neither reaction felt right. Why covet it? It was mine. Why loath it? It was what I'd yearned for! I might not fully understand it, I might have to decipher that unknown language, but there *was* obvious and genuine power here! I just needed more information.

And I knew where to get it.

Most of the day had passed as I lay insensate. I rushed across the street to the lodge, where the preview was already underway. The death of the night watchman appeared to have caused little disruption in the scheduled proceedings.

I regarded the hallway at the top of the stairs—where we'd collided, where he'd died—with morbid fascination. But I saw no evidence of police presence or medical examiners. The ruse must have worked. A simple heart attack, nothing more.

A modest crowd circulated in the basement, inspecting the lots to be auctioned. Many, I recognized as colleagues and fellow scholars. I ignored them, however. I was not here for idle chit-chat.

Only gradually did it occur to me that I was the subject of low murmurs and askance looks.

"Isn't that Sebastian Drewe?"

"Do you think he's all right?"

Then came realization. In my haste, I'd given no thought to anything but my mission. Here I was, unwashed and unshaven, hair in corkscrew disarray, yesterday's clothing rumpled and disheveled. Were my eyes wild? Was that a coffee stain upon my shirtfront?

I stammered some inarticulate half-excuse to no one in particular, and hurried from the room.

At the top of the stairs, I nearly collided again with someone else. Jerking back with a gasp, I then nearly tumbled backward down the steps, but caught myself on the handrail.

It was *her*.

The woman in the hat and scarf and long ragged coat. My lady-of-tatters, standing hunched and frail upon the very spot where the watchman had fallen.

I shrank from her. I clutched at my chest, much as the watchman had done... only, unlike him, it was not my stricken heart that I clutched at, but the slim journal tucked with such perfectly-tailored hidden discretion in my inner pocket.

She held out an expectant, gloved hand, delicate fingers uncurling.

I shook my head. Or, rather, my head shook itself side to side as if of its own accord.

Her gaze, star-shining, twilight-on-the-lake, regarded me with cool dispassion. Oh, and yes, she was exquisite, young and beautiful, skin of ivory silk, hair a fine platinum-blonde.

Maybe it *was* my stricken heart that I clutched at after all.

"Return it," she said, and her voice was the soft susurrus of wind over sand.

"I found it." The words—childish, petulant words in a childish, petulant tone—spilled from my lips. "I found it first."

"You stole it."

"I—"

"You killed for it."

"No, I—"

"And yet, for you, it is still not too late. Give it to me."

"What is it?" I demanded. "What does it say? I want to know!"

"Why should *I*," she replied, "care what *you* want?"

Enough of my ego remained sufficiently intact to be affronted, but not enough of my wit to formulate a reply. I just shook my head again—of my own will this time—and stared back at her, my breaths short and rapid.

"You have *seen*," she went on, "but you do not *see*. This is nothing to you. A path to places you do not wish to go."

"A path to knowledge," I said, finding wit and voice again. "To power and truth!"

"To danger and madness and darkness and death."

"I've spent my whole *life* searching for—"

"Your whole *life?*" she echoed. "I have searched for more lifetimes than you could possibly comprehend!"

I… believed her.

In that moment, I perceived distances and eons and a vast, cavernous room where arched pillars rose to a crystal-paned ceiling. In the black sky above, blacker stars whirled by the thousands, dancing clusters of constellations few sane eyes had beheld. I saw shelves, an infinite archive of shelves holding countless upon countless slim indigo journals… countless upon countless, yet barely filling half that infinity… the collection still far—still *so* far, so achingly far!— from complete.

I perceived, and believed.

My challenge and stubborn defiance melted. "Then, show me," I pleaded, sinking to my knees. "Teach me. Help me understand."

Her own aspect softened, her own stern tones gentled. "Is that truly what you desire?"

"Yes!"

Once again, she extended her expectant hand.

I fumbled the journal from my inner pocket. The sigil embossed on the cover, had I seen the same design done large, set in citrine mosaic into the archive's mirror-smooth floor? I had, yes, I had… and she would show me, she would teach me… I would have the knowledge of universes, the power of dimensions, the truth of the cosmos unmeasurable by man!

Delicate, gloved fingers plucked the journal from my grasp. A radiant light burst around us. The woman's mismatched layers, ragged garments, and tattered coat fell away. She stood now as I'd imagined: tall and regal, gowned in ambergold satin, arrayed like a queen.

She smiled on me, exquisite, beatific.

And then, she laughed. "Fool."

With that, she turned and was gone. Gone, leaving me kneeling alone on the carpet. Kneeling there wild-eyed and disheveled in the hallway of the lodge, while people coming up the stairs paused to whisper and gawk.

I think I collapsed, fell unconscious, took leave of my senses.

There followed a confusion of doctors and hospitals, concerned colleagues, scandalized family, medications, a quiet asylum, recuperative rest cures. At last, I regained myself sufficiently to be released.

I went home. I withdrew from society and social functions. I let my studies lapse. I became indifferent to keeping up with fashion. My wardrobe suffered, as did my reputation.

She'd told me I had *seen,* but did not *see.*

Perhaps she'd been right. But, I *had* seen… and *what* I had seen was that infinite archive of half-filled shelves… countless upon countless indigo journals… the collection still so far from complete.

Which meant there were more of them yet to be found.

Which meant this wasn't over.

My lady-of-tatters, my exquisite queen.

Next time, she would not call me a fool.

AT THE CROSSROADS

This has been my home for all my life. It has been my family's home for generations, my mother's before me, and my grandmother's before her, and so on back through the ages. Since the metropolis was a city, the city a town, the town a village, the village a settlement, the settlement a lone homestead claim by a grieving widow woman.

She lost her husband, that great-ancestress, in the ocean crossing. A less-stalwart spirit might have given up the difficult dream of a fresh start in a new land, might have returned with her unborn child to the place from whence she'd come. But, she did not. She stayed. She struggled and persevered. She built her cottage, tended her garden, raised her daughter, lost her son.

Over time, just as the homestead became a settlement and the settlement a village and so on through the years, that humble little cottage grew into a fine house, with cone-capped turrets at the corners, neat white shutters, a long covered porch. Its garden went from herbs and vegetables to prize-winning roses, its yard a lush green tree-shaded quietude behind its ivy-climbing fences.

And the roads went this-way that-way all around it, first simple country lanes, then bricks and cobbles, then paved and widened with traffic lights and bustle. Neighbors crowded ever more and ever closer, shops and taverns, schools and churches, a town square. Buildings rose ever higher, apartments and hotels, offices, shopping malls. These days, it is bus routes and businesses, condos, commuters, taxi-cabs.

While still, amid it all, the house remains. Older now, as I am. Weathered and worn down. It still sits behind its ivy-climbing fences in green tree-shaded quietude, though the roses have gone wild and not taken prizes in many years.

The house, and I, are surrounded by the bustling, growing change. I've watched skyscrapers go up, and highways. When I was a little girl, I knew everyone on the crossing streets. People strolled and chatted, brought each other plates of cookies, helped with raking leaves or shoveling snow.

I see them now, so many strangers. So many hurrying strangers, wrapped up in their own worlds. No one strolls. No one chats, unless it is on their phones, and even then it is brusque more often than not, brusque and curt, loud.

When my own girls were little, before their father died, I would send them with plates of cookies up and down the block. They had a lemonade stand every summer at the corner of our yard where the busiest roads met. During the rest of the year, I would be out there every morning and afternoon, wearing a bright smock and cap, a whistle hung around my neck, my trusty STOP/SLOW sign in hand, to cross the children on their way to and from school.

My girls are gone now. Grown up and moved away. They didn't want to stay. They didn't want to keep the house the way it was. Sell it, they urged me. Sell it and let them put up more condos or a fancy hotel. Location, location, location! We'll make a fortune!

This has been our *home,* I told them. Our home for generations. Your grandmother and hers before her—

We *know,* they'd say, and roll their eyes. That doesn't mean *we* have to be stuck here.

I thought they'd reconsider. One, at least, would see my side. Would appreciate the dedication, the dream so long sustained down our family line.

Instead, I'll occasionally get letters. Cards for holidays. A rare, dutiful phonecall. I have grandchildren who've never been here.

Great-grandchildren I've never seen. Every so often, one of my girls—women now, mature women, some grandmothers themselves—will ask if I haven't come to my senses yet. They'll send me brochures for upscale 'senior living' complexes, and property value estimates from real estate agents. They drop strong hints about the costs of college tuition, car troubles, vacations.

Now, they just wait for the inevitable. For me to get too old, too infirm. For me to fall and break a hip, start forgetting to turn off stove burners or forgetting my own name, have a heart attack or stroke. Until they can *put* me in one of those places... or until they put me in the ground... and *then,* they think, the house will be theirs to do with as they please. *Then* they can sell the land to some developer, who'll tear down and uproot and pave over, and build some towering anonymous facade of glass and steel.

These fruit trees your ancestress planted—

Yes, nasty, mealy, full of worms; it all just falls and rots anyway. Even if someone gathered the harvest, not like you can sell it to a store. No farmer's markets around here. Not like anybody cans or makes preserves anymore.

The roses—

Who has the time or patience? You can order a bouquet online and have it delivered anywhere in the world.

This handmade—

Impractical, uncomfortable, old-fashioned, ugly.

And, no. And, no. And, no.

So, they wait, disgruntled. They tell their children and grandchildren who-knows-what, but whatever it is, they must believe them. I get obligatory announcements—graduation, wedding, baby shower—but no invitations.

I get told I should try email, facebook, snapchat, instagram, a thousand other things I don't understand. I get told it's the only way to keep up, to keep in touch.

When I used to just be able to step outside. When I used to be at the intersection morning and afternoon, rain or shine without fail. When people would smile and say hello, greet me by name. When I'd hold up my sign and cars would stop, and their drivers would nod and wave. First-day-of-school jitters, students excited or anxious, parents the same. Last-day-of-school jubilation, no more pencils no more books no more teachers' dirty looks. Art projects, A-pluses, lunchboxes, mittens. The same familiar faces, going from chubby-cheeked babies in strollers to gap-toothed and bright-eyed kindergartners, from kids on big-boy and big-girl bicycles into teenagers, crossing for the bus to the high school or walking with younger siblings.

When the men had their lawns and their cars and their bowling, when we women had housework and recipes and bridge parties, when we'd ask after relatives and did-you-hear-about this or that; yes, sometimes gossip, sometimes spiteful and mean, but not often, not as often as you might think.

But that's all gone now. Gone like my daughters, moved away, moved on. Bigger and busier and louder and faster. I sit at my window or stand on my porch or lean on my gate and watch them go by. Countless hurrying strangers with heads bent to phone-screens and thumbs flying, with earbuds and sunglasses, with briefcases and computer bags, with take-out and delivery and on-the-go instead of home-cooked sit-down meals. With no eye contact, no smiles, no friendly hellos and companionable conversation.

I don't know them. They don't know me. They see, if they see me at all, white hair and wrinkles, a stooped back, bunch-knuckled hands gripping a cane instead of the sign I once held, drab shawls and sweaters in place of the bright smock and cap.

They see the house and it is a passing curiosity to them, the tree-shaded quietude an oddity amid the tall towers of brick, steel, and glass. It isn't part of their world. It seems out of place. At the most, they might pause to wonder if it's some historical site, for, what other reason could there possibly be? Not that it matters. Not that they care.

People used to care, to talk and to listen. To share stories, experiences, travels, their lore and their lives.

I'm told they still do, just…

Things have moved on, crossed over into a realm beyond my understanding. A realm so faraway and exotic, it may as well be some other reality. Intangible. Ephemeral. It's all aether and cloud, digital, electronic. It exists without existing, everywhere and nowhere, everything and nothing, simultaneously. With its own languages, its own customs and currencies, its own rules and laws, crimes and punishments, its own wealth and wonders.

All the people who rush by, day after day, who crowd the sidewalks and cross the streets as car horns honk and sirens wail, all the people with their heads bent to their screens and thumbs flying, they are the travelers who don't even know where they are, the dreamers who don't know they're dreaming… and making their own dreams, their own nightmares, as they do.

They move in the real world, they live and breathe in it, and barely notice. They follow the enticing lure of phantoms and phantasms. They sail on vast oceans of information and entertainment, truth and lies intermingled.

While I, I am here. Alone, isolated, lonely as a lighthouse keeper… tending a fading beacon that no longer guides anyone's way, a fading beacon of memory and nostalgia… important only to me, as the rest of them hurry by without so much as a flicker of acknowledgment.

Can it be so fascinating, that unreality? So captivating?

I sit by my window or stand on my porch or lean on my gate and watch. Watch them rushing, crossing, back and forth, this way and that, here but not-here, elsewhere. More interested in their glassy portals to ephemera than in what's going on around them.

But then, this evening as I'm out in my gone-wild garden, fireflies dancing in the dusky gloom, leaves whispering their mysteries, the scent of roses fragrant in the cooling air, a beam of moonlight paints a silver-white path. It leads to the side gate, which I see is standing open. Leaning upon my cane, I make my way toward it.

Traffic rushes up and down the street, as it always does. Cars and cabs, buses, bicyclists weaving from lane to lane. The intersection where I used to cross the schoolchildren is an orderly chaos of stop-lights and signs, brake lights and blinkers, flashing lights and reflec-tors. Horns beep. Strains of music compete. In front of the bank, the big clock displays the time in glowing numbers. The interiors of vehicles are awash from within by bluish screenlights as people check their phones, text their messages.

At the curb near my gate, a single car idles, placid and serene. Others veer around it but without honks or shouts or irate gestures. It simply waits there, like a moored ship. It's of a make unfamiliar to me—so many are, nowadays. One of those hybrids they talk about, maybe? What I do know is, it's strangely beautiful, strangely inviting. Clean and white, sleek and pure, opalescent. Its smooth windows seem more crystal than glass.

The passenger side window lowers in a silent glide. I see the driv-er behind the wheel, leaning to look at me. She is very young, very lovely, her hair a pale shimmer. Something about her reminds me with painful yearning of my girls, my daughters before they grew up and we grew apart. It even crosses my mind that this could be one of their descendants, one of those grandchildren or great-grandchildren I've never met.

She smiles. I have come all the way to the open gate, follow-ing that silvery moon-path, as if unaware of my steps. I hold my cane barely leaned-upon. Though the sidewalk jostles with pedes-trians—business suits and briefcases, power-parents pushing jog-ging strollers, dog-walkers with leashes in one hand and phones in the other—the span from my gate to her passenger door remains oddly clear.

Everyone else seems oblivious to her, to the white car, and to me. Lost in their own dreamlands and virtual worlds.

With a muted click, the car door unlatches and swings welcom-ing-wide. The seat looks soft, looks comfortable, looks like cloud-stuff and moon-stuff. It *is* soft, I find as I ease my old bones gently into it. Soft and comfortable. I lean my cane by my side. The door closes again. The window glides up. We are in serene, crystal silence. Outside, around us, the traffic continues to rush and veer. The people continue their hurried passage.

I don't say anything. Neither does she, not at first. She merely drives, navigating the intersection as if she's done so a thousand times. The metropolis—once a city, once a town, once a village, once a settlement, once a homestead—lifts its glittering skyscrapers, arches its steel-span bridges, blares its marquees and electronic billboards, sweeps searchlights through the spangled night.

Where are we going? I do not ask. It does not matter. The girl drives with purpose, destinations in mind. She never has to stop, never slows, never seems lost or uncertain. It is as if she follows a guide I cannot see.

Soon, an eternity later, the scenery changes. I behold unfamiliar places, impressive and majestic, daunting, intimidating. But the girl, in a gentle language I should not be able to comprehend, begins to speak. Here, there are fabulous sights, mysterious wonders.

They are like islands, each unique and of itself, but interconnected. Archipelagos joined by countless crisscrossing latticeways, along which this girl steers the little white car with ease. As she explains, in her gentle manner, understanding slowly comes to me.

These places are real. They may have no native inhabitants, just untold visitors, travelers passing through again and again, but commerce is done, information exchanged, experiences shared. Relationships form sight unseen, friendships, romances... form, and fracture. There are joys and terrors, delights and dangers.

She shows me, and I learn. Where it is safe to go, where it is best not to. Where many gather, giving, generous, and kind... where others gather, sour, bitter, and cruel.

I behold archives, vast libraries, universes created solely from thought. I behold hollow, hateful echo-chambers where spite and ignorance recurve and redouble. Each who wishes it has his or her own realm, his or her own fiefdom. There are memelords and edgelords, SJWs, MRAs. I marvel at the treasure troves of pinterest, the benign madness of tumblr, the vilest cesspits where redditors eat their own young. I witness the fiery flamewars, the scammers and thieves, the death-threats and rape-threats and worse... yet I also witness love and compassion, I attend fairytale weddings, see babies take their first steps. Moments are preserved, some poignant, some funny. Messages are sent, tributes and testimonials given.

She points out the worst regions where dark webs are spun, realms of overwhelming evil and depravity from which escape is nearly impossible and what has been seen cannot be unseen, what has been known cannot be unknown. Yet, not all is horrific. Horror may loom large, may appear to blot out the goodness... but much of the horror is elongated shadow, disproportionate, exaggerated... while much of the goodness is humble, simple, quiet, small, and steady.

And I find, oh, I find great affection for history, for nostalgia. Amid this dazzling wealth of new knowledge thrives a yearning for the past. For roots and connection, anchorage, lighthouses through time to remain blazing steady and solid as beacons, even while advancements fly ever onward fast and fleet as birds.

The birds, yes, the birds, the girl shows me the birds. Azure, cerulean, brilliant blue, as they dart and flit and twitter. Theirs is the brief thought-song of waking dreams, from the clamor of kings to the chatter of rabble. A single bird on a branch might pipe its opinion, or monstrous flocks of them descend in teeming, tweeting frenzies, maelstroms picking and pecking and fighting until scraps of words and blue feathers litter the ground.

I am, I think, not yet ready for that. I tell the girl so and she laughs a gentle, melodious laugh. In time, she says to me. In time. I have begun my forays into these new lands of living dreams and unreality. It is a start, she says. I will find my way. I may even find my family, connect with those great-granddaughters I've never met. Who knows? If some of them share the sense of nostalgia I found, the longing for a steady faithful lighthouse beacon of the past, they might come to me. They might cross the distances, literal and metaphorical.

While saying these things, she has gone on driving, piloting the little white car with effortless skill. I'm not sure how we make the return trip so quickly, but soon she has pulled up again alongside my gate.

Here stands my house, as ever, in its tree-shaded quietude amid the rushing crisscrossing bustle of the streets. The cool air still smells of roses. Moonlight still silvers the path, the moon itself unmoved. I feel as if I've been away for hours, if not days, yet it also seems no time at all has passed.

I turn back to speak to the girl, the driver. To ask more questions? To thank her? But she is gone, she and her car both, as if they'd never been there. The traffic sweeps on, ceaseless automotive currents mingling and merging. I go to the curb and look both ways, look all ways, up and down, across. But, the white car is gone.

The big clock outside the bank displays the same glowing numbers as before. I lean on my cane and watch it, waiting, until it *does* change, a minute ticking by to prove to me the world isn't somehow frozen or suspended.

Now, people are not utterly oblivious to my presence on the sidewalk. They bump and sidestep and mutter, irritable, irritated, having to raise their gazes from their devices. I decide to move out of their way. To go home, go inside, brew some tea, ponder what I've witnessed and learned.

As I reach my gate again, a sweetly youthful voice calls out, ma'am, ma'am, you've dropped your phone. A child scurries up to me, her pale hair and white dress shimmering, her tiny hand outstretched.

I start to speak, to say, no, that isn't mine, someone else must have dropped it.

But then I pause, gazing at the proffered item, which gleams crystal and moon-silver. It has somehow made its way into my own frail and wizened hand. It feels cool and smooth and vibrant, both world-window and key.

I start to speak again, to thank the child... only to find that she, too, has vanished into the rushing crowd.

In my hand, the phone hums softly. Its screen becomes luminous, alive. Suspended within its smooth glassiness, like a dream held in a mirror, is the bright blue image of a cerulean bird.

So, I take it with me as I cross the darkened yard. As I cross to my familiar, beloved house... which, somehow, no longer feels so isolated or alone.

KEEPER OF MEMORY

"T he gods, once, were kind."

Laughter greeted this, but the old woman merely smiled.

"Oh, yes," she said. "They were different gods then. Kind gods. *Our* gods. The gods who made and loved us. We spoke to them in prayers and praises, and they heard, and answered."

The laughter turned, for the most part, to smirks. *We may be young, but we are not fools,* their looks—again, for the most part— declared. *Kind gods, indeed.*

Still, they'd gathered eagerly enough around when invited. It was a change from the sameness of their chores, a reprieve from cutting reeds and dredging mud, gutting frogs and hauling water. Entertainment, novelty, and rest were rare. Already, these children knew that all too well.

Some of them might have never in their brief lives seen outsiders before. Let alone outsiders who traveled with hide-covered huts built on sledge-rafts, pulled by harnessed many-legged beasts. Outsiders who wore strange garments and stranger ornaments, who brought strange things from stranger places.

Who brought this old woman, with her wizened head and matted strings of pallid hair. A knobby hump of flesh rose above her bent back; a loose skin-wattle drooped below her neck. From her fingertips curled long nails in thin and yellowish chitinous spirals.

"I am Mema," the old woman said, "though you may call me

Grandmother, if you like. I am the Keeper of Memory."

She sat on an upended water-worn stump put to use as a chair, its roots cradling her limbs. A canopy of broad-fronded leaves held up on bent poles provided some shelter from the steady dripping of the mist.

"This is Nemon, my granddaughter's daughter, who will become Keeper after me."

Nemon dipped her head as she poured mossbark cups of juice pressed from lilyberries. Just as they—she and Mema, their fellow travelers, their sledge-rafts and their tamed, harnessed beasts—were the objects of scrutiny, so too did she examine with interest the crude village and its inhabitants.

Irregular hills rose low from the morass, topped with clustered dwellings made from sticks and mud. The shape of them was like that of wader-birds' nests overturned, or the lodgings of oil-furs moved to higher land. Meandering paths of stepping-stones crossed slow-coursing waterways. Fresh catches from fish- and frog-traps hung on lines, near bundles of harvested reeds with pulpy, fibrous tufts.

"In the time of my grandmother's grandmother's grandmother," Mema went on, "our people were numerous, and powerful, and strong. We held this world and ruled it, and our gods were kind."

Again, her words were met—for the most part—with those smirking looks. *Silly old woman and your fancies, your made-up tales of a never-was.*

The children who did *not* sneer and smirk, however, Nemon watched with close intent, but discretion. The ones who listened to Mema with attentiveness, with curiosity... whose expressions showed something more... something *other*... those were the ones she made note of.

The ones who thought, and questioned. The ones in whose minds lived something other than necessity and survival.

"They granted wishes and gave us gifts," said Mema. "If we were hurt or ill, they healed us. They protected us. They provided us with bounties of food and clean, clear water."

"What did they look like?" asked a little boy called Lut.

Yunnig, a larger boy, nudged him, nearly knocking him over. "Don't be a hoot-head. Everyone knows the gods are indescribable."

"That's not true," said Tesya, who wore her hair woven into several thin braids. "The Mindless in the Dark-Between has no head and no body."

"You can't describe something by saying what it hasn't," a girl named Anith said, then looked to Yunnig as if for his approval.

"My papa told me that the deep-folk by the ever-waters say their god is bigger than hills upon hills, with wriggling feelers like handfuls of worms where a mouth would be." Paulph held a hand against his lips and wiggled his fingers to demonstrate.

Nemon, observing the boy's wide-set bulging eyes, supposed that his papa may have come by that lore with good reason.

"And the Over-Seer of the Under-Seers is all shiny slime-bubbles and glow-bulbs," Tesya said, persistent.

"Our gods were beautiful," Mema told them. "They looked much like us, because they made us in their own shape and image."

"This is *gone-world never-was* talk," Yunnig said, scoffing. "You'll be telling us about fire and fairies next."

Tesya threw a mud-clod at him. "I want to hear."

A few of the others voiced their agreement. More joined in when Chayg pointed out that it was better than going back to their chores. Shurg, his twin, asked if they could have more lilyberry juice as well, and that convinced the rest.

Meanwhile, over by the largest of the mud-and-stick dwellings, the usual trade negotiations were being helped along by the sharing of a foamy brew made from pounded yeast-roots soaked in stone troughs. The travelers had picked it up at one of their previous stops, and, judging by the jovial tone, its heady effect was already taking hold.

"Well, then," said Mema, as they settled themselves on hummocks of damp grass. "Much of what I know has been passed down to me from my grandmother and her grandmother and her grand-mother before that. It was a very different world, then. Before the new gods came, bringing the mists. When we knew night and day, *real* night and *real* day. When there were seasons other than warm-steam and cool-fog."

The children laughed again at this, at the very idea. And, again, Mema merely smiled her toothless, indulgent smile.

"There was a sky beyond the mists, and lights hung in that sky. Lights so very bright and brilliant, brighter than anything you could imagine."

"But lights hang in the sky now." Paulph peeked from under the leaf-canopy, up toward pulsating lambent orbs within dark shad-ow-shapes.

Dark shadow-shapes, undulating in slow courses through murky striations of grey-upon-greyer clouds… the Under-Seers with their under-eyes… never blinking, never closing to sleep… sometimes shedding forth gleaming beams, sweeping back and forth… eter-nally watchful, but for what?

"Yeah," Yunnig said. "And if you look too long, they'll reel down their suckery ring-toothed tendrils and pluck you up for a snack."

The younger children squirmed and hid their faces; even some of the older ones made sure to avert their eyes from the cloudy expanse overhead. Lut hunkered beside Mema's stump-root chair. "I don't want the Under-Seers to eat me," he said. "I don't want the lights in the sky."

Mema patted his tousled hair with her long-nailed hand. "Not those lights, no. I meant the lights from before the mists. Oh, such wonderful lights. Why, when the sky was blacker than black, they say a pale shining stone would float high up in it."

"Stones don't float," said a girl named Oalthi, rocking a hollowed bark-log in which her baby sister slept.

"This one did, for it was a great stone of magic. Sometimes it would be round like a paddler's egg, and sometimes only the thin-nest curve like a shard of egg-shell. The Muen, it was called."

"Muen," Tesya murmured. She, as she listened, had idly plucked many long blades of grass and was experimenting with ways of twining and lacing them together.

A weaver, Nemon thought. The girl with the intricate braids might one day become a weaver, a maker of baskets and cloth, an artist of patterns and design.

"There were also points of light," said Mema, "thorn-sharp, dotted across the black sky, like a vast swarm of fireflies, but motionless, white as bone, clear as water."

"Stars!" cried a boy who, up until that moment, hadn't seemed to be paying attention in the slightest. "The stars were wrong, so the gods waited and waited, and then the stars were right and the gods came!"

Nemon caught her breath, but Mema remained calm. "What was your name, child? I don't think you said."

He didn't answer. Sticking his grubby fingers into his mouth, he resumed staring off at nothing.

"That's Zath." Anith rolled her eyes and heaved an exasperated sigh. "My stupid little brother."

"Were they stones, too?" Oalthi asked, when Zath showed no signs of speaking further. "The stars?"

"No one knows, dear girl," Mema said. "No one knows. But, the brightest light of all, so bright it dissolved the sky-blackness into the clearest and most beautiful blue, was called the Sunn. Which was more than bright..." Mema leaned forward, pausing with each word. "It... was... *hot!*"

Paulph tilted his head. "What's 'hot'?"

"Hot is like warm," Oalthi told him. "Hot is warmer than warm."

"Like at the spitting pools," Shurg said. "Our uncle fell in once."

"That's how he got those scars," Chayg finished.

"Shh," said Lut. "I want to hear about the Sunn."

"It was hot," Mema repeated. "Hot enough to *dry*, children. Why, there were places so dry, the mud went away, and rain didn't fall for days on days, and water sank far beneath the ground."

They fell silent for a moment, pondering this. Even Nemon, in all of her knowledge and all of her training, could barely just begin to imagine what it must be like to be *dry,* fully *dry.* Or to walk on sand, not clammy silt-mud sand but Sunn-heated *dry* sand.

Nor could she quite envision some of the other truths Mema had taught her, truths of places colder than cold, so cold that lakes turned to stone. She did not *doubt* them, but such a reality would not fit well into her comprehension.

"Never-was stories," Yunnig said. "I told you she'd be talking of fire and fairies next."

Or fire… Nemon didn't know what fairies might be, but Mema *had* now and then spoken of fire, that it *was* real, that people had once possessed the secrets of stealing it from sky-storms or springing it alive out of wood and stones. Fire, also bright and hot like the Sunn, also with the magic to *dry.* Fire, which ate and consumed, which had to be fed, but which could be controlled, and killed.

"I'm only telling you of our once-world," Mema said. "When the land itself was larger, and the waters not so deep. Much of it, I learned from my grandmothers down through the ages. More, as I said, we have learned in our travels. Why, we have been from the fog-forests of the mountains to the rocky salt-shores. We have seen the hoof-prints of the goat-folk stamped into the soft black loam, and we have seen the deep-folk swimming toward the endless waves."

"Ohh," Paulph said.

"And we have seen the immense clay-mounds formed by the colonies of one will and mind, clay-mounds ever-growing in chambered tunnels around the rugose and oozing nodules of their Masters. They devour their own dead, you know. All waste is cast into the rendering pits, and flows into the food-trenches. If babies are born thought-deaf, of no use to the colony, they too are thrown into the pits. Yet, even they—even *they,* dear children—were once like us. Oh, yes. Long ago, when we were of one people, and this was our world."

"Our world," Tesya said, sounding wistful. "Was it pretty?"

"So very pretty. Plants of so many kinds… flowers of every color, flowers that smelled sweeter than sweet-nectar… fruits too big for one person to eat… trees as tall as the clouds…"

"Were there animals like now?" asked Lut.

Mema patted his head again, ruffling his matted curls. "Far more than there are now. Some ran faster than anything. Some had fur, not wet and oily fur but thick and soft. And there were birds, not just paddlers and waders but birds that flew all the time, flew high and far—"

"Without getting snared by the Under-Seers?" Paulph's wide eyes widened further.

"There were no under-seers then."

"You can't know any of that," Yunnig said.

"But we've seen them, in ancient make-arts, and in the relics." Mema's old eyes twinkled. "Would you like to see, my dear ones?"

"Yes!" Tesya bounced up and down.

"Pleeeeeeease!" Lut added.

Those two were the most eager, capering in their excitement. The others ranged from interest to skepticism, but they did crowd closer. Only Zath, sitting slack-mouthed with a vacant stare, appeared oblivious.

"Now, let me see…" said Mema, rummaging in the folds of her voluminous scrap-hide robe. She drew from within some inner pocket a small item, pinched in the yellow spirals of her nails.

It was the figure of a bird, unmistakably a bird, but like no bird any of them had ever seen. No squat pond-paddler, nor gangly stick-legged wader… this bird was sleek-bodied, feet curled into claws, head cocked, beak hooked, and wings outspread in magnificent sweeps.

Even Yunnig, the most skeptical, was momentarily dumbstruck. They all simply gazed at the bird, at the intricate precision of detail, each feather, each tiny eye, so lifelike they might have expected it to flap and flutter in Mema's grasp.

Tiny flecks of pigment in the deeper crevices suggested it had once sported full glorious plumage, but the colors had been weathered away by the ages until only the shape remained, the shape in its strange substance and solidity, its strange uniform opacity.

She held it out to Tesya, who hesitated and curled her hands shyly against her stomach.

"Oh, it's quite all right, child," Mema said. "You won't damage it."

The girl, emboldened, extended cupped palms and let Mema drop the bird-relic into them. As she examined and felt it, her confidence grew, and she looked up at Mema with wonder.

"It's so light!" Tesya said. "But so strong! Not wood, not stone, not... I... try it, touch it," she added, turning to the others.

When those brave enough had tested their nerve, Mema brought out another figure. This was larger, vaguely hound-like in form, but with upright points of ears, an erect posture, un-bowed limbs, and a tail resembling the bushiness of a chaff-frond about to go to seed. More pigment remained on this relic than the bird, showing a grey hide with whitish undersides and darker grey markings.

She showed them still others: a lizard that went on two strong hind legs and had gaping, toothy jaws... a graceful-looking creature with flowing hair along its neck and a single twisting horn... a chubby figure with huge round head and eyes, a yellowed face and belly, and the faded vestiges of dark stripes.

"So, you see," said Mema, "our people knew all these animals, and many, many more. More kinds than you could count. Some were hunted for food, yes, like now. Some were tended for their eggs, the way you might visit a paddler's nest again and again. Some even gave milk that people could drink!"

"Eew!" chorused several of the children. "Milk from *animals?*"

"Milk from animals. Others did work, the way our beasts pull our sledge-rafts, and some let people ride upon their backs. Still others, people kept as friends and companions, and taught them to do tricks."

"Oh!" Tesya clapped. "I found a little oil-fur once, all lost and alone. I wanted to bring it home, feed it, take care of it…" Her face fell. "But everyone said no."

"Where did they all go?" Lut asked. "All the animals?"

"They died and drowned and got eaten by the Under-Seers," Yunnig said. "Tff. Hoot-head. Duh."

"Many did, that's true," Mema said. "But, there are places, my dears… magic places, wonderful secret places… hidden far beyond the reach of the new gods. In these places are chambers filled with seeds, and pods, and eggs, and sleeping unborn babies of every animal that ever was… waiting… waiting for a time when the stars change again."

She paused, glancing at Zath, but the boy still seemed far off in some secret place of his own. Then she continued.

"When that happens, the mists will lift… the lands will rise from the waters… the Sunn will shine in a blue sky by day and the Muen in a black one by night… and the world will be renewed."

"You mean, the gods will go away?" Paulph's voice wavered like a strand of sea-kelp caught in an uncertain current.

"And our own gods will return?" Tesya added. "The kind ones who love us?"

Anith snorted. "The gods that look like *people!* Sure, they will!"

Mema brought forth another relic, the torso of a goddess-figure, one who could be none other than a goddess of eternal beauty and youth. Ideal, ideal to perfection and beyond… high-breasted, the narrowest tapering of waist, smooth loins. Where a head might have been was a slim neck ending in a rounded knob. Empty sockets showed at the shoulders and hips.

"We've found many of these, across the land, from the mountain edges to the salt-shores," Mema said. "None complete, but all identical in form."

The color of the idol's substance was a vivid peculiarity for which Nemon never had found fitting words. It reminded her of the innermost surface of a speaking-shell, or the fleeting blush at the heart of a just-blooming lily, or the raw-meat slice of a wader-bird's flesh.

"Our goddesses looked like *that?*" Yunnig glanced from the idol to the girls around him, raising his eyebrows. Anith flushed, tugging at the front of her knotted sedge-grass dress.

"Identical?" Oalthi asked. "How can that be? No two things are *exactly* the same! No two leaves, no two stones, no two seed pods—"

"No two twins," Chayg put in, and Shurg nodded.

"—or frogs... *nothing* grows that way!"

"They didn't grow," said Tesya. "They were... made."

"Nothing is made that way, either," Oalthi argued. "Nothing *can* be! No two mud-pots, no two stick-houses—"

"These, we believe, were hero-gods," said Mema, bringing out two smaller figures. "Mighty warriors, fighting evil. You can see how very strong they were, how muscular and powerful."

Anith stuck her tongue out at Yunnig. "Our *gods* looked like *that?*"

Tesya traced the supple curve of a design upon one of the figure's chests. "We... we had *symbols?* Of our *own?*"

"His looks scary," said Lut, pointing at the other.

"Like the wings of a gloom-gaunt," Shurg said. "Our uncle saw one, once."

Chayg nodded. "It had little horns that stuck up like that, too."

"Our own symbols." Tesya shook her head, amazed, thin braids swinging. "Did we have... were we allowed... *books?*"

"Oh, stop it." This time, it was Yunnig who threw a mud-clod at her. "It's only stories, no more real than the Cities of Lines!"

"But the Cities of Lines *are* real," Mema said. "We've seen them. What remains of them, their ruins. Cities of the gone-world, *our* gone-world. The waters have not yet claimed everything. Structures rise above the shallows, structures of stone and stuff harder-than-stone. Crumbling, yes. Rotting like carcasses from strangely-bleeding skeletons. But real. In some places, paths can be seen, paths that do not meander for hill or hummock."

"In..." Paulph swallowed, throat making a thick gulping sound.

"In *lines?* You don't mean, they really *do* go in lines?"

"In lines," she said, nodding gravely. "In *straight* lines that meet in right-angles and squared corners. There are steps, steps stacked one atop another atop another, climbing toward the clouds."

They listened, some agog and some askance, as Mema continued describing the ruins of the old-places. Bridges and towers, circles and arches, and other words all but meaningless. Even for Nemon, who had seen for herself, much of it sounded impossible. That there had been such cities... that there could ever have been, and were... cities built by the hands of *people*... *their* people... people who had *symbols*... idols and art and lore of their own...

That they could have had all that, and done all that, and lost it forever...

She watched as the full, awful extent of that loss and horror sank into Tesya's eyes like a stone dropped into a deep pool. She watched Lut's chin began to quiver, his lower lip down-turning.

Those two, yes, those two. Their minds could envision, could imagine, could invent and create. Could think in clever ways and try various ideas. It had not yet died from them, not yet been pressed and crushed by the drudgery of simple survival.

If they lived, if they were allowed to live and to grow, and to thrive... if that difference of other-thought lasted...

It would be them, ones like them, who'd be chosen. Who'd be led to the secret places of which Mema had spoken, the chambers filled with all the waiting treasure-troves of the world's renewal.

Zath, who had been quiet since his earlier outburst, staring vacantly off into the mists, voiced a sudden shrill cackle. It made the rest of them jump, even Mema.

"Cities!" he cried. "Rich cities, sin cities, great vain folly cities! Lines and order from chaos, nature cut to man's whim! Sky-scrapers, sub-ways, transit-stations! Palaces of crystal and streets paved with gold! Chicago! Paris!"

Uneasy shudders crept through Nemon with each of the boy's utterances. His words tingled along her nerves and in her marrow-bones, resonated in the deepest caverns of her mind.

"Miami, Cairo, Istanbul!

"Hush, now, child." Though she tried to sound soothing, Mema's voice stretched taut with tension. "Hush, now. That's enough."

"Are those… *names?*" Tesya asked.

"Machu Picchu! Quebec! In their houses at Parliament, at Congress, they die dreaming! Tokyo and Boston! The wheels on the bus go 'round and 'round and all roads lead to Rome!"

Oalthi's baby sister began to wail, waving tiny fists. Paulph backed away, eyes nearly bulging from his head, rubbing fitfully at the flap of skin between his forefinger and thumb. Tesya trembled from head to toe.

"What's wrong with him now?" asked Shurg.

"He's not making any sense," Chayg said.

Nemon saw that Mema had taken on a sickly pallor, the sagging wrinkles of her skin hanging from her skull. At the old woman's temples and in the center of her forehead, veins pulsed like unearthed worms. In the sunken hollow at the base of her throat, something seemed to throb.

"They come from Memphis and Madrid. They go to Sydney, Dubai, Saigon! Next stop all aboard! Vienna!"

Yunnig gave Anith a dig in the ribs. "He's *your* brother, make him stop!"

"Za-a-ath, quit it!"

"The city, the city, the city that never sleeps! What happens in Vegas stays in Vegas! London bridge is falling down, falling down!"

"I mean it, Zath! I'll tell—"

Ignoring his sister, he turned to Mema. His smile was pure innocence, but something rippled in his eyes. In them, or behind them. A shifting, shimmering veil. "Did you think no one would notice you, old woman?"

Mema went paler yet, clutching at her thin chest. "Wh… what?"

"Moscow nonstop New York! Did you think you were unknown, unseen?"

"He's scaring me," Lut said, clinging to Mema's knee.

"*She* means to steal you from your home, you and Tesya there, steal you from your home and take you away forever, but *I* am scaring you? Copenhagen, Glasgow, Buenos Aires! Look on ye works, o mighty, and despair—"

"Zath?" Anith asked, sisterly severity giving way to genuine worry.

"I don't think he's Zath right now," Tesya said.

"Stop him," said Mema, in a harsh whisper. "He must be silenced."

Nemon took a step toward the boy, but before she could take another, he sprang away. His strange, rippling gaze met hers with an intensity that stunned her to the core. For a moment, he seemed calm, even reasonable.

"It was too late in Babylon," he said. "*Much* too late in Athens."

"What was too late?" Nemon heard herself ask, as if from very far away and through numb lips that did not feel like her own.

"No, Nemon! Do not listen—"

"It was too late already in *Jericho* and *Ur!*" With a final cackling cry, both hideous and triumphant, Zath clawed at the sides of his head. His fingers sank in knuckles-deep, popping through the skin.

The children screamed, stumbling and tumbling backward. Nemon felt mired in cold, sludgy mud. She could not move, could not even look away, as Zath worked his fingers deeper into his own flesh. The noise of it was a wet squishing; fluid too dilute and pale to be blood spurted from the wounds and trickled down his neck.

He peeled off the wholeness of his face like the rot-softened rind from a decaying fruit. Underneath was not a raw, flayed skull… nor a gaping hollow… but a slick mass of slimy bubbles and myriad glowing orbs. They oozed, bulging and receding, moving over and around each other in a strange, oily effluence.

More screams erupted all around her, but Nemon still could not move. She stared at the spreading horror birthing itself from the boy's collapsing form. Its smell was both bitter and sour, insinuating itself into her nose, coating her tongue and throat with a lingering foulness.

Above them, the gloom-darkened clouds grew even darker as immense shadow-shapes converged, and shifting lambent beams wavered through the mists. The air seemed to have thickened, become clammier with a tangible, gelatinous chill.

The beasts went mad in their harnesses. Some broke free and fled, crashing through mud-and-stick dwellings, trampling anyone in their path. Others fell, half-entangled, tipping sledge-rafts, kicking and biting.

Villagers and travelers alike succumbed to shrieking panic. Nemon saw from the corner of her eye Chayg and Shurg running in opposite directions, Anith on her knees sobbing, Oalthi abandoning her howling baby sister, Paulph diving into a much-too-shallow pond, Yunnig on the ground with his arms over his head.

The thing that had been Zath loomed up before her, bulbous and writhing. In its faint vile sheen, Nemon saw herself reflected untold times, reflected in mockeries and distortions. Mouthless now, voiceless, a loathsome gurgling hiss was its only speech... yet, somehow, she understood.

"You know what will happen if you do what she wants. They will die, you will die, in the end you all die. Why make it worse? Why such torment, such poison suffering? Let it fade. Let it be forgotten. It is the only kindness you have left, the only true gift you can give. Remembrance is pain. Hope is cruelty. Spare them."

All at once, Mema was there, Mema terribly illuminated in the questing rays of the Under-Seers, looking more ancient and haggard than ever. Tesya and Lut were by her side, each clutching precious relics of the gone-world tight in both hands. They, alone among the tumult, looked serene... hypnotized, almost spell-struck.

"Did I think no one would notice me?" Mema asked. "That I was unknown, unseen?" She laughed, fearless in the face of the monstrous entity before her. "You noticed, but you did not comprehend. You thought you knew, but you were wrong. You saw...

but you did not *see!*"

The Zath-thing recoiled in uncertainty. Under its slimy iridescence, orbs rolled and bubbles roiled. In the mist-thick clouds above, the coursing shadows hesitated. More of their beams converged, bathing the gloom in a seething, murky light.

"Take the children," Mema said, pushing them toward Nemon. "You are Keeper now. You know where to go."

"Where we took the others," she said, hefting Lut onto her hip and grasping Tesya's arm. Neither child resisted. "But, Mema—"

"Our comprehension is beyond yours, greater than you guess!" came another noxious, gurgling hiss from what had guised itself as a boy. *"If you had left them in dull nothingness, we might have let them live out their lives!"*

"Nemon, go!" The old woman suddenly stood taller, straighter than it seemed the bowed hunch of her spine should allow, and cast aside her scrap-hide robe.

"Instead, let them be consumed and dissolve a thousand years in the mindless madnesses Beyond!"

Nemon turned to run, pulling Tesya with her. Their feet slipped on rain-slick grass and splashed in sloppy mud. They hadn't gotten more than a few paces before the sounds of ripping meat and cracking gristle reached their ears.

"They *will* remember!" Mema cried from behind them. "They will rebuild, and they will *renew!*"

A keening screech of otherworldly agony split the air. Almost despite herself, Nemon risked a quick glance over her shoulder, and wished she hadn't.

The knobby hump on Mema's back had split apart, bones forced up in jagged quills strung with glistening strands of slime. From her temples, her brow, and the base of her throat, wormlike segmented lengths extruded, black eyes opening wetly at the ends of whip-thin stalks.

"And as for you—" The thing that had been Mema laughed again, as the thing that had been Zath writhed dripping in her grasp. "Now that you've revealed yourself, oh Over-Seer, you are *mine!* For we *were,* we *are,* we shall *always* be!"

Clinging to the children, as more shadows converged in a malevolent gathering above, Nemon, now Keeper of Memory, fled toward a promised future with no more looking back.

COPYRIGHT INFO:

ABOUT THE AUTHOR

After several recent difficult life-upheavals, Christine Morgan now resides in the California high desert, at her father's rustic and remote homestead. There, she's focusing on writing, editing, and reviewing, as well as continuing to dabble in weird crafts and baking. Her bedroom is dinosaur-themed, her bathroom shark-themed, and she spends most of her time getting bossed around by cats. Info about her various works can be found here: https://christine-mariemorgan.wordpress.com/

www.ingramcontent.com/pod-product-compliance
Lightning Source LLC
Chambersburg PA
CBHW020543020726
47494CB00006B/1892

the left hip and saw the reporter approaching him. The lights and the man with the minicam were right behind him. The reporter shoved the mike toward Wilt.

"Sheriff Drake ..."

"Not now," Wilt said. "I've got an investigation to conduct."

"Sheriff Drake ..."

"I'll talk to you in the morning when I know more. Now, if you'll cut off those lights and get in the van and ..."

"The people have a right to know what happened here tonight."

"They will know when the time is right," Wilt said.

"The little girl ... was she assaulted?"

"The people have a right to know that?" Wilt glared at him. "Before the medical examiner knows? Before her parents have been informed?" Wilt saw the impact, the way the reporter backed away a couple of steps. Wilt used that moment of uncertainty and grabbed the mike and tossed it to the camera operator. "You," he hissed at the reporter, "you get the fuck out of here before I break your head."

Doc pulled his slicker sleeve and dragged him away. "Easy, now you be easy."

He escorted Wilt to the medical examiner's car and pushed him into the passenger seat. He closed the door on Wilt and walked to the rear of the ambulance. Wilt rolled down the window and watched Doc as he oversaw the loading of the body into the ambulance. Near the television van, Joe was doing the interview the reporter wanted, filling in.

Doc trotted back to his car and got behind the wheel. He shivered and poured half a cup and slugged it down. Then he passed the thermos and the cup to Wilt.

The interview continued near the Van. Doc looked through the back window. "That bother you?"

"What?"

"The flair Joe has for courting the media."

"Should it bother me?" Wilt sipped the coffee mixture.

"It doesn't bother you, it doesn't bother me." But Doc gave Wilt an odd stare. "You leave me any?"

"Maybe a swallow." Wilt passed the cup.

Doc poured. "Nasty business down there. It was almost more than I could take and I thought I'd seen everything."

"Raped?"

Doc nodded slowly. "Vagina and rectum."

"Cause of death?"

"Strangulation or a blow or blows to the head."

Wilt took the thermos and shook it near his ear. It was almost empty. He drank from the mouth of the thermos. "The panties … where are they now?"

"In an evidence bag with the body." Doc drank the last drop. With a mock sad look on his face he capped the thermos. "Odd thing. I asked Joe if he'd gathered all the child's clothing. He said he had but he didn't find her underpants."

"A trade?"

"Maybe. Or maybe you'll find those underpants when you do your search in the morning."

Seven in the morning. That didn't seem far away, not with all he had to do and some sleep to fit in if he could find a time for it.

The lights went off at the television van. It was loaded and back on the road about as fast as he had arrived. Wilt looked over his shoulder and watched the dark shape of Joe Croft heading toward Wilt's cruiser. "You talk to Amos tonight?"

"I had about as close to a conversation as a man can have with a dumbass." He rolled down the window on his side of the car and tossed the soggy cigar stub away. "One favor Amos did you. He told me he'd send the Dobbs' preacher over to tell them about the death of their child."

"I knew Amos wouldn't do it himself."

"But he's all heart."

"One hundred percent." Wilt put his hand on the door handle. Now that he was warm he didn't want to leave the shelter of the car and step into the cold rain again. "I've got to confer with Amos. I guess tonight is as good a time as any."

"Don't confer. Advise. Amos doesn't know his armpit from a posthole about police work."

Wilt laughed. He felt lightheaded from the rotgut bourbon. "I quote you, Doc?"

"Do what you think best. It's no red off my candy what Amos thinks of me."

A pull at the door handle. Wilt stepped into the rain. "Call me tomorrow."

Doc nodded and waved.

Joe and Floyd waited for him in Wilt's cruiser, officially known as Car # 1. Wilt tipped his cap over his eyes and headed in that direction. It was time to give Floyd the bad news. He would stay at the crime scene until midnight or one. Then he'd be relieved by someone from the off-duty roster.

He settled that in his head.

A couple of minutes later, he left Floyd in Car # 2 to begin the watch. He let Joe drive his cruiser back to town while he slouched in the passenger seat with his eyes closed.

A few miles from town, after a silence that had lasted all the way from the Henshaw place, Joe looked around at Wilt. "What did Doc say about the little girl?"

Wilt shook his head. He didn't want to talk about it.

Joe let it drop.

After another minute or so Wilt sat up and looked at the approach to Edgefield. The lights of the growing town formed an ugly rainbow across the horizon.

CHAPTER FOUR

Chief Amos Wilson sat directly under the huge picture of himself as a Carolina football player. A can of Diet Pepsi was almost completely engulfed by a puffy hand with fingers like sausages. His jowls were spreading. His eyes were pale and watery. Red drinker's veins spotted his face and nose.

The other man in the Chief's office when Wilt came in was the mayor of Edgefield, Ben "Red" Colson, who was seated on the right side of his desk.

The office of mayor was mostly honorary. It was an unpaid job and it was passed around from one prominent townsman to another. Colson was in his late thirties. He was tan and slim and athletic. He was a Carolina graduate too, a former fraternity man who'd never grown past the glad-handing and the back-slaps. He could small talk with anyone about anything and he was equally at home in church praying or at some men's club telling a dirty joke.

The Colson family had been in business in Edgefield from the time real estate meant selling a downtown building or a home or a plot of farm land that would be used for farming. How well he'd done was obvious from his new offices that overlooked the town square.

Colson wore tan twill trousers and a British tweed hacking jacket with leather elbow patches. His lowcut black English boots were spotless, as if the weather outside hadn't bothered him.

Amos motioned Wilt to the other chair. After Wilt was seated Amos took a gulp of Diet Pepsi and belched softly. "Is it as bad as they say?"

"Worse." Wilt let it go at that.

"Doc Simpson called me. He said you might have some ideas how we could coordinate our efforts so we won't both be doing the same thing."

That was the Chief's way of asking for help, as close as he could force himself to ask with Mayor Colson listening to them. Wilt wasn't certain what Colson thought about Amos Wilson's abilities. If Colson had doubts, he kept them to himself.

He considered letting Amos squirm. It would be a payback for several slights he'd had at the hands of Amos. But that thought passed. The killing of the little girl was too awful to play politics with. He couldn't take the risk that, while he and Amos were having their petty war, the killer might use the time to cover his tracks.

"Like we talked about earlier ..."

Amos blinked and held his breath.

"... the first step is to send a team of policemen to the West Oak and 12th area, where the school bus dropped the little girl this afternoon. We need a door-to-door interviews. Did anyone see the red and white 1980 or 1981 Thunderbird? Did they see the driver? We need descriptions of anyone on the street around the time the girl was kidnapped ... anyone who might not have belonged there. Strangers. That kind of person. And it's got to be a real door-to-door. Every house, every apartment checked. If there's no one at home, the address has to be noted and there'll be a callback later. We've got to touch all the bases this early in the investigation."

Amos nodded. "I'll have a team there in twenty minutes."

"And there was that other idea you had, Amos. I think I'll go along with you. You handle the in-town part of it and I'll put two cruisers to work on the county part of the job." Wilt couldn't resist letting Amos sweat for a few seconds.

"What idea was that?" Amos fumbled. "We talked about so many."

"Gas stations," Wilt said. "If the man driving the Thunderbird lives in the town or the county, he's got to buy gas now and then."

"Oh yeah, *that* idea." Amos grinned.

"That's the one. Your men check every gas station within the city limits. Those outside fall to me. And again, no skips, no misses. Return trips when we have to. Until we've covered every station. One bit of luck and we get a description or we put together an identi-kit." Wilt stood. He could taste his boozy breath and he wondered if the smell carried across the desk to Amos or to the mayor. But the alcohol was wearing off and his hip was stiff. He could feel the pain from his knee to his shoulder, all down his left side. "We stay in touch. We share what we learn."

"That sounds good to me." Amos was relaxed, off the hook. He hadn't lost his credibility with Mayor Colson and he'd acquired the first two steps in the investigation. "Appreciate you stopping by, Wilt."

Colson followed Wilt toward the office door. "I assume everything's been taken care of at the Henshaw site."

"I've got men watching the crime scene tonight and first thing in the morning we give it our best close look to see if the killer got careless."

"I know you're doing your best, Sheriff." Mayor Colson extended a hand and gave Wilt his best tennis grip. "It's too bad the incident had to take place at the Henshaw site. It could have happened a hundred other places."

"If it had to happen at all." Then Wilt remembered that development of the property was the work of the Colson company. Colson had his money tied up in it as well as funds from out-of-state investors. The investors wouldn't be happy with the child molestation and killing at the still undeveloped property.

Wilt found his cap on the coat rack by the door. Water had run from it and pooled on the floor beneath it. "Six o'clock comes early. I've got to tie up some loose ends, get my supper and a few hours of sleep."

Colson followed Wilt from the office. Outside, Wilt turned and saw Amos Wilson still at his desk. The meeting, he guessed, was not over yet.

Colson stepped close to Wilt, so close the cologne or after-shave gagged him. "Let's get that cocksucker," he said in a low voice. "For the good of the town."

And to wipe the stain off the Henshaw property.

"I'll do my best," Wilt said.

Colson's tanned hard hand patted his shoulder and remained there until Wilt walked away from it.

Wilt sat in his cruiser in a space outside the Police Department. He felt the weight of the day, the bitterness of the evening, and he couldn't find the energy to move. The gut-deep well of energy that he usually had just seemed to dry up. The pump had stopped. And the rain that pounded the car's roof reminded him of his childhood and rain on a tin roof and being very small and very warm, at a time when the whole world seemed stretched out before him. All he had to do was reach out...

That against the reality of now.

The restlessness was in him, the go-to-hell. But he knew he was too old, too settled for that. He didn't have the flow, the gush, the river running in him.

One person. Diane. He wanted to see her, but he knew that an interest in her would compromise him. Between the time he revealed it, and the Biker Mafia tried to use it against him, that was only a finger-snap or the blink of an eye. Only a matter of time before they decided they could buy him by the pound, badge and balls and all.

It would be better for him to drive to Raleigh, where he wasn't known. Better even to see Widow Thumb and her four daughters at the whorehouse there. Anything but stepping into that honey trap when he knew better.

But Diane was the only woman who'd interested him since his ex-wife Mary Ellen left him while he was recuperating in a California army hospital from the sniper shot that blew out his hip.

Oh, there'd been other women. He wasn't a monk. But this one, for all the absurdity that was involved with it, was the only one that made him think there could be more to a relationship than a grope, a fumble and a few grunts in the dark.

He'd reached for the ignition. He'd just have a drink. And if Diane was there, he'd say his hello and that would be all there was to it.

A hello didn't compromise a man. A hello didn't commit a man to anything. Not even to saying hello the next time he saw her.

CHAPTER FIVE

Wilt parked as close as he could to the entrance to the Blue Lagoon. The rain had slowed some. There was a chill wind across the open parking lot.

He stepped from the cruiser as soon as he switched off the engine. Any delay and he might change his mind. He might back and turn and roar toward town.

You're on parade, he told himself. On fucking parade, no matter how you feel. And by the time he reached the door to the Blue Lagoon, he'd adjusted his stride so that the limp hardly showed at all.

A fleshy man with a scraggly red beard was behind the counter just inside the entrance. He wore a new black leather jacket without a club insignia. He was counting bills into a cashbox when Wilt reached the counter. He didn't look up. "That'll be three dollars door fee," he said.

Wilt dislodged a few drops of rain from his cap by slapping it against his leg. He didn't offer the three dollars.

"I said that'd be three dollars…" Irritation clouded the big man's voice. But he broke off when he looked up and saw Wilt. "Oh, it's you, Sheriff. Walk on in."

"Even if it's not business, Kyle?"

"Especially if it's not business."

Wilt nodded. He circled the bar and moved past it. The outer room had three pool tables. A couple of players at the nearest table looked at him, at the yellow slicker, and went on with their game. At the middle table a sallow, balding man in blue coveralls stepped away from a shot he'd lined up and racked his stick. He tossed a crumpled five on the table and said, "I'm running late."

Wilt watched the man leave. He didn't know the man and he didn't fit any of the descriptions of men who were on the wanted list. It was more likely the man was afraid he'd be pulled with booze on his breath and wanted a head start. The new state laws on drinking and driving were scaring a lot of people.

At the counter, Kyle shook his head. "You're ruining my business."

Wilt stepped back to the counter. "There are a lot of ways to ruin a man's business. That was one of the easy ones."

"A brag," Kyle said.

"A fact." Wilt held Kyle's eyes until Kyle lowered his head and began counting again. "Not ready to go the whole way, Kyle?"

Head still lowered, Kyle said, "I'll let you know when, Sheriff."

Time. In time.

Wilt turned and moved to the doorway that led to main part of the club. He stopped here and unsnapped the slicker. The dancers weren't on yet. But it wouldn't be long. Wilt could see the head and shoulders of the man in the sound booth, the one who announced the dancers and played the tapes. He was hunched over with a cigarette pasted to his bottom lip and smoke curling upward into his eyes.

The stage faced the doorway where Wilt stood. It was roughly thirty feet wide and somewhere between fifteen and twenty feet deep. There were narrow walkways from the wings on each side of the stage. Four thick posts supported a canopy where the colored lights were concealed.

The main seating was in tiers, small tables on the levels down the center and booths on both sides. Nearer the stage, at the edges on all sides, there were bar stools and a narrow bar counter where the customers there could place their drinks.

Even early, several of the tables and booths were taken. And what seemed to be college students had taken some of the bar stool close to the stage.

Wilt settled on a table near the center halfway toward the stage. It was cool enough so he decided to keep his slicker on. The uniform might run some more of the customers away. He placed his cap in the chair beside him and waited for one of the waitresses to take his order.

The waitress approached him from behind. Her recital was by rote. "The show starts in ten minutes. What'll you have ?"

He looked over his shoulder at her. Her face was down, eyes intent on a stack of guest checks. "How about a bourbon on ice, Erlene?"

The waitress circled the table and stared at him. "Wilton … it's you?"

They'd been in high school together. He'd been in the 12th grade and she'd been in the 9th. He'd been the big man on the high school campus, basketball and baseball and she'd been timid and shy, with the look that said she had a crush on him.

He hadn't seen her since high school and to tell the truth he hadn't even thought about her. No, that wasn't true. Four or five months ago, he'd heard that Erlene's husband had done a backwoods buck and wing and left town, leaving Erlene with two kids, on welfare and food stamps.

"I didn't know you worked here." It wasn't a good thought, her working for the bikers. Not with all the crap that was usually a part of the job. But as he looked her up and down, he decided that it wouldn't be as hard on her as it would be with some girls. Faded the way she was, age and the weariness on her, it wasn't likely she'd be hassled for more than a cut of her tips. That was much better than the way it was if the girl was young and the bikers thought the girl's flesh had some commercial value.

"I started last week," Erlene said. A sad shake of her shoulders. "A girl's got to eat, Wilton."

"There's no problem if they treat you alright."

Her voice was low. "They haven't been bad to me or anything."

Wilt motioned her closer. "You tell me if it gets rough. And just to be on the safe side, let it be known you're a good old friend to the Sheriff."

"Thanks, Wilton." She started to move away. "You're not here on business tonight, are you?"

"If it was business, I wouldn't want that drink," he said. "If I ever get it."

"Sure, Wilton. Sorry." She gave him a trembling smile and rushed away.

Wilt waited a count of five and looked over his shoulder. It was as he'd expected. Two bikers had Erlene cornered in the doorway. One blocked the entrance to the bar. The other one caught her arm. The one holding Erlene's arm asked something. Erlene answered and shook her head. The biker released her arm. The other one stepped out of her way. Erlene scooted past them and into the bar.

The bikers stood shoulder-to-shoulder and stared at Wilt. He met their eyes and, before it became a contest, he turned away. It wasn't worth it. Cheap rooster cock games and those didn't prove anything.

When Erlene brought his drink, she leaned over him and said, "Kyle wants you to know it's Black Jack Daniels and it's on the house."

"Thank Kyle for me." He dropped a couple of ones on her tray. "And thank you too."

"Aw, Wilt, you don't have to do that."

"A girl's got to eat," he said.

She backed away and scamped to the next table. Wilt had a swallow. It was Daniels but he couldn't tell for sure that it was Black Jack. Another swallow and he left the table and headed for the bank of phones beside the Men's Room. He dialed the Sheriff's Station. Joe Croft answered at the switchboard.

"I'm at the Blue Lagoon."

"I had a feeling. It was a look you had."

"You're too smart to be just a chief deputy."

"I know," Joe said.

"Hey, don't agree with me so fast."

"Yes, boss."

"You need me, you call the bar. Kyle knows I'm here. I'll check in before I head home."

"Enjoy yourself. It's a slow night. I called in Frank Boyle and put him to checking all the gas stations that are still open. He called in a few minutes ago. Nothing so far."

"Call me if you need me."

"That Blue Lagoon. I got to make a run there with you one night."

"I'll send you in undercover one night," Wilt said.

"Make the plans," Joe said.

Wilt was on his second drink when the house lights dimmed and the colored ones came up hot and bright. The M. C., the one in the sound booth, wasted no time with the introduction. "Ladies and gentleman, the Blue Lagoon wants you to welcome Tanya."

A leggy blonde in cowboy boots, a ten-gallon hat, a vest and a skirt made to look like fringed buckskin pranced in from the wings to the right and started a dance that was half shuffle and half walk. At the end of the first number, timed to fit it, she tossed away the vest and stepped out of the skirt. Her breasts were long and pear-like. The bikini bottom was narrow at the crotch. It was pulled high so the buttocks were almost bare. There was a hand-shaped bruise powdered over on her right cheek.

Erlene passed Wilt's table on the tier below him. He motioned toward her. Erlene stopped. "Another one, Wilton?"

"Is Diane working tonight?"

"Miss Mills? I don't think she's dancing tonight." A turn and she looked at the doorway near the corner of the room, to the left of the stage, "I think she's in her office."

"Where?"

Erlene pointed. "Where that man's sitting."

There was a man seated there on high-backed bar stool. He was young and thick-shouldered with the neck of a weight lifter. Thick arms were crossed over his chest. His eyes roved the crowd. Each sweep ended with a lengthy stare at the dancer. His eyes were those of a snake watching a bird.

Wilt tucked his cap under his arm and picked up his drink. He headed toward the door and the young man who guarded it. He was four steps away from the door when the man edged forward on his stool seat.

"Nothing for you over here."

Wilt stopped. "You wanna bet?"

The young man tipped his head. "The pisser's over there or you can leave the same way you came in."

"Miss Mills," Wilt said.

"She can't see you."

Wilt stepped around him. He grabbed the doorknob. "She'll see me."

The young man looked him up and down. He looked at the uniform pants that showed below the slicker and the cap crushed under Wilt's arm. "You law?"

"County," Wilt said. He pulled the front of the slicker aside so that the badge and the uniform jacket showed. "You going to stop me?"

The young man hesitated. "Kyle know you're here?"

"He knows I'm in the club. That's all."

"I guess you can go on up." The man settled back onto the bar stool.

Wilt opened the door and found a narrow staircase leading up one flight. He started his climb. No matter how bad the pain was, he didn't let the left leg drag.

The man behind him cleared his throat. "And … knock."

"I always do," Wilt said. "That's to show I've got manners."

The man put out a huge hand and slammed the door shut between them. Wilt grinned to himself and grabbed the bannister to support his hip. Climbing steps wasn't his favorite kind of exercise.

He was sweating when he reached the landing. The door was straight ahead. He stopped and wiped his forehead with his hand. While he waited for his breath to even, he looked around. There was a hall and an entrance way to his right. A flimsy bead curtain hung there. Any shift of air set the glass beads to clattering.

Wilt walked to the curtain and used a hand to peel a section away and create an opening. There wasn't much to see. Only another hallway and closed doors facing each other.

Wilt released the curtain so the beads didn't clatter. He returned and stood facing the closed office door while he took a few deep breaths. A taste of the Daniels and he thought he was ready.

He knocked. After a few seconds he heard footsteps.

"Yes?"

"It's Wilt."

"Who?"

"The Sheriff." That tore it. She didn't even know his name. "I was just passing by."

The lock rasped. The door opened a few inches and then spread wide. Diane stepped back and released the doorknob. "Just passing by and you couldn't find a phone anywhere?"

"Don't use your spurs on me." He brushed past her and stopped in the center of the room. "It's been a rotten day." A subtle perfume he couldn't identify brushed at him.

It was a wallboard office. There was no attempt at decoration. No paintings, no prints. Even the paint job on the wallboard was the bare minimum, a single coat that hadn't done much to disguise the texture of the walls. The furniture was from any of a dozen discount stores. There was a pine desk, a captain's chair behind it and a leatherette-covered lounge chair to one side. "Who's your decorator?"

"Army surplus," she said. She turned and closed the door with a firm push.

"My decorator too," he said. He realized he hadn't really looked at her yet. It was time. He put his weight on his good leg, his right, and swung around to face her.

Diane Mills was tall, about five-six or seven. Dressed, she looked thinner and more fragile than she really was. Undressed, there was that beautiful body with the colors on it as surely as any biker ever wore colors on his jacket. He saw it each time he watched her dance. The tattoo of an open road heading into the horizon that began high on her right shoulder and flowed downward and covered the top half of her breast. Maybe that meant she was a biker mama or had been. At least that was what he'd heard.

He guessed her age at thirty and he didn't think he was off one year on either side of the line. It was the special kind of beauty that caught him. The beauty, he'd heard one fellow Marine officer say, that was a woman at her full ripeness, the high arc that lasted a few years before she had to fight off the years.

Tonight, she wore designer jeans and a white soft wool sweater. She seemed shorter and he realized she was in stockinged feet. Her boots were lined up in front of the desk.

She'd been smiling. But as his appraisal lengthened the smile vanished and a thoughtful look replaced it. "The way you're looking at me … did you think I was dancing tonight?"

"It wouldn't hurt my feelings any if you stopped dancing altogether."

The smile returned. "And give up show business?"

"So that's what it is."

She circled the desk and stood in front of the chair. It was, he decided, a move to put space and a solid object between them. "I understand Erlene is an old friend."

"We go back to high school." He tossed his cap on her desk. When she didn't sit, he moved to the lounge chair and eased into it. "Word travels fast out here."

"Kyle called me."

"Let's see how the plot went. Erlene finds out I'm not here on business. She tells the two bikers who put the question to her in the doorway. The bikers pass the word to Kyle. Kyle calls you because if I'm not here on business then I must be here to see you. Am I close?"

"Me?" She laughed and batted her eyelashes at him. "You came to visit little me? I'm not immodest enough to believe that."

"Kyle probably believes it."

Diane shrugged.

"The truth is you do interest me."

"No, I bother you. You don't know what I am yet. You don't know how to classify me."

The conversation had drifted in a direction he didn't like. He took a deep breath and a jolt of the Daniels in preparation for getting to his feet. "And when I decide?"

"One of two things happen. You make a grab for me or you bust the club because you've decided I'm a hooker."

"Only two choices?" He used the edge of the desk to pull himself to his feet. "I thought there was at least one other possibility." He hesitated and got his balance. "It must be great to have all the answers."

"No, it's not."

"You went to college … where?"

"Coker … that's in South Carolina. A girl's school that teaches a young woman to be a proper lady."

"I never heard of it."

"I'm not surprised." Her hair, when she was under the gels on stage, appeared to have a copper glint to it. In normal light, it seemed softer, blonde with a mild red tint to it. Her eyes were the pale green of a watermelon rind.

RALPH DENNIS

"Take some time off. Let's have a drink or a coffee somewhere."

It was the third time he'd asked her. The other two times had been nights she'd danced. Now, for a long moment, he thought she'd refuse again.

"Why not?" A dip of her head. "It's a slow night." She circled the desk and put on her boots.

Wilt looked around and found a dark tan trenchcoat on a wall peg near the door. He held the coat while she slipped her arms into the sleeves. He followed her outside and waited while she locked the door. When she turned for the stair, he stopped her with a touch of his hand.

"What's down there?"

"The brothel." She moved away from his hand. "Isn't that what you think?"

"Just so nobody lives there. It's against Beverage Control laws for anyone to live on the premises where alcohol is sold."

"Is that right?"

"That's the law," he said.

"But it's alright for me to have dressing rooms where the dancers change into costume."

"Sure."

The young man stepped down from the bar stool and gave Diane a questioning look. "Everything alright, Miss Mills?"

"No problem, Marky." A wave of her hand toward him and she led Wilt through the audience. She stopped at the entrance way and ran her eyes over the audience, as if doing a rough count of the customers.

The dancer on the stage had long black hair and a body out of a Rubens painting. Diane looked at Wilt and then down at the stage. "That's Rachel. She's new."

"But old from somewhere."

"Aren't we all?"

At the bar, he stood back a distance while Diane had a whispered conversation with Kyle. Kyle, his eyes on Wilt the whole

30

time, nodded a time or two. The eyes were in shadow and Wilt couldn't read much into that stare.

It was still raining when they stepped outside. A shiver ran the length of her when the first gust of wind struck her. She leaned back against him. "You sure we have to go out for this drink?"

"Don't be a baby." He opened passenger door of his cruiser and waited while she seated herself. Before he could step back and close the door she said. "Aren't you curious? Don't you want to know why I pointed Rachel out to you?"

"If it's important, you'll tell me."

"She available. Kyle could send her to you. It would be a freebie."

"How about you? Would Kyle send ...?"

"Nobody sends me anywhere. Ever. But Rachel ...."

"No pimping." He closed the door.

During the drive she leaned back, her legs tucked under her. Her arms hugged her chest. Her eyes were barely open. He could see a bright gleam from her slitted eyes. Involved in her, concerned for her, he wasn't even sure where he was going. His mind wasn't on a drink or where they would have it. Driving by reflex, this way and that, until he was sure he was lost. Then he reached a dirt road and he wasn't lost anymore. Smiling to himself, he continued on the road until it dead-ended.

He'd parked on a ledge that overlooked the lake. It had been a long time since he'd been there and almost that long since he'd thought about the lake. That was over twenty years ago when it was a favorite high school petting place. He remembered, with a rush, a party he and his pals had there with their girls the night they graduated from high school.

He switched off the headlights. He put both hands on the steering wheel. He shifted the muscles in his back. A long day, a very long day.

"Where are we?"

"Dead Woman's Lake." It hadn't always been called that. It had been Harper's Lake until the body of the woman from Durham floated to the surface one day. Her throat had been cut from ear-to-ear. From that time on it had been called Dead Woman's Lake, until even the area maps listed it that way.

"What a romantic place to bring a girl."

"You're not a girl. You're full grown." He cracked the window an inch or two and reached for his Chesterfields, "I thought a visit here might get your attention."

"I'm not a girl and you want my attention?" Diane kicked out her legs like they'd gone to sleep. She sat forward and stared at the rain sheeting on the windshield. "Let me make a guess."

"Make two or three. They're free." He lit the Chesterfield and blew the smoke toward the window opening.

"I think this is the moment when I melt into your arms…."

He laughed. "Sounds good so far."

"We kiss with passion …"

He didn't interrupt.

"My breath grows uneven…"

A strong wind blew leaves against the hood. They scuttled across with the sound of crabs.

"You unzip your fly…"

He whipped his head around and stared at her.

"And I give you the blowjob of your life."

He pushed the cigarette through the narrow opening. He leaned forward and twisted the ignition. He backed down the wet road until he found an opening where he could make his turn.

During the drive back to the Blue Lagoon, she huddled against the door, head down, and her eyes closed. He pulled into the parking lot and parked the cruiser as close to the entrance as he could. She didn't move.

He got out and walked around to the passenger door. He opened the door and waited. She opened her eyes and stared at him for a long time before she swung her legs around and stepped from the car.

He walked beside her to the door. "What if I'd said, yes, it was time for you to melt into my arms ...?"

"You won't know now, will you?"

"But Rachel's still available?"

She didn't answer. He stood and watched the club door close behind her.

The cruiser was full of her perfume all the way back into town. Even lowering a window didn't sweep it away.

Five minutes after he reached his apartment and called in to the Station he was in bed. He was asleep a few seconds later.

CHAPTER SIX

The rain ended sometime during the early morning hours. There was a dull rattle on the bathroom window when Wilt's bladder awoke him. By six, after he'd shaved and showered, he stood in the cramped kitchen and drank a cup of coffee and listened to the grim howl of the wind that followed the rain.

The sky, gray and boiling with angry clouds, suggested snow but it didn't snow often in Webster County. The cutoff line for snow was probably Greensboro. East of that city, it was more likely to be rain or ice rain.

Joe Croft called while he was dressing. They arranged to meet at the Henshaw place. That would save a drive into town later in the day.

"Bring your own coffee," Joe said.

"Bring your own Bromo."

"I didn't have that kind of night."

"What other kind of night is there?" Wilt laughed and broke the connection.

Joe's cruiser was parked next to the barn. Wilt pulled in next to it. He carried a thermos he'd filled at a 7–11 back on the highway. He found Joe standing beside the tarp they'd left to cover the spot where the little girl's body had been found. Water pooled on the surface of the tarp and the rain had been so steady that it had seeped under at the edges.

Joe drank from a pint milk carton. He lowered it and wiped his mouth. "I sent Floyd home when he was relieved at one by Frank. He's due back at nine. I relieved Frank about ten minutes ago. He'll check back at two or three, according to how he feels." Another swallow from the milk carton. "That arrangement suit you?"

Wilt said it did. "But it means a lot of overtime."

"Maybe not. If this breaks open early, we can give time off and shave the bulge as much as we can."

Wilt walked around the tarp and faced Joe across it. "Let me know when it slows down. I'd like a long weekend off myself." He leaned over. "Ready?"

They worked the dry space under the covering first. A careful search produced nothing. Then, starting at the outer edges of the dry area, they moved in ever-widening circles, heads down, kicking at the ground debris. After a time, fifty yards or so had been searched. Wilt leaned against a pecan tree and shook his head. "I don't know which is worse."

Joe lifted his head. "Huh?"

"Believing all that Sherlock Holmes crap. That there are clues all over the place and all I have to do is find them. Or knowing better. Knowing that there aren't any clues that matter. That this bastard'll get caught when he runs a red light and gets stopped. This cop is writing the ticket and he looks at the car and he asks himself, *now wasn't there something about a red and white Thunderbird?*"

"But, since we're already here..." Joe said.

They spent over another hour in their search pattern. Wilt poked and kicked his way through wind drifts of leaves while Joe worked low scrub and bush. They found old wine and beer bottles with the labels rotted away, some rusted steel cans and even some cans that looked like they'd only been in the weather a few days. There were Kentucky Fried Chicken boxes and Whopper containers and the flat shapes of pizza boxes.

At eight-thirty, Wilt called it off.

Joe followed Wilt to Car #1 and waited while the Sheriff worked his leg into the right position. If Wilt's difficulty bothered him, his face didn't show it. He watched while Wilt poured coffee into the cup-top and gulped a swallow or two.

"I've got a list of the gas stations that were checked last night," Joe said. "I thought I'd go on with the rounds, if that's alright with you."

"Might as well. I'll have breakfast and see if Chief Amos is in his office yet."

"After that, you'll be at the Station?"

"And I've got to see Doc about the autopsy."

Joe shook his head slowly, "I'd rather wrestle a sick bear in a grease pit."

"Good country image," Wilt said.

They split at the secondary highway. Wilt headed toward town, Joe pointed his cruiser deeper into the county.

Wilt ordered his usual at the Egg 'n' Biscuit Cafe and he was so tired he couldn't, for the life of him, remember what the usual was until the counter woman, Edna, placed a plate with scrambled eggs, salt cured ham, grits and two toasted corn muffins before him.

He loafed over a third cup of coffee.

Once, looking up suddenly, he found Edna watching him with a curious smile. He paid his check and left and he was a block from the Cafe before he realized what the smile was about.

They'd been eight that summer, both of them, and he and Edna went into the woods and played "doctor." Now, from the distance of time, he couldn't remember what there had been about her that interested him. Probably nothing. Probably just a body.

A body. He almost stopped dead in his tracks. A surprising flush burned his face. Diane's body. On that beautiful body, her tattoo was as awful a scar as the one that puckered his left hip. Her scar and his, neither of them, he thought, with any real honor involved. Hers for some reason that he didn't care to speculate about. His in that peace action in Lebanon. He'd been standing beside a jeep having a smoke when a sniper, probably using a scope, put a round through his hip. It hadn't been a war, there wasn't the glory the Marines believed in. Only dirt in his mouth on a road and the terrible, terrible pain that never ended. A steady gnawing pain.

Screw it. After last night, he wasn't sure there would be any pleasure visits to the Blue Lagoon. The next time he went there, it would be to bust heads for drug sales or gambling or the girls. Or to check the rumors there were after-hours beer and booze sales. It would be easy enough to spot. And if the rumor checked out, he would alert the ABC and have them try a bust. If the bust held up, there went the license and the club closed and all those assholes in leather jackets could move on. Laughing out of the other side of their mouths. Not the way they'd probably laughed last night when Diane told her funny story about what happened last night at Dead Woman's Lake.

The flush returned.

Let them laugh while they could.

Amos Wilson arrived at the Police Station ten minutes after Wilt got there. He was puffing hard, as if he'd run from his parking space out front. Wilt settled into a chair in the Chief's office while Amos stopped off at the bathroom to catch his breath and run a wet paper towel over his face.

They spent the first few minutes comparing notes on the investigation so far. The checks of the gas station within the town had uncovered nothing and the door-to-door in the west oak Street and 12th area had drawn a blank as well.

Wilt drew an ashtray toward him and lit his first smoke of the day. "Garages too," he said.

"What about them?"

"Let's throw in garages too, the legitimate ones and the shade tree ones. We do the same split as before. You in town, us with the county."

"I don't see..."

"We can slice the list to garages that do car inspections. And hand out stickers. Every car's got to have one. Could be we'll be lucky."

"It can't hurt." But Amos didn't sound convinced.

"In a case like this, it's always better to do too much rather than too little. Say we skip a step that might have solved this. Instead of being behind bars, he's out there killing another child. I won't live with that."

"Garages. Alright." Amos made a note on a pad.

Wilt mashed his cigarette and headed for the door. "One more thought. If you've got a free patrol car, you might have them cruise the grammar school when it lets out. Have them watch for a red and white Thunderbird."

"You think that'll do any good?"

"Maybe not, but it'll make me feel better. And I need something to make me feel better. I keep thinking about the woman's underpants at the crime scene. It might be a fetish, some kind of sickness. If this man's out of control, it might happen again."

"You know what?" Amos' face brightened. "We could hold a press conference and go on TV tonight."

"And what do we say?"

"I'll warn the parents that we've got a sex pervert here in town."

Wilt gave him his hard look. "There's no reason to start a panic. These parents are scared enough already. If I were you,

I'd stroke them, calm them. Just say that it might be better if mothers walked their children to the bus stops and waited with them until they boarded the bus. And that they ought to meet their children at the bus stops when they return in the afternoon."

"Calls I've been getting, there's already panic here in town."

"That's the best reason to be calm. In a panic everybody starts acting crazy. First thing you know, some worried father shoots some innocent man who just happens to be in the wrong place at the wrong time. An insurance man who's trying to sell a policy or a door-to-door salesman."

Amos agreed reluctantly. "If I do the conference, I'll calm them."

"That's the ticket."

"But what happens if another child is killed?"

"That happens, we're in trouble." Wilt felt a sickness in his stomach. "And it could happen."

On his way from the Police Station he stopped at the drugstore and bought a copy of the *Edgefield Herald*. He carried the paper outside and stood in the windbreak formed by the entrance and the jutting display windows.

The death of Cathy Dobbs and the investigation were the headline stories of the day. There were no details of the rape and really no mention that there had been a rape. That was the *Herald*'s editorial policy: nothing terrible or dishonest ever happened in the little village of Edgefield.

And there, at the end of the article, what Wilt couldn't control: the interview with Chief Amos Wilson. The lies: *our investigation is underway and we are pursuing leads that should result in an arrest in the next few days.* And the boasting; *most people don't know what a modern, efficient police department we have here in*

Edgefield. Criminals ought to think twice before they commit a crime in my town.

Wilt tossed the paper in a trash container on the street and drove to the Sheriff's Station. On his way through the lobby, Susie shook her head at him: there had been no calls.

"See if you can reach Doc Simpson for me."

He'd hardly settled into the chair behind his desk when she buzzed him. Wilt picked up the phone. Doc started talking as if they had already been in middle of a conversation.

"I'm not completely done," Doc Simpson said, "but I can tell you the major part of it."

"Cause of death?"

"Suffocation."

"He choked her?"

"That's what I thought at first. You remember those women's panties? On a hunch, I ran a test on the cloth. I found dried traces of saliva that matches samples taken from the child's mouth."

"I didn't know you could do those crime lab tests."

"It's easy if you've got a Dick Tracy crime kit." Doc said.

"So you think he stuffed the panties in her mouth to quiet her?"

"From the pattern of bruises, he stuffed them down as far as her tonsils."

"Tell me the rest."

"I've got a few more points to cover. Maybe half an hour. I'd rather write up the report and send it over to you."

"Fine by me," Wilt said. "I know how you feel."

"Hell, I've got a grandchild her age."

Wilt said he understood. He broke the connection and sat with his eyes closed for a time.

The morning dragged along. A few minutes before noon, Joe Croft called in.

CHAPTER SEVEN

Gus Triffon was short and wide-shouldered. He was in his late forties. His face was round and lumpy and there was a child-like expression he wore most of the time that deceived people into thinking he was simple. He wasn't simple at all, just contented.

Today that look was gone. He looked puzzled as he sat in the gas station office with Wilt and Joe.

There was a smear of grease on Gus's chin. He worried the cuts from two barked knuckles on his right hand.

The gas station had been in the Triffon family since Gus's immigrant grandfather saved enough from his years in the food business and bought the garage and filling station. Once, years ago, the old man told Wilt that he'd grown tired of smelling like cooking grease. He'd decided that gas and oil and grease had a more honest smell. The station, after the death of his grandfather and the disabling stroke that his father had, passed into Gus Triffon's hands four or five years ago.

Joe passed Wilt a covered cup of coffee, "I got these down the road while I waited for you."

Wilt perched on the edge of the desk in the station, the left hip carefully positioned to take the weight and strain off it. "Tell me about the red and white Thunderbird, Gus."

"It was a week ... maybe ten days ago. This 1981 Thunderbird pulls in. The driver wants five dollars gas and the oil checked."

"You notice the tag numbers?"

"No reason for me to," Gus said. "He paid cash."

"North Carolina tags?"

Gus closed his eyes. The strain of concentrating contorted his face. "I can't say for sure, Sheriff."

"Tell me what you remember about the driver."

"He was maybe thirty, a year either way."

"What else?"

"He was dressed...well, fancy. Black boots, those kind of shoes, and trousers with a knife crease to them. A black turtle-neck sweater. He wore a coat that looked like a raincoat but he was shorter and didn't go past his hips. And the lady in the car with him..."

"What lady?" Joe Croft looked surprised.

Wilt moved from the desk top so quickly he spilled some of the coffee. "You didn't say anything about a woman."

"I guess I forgot to tell about her. Anyway, she was maybe fifty. Gray hair but it was fixed fancy."

"How was she dressed?"

"Those expensive jeans..."

"Designer jeans."

Gus nodded. "And a full-length leather coat that probably cost four or five hundred dollars."

"Anything else about her?"

"Too much makeup. A lot of rouge and lipstick. Real dark eye makeup."

"Shape of her face, Gus?"

"Well...swollen."

"Huh?"

"Puffy, the way a woman's face gets when she's older."

Needs a facelift. "You saw the man and woman together. You think they might have been related? Mother and son?"

"I don't think so."

"Why not?"

"It's this way," Gus said. "He buys the five dollars gas. I check the oil but he don't need any. He give me a twenty. I go to the office to make change. I come back to give him his change and I see something."

"What?"

"The woman's rubbing her hand on the inside of his leg. Up near where his *business* is."

Older woman, young man. That new social tapdance. Wilt gulped his coffee. Well, why not? Wasn't turnabout fair play?

Joe Croft edged in, the notebook in his hand. "Give me the best description of the man you can."

"Like what?"

"How tall?"

"Six feet."

Everybody is six feet tall. At least, all the witnesses think they are. Wilt got a Chesterfield from his shirt pocket and lit it.

"Hair color?"

"Sort of brown. A light brown."

"Color of his eyes?"

"I didn't see them. He wore those wraparound sunglasses."

"Shape of his face?"

"Long and narrow. Thin."

"Kind of skin?"

"Pale, real white."

"Notice any scars?"

"A lot of them," Gus said.

"What?"

"Little places here and here." Gus touched his cheekbones.

"Acne?"

"The little pits. From bad skin."

"Any acne now?"

"Not that I saw," Gus said. "Just the dried pits."

Wilt looked around. He couldn't find an ashtray. He had another swallow of coffee and dropped the cigarette butt in the coffee. "This man and woman ... you think you'd recognize them if you saw them again?"

"Maybe not the woman, but I'd know the man for sure."

"Why?" Wilt knew the station was busy. A lot of cars and people passed through. Wilt knew the answer might be important later. It was the kind of question a defense lawyer asks.

"He was snotty, that's why."

"How?"

"He got the key to the rest room. He goes in there while I'm pumping his gas. He comes back a minute later and he screams at me that it is the dirtiest toilet he's ever been in. I tried to tell him that my cleaning man ain't been in yet but he's not listening. He shouts at me that the toilet ain't been cleaned for a month. So I just keep my mouth shut and let him wear himself out."

Wilt nodded. That would wash in court. "Set a time when Gus can come in and make a statement."

"What am I making now?"

"I mean one we can get typed up and signed." Wilt walked outside. The wind was drying the air, pushing the rain that had been over the area toward the coast. But it was cold, very cold.

Wilt dumped his coffee cup in a trashcan and got into the cruiser. A few minutes later Joe joined him. He leaned on the roof of Car # 1 and bent his head toward the open window.

"He'll come in at two-thirty or three, when his nephew relieves him."

"I hear the Police have an Ident-i-kit they've never used."

"That's the word."

"Who handles it for Amos?"

"I think Johnny Ferrell took the lessons."

"You know him?"

"Pretty well," Joe said.

"I can talk Amos into letting us use the kit. I want you to sit in and make sure it's good work, that it's not slipshod. You do that without hurting Johnny's feelings?"

"I think I can."

Gus Triffon stood in the doorway. He took a step toward them and stopped.

"I'd rather do it at our place. If Amos won't go for that, you'll have to work at the Police Department."

"Why make a case over it? We'll do it at their place and not ruffle any fur. Let the Chief think he's in charge."

"Sly," Wilt said. "You've got that streak."

"Not me, Sheriff."

"You ever get sly with me?"

"Not often."

"But you stroke me now and then?"

"Hardly ever. You've got thorns."

Wilt laughed. He was rolling the window up when Gus left the doorway and headed toward them. Wilt waited. There was always a chance that Gus remembered something else about the people in the Thunderbird.

"This is about that little girl, ain't it?"

Wilt said it was.

"This happens in Greece … the man who did it … they'd cut off his *business* and stuff it down his throat. This man … I knew as soon as I …"

"Gus," Wilt said, "driving a red and white Thunderbird isn't a crime. We don't know for sure that this is the man we're looking for."

"Well …"

"Keep this to yourself until we know for sure, one way or the other."

"Whatever you say, Sheriff."

On the drive into town, Wilt laughed to himself. The first humorous moment since the call came in the day before about little Cathy Dobbs. That Joe Croft. Saying he didn't stroke but doing it in such a way that it was, even in the denial, a masterful stroking.

Election was still a year away. He'd have to keep an eye on young Joe Croft. Maybe he'd learned enough. Maybe he'd decided that it was time for him to sit in the big chair in the office.

Joe wouldn't be a bad choice. But it would happen only when Wilt decided he'd had enough of the job. He had no plans to be pushed out by a new kid.

The new kid would have to wait his turn.

CHAPTER EIGHT

Susie flagged him down and passed him the brown envelope with his name written on it in the old looping Palmer penmanship method. "Doc said for you to call him if there was anything you needed explained."

Wilt stared at it. He didn't want to read any part of it. But that went with the job. The bad days that ruined the memory of the good ones.

"And this." Susie smiled and held out a memo sheet. "A woman called. She wouldn't give her name."

Wilt looked at the number. It didn't mean anything to him. "What's the smile for?"

"She said it was personal."

"I don't know any personal ladies," Wilt said.

"Maybe you're about to meet one."

"No such luck."

He carried the memo sheet to his office and punched in an outside line. He dialed and waited.

Her voice was throaty. She didn't have to identify herself. "I read the morning paper. Now I know why you were the way you were."

"Don't give me the benefit of the doubt. I'm always like that, Diane. Exactly that way."

There was a long silence at the other end of the line. Except for the steady, soft breathing he'd have thought she'd hung up on him.

"You want me to call you back for any special reason?"

"You bother me," she said. "You keep hanging around. I keep asking myself why and I don't come up with any answer I like. I think you've already decided what kind of woman I am and you don't like much of what you believe. I guess I don't understand why you drag it out and pick at it."

"All I said was that you interest me."

"How? In what way?"

"That's the part I'm having trouble with."

"Come by tonight. This time I promise I'll be good."

"That's part of the problem. I'm not sure I want you to be good."

Her throaty laugh got inside him and echoed in the hollow of his chest. "You had your big chance last night, buster."

"That wasn't a chance. That was a calculated insult and you know it."

"You understood that, did you? First thing I know you'll interest me."

"I doubt it. Redneck Sheriffs probably aren't your style."

"You're right. But it's a strange and confusing possibility that I might change. A one in a thousand shot."

He waited. He thought she expected him to say something more but he didn't.

"Bye, Wilt."

He punched the button and broke the connection. He waited a few seconds and punched in the outside line again. He dialed the Police Station.

"It's like a television screen." Joe explained the method while Wilt stared at the result of Joe's hour of work with Johnny Ferrell and Gus Triffon. "You've got a choice of a lot of foreheads, hair styles, and you match those with a chin. Then you settle on the kind of nose and the shape of the cheekbones. Then the eyes and the mouth ..."

"Gus Triffon satisfied with it?" The likeness had a certain mechanical quality to it.

"He says it's as close as he can get."

"It looks like it was drawn by a machine that didn't know what a man is."

"Well, it was drawn by a machine." Joe moved around the desk and stood behind Wilt. "What do you want done with it?"

"You think it's useable?"

"Probably. A photograph would be better but we don't have one."

"Copies. Enough for us, enough for the police and some spares. A hundred copies to start." He passed the drawing over his shoulder to Joe. "On the way back from getting the copies made, stop by the *Herald* office. Talk to Charlie Giddings. See if he'll run this on page one in the morning. Suggest a caption like *Do You Know This Man?*

"He'll do it."

"Sure," Wilt said, "but ask. Asking and thanking, that's good politics."

"The other area papers?"

"Might be worth a try. Have Susie type up a letter for my signature. Say a man fitting this description is wanted for information he might have on the kidnapping and murder of Cathy Dobbs, aged six. Keep it vague."

"A call from you to the managing editors of the papers might help."

"Could be." Who the hell was running the office anyway? All those ideas from Joe irritated Wilt. But he accepted them. That was the balance he prided himself on. Not to reject an idea just because someone else had it.

Joe left with the drawing. Wilt sighed and drew the phone toward him. He started with the *Raleigh News and Observer.* Within half an hour he worked through the *Durham Morning Herald* and *Sun* and even the *Chapel Hill Newspaper.*

At the end he decided the calls had been worth the time.

The afternoon dragged. Amos Wilson called and said that the door-to-door was completed in the West Oak and 12th area and they'd come up empty-handed.

Bad breaks. Nothing but bad breaks.

At four-thirty, he tired of listening to his stomach growl and sent out for two burgers from the Char Pit. He got a Coke from the Station machine and sat at his desk and ate one burger. He'd just taken a bite from the second one when Joe pushed the door open without knocking. The push was so hard that the door slammed against the wall.

"We've got another one, Wilt."

"What?"

"Another little girl's missing."

"Where?" Wilt wrapped the rest of the burger in the foil it came in and tossed it in the waste can.

"The call just came in." Joe lifted the pad and read from it. "Seven-years-old. Second grade. The child's name is Dana Moore. The Moore live in the county, in the Tall Pines complex."

Wilt grabbed his coat and cap. On the way through the outer office, he stopped long enough to tell Susie to call in all the off-duty deputies. After he talked to the parents, he'd set up a search pattern.

The sky was dark. It had all the makings of a miserable night ahead. As soon as it got dark, the temperature would drop like a lead sinker.

CHAPTER NINE

The apartment complex was in the western part of the county. It was an architect's hybrid idea of what an adobe complex in New Mexico might be like. The outside was constructed of imitation adobe and each unit had been painted in a pastel tone. The units faced a courtyard in which several yucca trees were slowly dying, leaf blade by leaf blade.

Parking was in the back.

The Moore family lived in Unit D, #3, an apartment that had been painted a dark clay color. In the parking space for Unit D, # 3, there was a Subaru station wagon and a Pontiac Firebird.

After Joe parked the cruiser, he and Wilt walked around the end of the complex and entered the courtyard. On the porch-landing, Wilt noted the bundle of red chilies, the functional decoration he'd seen passing through the southwest. While Joe rang the doorbell, Wilt put out a hand and touched the peppers. There was no real "give" to the pods and he realized that it was ornamental, made of plastic.

The woman who came to the door was in her thirties. Her dark hair was shaped and neatly arranged. She wore tan slacks tailored in the mannish way, a white blouse and wore a ski sweater over her shoulders. She might have been attractive on some days. Today she wasn't. Her mascara was wet and smeared and her eyes were red. A lacy handkerchief was pressed to her mouth.

Past her, Wilt saw a man about her age. He was seated on a sectional sofa, the central part, and he wore suit pants and a vest that was unbuttoned. A burgundy tie was loose at his neck. He clutched a drink in one hand and held a cigarette in the other.

Mrs. Moore lowered the handkerchief and Wilt saw the red bruise on the side of her chin. Then, conscious of Wilt's stare, she covered the bruise again. "You've found her? She's alright?" Tears pooled in her eyes. She wiped the overflow away with her free hand.

"Not yet." Wilt introduced himself and then told them who Joe was. He stepped past her and into the living room.

Mr. Moore stood. He placed his drink on the coffee table. There was a faint weave to him as he approached Wilt. "I'm Jonas Moore. This is my wife, Arlene."

Wilt pressed the manicured hand. "Just how long has your daughter been missing?"

Jonas Moore released Wilt's hand and turned and looked at the wall clock. "It's five-twenty now. The bus wasn't always on an exact schedule but she should have been here between three-fifteen and three-twenty-five."

Wilt opened his coat. The room was overheated. "Where does the bus usually drop her?" "Down the road. There's a yellow school bus sign. It's about two hundred yards from the bus stop to the entrance road to Tall Pines."

"You usually meet her or wait for her?"

"Today I didn't." Arlene Moore said. "I had an appointment at the beauty shop. The only open time Betsy had was at three. I left a note for Dana and I asked Mrs. Daley... Margaret to keep an eye on her until I got back."

"You got back... when?"

"Four-fifteen." She lowered the handkerchief once more and the bruise was visible again. "First thing I went to Margaret's. She said she hadn't seen Dana at all and she'd assumed I met her on the road."

"You should have been there," Jonas said.

She flared back at him. "You're the one who wanted to go to the Flexner's for dinner tonight."

They could argue and accuse each other on their own time. "That was forty-five minutes ago. What did you do then?"

"I called the school. I spoke to the principal, Mr. Garland, I'd hoped ... well, there was the chance they'd kept her after class or she'd missed her bus. Mr. Garland said he'd talk to Dana's teacher, Miss Prince, and call me back. When he called back, I talked to Miss Prince. She said she'd seen Dana get on the bus."

Jonas carried his glass into the kitchen. Through the open doorway, Wilt saw him pour a generous shot of Early Times and add an ice cube.

"I didn't know what to do," Arlene said. "I waited until Jonas got home."

Jonas carried his drink to the sofa and slumped down on it. "It was still light. We walked around the area, just in case she'd gone off to play with one of the other children in the complex."

"Then we decided we'd better call you," Arlene said.

"Just a few minutes ago the principal called back," Jonas said. "He said he'd been trying to get in touch with the driver. He'd call us back. That was ten minutes ago."

"What are the chances you'll find her?" Arlene asked.

Jonas looked at his wife. The drink shook in his hand. The ice rattled against the glass.

"If anybody can find her, we will." Wilt said.

"Alive ...?" There. It was out. And the moment Arlene Moore asked the question she probably regretted. it.

Jonas' face contorted. He caught himself. "Arlene ..."

"I don't know," Wilt said. "I'd be lying if I made promises to you. What we've got in our favor is that we've got an early start. With some luck ..."

The phone rang. Wilt felt that he'd been saved by the bell. He was running out of assurances. It was hard to lie to parents when the naked fear was on them.

Jonas Moore answered the phone. After listening for a few seconds, he said, "Mr. Garland, the Sheriff's here. I think he'd like to talk to you."

Wilt took the phone. "Sheriff Drake."

"Sheriff, this is terrible. I'm heartsick over what might have happened to little Dana."

"All of us are. Look, I'd like to talk to the bus driver."

"I've talked to him. He said he remembers that Dana left the bus at her usual stop."

"I still need to talk to him. I've got some other questions for him."

"I can assure you we did a thorough check on him before..."

"It's not that, Mr. Garland."

"I guess I overreacted. I'm sorry. I've got his name and address here somewhere. Here, His name is Bobby Turpin. He lives on the Akers place. You know where that is?"

"I do."

"He's there now. I told him Mr. Moore might want to talk to him."

"Do me a favor," Wilt said. "Call him and tell him I'll be there in ten minutes. That I want him to wait for me."

"I will and I hope you find Dana before... something terrible happens to her. What happened to little Cathy Dobbs..."

"We'll try our best."

"We'll be praying for her."

Wilt said his goodbye and placed the phone on its base.

While he'd been on the phone, Arlene Moore had left the room. Now she returned, carrying something cupped in her free hand, the one that didn't press the handkerchief to her chin. When she was close to him, she opened her hand and he saw that it was a photograph.

"I thought you might need this. It was taken at the school in September."

Wilt thanked her. He looked down at the child's face. Long straight blonde hair touched her shoulders. Her eyes were wide and innocent. She was smiling, only an instant away from a grin.

"This wouldn't have happened if you'd caught the man who killed the other little girl." The drink was getting to Jonas Moore and his speech was slurred.

"Jonas," his wife said. "That doesn't help."

"But it's true. It's the Goddam truth and the Sheriff knows it."

"All I can say is that we're making progress." Wilt got his coat buttoned and slapped the cap against his leg. "All I wish is ..." He caught himself. What he'd almost said is that he wished all the mothers in the county would take care of their children so this wouldn't happen. But he couldn't say that. "All I wish is that she's unharmed when we find her."

"Why our child? Why Dana?"

He had no answer for her. All he could do was shake his head slowly. "I'll call you as soon as I know something."

"Find her, Sheriff," Arlene said. "Please find her."

He said he'd do all he could.

CHAPTER TEN

The night air was colder. The temperature had dropped five or ten degrees while they'd been in the Moore apartment.

Wilt settled into the seat on the passenger side of the cruiser. There was a sour taste in his mouth.

Joe started the engine and let it warm up. "I thought he was going to blow up all over her and you too."

"You see the bruise? He's already had his round with her. And me … I don't think he wants any part of me the way I feel."

"That was a cheap shot he threw at us," Joe said.

"It comes with the job. What he really wanted to do was kick a few more lumps on her ass and he couldn't, not in front of us. So, he tells us it's our fault. That takes some of the pressure off him."

"Sometimes I feel like I wouldn't want your job,"

Wilt grinned. "And sometimes you do want it?"

"Not today."

"What you want to be is a fair weather Sheriff."

"You're right, Wilt."

Joe drove.

Wilt put his head back. He willed a darkness behind his eyelids. He didn't get that. What he got was the face of Dana Moore on the twisted, tortured body of Cathy Dobbs. It was like a nightmare and he opened his eyes and tried to shake the image away.

It lingered. It was stubborn.

❧   ❧   ❧

The Akers place still raised tobacco. The original allotment for leaf hadn't been large enough to make it worth the owner's time. But in Webster County, as in the rest of the state, there were allotments that got handed down in families. When the owner of the allotment was a widow, or an older person who didn't want to farm, it was possible to purchase these allotments on a yearly basis. A still active farmer could put together twenty or thirty or forty acres of these leases. Such small farming wouldn't make a man rich but it helped keep his books in the black.

The Akers family was a large one. Until around 1960, the farm had supported old Abner and three sons. But farming changed. In the late 1950s and the early 1960s, the sons married and moved away. Now Abner Akers lived alone in the big, main house that had been built to house a large family.

The smaller houses where the hired help had lived were rented now. It was Wilt's guess that Bobby Turpin lived in one of these.

On the drive toward the main house, Wilt had decided to stop by and see Abner. It had been two or three years since he'd seen him. Beyond the main house, he saw one of the smaller places where smoke billowed from the chimney. And there was a yellow school bus parked there, next to a Ford pickup.

The front door of the smaller house opened and a young man stepped onto the porch the moment the cruiser braked next to the school bus. He wore jeans, a red N.C. State pullover and heavy work shoes. His face was weathered and blotchy and he was trying to grow a beard. The beard was whispy and hardly showed at all at a distance.

"Bobby Turpin?"

He nodded. "You must be the Sheriff. Mr. Garland called me."

Wilt nodded toward the house. "Can we talk inside, out of the wind?"

"If you don't wake the baby. You wake the baby and my wife'll be on my back all night."

"In that case, we can talk out here." Wilt turned up his coat collar and shoved his hands deep in his pockets.

"Naw, come on in. It's too cold out here."

Inside, a roaring fire burned in the fireplace. An oil heater hummed on the other side of the room. There was a strong scent of pine. But, also, underneath that, the smell of diapers and urine.

"How old's the baby?"

"Three months plus a few days. It sure changes a man's life."

"For the better?" Wilt smiled.

"I'll have to wait and. see."

"The reason we're here ..."

"I know." A sober and sad look moved across Turpin's homely face. He motioned them to chairs. "That's a nice little girl."

"Mind if I smoke?" Wilt asked.

"Go ahead." Turpin moved around and stood with his back to the fireplace. "My wife's against it, but she seems to be against anything with pleasure to it."

Wilt laughed.

"You married, Sheriff?"

"Between wives." Wilt got his smoke going and tossed the match into the fireplace.

"Dana's a sweet little girl. Wasn't no bigger than a minute. But for her age, she's so ladylike. You know, she sits up straight, her knees together and her ankles crossed. It was like she'd been to one of those finishing schools, a place where they teach manners. She always got on the bus early and sat up front. That was because some of the kids got rowdy and she didn't like it. So she sat near me."

"You know Dana. You think she would get in a car with a stranger?"

"I doubt it."

"You think of any circumstance where she might talk to a stranger?"

"Well, she might answer a question or give directions. But that's just a guess."

"Tell me about today."

For Bobby, it had been like any other day. She'd boarded the bus early and she'd been just as quiet and ladylike as ever.

"She got on at …?"

"Roughly three o'clock."

"And she got off …?"

"It takes about fifteen minutes to run the route from the school to Dana's stop. In fact, I usually check the time at that stop. It tells me if I'm running late."

"And today?"

"It was three-fourteen."

Wilt took a final draw from the Chesterfield and stepped forward to toss the butt into the fireplace. "You see any cars parked near the stop?"

"No."

"You see any cars behind the bus that might have been trailing you?"

Bobby shook his head. "I'd have noticed. You see, by state law, cars have to stop when a bus stops. So I check behind myself all the time. It's got so it's reflex now."

"Dana the only child leaves the bus at that stop?"

"Yes."

"Today, when she left the bus, did she look around like she expected her mother to meet her?"

"Her mother never met her. Never."

That fit the image Wilt had of Arlene Moore. Too wrapped up in her own life to pay the time or the attention to the safety of her child. "You pull off right away?"

"Usually I do. Today I had to go back and quiet a couple of kids who were acting up. That took some time."

"You pass Dana down the road?"

"She was about halfway to the entrance road that went to Tall Pines. When she heard the bus, she turned and waved."

"You see any cars on the Tall Pines road?"

"No. No car." Turpin's face changed. It went frozen, thoughtful. "That was one thing."

"What?"

"A man with a dog."

"On the entrance road?"

"No, in the field between the highway and the complex."

"What kind of dog?"

"It was more a puppy than a dog."

"You know the breed?"

"I couldn't tell. I don't know dogs that well and this was a puppy."

"White, brown, black, spotted ...?"

"More white than anything else."

"What was your impression of the man?"

"It was at a distance. I couldn't see that much of him. He wore a tan coat. It might have been a raincoat."

Raincoat? That reminded Wilt of the man Gus Triffon had described. "A short raincoat? Or the usual length?"

"I think it was short."

"Old man or young man?"

"I wasn't close enough ..."

"I understand that. But think. How did he move? Like a young man or an old man?"

"The way he moved, I'd say young."

"Why?"

"Well, he had this stick and he was throwing it for the puppy. It was the way he swung his arm. It was easy and smooth, not jerky. And when he bent over to take the stick, it was easy and smooth. Like the way he threw the stick."

Wilt looked at Joe.

"It could fit," Joe said.

There was a loud squawl from a nearby room. It was breathless, nonstop shrieking. A woman's voice rode above the baby's cry. "Bobby, you see what you've done? I told you. You can't say I didn't tell you."

Wilt stopped at the fireplace and rubbed his hands in front of the flames. "Tell her it was my fault, Bobby."

Bobby Turpin shook his head, not at the suggestion but at the trouble he was in. "You can bet I will. Let her raise hell with the Sheriff and see what that gets her."

Joe backed down the road until he was beyond the Ford pickup and the school bus. He turned and they passed the Akers house. A cluster of chickens watched them from a shelter under the back steps.

"Our boy, whoever he is, probably changes his approach each time. What works one time will get him caught the next time."

"If the man in the field with the puppy is *our* man," Joe said.

"I wonder if anybody on West Oak and 12th saw a man with a puppy. That would spoil my guess."

"We should have gone along on that door-to-door with the city cops. I trust those boys as far as I can throw a police car."

"Slipshod work?" Wilt nodded. "It trickles from the top and Amos is at the top."

"The man with the puppy?"

"According to Bobby, there wasn't anybody else on the road. No cars on the entrance road to the Tall Pines complex." The heater air was changing. The raw chill eased. Wilt touched the vent and felt the warm air. "It's a good ploy." He checked himself. "No, it's a rotten trick. What kid can resist a puppy?"

"Even when the kid's been warned not to talk to strangers?"

"A puppy's not a stranger."

"Rotten and sleazy," Joe said. He drove for a mile or two in silence. "What say I drop you at the Station and pick up Floyd?

That's what you want, isn't it? A door-to-door at Tall Pines to see if anybody else saw the man with the puppy?"

"I don't know what I'm doing around here. You've got it all figured."

"You're around to crack the whip," Joe said.

"Some whip." But he relaxed now that that decision had been made. "Take along the composite Gus Triffon helped us with and show it around."

"I've got a glove box stuffed with them."

"Ask about strange cars around the complex today."

"Like a red and white Thunderbird? That's the second question."

Wilt leaned forward, eyes closed, and let the warm air blow across his face. "Write if you find work."

"Where'll you be?"

"At the office. I'll set up the search. After that, I'll be at my desk. All night if I have to."

"Put out the cot. Staying awake all night won't help us find the girl."

"I'm not sure I can sleep. I've got this bad feeling that when we find Dana Moore, it'll be just like the little Dobbs child."

"That hopeless, Wilt?"

"It's the grim horrors."

They approached the city limits. The fields, the woods gradually giving way to the first haze of lights and a sprinkling of houses that straddled the line where the city and the county merged. The way it was going, Wilt thought, in his own time he would see all this vanish and the concrete and the asphalt take over.

"I feel so helpless," Joe said.

Jerked back to now. Not fifteen years from now. He would quarter the county and parcel it out to four cruisers. Walk every inch of it, he'd tell them. And when the search teams left, he'd talk to Susie. Could she put in overtime? Could she stay at the switchboard and free a man for the hunt? He thought she would.

And later, waiting for the reports to come in, he would set up the camp bed and try to get a couple of hours of rest. Not sleep. Rest.

At the Station, Joe waited in the cruiser until Wilt sent Floyd to join him. Susie volunteered to stay on before he could ask her.

"Isn't it terrible about that poor little girl?" was all that Susie said.

Within five minutes, Wilt stood at his office window, the one that overlooked the back parking lot, and watched the cruisers pull away until only one remained, Car #1, his cruiser.

The windows shook and rattled in their casements. At the back of the lot, backlighted by a glare from the downtown buildings, he watched the old oak tree. Its upper branches writhed and twisted in the strong evening wind.

The autopsy report on Cathy Dobbs was still centered on his blotter. When he sat at his desk, he pushed the report aside. He didn't want to read it. Not now. Not ever.

Susie brought him a coffee.

Wilt sat and stared at the wall clock.

By nine, he'd heard nothing from Joe Croft at Tall Pines. That meant the interviews had produced nothing worth reporting. The four search teams called in at the half hour, giving their locations and what territory had been combed. It was going, for them, smooth as it was supposed to, but there was no sign of Dana Moore.

His stomach growled at him. He didn't want to leave his office for a burger. A burger wasn't worth the trouble. What he really wanted was a plate of chopped barbecue from the Open Pit. That and a bowl of cole slaw and about a dozen hush puppies. And sloshed over the pork, some of the special vinegar sauce the Open Pit made. And black coffee until it ran out of his ears. And lemon chess pie, home baked and offered in a generous wedge.

Nothing else he could do. He opened the office closet and pushed the folded camp cot aside until he found the box he thought of as his survival kit. He'd packed a one burner hot plate and a selection of canned soups. And, at the back of the box, a couple of tubes of saltines he'd double-wrapped in plastic.

With no special interest, he chose the Manhattan Clam Chowder. Within minutes the soup was simmering, about ready to be eaten.

Just as he reached for the sauce pan, Susie buzzed him. "It's Joe."

Wilt switched off the burner. He carried the pan to his desk and placed it on the blotter before he lifted the receiver. "Yeah, Joe?"

"I think you'd better get over here."

Wilt lifted a spoonful of the soup and blew across it. "You find someone who ...?"

"It's not that. It's a ransom note."

"The hell you say."

"It's what the note says, Wilt."

"I'll be there fast as I can. You put Floyd on the road now so he can handle the Station."

"He just left."

"And stop reading my mind."

After he broke the connection, he got down three spoons of the Clam Chowder before he burned his tongue. He left the pan on the desk.

His stomach rumbled at him as he rushed down the back steps to the parking lot. It seemed to be saying *more, more.* On the drive, he smoked two cigarettes in an attempt to dull the edge. It didn't work.

In desperation, he stopped at a closed gas station that had an outside snack area and bought a Milky Way and peanut brittle bar.

Then he was down to pennies and the machine didn't give credit.

CHAPTER ELEVEN

The note was on the kitchen table in the Moore apartment. It was pegged down at the top and bottom by oversized salt and pepper shakers.

On the way through the living room, Wilt had his look at Jonas and Arlene Moore. There were no new bruises he could see on Arlene. And the anger had been replaced by a desperate hope. For them, the note meant there was still a chance Dana was alive.

"I'd bet against any prints being on it," Joe said, lowering his voice so the Moore, who remained in the living room, wouldn't hear their conversation. "So far, the only people who have handled it are the Moores."

"Fingerprints are overrated." Wilt leaned over the note. It was block printed on a rough square of brown paper. The paper had the texture and thickness of a segment from a grocery bag.

If you want to see your girl again get $5,000 dollars and wait for phone call. Don't call the police.

"You think it's real?" Joe asked.

Only Five thousand dollars? It didn't seem to Wilt like much of a ransom demand. And why was there a demand this time and not before? It didn't add up.

"I don't think we have any choice," Wilt said. "We've got to act like we believe it is. How was it delivered?"

Joe shrugged. "They're not sure. Mrs. Moore says she happened to pass through the living room and saw it stuck between the bottom of the door and the doorframe."

"While you and Floyd were in the area?"

"I guess so." Joe shook his head. "Hell, we were busy. We were hardly outside more than a minute at the time."

"Damn."

"I'm not making excuses. This whole place is rented. There must be a couple of hundred living here and they're coming and going at all hours. It's hard to tell who belongs here and who doesn't."

"The disappearance of Dana. It make the evening news yet?"

"I think it made the news on two of the TV channels and there have been news flashes on the radio stations."

"You make a guess where they got their information?"

"Probably from Amos and from that school principal... what's his name?"

"Nobody tried to talk to me," Wilt said.

"I think you scared the shit out of them last night."

"That's my charm." He headed for the living room. Joe followed him.

Jonas Moore took his wife's hand from his shoulder and stood. He seemed oddly sober now despite the drinking Wilt had witnessed early that evening. "There's one problem I'd better tell you about, Sheriff. I can't get the money tonight. I can have it tomorrow as soon as the bank opens. But tonight, I don't know..."

"That's what you tell them," Wilt said.

"What if they don't believe me?"

"If they want the money, they'll have to believe you. It's that simple. The fact is that kidnappers know banking hours as well as you do."

"What do I say?" Jonas looked from Wilt to Joe and back. "I mean ... when they call."

"You tell them you'll have the money tomorrow." Wilt turned toward the front door and stopped. "They'll probably say fine, that they'll call you again tomorrow and give you instruction for handing the money over." He opened the front door and felt the raw blast of wind. "I'll be right back."

Wilt dug a transparent evidence bag from the box in the trunk of his cruiser. He returned to the house and edged the ransom note into the bag with the tines of a fork.

Joe blocked the doorway when he started back into the living room. "You going to call the Bureau?"

"I've got to," Wilt said.

He faced the Moore across the coffee table. "Here's how it is. I'm going to leave my chief deputy here with you. When the call comes in, he'll listen in with you. You do the talking, Mr. Moore. If anything comes up, and you don't know how to answer or what to say, you look at Joe. He'll nod or shake his head. You follow his lead."

"Thank you, Sheriff," Arlene Moore said.

"We're doing all we can." Wilt tapped Joe on the shoulder. "Let me see you outside for a minute."

Outside, in the glare of the porch light, head down against the cutting wind, Wilt said, "Keep them as calm as you can. And while you're waiting for the call, run it through your head and anticipate all the roadblocks that can come up. Do some coaching with Moore, what to expect and how to handle the kidnapper's moves."

"That's my next question. How are we going to handle it?"

"We want it tomorrow. We want as much lead time to prepare for it as we can pressure from them."

"You think we ought to tape it?"

"If we can. I'm going to see how much influence Amos has with Ma Bell."

Wilt walked through the courtyard. Joe slowed his pace to stay level with him. "You want me to send Floyd back?"

"If you can spare him. He can go on with the door-to-door by himself."

"He up to it?"

"Yeah." Joe stopped at the far end of the unit. "You going to call off the search?"

"No. You think we ought to?"

Joe shook his head.

On the way to the station, Wilt called in and told Susie to send Floyd back to Tall Pines. He passed the narrow offshoot road that led to the Blue Lagoon. He stared at the lights in the distance. He realized that he hadn't thought about Diane Mills for about eight hours. Progress.

Amos wasn't at the police department. In frustration, Wilt turned the hunt over to Susie. On the fifth call, she located him at the Moose Club. Wilt picked up the phone and filled him in on what had happened and what he wanted to do.

Amos didn't like the whole idea or want any part of it. "I can tell you ahead of time what that Bell supervisor is gonna say. Shit, Wilt, you know that's an illegal tap and it can't be used in court."

"I don't want to use it in court. And, anyway, whose rights are we protecting here? Dana Moore or the kidnappers?"

"Well…" Amos was still hedging.

Wilt could hear loud music in the background. "Amos, I've got the F.B.I. on the way here right now. You know those boys. You believe they'll think twice about the legality of this kind of tap when a child's life is on the line? My problem is that I can't wait for the F.B.I. to get here. That call might go through any minute."

"Where are you?"

"At my office," Wilt said.

"I'll try my best. I'll get back to you."

Amos broke the connection.

Wilt took a deep breath and drew the list of phone numbers for area law enforcement agencies toward him. He dialed the F.B.I. office in Raleigh and got a taped message that told him to leave a message explaining his business. His call, the cool voice said, would be returned.

Fifteen minutes after leaving the message, he got a call back from a supervisor telling him that Special Agent Harriman would arrive at the Webster County Sheriff's Station within an hour.

His private line phone rang as soon as he replaced the receiver. "Yes, Amos?"

He recognized the throaty laugh. "You give up on girls, Wilt?"

"How'd you get this number?"

"Oh, I have my ways." Diane said.

"I never said you didn't." He looked at the wall clock. He didn't want to tie up the line. He wanted it open if Amos called.

"I'm dancing tonight. I thought you might be interested." Her breathing stirred him. "You coming by, Wilton?"

"Where'd you get this Wilton nonsense?"

"From your friend, Erlene. She thinks you're quite something. You were a Marine hero and an officer and a gentleman and you even went to college. My, oh, my."

"Chapel Hill, if it matters. Navy R.O.T.C."

"Come out, Wilton. You can get your little boy thrills."

"You didn't hear?"

"Hear what?"

"It happened again. Another little girl's missing,"

He heard the sudden intake of her breath. "I'm sorry, Wilt. I've been such an ass."

"Another night I'll drop by and study your tattoo."

"Wilt ..."

"Got to go." He placed the receiver on the base.

A count of ten and the buzzer rasped at him. Susie connected him with the Chief.

Amos sounded smug. He'd worked his magic with Ma Bell. He'd invoked the power of the police, the Sheriff's department and even hinted at the F.B.I. The supervisor was driving in from home and he'd be met at the switching station by a police technician. A patch would be put on the Moore line and they'd record all incoming calls.

Wilt thanked him and promised, yes, he'd bring the Special Agent by for a talk as soon as the investigation was underway.

After the call, Wilt put his head on the desk and tried to rest. But he couldn't empty his head. He kept replaying the conversation with Diane over and over in his mind. If the man and woman mating dance was a war, then he'd won this round.

He knew, however, that it had been a cheap win. The bad feeling was in him. He'd used the shock impact, the missing child, to turn it back against Diane.

Cheap. A bad win that was hardly a win at all.

CHAPTER TWELVE

Every F.B. I. man Wilt ever met in his life looked exactly like every other one he'd met. Neat, hair cut just so and at the same length that could be measured from the shirt collar, shoes shined to a high gloss, his suit and tie tasteful, and a vaguely lean and athletic body. As if Edgar demanded of his underlings what he wasn't.

Special Agent Harriman had been stamped from the same mold at the same plastic factory. Windy as it was outside, not a hair was out of place and his shoes didn't show a speck of dust.

He was about thirty, with sandy blond hair, pale green eyes and he wore a pair of black-rimmed glasses. His suit was some kind of wool blend in a dark gray and he'd matched a black tie with that.

Wilt had Susie bring in coffee. Wilt motioned Harriman to a chair and filled him in on the death of the Dobbs child and the extent of his investigation into the disappearance of Dana Moore.

Harriman said little. He nodded now and then as if to encourage Wilt to continue. When the matter of the ransom demand came up, he took his time studying the note in the evidence bag. He appeared to be memorizing the note word-for-word. When he passed it back to Wilt, he took a sip of the cooked-down coffee.

"This doesn't make a lot of sense if it's the same guy who killed Cathy Dobbs," Harriman said. "Unless he killed her so the family of the next girl he grabbed would know he was serious about what he'd do if they didn't pay up."

"I don't think so. A man who'd rape and murder a child isn't in it for a payday. If this is the same guy, then Dana Moore is already dead."

Harriman looked down at his carefully clipped fingernails. Wilt thought he could read the Special Agent's mind. It was shaping up as a no-win situation for the Bureau. From the beginning, the Bureau liked good press too much to get themselves involved in losing situations. It was like the old doctor's advice to the new doctor who'd come to town to start his practice. *Young man, in your first year here, don't let anybody you're treating die.* And he advised the young man to send all the hopeless cases to North Carolina Memorial or Duke or Bowman Gray.

Susie buzzer ended that speculation. "It's Joe on the line."

"The call just came in, Wilt."

"Walk it by me."

"He was, the way you figured, a very understanding kidnapper about the money. He'll call back tomorrow and tell Moore where the money drop is."

"Anything else?"

"Whoever it was, I think he's been watching crime movies on television. From the way he sounded, I'd say he had a handkerchief over the phone mouthpiece."

"Where's Floyd?"

"With me. On second thought, I decided we ought to do the interviews in the door-to-door together."

It was Joe Croft's polite way of saying that, on second thought, he'd decided that Floyd didn't have the brains or the experience to handle that job by himself. "Okay, Joe, get back on that door-to-door."

There was a hesitation at Joe's end of the line. "It's getting late. We're going to get complaints if we roll people out of bed to ask them questions."

"Tell them to direct the complaints my way." He looked at Harriman. The F.B.I. man seemed preoccupied, even bored, and he stared out the window past Wilt. "Look, remind them we're talking about the life of a little child."

Susie opened the door and waited until Wilt looked at her and nodded. "It's the Chief on line two."

"Joe, work at it for another hour. Then come in. I think we both need a few hours of sleep. We've got to be at the Moore apartment tomorrow when that call comes in."

"See you in an hour."

Wilt punched in line two.

"The tape is on its way to your office," Amos said.

"That's great, Chief. I was just telling Special Agent Harriman that you could really get the wheels moving."

Harriman turned in his chair and stared at Wilt.

Wilt grinned at him.

"He's there ... right now?" Amos asked.

"Big as life," Wilt said. "Now, we're going to need to tape the next call, the one tomorrow."

"I don't know, Wilton. I stuck my neck out this time to get ..."

"Not the same way, Amos. Tomorrow we tape it from the Moore apartment. How about the loan of the same technician and his equipment tomorrow? Send him to the Tall Pines, D-3, at ten in the morning."

"I guess I can do that."

"I appreciate it and I know Agent Harriman appreciates it too."

When the call was over, Harriman stood and stretched. "You're free with my name, Sheriff. I'm not sure I like it."

"Sorry. But getting Chief Wilson to move on anything is like trying to kick Mount Rushmore one foot to the right."

"As long as you don't make a habit of it."

Wilt watched Harriman pull on his raincoat. "You staying the night?"

"I thought I'd let you recommend a hotel."

"The Holiday Inn's two blocks over. Nothing special but no bad surprises either."

Harriman said the Holiday Inn was fine.

Wilt followed Harriman into the lobby. He stopped by the switchboard. He told Susie to call the Holiday Inn and book a room for Harriman and that the Sheriff wanted the V.I.P. treatment for him.

Wilt walked outside with him and pointed him in the right direction. They agreed to meet at the Station at eight-thirty or nine the next morning.

After Harriman drove away, Wilt stood on the steps and let the wind beat against him. He took some deep breaths. After all the cigarettes and the coffee, the air was like cold spring water.

"Hello."

Wilt heard the shuddering, anxious breath Jonas Moore took before he spoke on the recording.

"You get the note?"

"Yes … yes, I got the note."

"Do you have the money?"

"It's not that easy. Please. The bank's closed. I can't get the money until tomorrow morning."

"But you'll get it then?"

"I promise."

"And you didn't call in the law?"

"No." A flutter of breath. "I did what you … said."

"I'll call again tomorrow."

"Wait a minute," Jonas said.

"What?"

Wilt guessed that Joe was prompting Moore.

"Let me talk to Dana. How am I supposed to know she's all right?"

"You don't … until we get the money."

"When?"

"When … what?"

"When will you call tomorrow?"

"When I feel like it."

A click and the call was over.

Jonas Moore didn't want to give up. "Wait…let me talk to Dana."

There was a second click. Wilt guessed that Joe had taken the receiver from Moore and placed it on the base.

Wilt took the tape out of the player. After he locked the tape away in the safe, he walked into the lobby, leaned on the counter and grinned at Susie. "How you feeling?"

"I'm fine. I really am." She covered a yawn and turned her head.

He considered her for a time. She'd been on all day with just rest breaks and now, by the wall clock, it was five of midnight. He could have asked her to stay another hour, until Joe and Floyd checked back in from Tall Pines. But he knew that was selfish. He couldn't ask it of her. That decided, he moved behind the counter and got her heavy coat and scarf.

"Home," he said. "And don't come in until you feel rested."

"Really, Wilt, you need sleep more than I…."

Wilt shook his head and held her coat for her. He gave the scarf three or so turns around her neck. "Shoooo."

"But you…"

He took her arm and walked her toward the front door.

"…you need your sleep."

He guided her down the steps. "And I'll get it as soon as Joe and Floyd come in. That ought to be in a half an hour or so."

He watched her drive away and then returned and sat in her chair at the switchboard. He dozed. At twelve-thirty, he made a fresh pot of coffee. Joe and Floyd arrived a few minutes later.

Floyd was fresher. He'd had a good night's sleep. Joe was bleary-eyed. Wilt assigned Floyd to the switchboard. Wilt left the Station while Joe was putting the camp cot together in the office.

Being head man had its advantages. He'd sleep in his own warm bed.

CHAPTER THIRTEEN

He parked the cruiser in his assigned space at the Martindale apartments. It was a squarish, brick building that had been a hotel into the 1950s. A new owner converted blocks of rooms into apartments. The apartments even came furnished but Wilt took a long look at the cigarette burns on the tables, the scarred dresser and the ratty rugs and drove straight to Sears and bought the complete outfit for the apartment.

He talked about bringing in a crew of painters but Joe said he and Floyd would help Wilt one weekend and get it all done. Wilt furnished the beer, all they could drink, and when they were done, knowing neither Joe nor Floyd would take pay, he gave each of them two quarts of Wild Turkey. One bourbon and one rye each.

Wilt settled in. A black woman cleaned two days a week for him.

At times, late at night, Wilt wondered why he just didn't rent a room somewhere. For all the time he spent in the apartment, for all the use he got of it, he might as well have placed a bed in the hall of the station and let it go at that.

When he slammed the cruiser door, he heard another slam a distance away. It was so close to him that he almost decided it was an echo. He turned and looked over the cruiser in the direction of the second door slam. What he saw was Diane Mills with a large bag of groceries in front of her like an offering.

"I bet you haven't had your supper."

Wilt locked the cruiser door and walked around the back of it to meet her. "Not unless you count a candy bar and a peanut brittle."

"Does that mean I can fix you supper?"

"They didn't call it dinner at Coker College?"

"I didn't."

He took the bag of groceries from her and led the way up the stairs and into the lobby. The old elevator clacked and rattled as it carried them to the third floor.

Wilt placed the bag on the kitchen table and returned to the living room to help her remove her coat. The coat was leather but it was as supple as the kind used in making gloves.

She turned slowly, looking at his furniture. "Sears 1984."

"Hey, it's older than that. It's Sears 1982."

"Antiques," she said.

"Only a young lady educated at the Coker Finishing School…."

"Or a Carolina Tarfoot…"

"… could appreciate such classy furniture."

"While we're talking about classy." She went into the kitchen and returned with a bottle of wine. "I wiped the dust and spider webs away after I selected it from my four thousand bottle cellar."

"Let me see it." He took the bottle from her and turned it in his hands. It was a Merlot from some California vineyard he'd never heard of. "An interesting coding system you have in your cellar. One-period-nine eight. What does that mean?"

"That it's not to be uncorked until January of 1998." A girlish shrug of her shoulders. "But for an occasion like this…"

"Touching. Sacrificed before its time."

"Why don't we open it? I assume you have jelly glasses. Such apartments usually come complete with a set of jelly glasses."

Wilt placed the wine on the table and found the cork screw. "I've got the most expensive jelly glasses money can buy." He pulled the cork and got down two wine glasses from the cabinet. They were from a good crystal set, a wedding present. After Mary Ellen vanished into Northern California, he'd received a bill from a storage company. They had used it to store their stuff during their last duty station move. There hadn't been that much there — a set of good dishes, some silver, the good crystal and bed linen that was still in the packages it came in.

He poured and handed a glass to her.

She smiled at him over the glass rim. "Since you wouldn't come to me …"

"I become a beast when I see your tattoo." He sipped the Merlot. It seemed thin to him.

"All you men are alike. All you want to do is talk about a girl's tattoo."

"True. A man never gets enough of that." He took a seat at the end of the small kitchen table, away from the stove. "You said something about supper."

She placed a package that was wrapped in butcher paper on the table. "Ribeyes. How do you like your steak?"

"Crust on the outside. Pink on the inside."

Diane cooked the two steaks in a huge cast-iron skillet that she insisted upon calling a "spider." She found a can of artichoke hearts on his vegetable shelf. She made a salad with those and part of a head of lettuce she found in the refrigerator crisper. She dressed it with oil and a dash of lemon juice.

During the cooking, he watched her. He liked her grace, the sureness with which she moved around the kitchen. And, when the meal was ready, he liked the appetite that she didn't bother to hide.

Later, the dishes rinsed and stacked in the sink, he clawed around the freezer among the frozen dinners and found part of a pound of frozen French roast Columbian coffee. He ground a couple of handfuls in the Braun and made drip coffee. There was part of a bottle of Armagnac he'd brought back from New York.

The ABC store didn't sell it. They didn't sell anything unless it sold so many cases a week. They sat at the kitchen table and sipped the coffee and Armagnac. He liked the raw burn of the Armagnac, the harshness that a good Cognac doesn't have.

Her glass was empty. He offered her more.

"You need your rest, Wilton."

He followed her into the living room and helped her with her coat. "I'm sorry you have to leave."

"It's for the best," she said. "I never show my tattoo on a first date."

"Damn your tattoo." He leaned forward and kissed her. It was a gentle kiss that held back his need. Her mouth didn't meet him fully but it wasn't slack either. When he backed away, he saw that her eyes were open. Her face was thoughtful, serious under his stare.

"I've got to go."

"I'll walk you to your car."

"No," she said firmly, "you go to bed."

"Tuck me in. I'll sleep better."

A smile, a shake of her head. "Not that even on the second date." She grabbed her purse and before he could protest, she was gone.

He stood at the living room window that overlooked the street. He waited and saw her come down the steps and stop on the sidewalk and look over her shoulder, toward his window. He didn't think she could see him. A few seconds later she was in her car, a silver-toned Celica. She drove away.

He set the alarm for eight. He poured himself another shot of Armagnac and sipped it while he undressed. He fell asleep with the burn on his tongue.

It was a deep, full sleep. If he dreamed at all, he didn't remember the dream the next morning.

CHAPTER FOURTEEN

By nine-thirty, the listening post setup was in place at. Tall Pines. The main element, the core of it, was plain dumb luck. Joe Croft, relieving Wilt the night before, happened to mention in passing that the apartment next to the Moore was empty. D-4, he'D called it. Wilt remembered that bit of information while he was in the shower. He called Joe at the Station. Joe said it sounded good to him. A hurried call to Southern Bell got the telephone truck to Tall Pines within minutes. The crew strung a line that bypassed the Moore outlet and directed all calls to the empty apartment. As soon as the telephone truck left, Amos Wilson's technician placed the tap for the tape recorder.

Any call intended for Jonas or Arlene Moore rang in the empty apartment. Jonas would answer every call. He was under instructions to keep the incoming calls as brief as possible. He was to discourage any lengthy talk without being rude, if that was possible and to be rude if the other methods didn't work.

At the Station, Wilt put together a makeshift crew that would handle the other business of the day. Susie was back at her switchboard. Charlie Reaton, one of the more dependable new deputies and still in training, sat behind Wilt's desk like he belonged there. One good day behind that desk and Charlie would probably decide to run for Sheriff, Wilt thought sourly.

Joe Croft, red-eyed and still groggy from his nap on the camp cot, arrived at the Tall Pines complex while Wilt was on his way to the Station. He scouted the near-by apartments and borrowed a card table and four folding chairs. To that Joe added an inflatable air mattress from the trunk of his cruiser. Wilt never quite got around to asking Joe how the mattress got there or what police work it was intended for.

There were calls from nine a.m. and on. Jonas was firm with the callers. He explained that he didn't want the line tied up in case the police called. It worked. The only long call Jonas allowed was from his mother in Syracuse. He talked to her for almost ten minutes.

The length of the call didn't bother Joe Croft. He and Wilt didn't expect the call with the instructions from the kidnappers until after dark. The money would be handed over in the dark and there would be little lead time given them by the kidnappers. Lead time meant the police could try to set a trap. The less time between the call and the delivery of the money the more holes in the trap.

The assignment editor of one of the television stations called and wanted to set up a live interview during the evening news. Jonas tried the best he could to explain that he didn't think an interview was a good idea at this particular time. The editor insisted and he argued that the live interview could be used as a platform from which Jonas could make a plea to the man who'd kidnapped Dana for a safe return of his daughter. When the editor became too insistent, and wouldn't listen to Jonas' refusal, Wilt took the phone and introduced himself. He told the man there wouldn't be interviews until there was some news worth communicating.

The other callers were friends and well-wishers. Jonas turned them aside, prayers and all, as politely as he could.

He's learning how to do it, Wilt thought.

At the edges of the activity, Special Agent Harriman wore his raincoat buttoned to the neck. There was no heat in the apartment. He had little to say. He split his time between a seat near the phone and a pacing area near the living room window. Most of the time, he stared out at the raw day. If Harriman approved of the way Wilt handled the situation, he didn't say that. If he disapproved, he was silent about that as well. He watched, he listened, but he didn't offer any advice.

By one that afternoon, the calls slowed and they had a makeshift lunch. Cold cuts, potato salad, cole slaw and coffee.

As the afternoon wore on, Jonas became more and more concerned about the ransom money. It was Wilt's decision that no arrangement was to be made to acquire the five thousand dollars. We'll do it with mirrors, he told Joe and Special Agent Harriman while Jonas was in the bathroom later that afternoon. But he had to deal with Moore, to calm him. He told Jonas that Special Agent Harriman had used his clout to assure that the money would be ready at the bank, even after the closing hour.

Harriman nodded uncertainly.

The call came in at three-thirty. Wilt was surprised. He didn't expect any contact with the kidnappers for another five or six hours.

The tape recorder was running. Moore answered.

"You got the money?" The voice had the same muffled quality, as if the man spoke through cloth.

Wilt nodded at Jonas, who said that he had the money ready.

"Unmarked money?"

Moore said it was not marked in any way.

"Put it in a gym bag."

"Wait," Jonas said. "How is Dana? Let me ..."

A click and the line was dead. Wilt saw the stricken look on Jonas' face when he handed the phone to the police technician. It wasn't pretty, it wasn't easy to look at.

Joe inflated the air mattress and got a pillow and blankets from Arlene Moore next door. He coaxed Jonas into stretching out and resting in the other room. Joe remained with him until Jonas wrapped the blankets around him and closed his eyes.

Harriman stood next to the front window and looked over his shoulder to be sure the door to the bedroom was closed. Harriman's voice was low. He was irritated. "What's that about me arranging to get the money, even after hours?"

"You think I'd use real money? When I'm ninety percent willing to bet the little girl is already dead?" Wilt shook his head. "My switchboard lady is cutting play money out of the morning paper right now."

"And what happens if he insists upon getting the money himself?"

"I let him write the check and give it to you."

"And I pretend to use my clout?"

"You've got it," Wilt said.

Harriman looked fresh. He was wearing the same suit but it looked like it had had a sponge and a press. He smelled of after-shave and talcum. His tie shirt still had the "bought and new" creases in it.

Wilt felt pretty good himself. His sleep, after the time with Diane, had smoothed some of the rough, tired lines from his body. Still, he knew next to Harriman he looked like a dirty sock.

"You better hope this works, Sheriff."

"Come on," Wilt said. "I know how you guys at the Bureau work. You lay out all this careful shit talk to cover your ass in case something goes bad. Okay, your ass is covered. You warned me. You want that in writing?"

"That won't be necessary," Harriman said. He'd stiffened. His feelings had been hurt.

"It's just as well you don't. I was going to put a heading on it: *Ass Covering Agreement for the Bureau.*"

"I'm not sure I like you, Sheriff."

"Hell, go ahead and dislike me. What else can you do to me, un-elect me? Try to set up a bribery attempt? Try to involve me in some scam that proves I'm corrupt?"

"That might not be necessary," Harriman said. "There's some talk that you have a tie-in with the biker gangs that operate clubs in your county."

"Do me a favor, Harriman. You make that charge in public, in the papers or on TV. I'll gut you and the Bureau like a fish."

"I'm not making a charge. I'm merely stating that ..."

"You'd better make that charge or wipe it off your books. As soon as this is over, I'll be in Raleigh to see what you have in your files on me. I might even know a lawyer who understands the Freedom of Information Act."

"It's nothing like that."

"It better be nothing at all, a clean slate."

Harriman stared out the window for a few more seconds. He looked stunned. People didn't talk to Bureau agents that way. When he got himself together, he said that he had some calls to make. He left without looking at Wilt.

Wilt took a slow look around the room. The police technician had his earphones firmly in place and his head was down. He was reading a magazine. Joe Croft stood with his back to the closed door to the room where Jonas Moore was resting.

Neither man gave any indication they'd heard the conversation between Wilt and Harriman. Not that it mattered with Joe. But he didn't want Amos Wilson spreading trash all over town.

Wilt took a couple of deep breaths and stretched. The suspicion, *that* was the price for showing an interest in Diane. The rumors that the Sheriff has a crooked back.

CHAPTER FIFTEEN

Jonas Moore didn't sleep or he didn't sleep long. Within minutes of stretching out on the mattress, he kicked the blankets aside and opened the door. He braced a shoulder against the doorframe. "It's past banking hours," he said.

"Don't worry," Wilt said. "Special Agent Harriman says he'll furnish the money from a special fund the Bureau has. You can give him a check later. You're good for it, aren't you?"

"I am," Jonas said.

"I want you to try to rest. It might be a long night. I want you fresh and alert."

"I don't think I can sleep."

"If nothing else, close your eyes and rest."

"If you're sure there's no problem with the money?"

Wilt assured him that the money was the least of their problems, the easy part of it.

Half an hour later, Wilt opened the door to the bedroom and looked in. Jonas was curled into a ball, snoring softly

Wilt decided that he would let Jonas sleep until eight or eight-thirty. Or until the call that gave the final instructions. Whichever came first.

Floyd arrived at Tall Pines around five-thirty. He said he couldn't sleep any longer knowing there was so much to be done. Wilt sent him off with Joe Croft to go on with their door-to-door interviews.

Wilt propped a chair against the wall and closed his eyes. He spent most of the time thinking about what was ahead that night. All the possible ways that the transfer of the money could be made and how he'd counter any tricky ones the kidnappers might come up with.

The rest of the time he thought about Diane.

The Tattooed Lady. Who needs a Tattooed Lady?

Maybe I do, he thought. But he wasn't one hundred percent sure. There were gaps and blank places and corners that were too much in shadow. The good warm sun didn't shine in there.

What kind of man needs a Tattooed Lady? That was one of the better questions.

He didn't have one of his better answers for it.

Joe returned a bit after seven. He carried two bags, "paper pokes" he liked to call them. The large bag held a number of foil-wrapped barbecue sandwiches. The other bag covered a six-pack of twist top Buds. He and Wilt and the police technician sat around the card table and had their supper.

Floyd looked in and left to relieve Susie at the Station switchboard.

"You ask all your questions?" Wilt asked between bites and chews and a swallow of Bud.

"Where's J. Edgar's boy?" Joe looked around.

Wilt ignore the question. "What have you got?"

Joe wiped his hands on a napkin and opened his notebook. "An older couple named Griffin say they saw a man and a puppy in the field between the complex and the highway. They're not sure about the exact time but it could have been around three o'clock or a few minutes after. The man was a distance away and neither of the Griffins can see too well. The composite Gus Triffon gave us wasn't much help." Joe flipped a page. "They think he was young. But when it got to how young … well, for the Griffins, that's anywhere from fifteen to forty."

"That's some range you've got there." Wilt finished a sand-wich. He did a count and saw there were four more. He took another one and peeled the foil away.

"Someone else saw a man in a raincoat. He didn't see the puppy. Out in the courtyard, we ran into Ellis Wilbur who deliv-ers the *Raleigh Times*. He was out here yesterday collecting. That was around three. He saw a young man in a raincoat in the field between the complex and the highway. He was over near the edge of the field, where the woods are. But he didn't see a puppy." Joe put the notebook aside and had a bite of his barbecue. "My guess is, if this was the same man as the one the Griffins saw, then the dog was in the woods when Ellis Wilbur passed by."

"An I.D.?"

Joe chewed and shook his head. He swallowed. "The man's back was to him."

"Where'd you get the barbecue?"

"Methodist church down the road."

"Yeah, but not the beer," Wilt said.

Most of the barbecue places in the south didn't sell beer or any kind of alcohol. That attitude went back to the old days when the churches all had barbecue suppers to raise money. The churches didn't approve of drinking and even if they had, they wouldn't sell it on the church grounds.

"Happened to have it in the cooler at home."

"You sure it wasn't in the trunk of the cruiser next to the air mattress?"

"Would I lie to you, boss?"

"Only if you thought you could get away with it." Wilt nod-ded toward the closed bedroom door. "What do we feed Moore?"

"I stopped next door. His wife says she'll fix him supper when he's ready for it."

"She alone?" Wilt had been holding back. Now he reached for the next to the last sandwich. He unwrapped it and tore it in half. He passed half of it to the police technician. He pushed the last sandwich toward Joe. Joe had been talking so much he was behind.

"Not alone," Joe said. "There's a classy-looking lady keeping her company. A divorcee."

"You get her phone number?"

"Not yet."

Wilt opened two Buds and handed one to the police technician. "Maybe I ought to look in next door. I might need a phone number myself."

"Not your type," Joe said.

"Why not?"

"You like your meat raw. This one's too ladylike for you." Joe opened the final beer. "You never did say where the Bureau man is."

"At the Holiday Inn. He's probably taking another shower and shave so he'll look and smell good tonight out in the moonlight. My guess is that was after he called the front office and told them how rude and crude and unfriendly I am."

Joe laughed. "Got your number early, didn't he?"

"It ain't hard."

Wilt checked his watch. It was right on seven-thirty. It was already dark outside. Though he knew Jonas needed all the rest he could get, he also knew he wanted the man fed and alert when the call came through. He stood. "I'll shake Moore awake. You see if his supper's ready."

"Don't throw me in that briar patch."

"You like briars," Wilt said.

Harriman returned while Jonas Moore was having his supper. He gave the empty beer bottles a sour look but he didn't say anything. He'd changed his shirt again. Now he wore a blue tie shirt and dark blue tie and he carried a dark raincoat. The raincoat looked new. Wilt wondered if that went on the expense account. Slung over one shoulder was what looked like a camera case.

"You going to take pictures?"

"It's a nightscope."

From the dark clothing and the nightscope, Wilt guessed that Harriman assumed he was going to be closely involved with the operation.

The hell he would. It didn't work that way, Wilt told himself. Harriman couldn't cover his ass and badmouth the way the operation was being handled and still wedge himself into the front-line action. Nobody got to have it both ways. If Wilt would be damned if Harriman got within a mile of the money while it was being delivered. And Harriman had picked his way without knowing it.

In the early evening, after the supper hours, there was a rash of calls. Dana's teacher called. The minister of Moore's church called and wanted to come by and offer such comfort as he could. An Associated Press stringer called and wanted to drive by for a short interview that would go out on the wire.

Jonas handled each call well. He was short and polite. After his rest, he seemed especially alert.

The call they were waiting for came in at nine-fifty-eight.

"You have the money?"

"Yes." Jonas said.

Wilt sat next to him. He'd taken the technician's earphones. He had a legal pad in front of him. If there was a question that Jonas wasn't sure how to answer, he would look to Wilt and the Sheriff would write the answer on the pad.

"In small bills?"

"You didn't say anything about small bills." Jonas turned to Wilt. Wilt scribbled on the pad: <u>In tens and twenties.</u>

"In tens and twenties," Jonas said.

"You called the police?"

"No, I didn't."

"Don't you lie to me."

"They're not involved."

"Here's how we do it. You know the bridge over Branch Creek?"

Wilt wrote on the pad: I know it.

"Yes," Moore said, "I know it."

"Exactly at eleven I want you to park on the side of the road that's south of the bridge. Two hundred yards from the bridge. What kind of car do you have?"

"A Firebird."

"You carry the gym bag and walk toward the bridge. If you're alone, if you're not being followed, you'll be met and you'll hand over the money. You got all that?"

"Yes, I've got all of it." Moore seemed to crumble inside. "My little girl … Dana … when will I …?"

"One hour later, after we've got the money, we call you and tell you where she is."

"How do I know …?"

"Repeat all of it for me."

Jonas repeated the instructions. Tears of frustration ran down his face.

"Good for you. You do it the way we say and your little girl will be with you by twelve-thirty. You get cute and you'll never see her again."

The line went dead.

Wilt met Joe's eyes. He nodded. "Why don't you take Mr. Moore next door? I'm sure he'd like to see his wife."

"But …" Jonas looked at the phone.

"They won't call again."

The technician stopped the tape and hit the rewind button.

Joe came back a couple of minutes later. He started to say something and then clamped his mouth shut.

Wilt nodded at the technician. "Play it again."

CHAPTER SIXTEEN

At five of eleven, Wilt parked the Moore's Firebird on the side of the road about two hundred yards south of the Branch Creek bridge.

The prior forty-five minutes had been busy.

His first stop was at his apartment for a quick change of clothing. He tossed his uniform aside and dressed in gray trousers, a plaid shirt, a dark brown pullover sweater and slipped on a pair of jogging shoes. Over the changed clothing, he put a hip length wool outer coat.

He found his gym bag on the closet floor. It was empty but it smelled of sweat and dirty socks.

The next stop was the Station, where Joe waited for him. On the way through the lobby, he left the gym bag with Floyd so that the money-sized bundles of cut newspaper could be packed in it. While this was being done, he entered his office and unlocked the safe. He got out his spare, a Dan Wesson .357 with a six-inch blue steel barrel. He loaded it with fresh shells and shoved it in his right hand, coat pocket. He counted six more shells from the box and wrapped them in a paper towel so they wouldn't rattle when he walked.

Floyd passed him the gym bag and said "Good luck, Sheriff."

Joe waited for him in the back parking lot. As soon as Wilt was seated, Joe said," It's been tested," and passed him a walkie-talkie, "But you check it again when you park by the bridge."

One more stop, at the Moore's, to get the borrowed Firebird.

All that hurry and he was early. A mile away from the bridge, Wilt realized he was ten minutes ahead of schedule. He pulled to the side of the road and let the time drift by.

Now, at five of eleven, he had parked with the bridge in sight. Early, but not too early if the kidnappers were watching. He lifted the walkie-talkie and checked the picket line.

Joe first. Joe was stationed half a mile away on the other side of the bridge. He'd taken the roundabout route so he wouldn't be spotted on the main road.

"Loud and clear and cold," Joe said.

The next call was to Special Agent Harriman. He was half-a-mile behind Wilt in the driveway of a farmhouse. There was a pickup and a flatbed truck in the same driveway and Wilt hoped the cruiser wouldn't be noticed in the dark.

"Read you loud and clear," Harriman said.

Deputy Charlie Reaton was in the cruiser with Harriman. Charlie was the driver. That was because Charlie knew the county and Harriman didn't. If there was a chase, it would be better to have Charlie behind the wheel.

What Wilt told Charlie was that this was an important operation and he didn't want Harriman playing cowboy and screwing it up. No matter what Harriman said, no matter what orders he gave, Charlie wasn't to leave that driveway until Wilt gave him the order. He was to be polite but deaf if he had to.

Eleven. The minute hand straight up. Wilt shoved the walkie talkie in his left hand pocket. Now he was balanced. He stepped from the car and dragged the gym bag after him. The night air was cold. He shifted the gym bag to his left hand and raised his collar. The wind was from the left side of the road, crossing him, and he thought he could smell the dirty socks. When this was over, he told himself, he was going to burn that damned bag.

A three-quarters moon. The sky was cloudless. The moonlight was bright. So bright he could see every clump of weeds or grass as he headed for Branch Creek bridge.

The creek wasn't wide or deep. The water, what there was of it, ran through a deep gulley and the gulley was the reason for the bridge. It spanned the banks and it was seventy or eighty yards from south end to north end. The construction was of concrete and heavy steel rails. Heavy steel rails bordered both sides of the bridge.

From a distance Wilt heard an anguished bellowing. If the wind were stronger, he'd have told himself that it was a sound created by the wind in the dense woods. Instead, it might be what it sounded like: a lost cow that needed milking.

The final hundred yards. He kept walking. He reached the near end of the bridge and paused. There was no sound from the water below the bridge and Wilt guessed that the level was so low that it was probably frozen over.

The new sound, when it came, startled him. It split the silence. Not there one moment and so loud the next that he almost jumped.

He must have passed it. Hidden in some road, in some clearing. He stepped onto the narrow pavement walk as the pickup truck's headlights brushed across him and the engine raced. He turned his head and tried to eye blink the glare away. It didn't work and he was blind when he turned his head away and walked on.

Split seconds later, he heard the hollow thump of the truck's tires as it left the road and touched the bridge.

The truck slowed. When the cab was even with Wilt the window cranked down. He saw a dark shape, head and shoulders and the man shouted, "Throw the bag in the back. Throw it in the back."

Wilt swung his left arm. The cab passed him and the bed of the truck was even with him now. He tossed the bag into the truck bed. Then he ducked and drew the Dan Wesson from his right-hand pocket. As soon as the bag hit the truck bed, the driver floored the gas. The pickup jerked, hesitated and lunged forward.

Wilt was directly behind the truck, three or four feet away, when he aimed at the right rear tire and pulled off three rounds. The tire exploded and bits of rubber slapped against Wilt.

The driver wrestled the wheel as the truck swerved. It wobbled from side to side. Wilt stood up straight and lined up the Dan Wesson. He was about to fire again when the truck made a wide circling half loop and struck the railing on the right side of the bridge.

Wilt trotted forward. Running jarred his left hip and he felt the hooks of pain. He slowed when he reached the rear of the truck. He listened. There was only the sound of the running engine and, below that, the clogged coughing of one of the men. He braced himself against the truck siding and limped to the driver's side. He prepared himself. Dan Wesson in his right hand. He grabbed the door handle and pulled. The door flew open. The overhead lights went on.

There were two young men, hardly more than boys, in the truck. The driver slumped forward against the wheel. His nose was broken and blood ran down and covered his chin and neck and the front of his jacket. As Wilt watched, this one coughed and spit up blood and mucus. The other boy, the one in the passenger seat, had his head back against the seat. A deep ragged cut on his forehead spilled blood down his face.

Wilt stepped back and took the walkie-talkie from the left pocket of his coat. "Joe, Harriman, I've got them. I'm on the bridge." He placed the walkie-talkie on the truck hood and reached in and switched off the engine. He stepped back and stood there, the .357 relaxed and down beside his leg.

He heard the sirens building as the cruisers came at him from both directions. At the last moment, at opposite ends of the bridge, both cruisers curled sideways and formed barricades. The bridge was bottled up.

"Call an ambulance," Wilt said when he saw Joe.

"Bad?"

"Not half as bad as it's going to be," Wilt said.

Special Agent Harriman trotted toward the wrecked truck. Wilt stared at him and smiled.

All those night operation clothes and that nightscope for nothing. The smile was all he'd allow himself. He really wanted to laugh.

CHAPTER SEVENTEEN

The interrogation room at the Sheriff's Station was crowded. The ambulance, on Wilt's orders, took the two young men to the Station rather than to the Emergency Room at the hospital. The ambulance attendants cleaned up the two boys and waited with them until a doctor arrived. Now the doctor, Walter Parsons, checked them for injuries besides the broken nose and the cut forehead. Floyd was there in case there was trouble with the boys and Joe Croft waited for the right moment to begin the questioning.

Wilt was in the observation room where the two-way mirror was. Joe hadn't looked in his direction but Wilt was fairly certain that Joe knew he was there.

Chief Amos Wilson stood shoulder-to-shoulder with Wilt. He'd been jerked from a warm bed and he was sleepy and boozy and needed a shave. He wore civvies, a topcoat over a rumpled shirt.

In the interrogation room ,the boy with the broken nose was starting to talk. "… but we didn't mean any harm. It was a joke."

Wilt leaned forward and switched off the sound.

"I know both boys," Amos said. "why, both of them are from good families and they're on the basketball team. I saw them play last week when Edgefield beat …"

"I don't care if they piss dark German beer and walk on water."

Amos held up his hands in surrender. "No, no, Wilton, what I mean is that I'm surprised. That's all."

"Let's leave it at that. You're surprised. Don't give me that shit about what good families they come from or what great jocks they are."

Amos nodded and gave Wilt his hangdog look. They left the observation room and entered the lobby. "Somebody call and get you out of bed, Amos?"

Amos almost choked on it. He got it out finally. "John Turner called me. His son is ..."

"The one who likes to play jokes, right?"

"Call me, Wilt, when you've decided what the charges are."

"You'll be the first to know."

Wilt passed the switchboard desk and nodded at Floyd. "I'll be in my office."

Special Agent Harriman was seated in Wilt's chair behind the desk and was on the phone. He got to his feet when he saw Wilt.

Wilt closed the door.

Harriman finished his phone call. "Yes, I guess that's about it, sir." He listened for a few seconds. "I'll stay over tonight and make sure this is wrapped up before I leave town. I should be back in the office after lunch." He listened a time more and smiled. "Thank you, sir. It's nice of you to say that."

Wilt edged around the desk. The pain in his hip had reached the toothache scale. Harriman moved aside and Wilt sat down. Harriman said his goodnight and placed the receiver on the base and pushed the phone into place at Wilt's elbow.

Wilt lit a Chesterfield and blew the smoke toward Harriman. Harriman looked startled and leaned away. He moved around the front of the desk and unbuttoned his suit coat. He unclipped a Police Special in its holster and placed it on the desk. "Keep this for me. I want a few words with the boys."

"Tell them to win one for the Gipper."

"What?"

"Nothing." The cigarette tasted like burning leaves smelled. "You going to take the credit for this one?"

"I don't know what you mean," Harriman said.

"Come on, Harriman, I know how you slickers work." He dropped the pistol and holster in a desk drawer and closed it. "You stand around the fringes and when the bust is made, you preempt it."

"There's enough credit to go around."

"After you covered your ass in case it went sour?" Wilt shook his head.

Harriman hesitated. It was probably a new experience for him. It wasn't often that other law enforcement officers confronted the Bureau so openly. "It's out of my hands." He reached the door and stopped with his hand on the door knob. "The district office does pretty much what it wants to."

"But you will spell my name right when you list the spear-carriers, won't you?"

"You've got a twisted sense of humor," Harriman said. He stepped through the doorway and drew the door closed behind him without looking back at Wilt.

He was gone about three or four minutes before Joe Croft opened the door without knocking and reached back and slammed it shut.

Joe's face was flushed and he looked about as angry as Wilt had ever seen him. "That shit…he's posing and posturing around like he had something to do with this. Our noble leader, I think it comes out."

"I've already had my words with him."

"The words didn't take," Joe said.

"I didn't expect them to." Wilt shrugged and then thinking, *oh, to hell with it*, he grinned. "I think we ought to read the papers in the morning and see what a really small part we had to do with tonight's work."

"It burns my ass."

"You can't blame him. It's a course they teach at the Academy. It's Stealing the Credit 44. It's required for graduation." Wilt rubbed his eyes. Clustered dust came away on his fingertips. "What do you think of the kids?"

"I'm a hundred percent sure they had nothing to do with Dana Moore or her disappearance."

"So, why'd they do it?"

"The money," Joe said. "They thought it was a small risk and they'd seen enough movies to think they could run this scam and not get caught. To tell the truth, it was the money that bothered me the whole time."

"Huh?"

"The money they asked for in ransom. Five thousand isn't enough for the risk. That should have clued us."

"Bothered me too. But five thousand is a fortune to them." He'd kept that doubt to himself. Until he knew better, he had to treat it as a legitimate demand and he wanted his deputies to do the same. "Tell me about the kids."

"Benny Turner, the one with the broken nose, is the brains."

"For the one with the brains he's still about half a load short."

"The way he tells it, he and his buddy ... George Hall ... heard about the little girl this afternoon or early evening. So, they decided they'd do a prank. And part of the prank was to see if they could pull it off without getting caught."

"A prank?"

"And a joke. Benny worked that word, Joke, into the conversation about as often as he wedged prank in."

"And the other kid?"

"George Hall. Mainly he's worried that we might think they really had something to do with the disappearance of the little girl. He kept telling us he and the Turner kid were at basketball practice until five o'clock or a bit after that."

"You check?"

"I called Coach Waters. He backs them. They were on the court until a little after five and they had to shower and dress."

"How old are they?"

"Seventeen, Benny's a couple of months older than George."

"Juveniles," Wilt said.

"Seventeen ain't like being twelve. I think they could do some time at one of the youth offender centers."

"Six months-to-a-year. I'm leaning in that direction."

"The judge in Juvenile Court..."

"Will get an earful from me," Wilt said. "Not only was this a nasty ball of crap, preying on the fears of the parents, but there's more. They tied up a lot of my manpower when I should have been out there looking for Dana Moore."

"That ought to read with the judge."

"What does Doc Parsons say?"

"Turner's got a busted nose. Might need an operation later to make it beautiful again. Hall's got about forty stitches on his forehead."

"What do you think we ought to do with them?"

"Bail?"

"Not this soon," Wilt said. "Parsons say anything about the possibility of concussion?"

"He said he didn't know for sure. Both of them are dizzy. Both of them took a lick when the truck hit that bridge rail."

"I say we put them in the jail ward overnight. For observation. Check that with Doc Parsons. See if he'll go along with it."

"My guess is that he will. Parsons not only didn't like being dragged out of bed, but he doesn't like their idea of a prank."

Joe left to check with Parsons.

Wilt put his head on the desk and drifted. He wasn't sure how long he was like that before he heard the door open and close. He lifted his head and blinked his eyes clear. Harriman got his coat from the peg behind the door. He folded the coat carefully over one arm and crossed to the desk and held out his hand. Wilt's mind was blank for a few seconds. Just before it got embarrassing, he remembered Harriman's holster and pistol. He dragged it from the desk drawer and placed it on the desk just under Harriman's hand.

"Thanks, Sheriff." Harriman clipped the holster and weapon on his belt just above his rump. He straightened his suit jacket. "I had a talk with the boys. They're harmless."

"Correct my understanding of English," Wilt said. "Harmless means they couldn't or didn't do any harm. Maybe you've got time to stop by and talk to Jonas Moore before you leave town. He probably thinks there was some harm done him in the last twenty-four hours. Or if that's out of your way, you can explain to me how extortion is ever, ever harmless."

"You know what I mean, Sheriff. They're kids. I think they've learned their lesson."

"For those two, school ain't even started."

"I think you're overreacting."

"Bullshit and you know it." Wilt stood. His left leg had numbed, gone to sleep. He shook the leg to get some feeling back in it. He wasn't sure which was worse, no feeling or the pain that came and went. "I'll check the morning paper to see what you say."

"You won't be left out," Harriman said.

"What I don't want to see in there is any crap about how harmless these two are. That shows up in your paper and you and I are going to butt heads."

"We're doing that already."

"But so far nobody's bleeding," Wilt said.

Harriman considered Wilt for a long time. He nodded finally. "There won't be anything in there about them being harmless. It's your county, Sheriff. I can't tell you how to run it."

"Thanks," Wilt said. "That's the way it ought to be."

Harriman sighed. He relaxed. "Call me as soon as you get a lead on the Moore child. I'm still involved. Keep me up to date."

"I'll call you when it's solved. That way you can save the government gas and motel rent."

Joe Croft passed Special Agent Harriman in the office doorway. He gave the agent a sour look and even bumped him with a shoulder. Joe didn't say excuse me or even act like he knew he'd touched Harriman.

Harriman looked at him and shook his head. He probably decided that it wasn't his kind of county, the kind where they kowtowed to the Bureau and said thank you a lot.

Joe closed the door. "Parsons says he thinks the jail ward is a good idea."

"The kids ready to move?"

"The Doc gave his okay."

"Floyd still here?" When Joe nodded.

Wilt said, "Here's how I want it. Have Floyd cuff them. I want you with a pump gun. I want you to lever a shell into the chamber right in front of them. I want it by the manual. *How to Transport Dangerous Prisoners.* No joking, no talking. They try to talk, you shut them up. I want them to feel we think they're Public Enemy Number One and Two."

"Got you." Joe stepped away. He stopped. "One problem. I let them make a call. That is, Hall made a call. Turner said he didn't have to. Anyway, there are a couple of pissed off Daddies there in the lobby."

"What they got to be pissed off about?"

"That their nice, God-fearing, clean-living and well-mannered sons are in our dirty slammer with ordinary criminals. Especially when everybody knows it was a joke and a prank."

"Lawyers with them?"

"No lawyers. A bails bondsman."

"Too bad there's no judge around at this hour to set the bail," Wilt said.

"Ain't it?"

Wilt followed Joe to the door. "Give me five minutes and then bring the kids through the lobby."

"Got it." Joe left.

Wilt closed the door after him. He stood and waited four minutes. When he opened the door and stepped into the lobby, three men were seated together on one of the benches. They got to their feet quickly. Wilt headed straight for them. He recognized the bondsman. Rollie Chessman was his name. He'd been a cop in Durham before he got tossed off the force for taking money for turning a blind eye on a fence that handled stolen goods.

Rollie spoke first. "Sheriff, I'm here with..."

"No bail's been set yet. It'll be morning before these two get in front of a judge."

Rollie turned and spread his hands toward the two men behind him, as if to indicate that there wasn't anything he could do.

The man behind Rollie on his left side pushed forward. He was a fleshy man with jowls that were just beginning to sag at the jaw line. Of the two men, he was the one with the expensive clothing. His tweed jacket wasn't off the rack and the trousers looked tailored too. The topcoat was five hundred dollars of Brooks Brothers. When he faced Wilt, there was a certain amount of arrogance, as if he wasn't used to running into roadblocks. What he wanted he usually got.

"These are juveniles we're talking about," he said. "We're not talking about hardened criminals. I don't even understand why we're talking about bail at all."

"You're...?"

Rollie introduced them. "This is John R. Turner. He's vice-president of Datatec."

"Your son, Benny, is the one who dreamed up this scam."

"I was assured by Benny that it was a joke, a prank."

"Everybody seems to be stuck on joke and prank. I wish somebody would come up with a different word, just so I don't get bored." He heard a door slam behind him and footsteps approaching. He didn't have to turn around. He could read what was behind him by the look on the faces in front of him. When this group was abreast of Wilt, he swung his head and looked at them. Floyd was on one side of the two boys, his hand on the butt of his holstered pistol. Joe was on the other side, a pump-action shotgun at high port.

"What are you...?" This was blurted by the other father, the one who'd remained in the background.

"They're going to spend the night in the jail ward at the hospital. That's for observation. We want to be sure neither of them has a concussion."

"Papa..." It was almost a scream from the shorter of the two boys, the one with shaggy hair that needed cutting. The patch of tape on his forehead identified him as George Hall. "Papa.." The boy tried to pull away from Floyd. The deputy put out an arm and wrapped it around his neck and pulled him back. "Papa, we didn't do anything."

"George." Mr. Hall took a step toward his son.

Wilt stepped between them. "This isn't doing any good. The night in the jail ward is the doctor's idea."

"This is highhanded behavior," John R. Turner said.

His son, Benny, tried to pull away from Joe. Joe moved in front of him and pressed him back with the butt of the shotgun. "This isn't fair, Daddy."

"It's as fair as extortion," Wilt said.

A long silence settled upon them before John R. Turner said, "That's the charge? The charge is extortion?"

"In all this talk," Wilt said slowly, evenly, "I never heard how the boys planned to return the money after the joke was over."

John R. Turner saw the trap there and slipped away from it. He lowered his head. Mr. Hall, not as quick, faced his son, George. "Tell them, son. You tell them."

The boy stared down at the floor. "We never ... got as far ... as talking ... about that."

"Enough said?" Wilt looked at both fathers. They wouldn't meet his eyes. Wilt nodded at Joe. He and Floyd marched the two boys down the back steps to the parking lot.

"I guess …" Mr. Hall's voice wavered and failed him. "I guess we can't say anything more about jokes or pranks."

"Go home," Wilt said. "Hanging around here isn't going to do anybody any good."

There was a plea in Mr. Hall's voice. "George's mother … she's worried about him."

"Tell her he's all right. The way this happened, he could have been killed. Tell her he was lucky."

Hall nodded. It wasn't much but it was something that he could carry home to his wife.

John R. Turner wasn't done yet. "My lawyer will be here in the morning with me."

"We have nothing against lawyers," Wilt said.

"When he gets done with you …"

"Don't make threats." Wilt reached into his shirt pocket and took out a single Chesterfield. He lit it. "You're on my territory now. And threats don't change the facts."

"My lawyer is …"

"Go home," Wilt said.

Rollie Chessman knew that Wilt had run out of patience with Turner's ways and his manner. Mumbling, whispering, he got Turner on the move toward the front door. But not before John R. Turner looked over his shoulder and gave Wilt a withering look.

Wilt thought, well, there's another vote I don't get next election.

"Erskine Hall," the other man said after the door closed behind Chessman and Turner. He put out a hand and Wilt shook it. The skin the palm of the hand was a hard as kiln-dried oak.

"A coffee before you go home, Mr. Hall?"

"That would be a kindness, Sheriff."

Wilt filled two cups at the urn. He passed one to Hall. He thought about the man's hand. "What do you do for a living, Mr. Hall?"

"I'm a foreman at the sawmill."

"The one Cooper owns? My daddy worked there."

Hall nodded. "I knew him. Robby Drake was a good man."

He had been, that was true. Until one night, he had too much white whiskey and tried to make a sharp curve into a wider one and ran off into the trees. The steering wheel crushed his chest.

Wilt had his look at Erskine Hall while they sipped the gagging, cooked-down coffee. His face was lean and bony and weathered. The suit he wore was brown with a muted stripe in it, probably his Sunday church suit. It was shiny at the knees and the elbows and, though Wilt couldn't see that part of it, he would bet the seat was worn smooth too. His shoes were cracked along the edges toward the soles but they'd been waxed and polished.

Wilt sat on the bench and indicated a place on his right. Hall sat. At first, Wilt had thought about using his office. Sometimes it was hard to get people out of there. If he used the lobby, Wilt could always say that he had business and walk away. "Tell me about your son."

"You might not believe me."

"And maybe I will."

"Mainly he's a good boy. It's just that sometimes, and it's hard for me to admit this, he don't seem to be very smart. Like this thing they're trying to call a joke or a prank. It's like he's always being led into things by other people. Like he believes if somebody else comes up with an idea, it's got to be a good one."

"Why do you think he and Benny pal together?"

"You know how it is in high school. It don't mean it'll last past then. They both play ball and George thinks the sun rises and sets on Benny. Another year and they'll be out of school. George comes to work for me at the sawmill and Benny goes off to some fancy college somewheres."

Wilt understood that. He'd seen enough of it in his own high school days. The close friendships that barely last past gradua-tion night and those parties. The ones that barely lasted through the summer. And the high school romances that went bloodless and died.

"You think a scare would do George any good?"

"I'd bet my life on it," Hall said.

"I'll make a deal with you." Wilt gave Mr. Hall his stern look. "You break this bargain with me and I'll come down on him so hard he'll wish he'd never been born." The coffee was undrinkable. Susie, who'd come in when she'd called in and heard about the capture of the two boys, was behind the switchboard. "Susie, how about a fresh urn? This is sludge." He turned back to face Hall. "You think you could make a bargain with me?"

"Yes, I'd trust you, Sheriff."

Susie and Mr. Hall nodded at each other. Then she kept her distance and got the coffee-making underway.

"I'm going to be around Webster county for some years. And I might even get elected two or three more times. I don't ever want to see that boy of yours in here again." Wilt lowered the cup of bad coffee into the trash can. "I'm going to put the fear of the Lord into those two young men. They're going to be so tight-assed they'll walk funny. The judge is not going to like what they did any more than I do. In matters like this, I usually get my say about what I think about the sentence. At the least I'd say a year of probation, reporting to a juvenile probation officer. Maybe there'll be a couple of hundred hours of community service for each of them. At the most, at the other extreme, they could get six months to a year in a youthful offender center. That and probation afterwards and the community service."

The relief showed on Hall's face. "His mother is going ..."

Wilt shook his head. "That's our deal. You made the bargain with me blind but that's the deal. Nobody's to know except you and me. If you tell your wife, the first thing happens she tells George and he'll start laughing behind my back and thinking he got away with something."

"It makes sense," Hall admitted. "But I wish I knew what to tell his mama."

"Tell her he's a minor as far as the law's concerned. He's not going to any prison filled with hardened bad-asses. And make it clear that it will be a lot easier on him if he shows he learned his lesson. At least, that's what you think."

"I can do that."

Wilt stood. He took the coffee cup from Hall and dropped it in the trash. "Good enough."

"You going to make the same deal with Mr. Turner?"

"I wouldn't trust him to keep it. He can sweat blood as far as I'm concerned."

Hall nodded. He probably understood the idea of getting even. And perhaps he wouldn't have trusted Turner, either.

"If you want to bring your wife over to the jail ward in the morning. I'll leave word she's to be let in to see her son."

"Thank you."

Wilt, watching him walk away, thought about his father again. He hadn't thought about Robby Drake for years. But he'd loved that man and there was a lot in Erskine Hall that reminded him of his father. The same dogged honesty, the same give-a-dollars-work-for-a-dollar work ethic.

The coffee was still dripping through. Wilt leaned on the counter and looked at Susie. "How you feel?"

"Fine," she said. "I got some sleep."

"You think this police work is fun?"

"I didn't say that, but it beats watching TV." She tilted her head toward the door where Hall was just leaving. "I heard you talking to Mr. Hall."

"You know him?"

"We go to the same church. He's a good man."

Wilt gave her a sour look. "Jack the Ripper probably had a nice daddy too." He rubbed his eyes. "When you start eavesdropping on my conversations, I start believing I've got to get you back on days where you belong."

"Don't talk tough to me, Wilt. I'll break down and cry all over you and that would embarrass you. You see, I know you. You've got a soft spot or two."

"I've got a heart made out of rusty old razor blades and you know it."

Susie said, still smiling, that he probably knew what his heart was made of better than anybody else did.

He couldn't sleep. The darkness bothered him. He was afraid if he fell into a sleep that was deep enough, he'd dream about Cathy Dobbs and Dana Moore. He fought sleep and at the same time needed it. In the end, he settled for switching on the light in the bathroom and a surface sleep that grew out of the almost daytime like circumstances.

By six-thirty, he was in the kitchen drinking coffee and yawning and watching the sun come up. The day was going to be cold and blustery. He knew if he had any sense at all he'd call and say he'd be late and he'd go back to bed.

Too late. He was wide awake enough to know all the jobs that had to be done. He couldn't sleep with that hanging around his neck.

He was at the Sheriff's Station by seven-thirty. Joe Croft was at the switchboard. Wilt tried the coffee. It wasn't more than an hour old.

"I relieved Susie and sent Floyd home."

"When do you sleep?"

"As soon as this is over." Joe brought him up to date. He'd called in everybody who was up to it and he'd set new search patterns.

"That it?"

"That Turner guy was here early. I told him, if I was him, I'd leave before you got here and kicked his butt."

Even though he'd made his decision about Benny Turner and George Hall, another massive wave of anger against the two boys swept over him. He'd lost a day because of them. It was enough to make him want to kick ass.

"That's not very politic of you."

"I don't have to be politic. I'm not the one running for office." Joe grinned. "Not yet anyway."

"Sounds like I might have competition."

"If you do," Joe said," it's because you taught me too well."

"Maybe I taught you wrong ... on purpose."

"It's not anything you said. It's how you did it."

"Shows how sly I am." Wilt carried his coffee into the office.

The autopsy report on Cathy Dobbs still waited for him, unopened. He sighed and broke the seal and read Doc Simpson's dry, spare, medical language. Bruises on her arms and wrists. Cuts and contusions on her face. Trauma in the vaginal and rectal area. The right leg dislocated at the hip. Death by suffocation.

He shoved the report back in its envelope and put it in a desk drawer and locked the drawer.

Damn all the crazies in the world.

"Thought you'd want to see this." Joe came in and dropped the *News and Observer* on the desk in front of Wilt. "You made page one."

He skipped through the short piece. It had all the earmarks of news that had come in late and had to be wedged onto the front page. The story was exactly what Wilt expected. The F.B.I., with Special Agent Harriman in charge, had foiled a phony extortion plot that had been concocted to take advantage of a missing child. Two young men, both juveniles, had been arrested. The F.B.I. had been assisted in the operation by Sheriff Wilton Drake. Harriman was quoted as saying that he could not have cracked the case without the dedicated help of the local law enforcement officers.

Wilt grunted and dropped the newspaper into the trashcan. He was still stinging from the writeup when Joe buzzed him.

"Charlie just called in from the city dump."

"Yeah?"

"You know Ernest Bishop?"

 "I know him."

"Ernest flagged Charlie down. From what Charlie says he thinks he's found the Moore child. At least he thinks it's her."

"Dead?"

 "Dead," Joe said.

CHAPTER EIGHTEEN

"Rats got to her," Doc Simpson said.

Wilt stood some feet away with Ernest Bishop.

Ernest was huge and black and had muscles on top of muscles. Some twenty years ago, he'd been a damned good defensive end. He'd been All-State in high school. There'd been hopes he would play his college ball at the University of North Carolina. His grades were a disaster. Some of the smaller black school came after him. Ernest said if he couldn't play where he wanted to, he wouldn't play at all. He took a job on a garbage truck and, in time, he worked his way up until he managed the dump.

"I guess she was there this morning when I got to work." Ernest said.

"But not there yesterday?"

"She wasn't here. We worked this area yesterday and I'd have seen her. Today we're working over there." He pointed east, where a city truck unloaded a mountain of garbage bags and loose refuse. "I was here a time and had a coffee and then I walked over there to see if yesterday's job had been done the way it was supposed to be. That was when I saw her. I was about to call you but I saw that cruiser."

Doc Simpson squatted beside the child's body, blocking Wilt's view of her. Doc looked over his shoulder. "It's like the other one, almost a carbon copy."

The photo Mrs. Moore had given him was in his pocket, Wilt stepped closer and passed the photo to Doc. "This who it is?"

"As far as I can tell."

Bracing himself. Wilt stepped around Doc Simpson and looked down at the body.

A broken doll. This time of real flesh. Not last year's Christmas doll that ended up at the city dump when it got broken. This doll bled and its flesh had been torn away and eaten by rats and other night animals that lived in the dump.

There was a pair of panties above her head.

"It's Dana Moore," he said.

Head on the steering wheel and eyes closed, Wilt sat in the Tall Pines parking lot. He'd left the minister with Arlene Moore. That was after the bad first moments. As soon as Jonas and Arlene saw Wilt and the minister, the hope ran out of them, what little hope there was after the bogus ransom attempt.

Comfort wasn't Wilt's real business. He stepped back, out of the sightlines and let the minister do his best. Part of that comfort was hugging and holding and mumbling about Jesus' overall plan. Arlene looked over the minister's shoulder and locked eyes with Wilt. "I want to see my baby. When can I see my baby?"

"Soon," Wilt said, "as soon as the autopsy's done."

"I want to see her now."

The minister drew her even closer. "The Lord will let you see her soon. He will and that is a promise."

Wilt touched Jonas Moore on the shoulder. "Let's get some air."

At the door, Wilt looked back. The minister and Arlene seemed to cling together like lovers. Wilt closed the door and stopped on the landing. "Smoke?"

Jonas hadn't worn his topcoat. Now he turned up his jacket. "No, thanks." He shivered.

Wilt cupped his hands against the wind and got his smoke lit. "See if you can talk your wife into waiting to see your daughter after she's been worked on at the undertaker."

"Why's that?"

Wilt stepped down into the courtyard. "Take my word for it."

Jonas shuddered and wiped a tear from his eyes. "The man who did this…?"

"I'll find him," Wilt said.

Jonas climbed the steps and stood on the landing. Behind him, the plastic chili peppers rustled in the crossing wind. "I guess I'd better go inside and help Arlene."

"That's the best you can do."

Jonas entered the apartment.

The hearing for the Turner and the Hall boys was set for that afternoon in Juvenile court. An hour before the hearing, Wilt put through a call to Judge Emily Walker and told her honor what had happened the night before. He surprised himself with how reasonable he was. It wasn't, he said, as if either of these boys was a repeat offender or a hopeless possibility as a person. But it was a serious matter. It couldn't go completely unpunished.

Judge Walker agreed with Wilt's suggestion that a stern lecture, a time of probation and a heavy load of community service was the least that the boys could expect.

"You know," Judge Walker said, "we're not supposed to have this kind of conversation."

"I don't see why not. Part of the punishment is the fear of God we're putting in them. We can't very well get that effect if we have this conversation in front of them."

"You'll be at the hearing?"

"I thought I'd send my deputy, Joe Croft. He was involved from the beginning and he knows as much about this as I do."

"You too busy, Sheriff?"

"I've got two dead little girls, Judge."

There was a hesitation, an intake of breath. "Is it two now?"

"It is," he said.

"I understand, Sheriff. Joe Croft will be a fine spokesman for the Department."

"And do me a favor. Watch for the magic words they're going to try to run past you. Joke and prank."

"I believe I can say ahead of time I don't believe much in that kind of defense."

"Give 'em hell, Judge."

He heard her laughing when he broke the connection.

At one-thirty he sent Joe to the jail ward. From there, he'd escort Benny Turner and George Hall to Juvenile court for the hearing. Next, Wilt called Doc Simpson, who sounded groggy.

"I just got to bed, Wilt."

"Sorry."

"I guess you want the findings on the Moore child. It's very close to the autopsy on the Dobbs girl." Doc summarized it quickly. "The difference is the cause of death. This time the larynx was crushed. No way of knowing if that was the result of a blow or if the killer pressed down on it to silence the child."

"Rape?"

"Same as before. Back and front."

"The underpants, Doc."

"That's different too. They weren't ever in her mouth. No evidence of saliva."

Susie brought Wilt a coffee. Wilt had a sip. At the other end of the line he heard a series of gulps. Doc was having a swallow or two but, Wilt guessed, it probably wasn't coffee.

"Doc, you know a psychologist or a psychiatrist who'll talk to me? Maybe some kind of profile of our killer would help."

"I know one. He's a shrink at North Carolina Memorial."

"You know him well enough to ask for an hour of his time?"

"His name's Rhyson. I think he'll do it if there's time in his schedule."

"You call him?"

"Right now," Doc said. "Call you back."

Doc was back on the line in fifteen minutes. "Ten tomorrow work for you?"

Wilt said it would. He took down all the information he'd need to find Dr. Rhyson at North Carolina Memorial. Full name, South Wing, the office number. Wilt folded the memo carefully and stuffed it in his wallet.

Joe walked into the office at two-thirty-five.

"That was short and sweet."

"It might have been short," Joe said," but it was not sweet. That lady judge tore the hide from them all the way from their eyebrows to their toenails. There was blood all over the chambers. That's where it was, in chambers. Just the boys, their fathers and the lawyer for the rich one, Turner."

"It satisfy you, Joe?"

"Next to a drawing and quartering, whatever that is, or fifty lashes with a cat-o-nine-tails, I guess so. What they got was a year and a half of supervised probation and a hundred and fifty hours of community work. All with the understanding that if there's a fuckup, just one, off they go to a youth offender center."

"How'd the boys take it?"

"Shaking and trembling and about to cry. And about to wet their pants."

"What you up to now?"

"Getting rich," Joe said. He reached into his hip pocket and pulled out a sheaf of divorce notices. "Lots of bitching from the lawyers because these notices weren't served. I handled four this morning and I'll do three or four this afternoon."

The notification was for the one being sued for divorce, giving the date and the time for the hearing. The lawyer paid twenty-five dollars to the Sheriff's department for delivery and then billed his client for that amount. A divorce couldn't be granted without proof of service.

"One day I'm going to get lucky," Joe said. "I'll have four notices all on the same floor in the same apartment complex." He flipped through the notices, checking the addresses. "No such luck this time." He flipped past one notice and then stopped and went back to it. "What's the name of the girl at the Blue Lagoon?"

Wilt held out a hand. Joe passed the notice to him.

Diane Hadley Mills.

"That the lady?"

"Could be."

"You want to serve that one yourself?"

"I could use the fresh air." Wilt stood and put on his heavy coat. He adjusted his cap. "Every leader ought to do some field work now and then."

"Sure," Joe said. "It makes the grunts proud to serve under him."

The address was apartment 28, The Towers. It was, he thought, a ritzy address for a topless dancer and manager of a biker club.

Wilt left Joe in charge. "I'll be gone half an hour."

Joe settled into Wilt's chair. "Hell, take an hour if you need it."

CHAPTER NINETEEN

The Towers was a huge column, mainly glass and stone, that looked like it belonged more in Atlanta than in the grassy farmland of Edgefield. Parking spaces, like spokes of a wheel, encircled the building. There was enough parking, Wilt thought, for a major league baseball stadium. He parked in one of the spaces.

Before Wilt got out, he sat in his cruiser and read the divorce notice. The one suing for the divorce was James Rodney Mills. The action was being taken in the Raleigh courts. The grounds given were the usual ones. Separation, six months living apart. It was the preferred grounds for people who didn't want to wash their linen in public.

The doorman at the Towers was a tall, wide-shouldered black in his early thirties. His gaudy uniform looked like it belonged in a comic opera. It was deep blue with gold braid on the cap, on the shoulders and on the stripe that ran down the outside seam of the trousers. His shoes were polished to a high gloss and his cap was exactly centered and squared.

The doorman, watching stepped into the wind when he saw Wilt start his walk across the parking lot. His eyes tracked Wilt and took in the uniform and the pistol on his hip. When Wilt was four paces away, the doorman lifted his hand slowly and touched the bill of his cap in what might have passed for a salute.

"Can I help you, sir?"

"I'm Sheriff Drake."

"Yes, sir. I've heard of you. Is there some trouble?"

"A minor matter," Wilt said. "Apartment 28."

"That's Miss Mills."

"Yes."

"But no trouble?"

"A minor legal matter." Wilt brushed past him and entered the lobby. He stopped and turned and inspected the electronic setup. On the wall, beside the doorman's station, there were two banks of television monitors. The top row covered the hallways. The two monitors below were larger and they showed the inside of the elevators.

Not the state of the art, he thought, but downtown for little Edgefield, North Carolina.

On the short ride, Wilt located the camera eye on the elevator and stepped in close and smiled and winked. He wondered how that went over with Soldier Boy.

"You found me." Diane stood in the open doorway. "Imagine that."

"It wasn't hard. I have my ways."

"Is this a pleasure visit?"

"Business," Wilt said.

His answer puzzled her. She stepped back and he followed her into the living room. He saw that she wore cutoff jeans and a blue pullover sweater. Her legs, as he remembered, were very, very nice.

The apartment was more than he expected. It was large and airy. The living room furniture was new and modern and looked expensive. The painting over the sofa was in style that made him think of Jackson Pollock and, here and there, were framed and glassed Dufy hunting prints. The drapes were thick and luxurious and the carpet, from the look, was real wool.

"What kind of business, Wilton?" She moved to a sectional sofa.

He followed her and extended the divorce notice. While she read it, he booked the receipt and noted the date and time. He passed the book to her. "You have to sign for it."

She signed. Then another look at the divorce notice. "Damn him."

"You're surprised?"

"Not really. One of us had to. I guess I outwaited him."

"Was he a biker?"

She stared at him in amazement for a long moment. That changed to a smile and then a cascade of laughter. When she could speak, she said, "Hardly. He'd be thrilled to know that you thought he might be. The truth is that he's a stockbroker and very, very good at it."

"The tattoo fooled me," he said.

"That came later, after I left him."

"I see." It was just something to say. The truth was that he didn't see at all.

"Poor baby," she said mockingly. "It's so difficult for you. You've been trying to put the pieces together and they don't fit. I'm this or I'm that and what I am at any one moment doesn't satisfy you at all."

"You do stir around in my head with a big spoon."

"Well," she said, "now you know that I'm married. How does that make you feel?"

"Do you mean does it make me feel guilty because you're married and I've been pursuing you?"

"Yes."

"I feel fine about it."

She tossed the divorce notice on the sofa. "You want a drink?"

"It's early."

"Without a drink in your hand, you don't get to hear the story of my life. The unexpurgated version."

"If I mix it myself. Just some color in the water." He trailed her through a dining room into the kitchen.

She pointed a hand at a cabinet. He opened the doors and saw, stocked with a dozen or so bottles as it was, not many of the bottles had been opened.

"Fix the same for me," she said.

He was heavier on the pour for her. He passed the drink to her and moved around the table, headed for the living room. She stopped him.

"You seem comfortable in kitchens. I noticed that about you." She pulled back a chair and sat.

He circled the table and eased himself into a chair across the way from her.

"Where do I start, Wilton?"

"At the beginning."

"That's an easy answer. But which beginning?"

"The one you're comfortable with," he said.

She'd been born Diane Susan Hadley in Charleston, South Carolina. Her father was a Lieutenant Commander in the Navy who was stationed there the first five years of her life. Near her fifth birthday, he was passed over for promotion for the second time and discharged. "Why does the service do that? Let a man spend all those years in the military and then pass him over and toss him out? It doesn't seem fair."

"It unclogs the line. It cuts the deadwood."

"I guess he was deadwood," she said.

Her father had a hard time finding himself after that. He went from job to job, hopeful at the beginning of each one and bitter when that job fell apart. She attended public school and she was a proper little girl. About the time she reached high school, he gave up on ever getting rich or finding the path to the good life. He settled into a final job as a leasing agent for a company that handled hundreds of apartments in the city and at the beach. He prospered to a degree and when Diane was ready for college, he could afford to send her to Coker.

"A liberal education?"

She smiled. "Of course. No typing, no shorthand. Just those courses that educate and prepare a young girl for a future as a wife and a mother."

Wilt sipped his weak drink. "That ought to take you up to when you're twenty-one or so and graduate cum laude."

"If we go too fast, we might miss something," Diane said.

"Like what?"

"We'd miss Jimmy Mills, the first man in my life. I met him when I was a senior. He was a senior at Davison. Girls from Coker were bussed to a dance at Davison. I met Jimmy at a mixer one Friday night."

"And?"

"He took my poor and worthless virginity one month later in a motel in Charlotte."

"Why was it poor and worthless?"

"You had to be there," she said. She waited, a finger tapping on the tabletop. "Aren't you going to ask me about it, Wilton?"

"What am I supposed to ask?"

"Did I enjoy it? That's one good question."

"Did you?" It was her game, her rules.

"Not very much," she said. "It was all mixed up and awkward and for all his big talk Jimmy didn't know much more about it than I did."

"So, you married Jimmy because you didn't enjoy it?"

"Exactly. And because I'd just about finished my course of study and I hadn't learned anything that would help me earn a living. And maybe because he asked me. And maybe because I thought you were only supposed to go to bed with someone you intended to marry. I'd been to bed with him, hadn't I? That had to mean I intended to marry him."

"It's a twisted kind of logic," he said.

"Isn't it?"

They'd married that June. Both graduated and the marriage took place about two weeks later. Her family approved of Jimmy because he seemed to have a future. His family approved of her because she was so completely a lady.

"So you marched off to face the world and you lived happily ever after."

"Something like that."

Jimmy was accepted into the M.B.A. program at Chapel Hill and they lived there for the two years it took to complete the program. "That's how I know so much about the Tarfoots."

She got her first job there, as a teller in one of the banks. With that income supplementing what his father furnished, they lived well and Jimmy worked hard and finished near the top of his class. The M.B.A. from the University of North Carolina didn't carry the weight the Harvard program did but he got a lot of good offers and he accepted one with a stockbrokerage firm in Charlotte. They did quite well socially, thank you, and Jimmy was so successful that he moved on after three years to a better position with a firm in Raleigh.

"That's too much about Jimmy," Wilt said. "What about you?"

"I made a comfortable home for us and we joined the country club and a tennis and racquet club. I sharpened my tennis and he played racquetball because that's the sport all the young executive enjoyed. Life went on. And on. And on."

"And on."

"I declare," she said mockingly, "I do believe you know about marriage."

"I have a few unsubstantiated clues," he said. "Children?"

"We were waiting for him to make his first million. We were waiting until we tired of the social life. Until we thought we were mature enough to take on the responsibility of raising a child."

Except for the part about the first million, her story matched the way it had been with him and with Mary Ellen. That was the surface. His secret reasons, the ones he never discussed, were more realistic. As a career officer, the time it took him away from home, he wasn't certain he'd be around a child long enough to be a good father. And the longer he lived with Mary Ellen, the less hope he had for the marriage.

"Let me make a guess. One day you looked around at your life, the way it was defined by all this social shit, and you bugged out."

"Not exactly." A brief shake of her head. "I didn't leave until I was fairly certain he felt the same way about me that I felt about him."

"Which was?"

"Bored, disinterested."

"He tell you that he was bored and disinterested?"

"Not in so many words. He demonstrated it. He did that by sleeping with his secretaries and even some of his women clients."

"He hurt your pride?"

"No, I was past that. I felt relief. So we split the blanket."

"I haven't heard that since I was a mountain man."

"In this case, it carried a lot more meaning. I asked for a big share of what we had in assets. You might even say I used a touch of blackmail to get the largest piece of the blanket. The merest mention of the names of some of the women clients he'd been sleeping with was enough to make him very generous."

"And then?"

"With that money, I bought myself a bar."

The thought stunned him. "The Blue Lagoon?"

"That surprises you?"

"A little." A thought pushed at him. "But you dance there."

"For two good reasons. I want to show the girls that I'm not too goody-goody to do what they do. And you have to admit, from the way it fooled you, that it is very good cover for me."

"It's a good cover. You fooled this farm boy."

"According to the books, the license, the club is owned by a corporation. I just happen to own ninety percent of the stock."

"And Kyle and the bikers?"

"Security. Hired help except for Kyle who owns the other ten percent in the corporation. You'd be surprised how much attention someone pays to the details when he owns part of the stock."

"That doesn't explain the drug sales, the after-hours alcohol sales, the women who sell their ass there."

"Not proven," Diane said. "There are no drug sales in the club. Nobody involved with the club, who works there, deals. That's my iron rule."

"Alcohol sales?"

"That's the first I've heard of it. I'll check and doublecheck. The club's no good without a valid license."

"The girls?"

"I can't control their private lives. But no selling is done on the premises. And no dates made for later. That is my other iron rule."

"That doesn't explain Rachel."

"What?"

"You said Kyle could send her to me."

"I think I knew you better than that. It was the insult you took it for. Though to tell the truth, many places the law is just one more item on the overhead."

"You have a talent for rubbing fur against the grain."

"It's a learned talent. And you'll admit you haven't been the perfect gentleman caller."

Wilt checked his watch. By the time he drove back to the Station, his hour would be over. "You didn't tell me about the tattoo."

"I'm not sure I know you well enough."

"I think you know me well enough," he said. "I think you like to keep a bit a mystery about yourself."

Wilt carried his drink to the sink and poured out what remained. She followed him to the living room and waited while he put on his heavy coat.

"You're a complex one yourself."

"What you see is what I am."

"That's too easy. Too obvious."

He opened the door and stood there while he seated his cap. "See you again?"

"If I said no, would that change anything?"

"Maybe. Maybe not. If you'd said no, I'd have to believe you were lying to me."

He backed into the hallway and pulled the door closed behind him.

CHAPTER TWENTY

He arrived in Chapel Hill by nine o'clock, an hour before his appointment at North Carolina Memorial Hospital. He parked his cruiser in the city lot on the corner of North Columbia and Rosemary. It was his first trip to Chapel Hill in years and he decided that a walk around the short main street, Franklin Street, and a look at the campus might stir some of the good memories that he had once had for the University.

The town had changed. Most of the places he'd known as a student were gone now. The block between Columbia and the post office now appeared to be home for a series of banks and other businesses that could afford the increased rents. The Goody Shop was gone. So were the cafeterias. Jeff's, Sutton's Drug Store and the Carolina Coffee Shop and a couple of clothing stores were the only ones that had outlasted the onslaught of record shops, electronic shops and the Carolina souvenir shops.

Saddened by the change, he put the town behind him and crossed to the old part of the campus. Silent Sam, the Confederate monument, was still there and near the back of this quad, Davie Poplar, and beyond that The Old Well and South Building. New brickwork paths had been laid everywhere. That was one change he'd always liked. As soon as the students wore a path in the grass, brick workers stepped in and made a permanent pathway of it. From a bird's eye view, the irregular design of the walks had to look like the web of a drugged spider.

⚜   ⚜   ⚜

Doctor Philip Rhyson was a pudgy man in his early fifties. His hair was long and had a reddish glint to it. His full mustache, on the other hand, was gray and brittle as straw. His eyes were flat black stones behind stainless steel rims.

After a handshake, Rhyson motioned Wilt to a chair and lifted a bulldog pipe from the edge of an ashtray. "You can smoke if you like," he said. It took Rhyson a couple of minutes to find his tobacco pouch.

Wilt lit a Chesterfield. Rhyson pushed the single ashtray to the center of the desk so they could share it. "How's my friend, Simpson?"

"Overworked."

"I thought Edgefield would have little need for a medical examiner. Small town life, the country, peace and quiet, all those are supposed to improve the quality of life."

"There's been too much growth too fast."

Rhyson got his pipe lit. The tobacco was dark and harsh and rank. "Simpson didn't tell me much about your case but I understand it concerns a killer-child molester."

Wilt talked.

Rhyson head back, eyes closed, sucked on his pipe and listened. At intervals, the Doctor lowered his head and asked a brief question. At the end of it, Wilt wasn't certain that he'd told all the important parts of it or what the important parts really were.

Wilt lit another Chesterfield and watched as Rhyson leaned forward and tapped the dottle from his pipe. He placed the pipe on the edge of the ashtray and clasped his hands together.

"First, I'd like to say that I wish I could furnish you with some facts, an outline of some kind. Unfortunately, it's not that easy. Every man involved in this kind of crime starts from some point entirely different from the point where another man with the same compulsions begins. What I can do is hazard a few guesses, what might be common elements in the profile of a man who preys on children."

Wilt opened his notebook and placed it on the side of the desk. He uncapped a pen.

"One element that is fairly common with these men is that, in seventy to eighty cases out of a hundred, this man as a child was also abused."

Wilt made a mark. "Sexually?"

"Not always. In some instances, they were battered children, children mistreated by their parents. And two. These men have low self-esteem. In the area of sex, this means that while the man may have a normal sex drive, he displays an inability to approach a woman. A mature woman presents problems that a child doesn't. A child is trusting. And the child is not judgmental about his performance as a man. That's the key. The abuse they took has made them, as adults, think of themselves as guilty and unworthy. A mature woman might sense this and use it against him. A child isn't that perceptive."

"Maybe they're ugly," Wilt said.

"If they're not, they certainly believe they are."

"Pock-marked skin?"

"That would certainly affect how they saw themselves." Rhyson motioned toward Wilt's cigarette package. "May I try one of yours. I'm trying to give them up ... but a pipe ... well, a pipe doesn't seem to make a good substitute."

Wilt pushed the package toward him and watched while Rhyson got a smoke going. He drew the unfiltered smoke deep into his lungs and coughed. "Often, with these men, there's a fear of being sexually inadequate. That leads to children."

"A girl child thinks what happens is what's supposed to happen?"

"Exactly."

"What kind of job would a man like this have? Would he take a job that would put him in close touch with young children?"

"Not always. In fact, in the case you've described, it's unlikely. Otherwise, the man would have made his approach to one of the children he has constant contact with. He would not be in the risky position of having to grab children off the streets."

"Why kill them?"

"The standard reason, of course. That he's afraid the child will identify him. Also, maybe in a way, it is rage and anger against her for what she has made him do. For the man who uses his position as a friend of a family to molest a child, it's quite different. He's established a relationship with the child. And after he molests him or her, he swears the child to secrecy. Often the child keeps this dark secret for years. In your case, the man has no relationship and he has no way to assure himself that the child won't incriminate him if he releases her. His safety demands that he kill the child."

"And the panties?"

"The women's underpants that are left with the body? Until you catch this man, until he's seated where you're sitting now, anything I say really applies to a hypothetical case. Nothing else."

"Give it your best guess, Doctor."

"It has the earmarks of an extremely powerful fantasy. In some twisted way, these women's underpants, and the way they appear to be substituted for the child's underwear, I'd say this is his way of convincing himself that the child is really a woman, that he's not molesting a child but making violent love to a grown woman."

"Jesus." Wilt closed his eyes and shook his head.

"I hope I've been some help," Rhyson said.

Wilt wasn't really sure he had. "Either you've cleared the water or muddied it, one or the other."

"I believe I know what you mean. So many factors have brought this man to the point where he is now. Ten different men and there are probably ten different roads that have brought them to murder and child molestation. I wish I could be more concrete, but ..."

Wilt stood. He turned for the door. "I think I understand the problem."

"Once you catch him, I'd like to examine him, Sheriff. If that's possible."

"Fine with me," Wilt said, "if he's still alive."

"That sounds..."

Wilt interrupted him. "I know how it sounds. It's not what I mean. But I have to be honest. If we find him, if he tries to escape, he might have to outrun a bullet."

"No matter how you say it, it has the sound of lynch law."

"If it comes to a crunch, if it's the choice between letting him get away and putting him down, I'll put him down. If I don't put him down, if he molests and kills another little girl, I'll have to live with the guilt. If he's in the hospital with a couple of slugs in him, if he's dead, I don't have to worry about him anymore. Hell, I'd run over him in a truck if that's the only way I had to stop him."

"What we're talking about is a mentally disturbed man who might be treatable."

"That won't hunt. No excuse in the world makes it with me. Not after what he did to those children. He might be crazy, mentally disturbed, but he's alive and those two little girls are very, very dead after he inflicted terrible pain and suffering on them. But if he gives up, I'll go along with the courts. I'll choke and swallow the puke when the court sends him off for treatment. Until he's well enough to go back on our streets. I'll swallow that whole mess but I'll be damned if I'll call it justice."

"An eye for an eye, Sheriff?"

"Whenever possible," Wilt said.

There was nothing more to say. By lunchtime he was back in Edgefield.

CHAPTER TWENTY ONE

"I had an idea while you were gone."

"You do that often?" Wilt was behind his desk. Joe was just back from lunch. A toothpick was lodged in his mouth and he swirled it as he talked.

"I went by to see Doc Simpson." Joe reached into his jacket and brought out a pair of woman's underpants in an evidence baggie. "This is the one that were found with Dana Moore. I compared it the one that were under the head of the Dobbs girl. They're both the same size and the same brand. Doc said I could borrow this one."

"For what?"

"To find where they were bought. To see if anybody remembers selling them to a man who fits our description."

Wilt extended a hand and took the panties. He read the label in the waistband. Seabreeze Fashions. He folded the underwear carefully and returned them. "My guess is that they're made in some place like South Korea. You'll find these are sold at any of a dozen discount stores."

"That's what Susie said."

"Susie's an expert on women's underwear?"

"Well, she's a woman and I couldn't just go on the street and stop some woman and ask her."

"Okay, try it. But I'll tell you right now this won't catch our boy for us. This is the ass-backwards way. If we catch him, this might be a nail in his coffin, proof that he bought this underwear. Catching him is the real business and we won't catch him this way."

"I take Floyd with me?"

"Sure. But if you get yourself arrested for flashing underwear, I never heard of either of you."

After they left, he leaned back and closed his eyes. Sparks and shadows danced behind his eyelids. And then, as if he'd willed it, the tattoo.

The Tale that Diane held back, to tell him later. Her version of the *Thousand and One Nights*. Only this was a simple tale, one that could be told in an evening. What could be complex about a tattoo?

The afternoon got busy.

With Joe and Floyd away, Wilt had to take patrol calls. A pickup had rammed a Mustang carrying four students home from high school at the crossroads near Gus Triffon's gas station. There were no deaths but some broken bones and a lot of blood and the sour odor of whiskey under peppermint on the pickup driver's breath.

He'd hardly completed his report on the drunk driving arrest when Elle Purdy called and said that her husband, Carl, was drunk and threatening her and her mother.

"You're the only one who can calm him down," Elle said.

So Wilt drove out to the Purdy farm and scared Carl into something like sober attention.

The Purdy incident wasn't worth a report.

Wilt settled in and waited for his six o'clock relief.

Joe returned at five-thirty. He dumped a stack of newspapers on Wilt's desk. "Guess what?"

"I really have to guess?"

Joe turned the top paper, a *Durham Morning Herald* toward Wilt. The composite drawing was centered under the headline: **Do You Know this Man?** The one below, the *Raleigh News and Observer* used the caption: **Wanted for Questioning**.

"They took their time."

"You know newspapers. They look on helping the police like it's some kind of public service, to be done when it fits their purposes."

"How'd the afternoon go?"

"I'd hoped you wouldn't ask." Joe turned and took a bag from Floyd. "You'd be surprised the crappy underwear a woman'll put under a hundred dollar dress."

Not really, Wilt thought.

Joe placed a package of underwear on Wilt's desk. "Bought these at Rose's."

"You get any idea how many pairs of these underwear a store like Rose's sells in a week?"

"A lot."

"How many Rose's did you try?"

"Three," Joe said. "I showed the composite. As far as I could tell nobody's seen him. In fact, the girls say not any men buy women's underwear."

Wilt pulled the package toward him and looked at where the panties were made. He'd been close. Taiwan, Republic of China. The package contained three pairs. "Any different packages? Six packs?"

"Three packs only," Joe said.

"So, say our boy bought one package. He'd used two pairs. That leaves one to account for."

"Or use," Joe said.

That was the chilling thought. One more pair. One more dead child.

Wilt didn't like to consider that possibility. He pushed his mind away from it and looked at the clock. "Charles due in?"

"Ten or fifteen minutes."

Floyd had come in at noon and would relieve Susie at the switchboard. Charles would take over and Wilt and Joe could leave for the night. But they were on call if there was a need for them.

"I'll split for the day," Wilt got his coat.

"Where'll you be?"

"At the apartment for a couple of hours. Then out."

"You want me to guess where?"

"I'll call in when I leave the apartment."

Joe nodded. He circled the desk and settled into Wilt's chair.

"You're beginning to like that chair too much."

"Comfortable," Joe said.

"Enjoy it while you can."

Joe gave him a wave and a lazy grin.

In his apartment, Wilt stood at the living room windows and watched the full darkness come. The new carbon arc streetlamps flared and crackled in the distance. A young couple passed on the other side of the street, arm-in-arm. The man caught the girl and turned her and kissed her. The carbon arc halo blurred above them.

Wilt backed away. He didn't need to watch young love.

He opened a beer in the kitchen and carried it into the bathroom. Between sips, he ran the electric razor over the day's growth of beard. He finished the beer and the shave at about the same time. He tossed the beer can into the trash and undressed and showered.

He dressed in gray slacks, a blue tie shirt without a tie and a tan tweed jacket. His black loafers were dusty. He used a dirty sock to wipe the dust away. He was ready to go. But go where?

There was Charlie's Apple. It was a new singles bar half a mile over into the county. Flashy but almost in good taste for that kind of place. A long bar and a piano player during the week and a jazz combo on the weekends. And women, women, women... Or the Blue Lagoon.

He avoided the thought and the decision by putting a Stouffer's frozen entree into the oven. Shrimp in some creamy sauce. When that was ready, he opened another beer and switched on the TV set. He ate the Stouffer's while he watched a game show. God, how he hated game shows.

He sopped the sauce with a wedge of sourdough bread. He watching a giggly woman trying for a fancy car as the grand prize, rooted against her and was pleased to see her disappointment when she lost.

That was the real American dream. The losing.

Another beer. He cut off all the lights and sat in stuffed chair and listened to his heart beat, the slow and even thump of it, until his body clock told him it was eight o'clock.

CHAPTER TWENTY TWO

Kyle waved him past the cash register. For the first time since Wilt started dropping by, Kyle didn't seem grumpy about the free admission.

"I'll send your favorite waitress by," Kyle said.

Wilt wasn't sure when Erlene had become his favorite waitress. But he couldn't deny she was, not without putting back on her some of the pressure that being a close friend of the Sheriff had taken off her.

He skirted the pool tables and entered the main room. Erlene arrived at his table only seconds after he sat down.

"You want Daniels. Wilton?"

"Well, actually I wanted a glass of milk, but since I'm here …"

Erlene giggled and moved away.

It was a big crowd. Half the tables were taken and most of the booths. All that and the girls hadn't started dancing yet.

Erlene leaned over him when she brought his drink. "They're all nice to me now that they know I'm a friend of yours. Especially Miss Mills."

"What does …?"

"She always asks how I am and how the kids are and I think she told the guys to leave me alone."

"I thought you said they weren't bothering you."

"Well, you know … saying things. That's all."

Wilt knew that kind of verbal hassle. The kind some men might dump on a girl if they thought she was vulnerable.

"It's not happening anymore." Erlene's smile was fragile, tentative.

Wilt dropped a couple of ones on her tray. "Baby might need a new pair of shoes."

"My oldest baby is ten," she said.

He watched her walk away, a sadness in him. Not the plastic sadness of the new country and western music. The real thing. A husband bugs out and leaves a woman with two kids to raise and she's past the age when she interests men much or she'd let herself go during the marriage and there was too much to reclaim. And all those old hopes, what she expected when she was in high school, have soured. Old dreams to throw out with the day's trash, the week's trash, a lifetime's trash.

A sadness that he had to shake off his back.

Or shock himself so that he could distance himself. What is so goodam great about your own life, Wilton Drake?

Answer that.

Erlene must have timed him. She brought another drink just as he finished the first. She hesitated. "I think Miss Mills is dancing tonight."

"Is that right?"

"That's what I heard."

For the first time, he felt embarrassed. The other times he'd watched her dance, he'd come to see the body, the fine legs and the breasts. He'd been just another customer looking at the girls. That had changed now. He realized that Kyle knew why he was here and Erlene knew and God knows who else. He felt foolish and very much like a teenager.

The room lights dimmed. Colored spots washed across the stage and the first girl was announced. It was the big girl, Rachel, the one Diane had used to bait him. He watched Rachel *galump* around the stage and told himself, no, never, not even on his worst day...

Another girl, tall and bony, followed and then, off in the wings next to the sound booth, he saw Diane. She was dressed in a robe and she leaned in to talk with the man in the sound booth.

Wilt got to his feet and carried his empty glass to the bar. Behind him, he heard Diane announced. He didn't look back. He saw that both tables were empty. He grabbed a pool cue and carried his glass to the bar. Kyle tossed in a couple of ice cubes and a long pour of black Jack Daniels followed.

"The girls don't interest you tonight?" Kyle pushed Wilt's money back toward him. Wilt grabbed the bills and stuffed them in the tip jar.

"Didn't you know I was gay?"

"Unlikely," Kyle said.

"In a mid-life crisis, anything's possible." Wilt carried his drink to the nearest pool table. He racked the balls and broke and ran off a few standard shots. He wasn't good at pool. The hand and eye coordination wasn't there. With a piece, a weapon, maybe, but not with a pool cue.

A biker wandered by the table and watched for a few shots. Then he laughed and walked away. He swaggered to the bar and said something to Kyle and laughed again. In the blink of an eye, Kyle had him by the collar and halfway over the bar. He said something to the biker and pushed him away. The biker straightened his coat. "How the hell was I supposed to know he was law?"

"Go home," Kyle said.

The biker slammed the door on the way out.

Wilt continued his listless practice until the next dancer was announced. Then he put the stack away and eased his way to the bar. Kyle added a trickle of Daniels to top off Wilt's drink.

"You're hard on your friends."

"That loudmouth?" Kyle shook his head. "He's no friend of mine."

"That wasn't necessary. I've been changing my own diapers for years."

"I never heard otherwise about you," Kyle said.

"As long as you know."

"I thought it might not be a good time for that child to get on your wrong side."

Wilt thought about it for a few seconds. One possibility was that he was talking about Diane. "Could be," he said.

"Those child-killings, that's what I mean."

"It's a bitch," Wilt admitted.

Kyle straightened up, like he went to attention. "Good evening, Miss Mills."

"Don't be formal just because the Sheriff's here, Kyle."

"Okay, Diane."

Kyle backed away and ran water in a wash sink. But he watched Diane and Wilt.

She'd done a quick change. Now she wore jeans and an off-white sweater in a fisherman's knit. "I dance for you, Wilton, and you don't even watch."

"Don't dance on my account."

"I'll stop dancing."

"That a promise?"

"No more dancing tonight. That's the promise." She looked past Wilt and nodded. Kyle placed a glass on the bar, added two ice cubes and poured scotch over them.

"Want to sit down?"

"Not in there," she said.

"In your office?"

"Depressing there."

"You got any ideas?"

"You didn't tell me why you took me to that lake."

"It used to be a necking and petting spot for the high schoolers."

"You think it's still there?"

"Probably," he said.

Another swallow of the scotch and Diane placed the glass on the bar. "Kyle, give me two tall Buds in a bag." She grinned at Wilt. "Wilton's taking me to Dead Woman's lake. You know where that is?"

"I know."

"You know what the lake used to be?"

"Can't say I do," Kyle said.

"It's a necking and petting place."

"That's interesting." But Kyle really didn't sound very interested. He placed the bag on the bar. "You sure two cans are enough?"

At the door, before they stepped outside, Diane stopped. "Did you take Erlene to the lake in the old days?"

"Erlene was just a kid then. I messed around with the fast girls."

"Like tonight?"

"Just like tonight," he said.

He parked the cruiser on the shoulder high above the lake. In the moonlight, he could see the near edge of the lake and the trees and undergrowth. The far bank and that part of the lake were in darkness. The surface water seemed to be polished stone.

He rolled down the window a couple of inches. "Tell me if you get cold."

"Don't you have a blanket? I understood the boy always brought along..."

"That was a hundred years ago. I don't remember." He pulled the tabs on both tall Buds and passed one to her. A swallow and he lit a Chesterfield.

"Tell me how it was then."

"Probably like it was in Charleston."

"We had the beach there."

"This was clean water then, fed from an underground spring. No matter how hot it was, the water was only warm for a few inches. Below that, it was like ice. Hot afternoons or muggy nights we'd collect some beer and some hot dogs and we'd spread blankets near the water. And we'd go swimming."

"With or without suits?"

"Without some nights. Suits during the day.

"Get laid much?"

"Jesus, you have to ask that question?"

"That's not an answer, Wilton."

"There were a lot of virgins around here in those days. Boys and girls."

"Just like Charleston."

"Tell me about the tattoo."

"Even though you didn't want to see it tonight?"

"I chickened out," he said.

"Nothing wrong with being honest about it."

He shook his head.

She turned slightly and put her shoulder against the car door. Her head was up and he could see the shadows in the hollow of her throat. "Let's see. Where was I then? I think I'd just split with Jimmy and I'd gone off on my own."

"That was where you were."

"I felt like doing something go-to-hell."

"Was that before or after you met the biker?"

"What do you know about any biker?" She waited, as if for him to answer. When he didn't, she went on. "It was after. He liked tattoos on his women."

"How did you feel about the tattoo?"

"That it didn't matter. That it was something to put on a body. Especially a body that I didn't care that much about."

"Punished the flesh, huh?"

"He punished it for me and he did it very well, thank you."

"You've got spurs, lady."

"I wasn't born with them. I grew them. I put all that divorce settlement money in the bank and forgot about it. I played biker mama for a few months. I smoked all the funny cigarettes I wanted, I tried other drugs, I screwed all I wanted and when it was time to move on, I didn't feel any better or any worse for the experience. I peeled away the old skin but the new skin under it was very much like the old one."

"Except for the tattoo."

"I like it," she said. "You know, in the dark, the tattoo feels just like any other patch of skin."

"Now I know."

"Take my word for it."

"Knowing that takes all the suspense out of my life."

"You didn't tell me it was important."

"All the good puzzles are solved before we get a chance to accept the challenge."

"Poor baby, one more time." She shivered. He tossed his cigarette through the opening and rolled up the window. "Tell me about your marriage, Wilt."

He noticed that she'd called him Wilt for the first time. Whatever that meant. If it meant anything. He took a long swallow of beer and cleared his throat. He told her that after he was shot by the sniper in Lebanon, he was sent to Oak Knoll Naval Hospital near Oakland, California to recover. One surgery after another.

It was while Wilt was at the hospital that Mary Ellen left him and started the divorce. She said she just didn't love him anymore and she didn't see any point being married to a man who spent about every other year away from home on sea duty or posted to some hellhole where a wife couldn't be taken along. Her mind was set. It was a firm decision. He didn't contest the divorce. There wasn't much community property. He gave her the car and the household goods. The divorce was granted and she disappeared from California. He never heard from her again. That was easy enough and perhaps it was the best way. There were no children and, therefore, no reason to stay in touch when the marriage was over.

The odd part was, when the medical miracle didn't come about, when he received his discharge, he realized there would be no more sea duty, no more hellholes he would have to staff. She would have had what she wanted.

"You think she deserted you?" Diane asked.

"I guess I did at the time. In bed all day, the operations to try to rebuild the hip and all the pain. I had a lot of time to feel sorry for myself."

"And now?"

"It's old news. It's nothing that concerns me anymore, like it happened to someone else."

"You ever wonder how she's doing?"

"No."

He finished his beer. He placed the can in the paper bag.

"That hip. It slow you down?"

"Only in the short dashes."

A smile. "But not the distance events?"

"I never was one for the dashes. You've hardly got started and it's over."

At first, he thought the talk about dashes and distance racing was a sexual game talk. Then he wasn't sure. Maybe she was talking about something else: a relationship that lasted, the staying power over a long period of time.

Before he could follow up on the metaphor the radio crackled at him. "Car number one, you there, Sheriff?"

"Go ahead."

"I hate to bother you. Joe says to call you. We got a phone call. It's a possible on the composite. Joe says to meet him at the Station."

"I'll be there in twenty."

Diane rolled down the window on her side and poured the last of her beer onto the ground. He took the can and placed it in the bag.

"You think this is important, Wilt?"

"It better be. We need a break on this."

He started the engine and backed down the road until he saw the space where he could turn around. He headed for the highway.

"You're always on the edge," she said slowly, "but you never walk over the bridge."

"I never cared much for making out in cars."

"You know that wasn't what I meant."

He felt a hard core of anger in her and he kept his eyes on the road. He reached the highway and turned in the direction of the Blue Lagoon.

"You misunderstood me on purpose," she said.

"You've got my head all scrambled."

"One day it would be nice to have all your attention. When your mind's not chasing after killers and child molesters."

"That's my work." He said.

"I guess I'm being childish."

"A little, but it's flattering."

He pulled into the Blue Lagoon parking lot and circled until he was close to the entrance. He braked and got out and walked around and opened the door for her.

"Damn you," she said softly as she brushed past him.

"You can't damn the already damned,"

She came back and stared at him, close up, and leaned forward and kissed him, "I know it's important, Wilt."

He waited until she entered the club.

A different music in him now. A sadness but a sweet sadness in him. He drove the miles to the Station without noticing much of the night. Her perfume, her scent, teased him.

Pure crazy or pure happy, he couldn't decide where or what he was.

CHAPTER TWENTY THREE

The sprawling grounds around the house looked like they'd been landscaped to resemble those at some English manor house or a summer place at Newport where the rich spent their leisure time. The lawn was about the size of three football fields edged together and, except for the fact that it seemed to roll downward toward the highway, it was as flat and even as any football field in the country.

Thick stands of pine bordered both sides of the drive that ran, straight as a plumb line, from the highway to the house, which was in the center of a large tract of land. The blank, even face of the home was what Wilt thought they called Federalist architecture. There was no decoration, no frills, and it lacked a porch. A number of steps led to a large door and there was only the barest suggestion of a landing.

And the house was white, white, white. Nothing but white except for the rows of windows. Even the curtains that covered the windows were white.

"Like this?" Joe asked as he pushed the cruiser forward and inserted it between a dark blue Mercedes and a tan late model Ford station wagon. Joe braked and nodded in the direction of the station wagon. "Probably belongs to the hired help."

Wilt punched open the glove compartment and raked around until he found a package of breath mints. He popped one into his mouth and, on second thought, added a second. He dropped the rest of the pack into his tweed jacket pocket.

Joe watched him. "Ready?"

"My breath is," Wilt said.

"I ruin your evening? I got that feeling."

"Don't get sensitive on me. It doesn't suit your style."

They climbed the smooth stone steps to the narrow landing. Wilt gave the brass door knocker a couple of sharp raps. "Who is this again?"

"Charlotte Winters. Money, stock and real estate. A heavyweight in all of those."

"She's got so much money, you'd think she could afford some do-dads on the outside of her house, wouldn't you?"

"On this style of house, that would be bad taste," Joe said.

"You seem to know a lot about this lady."

"I read the society pages."

"Bless me," Wilt said.

"The Edgewood paper, if you don't read the society pages, it's so thin it won't last through breakfast."

"You didn't say anything about what the husband does."

"She's a widow," Joe said.

"Ahhhh …"

"What does that mean?"

"You wouldn't be interested in this lady?"

Joe stiffened. "I can't say I've met her."

Wilt could feel the resistance, the pulling away, as Joe tried to find a comfortable position and an answer that would cover him. "Like my daddy said, it's as easy to love a rich woman as it is to love a poor one." His laugh was nervous. "Only you live in better surroundings with the rich one."

"You've seen this lady before?"

"Once or twice at the polo matches."

The door opened. A slim, light-skinned black girl in a movie set maid's uniform, a black dress with white trim, a white apron and a frilly cap, asked them in. Wilt leaned towards Joe as they followed her through an entranceway and into a large reception area. "What the hell were you doing at a polo match?"

"You remember," Joe said, "it was that BMW that was involved in the hit and run. I thought this polo business, the fans and such, showed more BMW's than an Atlanta dealership."

The maid stopped in the high-ceilinged reception area and took Joe's topcoat. She made a move toward Wilt before she realized he wasn't wearing an outer coat. There was a moment's wait while she put the topcoat on a wooden hanger and placed it on a rail in a small closet below the stairs. While that was being done, Wilt looked up the stairs. The same bare functional look to the stairs and the hallway there.

Quaker architecture? He wasn't sure.

He wasn't even sure there was such a thing as Quaker architecture.

"This way, gentlemen." The maid led them from the reception room into a large book-lined room. Here it was different. The wood panels were dark and polished, the rug a heavy oriental and the furniture looked comfortable and slightly over-padded.

There was a stonework fireplace and a roaring fire in it. Wilt rubbed his hands together and drifted in the direction of the warmth.

"Miss Winters wants you to make yourself at home. She'll be right down."

Wilt leaned over the fire and soaked in the heat. "You never did catch that hit and run driver in the BMW."

"But I discovered polo."

"Anything else?"

Joe shook his head. He stood next to a heavy oak desk with brass fittings. A hand, almost as if he didn't know what he was doing, slid across the smooth patina of the wood.

"Yes, you did. You discovered the high life and a rich widow."

"Hell, Wilt, that isn't fair." Joe colored and looked away.

Got to tell that boy the high price of upward mobility. *It ain't free.*

There was a tapping of heels in the reception area outside. Wilt gave his hands a final rub before the fire and straightened and turned to face the doorway. In that sudden movement, he caught Joe in the process of preparing himself, putting on his serious working face. That and a puffed-out chest and a squaring of his wide shoulders.

Charlotte Winters entered the room at a walk somewhere between a glide and a float. She wore a gray knit dress that pushed out at the right places and had the proper tucked-in lines at others. Angles and half-circles, Wilt thought. All the right ones.

She was certainly attractive. Wilt guessed her age somewhere in the early forties but she might have passed for the mid-thirties in the right light or in the shadows in a bedroom. Her blonde hair was shaped and cut short. What that did, Wilt realized, was draw attention to her firm throat. There was no sag to the jawline. Her eyes were green and the full mouth had a girlish pout to it.

When she seated herself, her dress rucked a bit and not a lump or a blemish showed on the slender legs or the portion of revealed inner thigh.

Wilt did the introductions. With those completed, she asked in a husky voice if she could offer them a drink.

"Not for me." Wilt backed toward the fire.

"Thank you, no," Joe said.

Wilt stared at Joe. He couldn't believe that Joe had said that. The stiff formality of an English drawing room conversation didn't mesh with what he knew about his deputy.

He nodded at Joe. It was Joe's game. He might as well let Joe play it any way he wanted to, even if he ended up sounding like a fox hunter. One thing was certain to Wilt: a look from Charlotte Winters and her reaction to him had been an immediate rejection. Her eyes buffed and polished Joe. That was where the real meat was and she knew it.

"I believe I've seen you» before, Mr. Croft," she said.

And she remembered his name. Wilt would bet a month's pay that she didn't know his last name was Drake. Hell, make it six month's pay.

"I didn't know you'd seen me."

Charlotte Winters raised an eyebrow toward Joe. Wilt, watching her, realized that she damned well knew where she'd seen Joe but it wasn't a woman's role to admit it.

"At the polo matches," Joe said.

"Yes, that's where it was." A blinding smile. "At the Mayor's Cup match?"

"I believe it was." Joe's nod was almost a bow toward her.

"Do you play?"

"I ride," Joe said. "However, I've never played."

"Too bad." Her voice was almost a purr. "I'm certain you could pick up the game in no time at all."

"It's harder than it looks." Joe was as close to blushing as Wilt had ever seen him.

The blush was just the right touch. Wilt squirmed and wanted to look away. Joe's reticence brought out the hunter in her, her strength against what appeared to be the weakness in his modesty.

Wilt decided that was just enough small talk and courtship. "Mind if I smoke, Mrs. Winters?"

"Not at all." Her eyes shifted toward Joe. "You may smoke, Mr. Croft, if you like."

"I don't smoke," Joe said.

Joe's answer seemed to please Charlotte Winters. To hell with them. Wilt got a Chesterfield burning and blew the smoke toward them. Might as well get the train on the right track. "I understand you think you might know the man in the composite drawing that was in the newspaper. Is that right?"

"A drawing isn't exactly a photograph," she said. "There is, however, a resemblance to a young man I've met a few times through a friend."

"Who is this man?"

"I wouldn't want him to think I've accused him of anything, Sheriff."

"You're not making an accusation," Wilt said. "Your name won't come into this at all. It's not as if you have any evidence that connects him with a crime that's been committed."

"If you're certain ...?"

Joe took a step forward. It was then that Wilt realized Joe was wearing a new tailored uniform, one that Wilt hadn't seen before. Now, when the hell did Joe have time to dress himself in high style for this encounter? Then he remembered. Joe had been at home when the call came through the switchboard at the Station. Floyd had routed the call to Joe for screening. When Joe heard who the caller was, he'd unwrapped his new uniform and probably waxed and buffed his shoes. The question was: if the call hadn't brought Joe and Charlotte together, how had Joe planned to use the uniform? Had he planned to lurk around the highway near the Winters home and give her a speeding citation? The way Joe was acting, that was as likely a script as any Wilt could devise.

Joe leaned over Charlotte. "All we need is a name. From there on we do our own checking. Our investigation will tell us if this is the man we're looking for. If he's innocent, we'll find that out. If he's the man we're looking for, then we put the proof together and arrest him. Your name won't be mentioned at all. It won't even appear in our reports." Joe looked at Wilt.

Wilt nodded.

"I know him because he is a friend to a girlfriend and her husband."

Joe opened his notebook.

Charlotte wasn't ready to end the guessing game yet. "He seemed, at first, to be a rather nice young man. But lately he seems nervous and high-strung. And I'm not certain that this relationship is a healthy one for my girlfriend."

"His name?" Joe waited.

"Raymond Thorpe." Charlotte released a sigh. "He likes to be called Ray."

Joe had written the name. Now the pen was still poised. "What does he do?"

She gave Joe a puzzled look.

"For a living."

"I believe he is somehow involved in insurance. Yes, I remember she said it was insurance."

"You know which company?"

She shook her head. "He's rather a newcomer to our area and certainly a newcomer in our group. What a person does for a living isn't usually a matter that concerns us."

It was a lesson in class. Of course, he and Joe, because of their upbringing, would always ask. A lady or gentleman of Charlotte's class wouldn't. Information about money and money matters was between a person and her lawyer or stockbroker. Between members of the group such information was always given indirectly.

Wilt took a last draw from the cigarette and tossed it in the fireplace. "This girlfriend of yours…?"

Charlotte looked at Joe, as if to ask if she had to answer the question. Joe nodded, encouraging her.

"Missy Plowden. Melissa Plowden. Her home is on Old Oak Terrace Road."

That was fancy. No number, just the road. Anyone who lived on the road would know the Plowden home. Wilt knew the road pretty well. There were only six houses on the road. Each one was almost an estate.

"This Raymond Thorpe," Wilt said, "where does he live?"

"At Missy's." Charlotte stopped and pressed her lips together. "In the Plowden guest house. Not in the main house."

Of course not, Wilt thought. That would be too obvious.

"It was a gardener's house," Charlotte said. "Missy redecorated it and transformed it into a guest house."

"You said Thorpe is a friend to both Mrs. Plowden and her husband?"

"They're my closest friends. Missy and I have known each other since college. Jonathan ... well, Jonathan has been ill for several years." Charlotte hesitated, as if she realized she hadn't answered his question. "Thorpe and the Plowdens are friends but I have trouble understanding exactly what they see in him."

"I have a feeling you don't approve of Mr. Thorpe."

"He's charming enough, at times. But his influence on poor Missy seems to be much stronger than I think it should be."

That attitude. Protection for the woman her age who was in the position where she might be used, or was already being used, by a younger man. When there was money there was always a young man who knew where it was and how to get his hands on it.

Wilt looked closely at Joe. He wondered if Joe thought of himself in the terms that Charlotte had used. That if he got close to Charlotte, he might be considered a "user" by Charlotte's friends. It was not a pretty position for a man. Wilt wondered if Joe was perceptive enough to realize what the dangers were.

Another close look at Joe and Wilt realized that Joe was still innocent enough not to notice or consider such a possibility.

Joe closed his notebook. "Thank you, Mrs. Winters. You've been a great help."

Wilt nodded.

"I'm pleased that I could be helpful. But I'd hate to think that this might involve Missy in any scandal if Raymond is implicated in any crime."

Wilt shook his head. "I'm sure that this can be handled so that it doesn't reflect unfavorably on Mrs. Plowden."

Wilt headed for the door that led to the reception area. He reached the doorway before he realized Joe wasn't with him. He turned. Joe stood close to Charlotte. She'd stood and Joe towered over her.

"I'll be with you in a minute, Wilton."

Wilton? That was fancy. He dipped his head and left them. The maid waited beside the closet at the foot of the stairs. As he moved past her, she reached into the closet and turned and offered him the uniform topcoat.

"His," Wilt said.

He stopped on the narrow landing outside and stared at the sky. The stars were bright and icy. It was a clear cold night when the wind had blown the clouds away.

He limped to the cruiser and got into the driver's seat. He started the engine and slid across the car and settled into the passenger side. The air from the heater was cold. He switched it off and hunched forward and stretched his back muscles to get the warmth flowing. He closed his eyes.

The cruiser door opened. The overhead light flared. Wilt opened his eyes and blinked into the glare. He leaned forward and switched on the heat. The air was warm now and he held his hands over the grill until the chill was gone from them.

"Going riding with her, huh?"

"How'd you know?"

"A lucky guess. She'll want to see what kind of seat you have in a saddle. And I've got one more guess."

"What's that?" Joe backed the cruiser and made his turn. He pointed it down the drive toward the highway.

"That you're not rich enough for this one."

"Funny thing about money," Joe said. "It don't make a man's dick stiff."

"And wanting money does?" Wilt said.

At the Station, Floyd saw them enter and he made a sprint for the restroom. Joe waved at him and moved behind the counter to cover for him. Wilt remained on the other side of the counter.

"Say it, Wilt."

"Say what?"

"What you're thinking," Joe said.

"Okay. Marrying money is a hard way to get rich."

"Who said anything about getting married? That lady gets my motor running."

"When are you calling her?"

"A couple of days. No hurry. I mean, I have to do her the courtesy of letting her know if her information was useful."

"You think she'll remember you?"

"I'd lay a year's pay on that."

Wilt leaned on the counter between them. "Since you're about to move into society, I guess I ought to school you for it."

"Yeah?"

"Don't chew toothpicks or clean your teeth in public. Picking your teeth is one of those private matters, to be done alone like taking a crap. And buy yourself some boxer shorts. No one in her circle wears jockey shorts. And keep your nose hair and the hair in your ears trimmed."

"And that's all?"

"I'll add to the list as we go along."

"How come you know so much?" Joe asked.

"I used to be an officer and a gentleman."

"That."

"I even know how to use a fish knife. I bet you don't even know what a fish knife is."

"A knife for cleaning fish?"

"Table manners and use of strange utensils, that's going to be lesson number two."

Before Wilt left the Station, he told Joe to wear civvies the next morning. They were going to do some stalking and walking and it might be better if they didn't look like the law.

⚜   ⚜   ⚜

Wilt reached his apartment and stood beside the cruiser and looked around. There was a faint hope in him that he'd spot the silver-toned Celica. No such luck. No sign of it.

Diane was probably showing her tattoo to strangers at the Blue Lagoon.

Climbing the stairs to the front door of his apartment building, he felt disappointed and even a little hurt.

CHAPTER TWENTY FOUR

Wilt arrived at the Station about twenty after eight. He looked like he hadn't slept well. The skin of his face had a corrugated look like he'd slept on a bundle of steel tying iron rods. He gulped coffee. A cigarette curled smoke into his eyes as as Joe popped his head in.

"Morning," Joe said.

"Old Oak Terrace Road," Wilt said. "We have any complaints out there recently?"

"Something a month ago ..." Joe stopped. "Let me check the reports."

Wilt was on the phone when Joe returned with the stack of complaints. The one he'd selected was on the top of the pile. He placed the stack on the desk and turned it toward Wilt.

Wilt leaned over it while he talked. "... to hold the desk down while Joe and I are away for a couple of hours. Hell, I know you need sleep. Everybody here needs sleep. And you can forget the shower. Won't be anybody here who'll notice but Susie and you know she likes her men overripe." He nodded and listened. He tapped the report. A shake of his head meant he didn't agree with Joe on his choice. Joe reached across the desk and uncovered the second report. While he read, Wilt said, "Make that ten minutes and you've got a bargain, one we can live with."

The call completed he said, "This is the better one. Just vague enough."

Five minutes after Buster arrived at the Station, Joe and Wilt were on Old Oak Terrace Road, the far end of it, headed for the Plowden estate.

Wilt decided that Joe was moody this morning, even disgruntled. And to tell the truth, it didn't matter a gnat's ass to him, just as long as he did his job and his scrambled emotions didn't cause any screwups.

If Wilt had to make a guess, he'd say Joe's mood had something to do with Charlotte Winters, the rub and smell and spur of her. But it wasn't only the woman. There was a touch, a smell, and a claw to money. Well, he'd learn or he wouldn't learn. And Wilt believed a man learned as much from his bad choices as he did from the good ones.

The Plowden home sprawled, it angled away from its center in several directions. One could play a game called Find the Original House, what was there before the owners decided that improvements were needed.

What looked permanent was the heavy log fence that bordered what was either a large lawn or a small pasture. The logs were stripped and aged and unpainted.

Joe didn't find a parking area at the front of the house. He followed a curving road that ran around the right side of the structure. The road continued about another quarter of a mile toward a small house that sat on the edge of a deeply wooded stand of second growth. The guest house, Wilt thought.

The parking spaces were behind the main house, on the edge of a slope that overlooked a patio where there was a sunning platform and roofed-over jacuzzi.

Joe braked the cruiser between two cars, a lipstick red Porsche and a white Thunderbird. The Thunderbird was on the driver's side. After Joe stepped from the cruiser, he tapped the Thunderbird on the hood and looked over his shoulder at Wilt.

Wilt nodded. A possible. A very good possible.

From the front, it had looked like the Plowden house had two floors. At the back, from the side, it was obvious that the building had been done on a hill or the earth had been scooped away so that two additional floors could be inserted. In contrast to the home's front, which was more traditional in the placement of windows, the back of the structure was a hodgepodge of many windows and sliding glass doors and natural wood terraces.

"Like it?" Wilt asked.

"I could get used to it."

"I bet you could."

A staircase of wrought iron and stone ran in a straight line from the slope down to the patio. In the patio, after the climb, Wilt stopped to give his hip a chance to recover. He filled the time by looking around.

"How's your suntan? You ever been in a jacuzzi?"

"I'm about bleached out and no, I've never, but I'm looking forward to my first dip."

Wilt headed for the door that was off-center in a wall of plate glass. A soft glow of light showed beyond a cloudy condensation.

A minute passed after he first knocked. He knocked again. He'd lifted his hand to try again when the door opened with a sliding sound and the maid stood there. Her black face was thin and disagreeable.

"Sheriff Drake and Chief Deputy Croft to see Mr. and Mrs. Plowden."

"You call 'head of time?"

"No, I didn't. My visit with the Plowdens is official, not social. Part of an investigation."

"I ain't sure what time Mrs. Plowden can see you."

"She'll see me one way or the other. The easy way or the hard way."

"I see if she 'vailable."

"Do that." Wilt took a foot and placed it forward, ready to step inside. The maid, without seeming to notice his intention, slid the door closed in his face.

Joe stood a step behind Wilt. "I'd say she doesn't like the law much."

Almost five minutes passed before the maid returned. The warm air as it rushed past her carried on it the breakfast smells. Eggs and bacon and coffee. And the burnt dry scent of toast.

"She say she see you for a minute."

Wilt and Joe followed her inside. The room they entered was set up as a bar. To one side there was the deep dark glow of burnished wood and bar stools that were arranged along a c-shaped bar counter. There was a gleam from racked glasses and the colorful patchwork of bottle labels.

To the left, there were tables, a grouping of marble-topped and wrought iron stands and captain's chairs. Wilt stopped when he saw the woman seated at a table next to the glass wall. The table had been converted into a breakfast nook. Seated there, with a single service and a silver coffee pot was Missy Plowden. The serving dishes were arranged over a low gas flame unit.

Her hair was gray but, on her, with whatever help the beauty shop contributed, the color seemed almost platinum blonde. She wore no makeup this time of day and her skin, while it was tight and almost without pores, looked thin and brittle.

It was a casualness, a studied one, that let them know how unimportant she considered them. Otherwise she wouldn't have received them with so much truth showing. As if she considered them on a scale with the maid or the gardener. Menials didn't matter, that was what she was saying to them.

"You wanted to see me?" Her voice was soft and tinged with a southern accent. Each word was carefully enunciated, as if she'd had a voice lesson or two, perhaps back in her college days. It was fine to have the charming southern accent, she seemed to have learned, but there is no reason to speak like a field hand.

"You're Mrs. Plowden?"

"Yes." She buttered a toast corner and placed her knife carefully at an angle on the back of her plate. The plate contained enough breakfast to feed a field hand, a generous serving of scrambled eggs, several slices of bacon and a mound of grits. To one side there was toast, honey and butter.

After he introduced her to Joe, Wilt did his verbal tap dance. The call was about complaints he'd received about teenag-ers using Old Oak Terrace Road as a drag strip late at night. Had she heard the noises?

"Goodness," she said, "it would be impossible not to."

More tapdance. Had she seen the cars? Did she know if any of the young drivers lived on Old Oak Terrace Road?

"Certainly not." Her kind of people didn't let their children run wild. More was expected of them.

"Anyone else in the house who might have seen the cars?"

"Jonathan, my husband, is ill. He hasn't mentioned being disturbed. However, he's under medication and he wouldn't notice even those loud noises at that hour."

"If I could speak with…" He broke off when he heard the whine, a mechanical grinding. The maid stepped around Wilt and stood beside what looked like an ordinary door. The whine ended. The maid opened the door and revealed the cage front to a narrow one-man elevator.

The maid pushed the cage front open and a man in a wheel-chair rolled himself from the elevator. He stopped about three feet from the elevator door. The maid circled him and grasped the wheelchair handles and pushed him toward the breakfast table.

"I didn't know you had visitors," he said.

The voice was thin and reedy. The pitch, the weakness went with the rest of the man. From the bones, Wilt could tell that the man had been large and heavy-shouldered at one time, before the flesh melted away. Now he was a dry, dying tree waiting to fall. His hair was neatly cut but it looked damp and brought to Wilt memory of a dying father, the lifeless feel of his father's hair and the smell that was sour.

"I think we're going to be arrested." Missy lifted her head and laughed. "I believe the Sheriff is going to arrest either you or me for drag racing on the road."

"It's an excellent idea," Jonathan Plowden said.

Play the game a bit. Wilt laughed. "I don't think anyone could out drag you in that Thunderbird."

"I think it's seen its best days," Missy Plowden said.

"But the Porsche ..."

Missy smiled at her husband. "Jonathan prefers the Porsche."

"It's a beauty," Wilt said. He looked over his shoulder at Joe. Joe had his notebook in his hands. It was his service, his question.

"Is there anyone else in the household who ...?"

"No," Jonathan said. "There's Raymond."

"Raymond?" Wilt kept it lowkey and casual.

"Raymond Thorpe," Missy said. "He's staying in the guest house." A wave of a hand indicated the location, the small house Wilt had seen. "Raymond is my husband's friend, his guest."

"Do you think we could talk to him?" This from Joe. "We might as well touch all the bases."

"By now he should have left for work," Jonathan said.

"Does he work in Edgewood? We could drop by on our way to the Station."

"His firm has offices in Raleigh." Jonathan didn't look up or acknowledge that the maid had placed a cup of hot tea in front of him.

"Too bad. Which firm is that? We could give him a call."

"Weigard & Timmons. Insurance."

Joe had him spell "Weigard" for him. Then he closed the notebook. Wilt knew he was aware that they were in danger of stepping across the line. One or two more questions, and the Plowdens might be alerted to the fact that the law's interest was far more than just a routine investigation.

"I don't think he'd like to be bothered," Jonathan Plowden said.

"We'll be brief," Wilt said.

"I'm sure he knows nothing. The guest house is so far from the road that I doubt he even hears the cars at all."

"Then we probably won't have to talk to him at all." Wilt closed and buttoned his topcoat. He made all the motions that meant he was ready to leave. "Appreciate you taking the time to see us."

"We'll let ourselves out," Joe said. He almost bowed over Missy's hand when he said his own goodbye and thank you.

They stepped through the doorway. Just before he and Joe pushed the door closed, Wilt heard Jonathan protest that he wanted some bacon with his eggs. And Missy telling him that he knew how bacon acted on his stomach. Then the door was closed and they were in the harsh morning wind again.

Wilt was halfway up the stairs when he saw the man standing at the top of the slope. He was five steps from the top before he was close enough to get a close look at the man. His heart thumped in his chest. The likeness was that good. The lean face, the bleached-out acne scars.

The man waited until Wilt reached the top. Joe was a step behind him. The man gave way and then stepped by Wilt and Joe. His foot was on the top stair when Wilt's voice stopped him. "Raymond Thorpe?"

The man turned and stopped. "Yes."

He was dressed for the office, a suit and a topcoat, a tweed hat. The hair that showed under the hat was lighter than Gus Triffon had said. And under that clothing the solid feel, the sense of strength and power in a trimmed-down body.

"We've been talking to the Plowdens," Wilt said and introduced himself.

Raymond Thorpe waited. His face revealed nothing, neither interest nor impatience.

Wilt had to give in first. Otherwise, he had the feeling that Thorpe would walk away. "It's about the drag racing on the road. Have you noticed anything? Seen any cars that you can identify?"

"No to all of that," Thorpe said. In the harsh wind, the pocks were redder now, as if the cold swept about fifteen years away and left him with the skin he'd had as a late teenager.

Thorpe moved down two steps and looked over his shoulder. "That all your questions?"

"That's all. Thanks."

"You're welcome, Sheriff."

Wilt turned away. Joe followed him. A black BMW was parked on the other side of the red Porsche. Wilt nodded at Joe. "Get the tag numbers."

CHAPTER TWENTY FIVE

Later, in the car, headed for the straight flat length of Old Oak Terrace Road Joe said, "He's our man. I've got the feeling."

"Feelings aren't doodly-squat in a courtroom."

"That one, I get the smell off him."

"We need a case," Wilt said.

"What now?"

"Back to the Station."

"Aw, Wilt..."

"And at the Station we trade this cruiser in for some unmarked car."

"And then?"

"Raleigh. We follow our number one boy around all day."

"He'll probably know us," Joe said.

Wilt grinned. "Now wouldn't that be a terrible thing? It might even make him nervous."

"That's an interesting concept."

"Not really." Wilt shook a cigarette from his pack and lit it. "He already knows we're bird-dogging him. That is, he's guessing. Now, if we have to, we let him know for sure."

Joe whapped the steering wheel with a palm. "I like it. I like it."

Wilt rolled down the window and tossed the match out. Joe was so easily pleased. Why, for a moment there he'd probably even forgotten about Charlotte Winters.

✤ ✤ ✤

It wasn't a prestige address. Not like downtown where some form of urban renewal was always going on at one street corner or another. The buildings where Weigard & Timmons had their offices were old and most well-kept. Most of the businesses concerned themselves with the care and feeding of North Carolina State, The State campus buildings towered over the street. The modern architecture overpowered it.

Joe found a parking slot down the street, about half a block from the sign hanging from the second-floor level: **Weigard & Timmons, Insurance.** The engine wasn't completely cold before a stocky, dark-haired man in a Durham Bulls ballcap and wearing a dark blue windbreaker stepped from the doorway of a cafe and stopped next to Wilt's window, the one on the passenger side.

"Sheriff Drake? I'm Billy Egan."

Wilt lowered the window. "Wake County Sheriff's office?"

Egan nodded.

Wilt nodded him into the backseat. Egan got in and peeled the windbreaker away and dropped it on the seat.

At the Station, before leaving for Raleigh, Wilt had placed a call to the Wake County Sheriff's office. He stated his business and that he would be moving across county lines. The man he talked with switched the call to Egan. Egan said he understood and that he would meet him, just to keep the visit and the protocol in place. "Not to look over your shoulder," he said. "Say I'll assist you if you need it since your jurisdiction doesn't extend beyond the Webster County line."

Now, in the backseat, Egan blew on his hands to warm them. "It's a bitch out there today."

"Breezy," Wilt said.

"Heard about your troubles, the two little girls. That's a bitch too. I could blow the asshole who'd do that away and not have a second thought about it."

Wilt nodded that he understood and changed the subject by introducing Joe Croft.

Egan shook hands. "Call me Billy."

"Glad to have you along."

"You got some drill in mind?" Egan asked.

Wilt explained it, including the fact that he didn't mind if he followed Thorpe around uncovered.

"It's a bitch of an idea," Egan said.

Wilt decided that Egan had fallen into a pattern and that bitch was his favorite word for the week.

Egan put on his windbreaker and replaced the Durham Bulls cap with one that was folded and carried in his jacket pocket. This one was black with *Wake County Sheriff's Office* stitched on it. He trotted across the street and entered the building through a door directly below the hanging sign. He was gone for ten minutes. During that time, Joe went into the cafe and got Wilt a cup of coffee and a milk for himself.

Egan got into the back seat and grinned. "I did it," he said, "but I don't know exactly what I did."

"What was your approach?" Wilt asked.

"A fender bender where the driver of a 1982 blue VW left the scene of the accident. Wanted to check to see if any claims had been made by someone with a car that fitted. Maybe one where the owner explained the fender in some other way."

"You see Thorpe?"

"He came out and listened to the last part of it."

"Any reaction?"

Egan shook his head. "That one's a stone face."

"But he listened?"

"He listened." Egan waited. He looked from Wilt to Joe. "What the hell was I doing?"

"Look at it this way. Our man, Thorpe, he's probably worried now. If I didn't worry him this morning you did. It's likely there hasn't been a policeman, any kind of law, around him for a month, maybe months. Now, all of a sudden, in one morning the Webster law and the Wake law are walking around him. You were Thorpe, would that bother you?"

Egan grinned. "Hey, this is fun."

"Ain't it though?"

"What now?"

"We wait," Wilt said.

A long-legged girl in a tan coat came through the door that was beneath the Weigard & Timmons sign. Egan turned and froze like a birddog. "That's one of the girls I talked to."

"You sure?"

"I have reason to remember her. With lungs like hers she probably doesn't have to type."

"Lunch time," Wilt said.

Joe kicked over the engine. He pointed through the windshield. "He goes in that direction we're good. If he goes that way, we're in trouble." Joe hooked a finger toward the rear window.

"Make a u-turn," Egan said.

"I can do that?"

"With me along, you can do anything but make an arrest." Egan took his eyes from the girl and looked at the building front and the door. "That him?"

Raymond Thorpe stopped on the sidewalk. He looked in both directions. Then he turned to his left and headed down the street toward the unmarked car. He was on the opposite side of the street.

"Tell me when," Joe said.

"When he reaches the corner," Wilt said. He looked over the seat back toward Egan. "Is there a parking lot or a garage down there?"

"A big municipal parking lot."

"That'll be it." Wilt picked up Joe's notebook. He found the tag numbers. He read them off. "A black BMW."

Ahead of them, Thorpe reached the corner, looked back over his shoulder and then turned left and went out of sight.

"Go," Wilt said.

Joe pulled into the traffic. He did some reckless driving to get in the left turn lane. A VW with a fat lady in it almost lost a fender. She leaned on the horn. Joe waved and smiled.

To reach the turn lane, he had to play a game of chicken with late model white Mazda. The driver of the Mazda backed off rather than risk a dent, a ding or a crumpled fender. Joe waved and smiled.

They caught the red light. Joe looked at Wilt to see if he ought to try some way of getting past. Wilt shook his head. "Plenty of time. He's got to buy his way out of the parking lot."

He called it close. The light changed and Joe made the turn. He moved slow. As they approached the entrance to the parking lot, the black BMW pulled away and cut into the traffic ahead of them. Two cars separated them. Wilt patted Joe on the shoulder. "That's what I call timed arrival. Keep it this way, two or three cars back."

Egan leaned forward and put his elbows on the seat back between Joe and Wilt. "Any guesses?"

"He's going to have lunch," Wilt said.

CHAPTER TWENTY SIX

Wilt didn't know Raleigh well, not anymore. Everywhere he looked something, had changed. Ahead of them, the black BMW worked into the turn lane that led to a mall that he'd never seen. He read the big sign. Heritage Mall and Shopping Center.

They followed the BMW into the mall and watched it brake in a space outside a restaurant. Thorpe left his car and walked quickly, roughed up by the wind as he went, to the front of the restaurant.

"Move on past," Wilt said.

Thorpe entered without looking back. Joe drove a hundred yards past and then found a place to turn around. Wilt indicated a space a couple of doors down from the restaurant. There was a hardware store there.

Joe cut the engine. "We wait?"

"Not this time. I think I'll check the menu and maybe have lunch. Can I bring you two a hot dog?"

"A hot dog in there will cost ten dollars," Egan said.

"I think I can spring for that."

"Only if it's not too much trouble." Joe smiled.

"If they have hot dogs," Egan said.

Wilt entered the Bird and Bottle. The host met him and stopped him. Did he want to dine?

Wilt shook his head. "A drink," he said.

The host waved him in the direction of the bar. Before he reached the bar, Wilt located Thorpe, who was with another man. Thorpe sat at a table against the far corner. His back was to Wilt and the front door. Wilt took a look at the man with Thorpe.

The man was tall, an inch or two over six feet, though it was hard to tell, since he was sitting. What had been jet black hair now had threads of gray in it. Gray also frosted his sideburns. His skin was deeply tanned for this time of the year and the tan made the long, bony face almost look like he had Indian blood. His eyes were flat and green. He wore an expensive black blazer over gray slacks. His opened shirt was oxford cloth and so white that it almost dazzled Wilt.

There was a seat at the corner of the bar near the door to the restaurant. Wilt took the seat and ordered a black Jack over ice. He sipped it while he watched the two men. He wished he had some way of knowing what the two men were talking about. Thorpe's face, no matter what he was saying or how important it was, was impassive, without any expression that Wilt could detect. Hell, with Wilt's luck, Thorpe could be trying to sell an insurance policy. That and nothing more.

Wilt checked his watch before he ordered a second drink. While he sipped that drink, he realized that the weight of the conversation had shifted. Thorpe said very little. A single word now and then or a nod, that was all. It almost looked like a lecture from the older man. His face was serious. His lips were tight, in a line, almost ruthless.

A half an hour after Wilt entered the Bird and Bottle, the man in the black blazer pushed back his chair and stood. He crossed the restaurant area in long strides and headed for the bar. Wilt turned his stool and pushed his glass toward the bartender.

"One more," he said. Wilt turned away when the man in the black blazer reached the entrance to the bar.

The man followed the line of the bar and entered the men's room. He didn't look back.

Wilt relaxed. For a second, he thought the man was going to brace him.

A couple of minutes later, the man in the blazer left the men's room. His head was down as he moved toward the corner of the bar where Wilt was. At two or three paces from Wilt the man slowed and lifted his head. There was an insolent grin on his face and his eyes went blink… blink… like a camera shutter.

The wiseass S.O.B. had made Wilt. And let him know he did.

Wilt finished his drink. Lunch was being served at Thorpe's table. Wilt paid his tab and tipped the bartender. He felt the man's eyes on his back as he left the restaurant.

Wilt stood in front of the cafe and took a couple of breaths. *Son of a bitch.*

No, this one wasn't buying an insurance policy.

Wilt eased into the car next to Joe Croft. His eyes were fixed on the front of the Bird and Bottle. "That topcoat warm?"

"Yeah."

"A man's having lunch with our boy. My guess is that they'll leave separately." He described the man in the black blazer, his height, his tan, and the gray hair. "I want his tag numbers. Maybe we can get a fix on who he is."

"You don't sound happy."

"Worse than that. He made me, just like that. He played *got-cha* with me. He did everything but point his finger at me and say, *bang*."

"Thorpe see you?"

"I don't think so. This one is sharp."

Joe left, turning up the collar of his topcoat. Wilt leaned back and closed his eyes. He felt weight on the seat back. He didn't open his eyes.

"You think you flushed him?" Egan asked.

"Likely."

"Where'd he run?"

"The tag might tell us." He could taste the bourbon. It felt like a thin layer of skin on his tongue. It was too damned early to have a taste like midnight in his mouth.

Time passed. Wilt shut out the heavy breathing from the rear seat. And then he was jerked upright when the door on the driver's side opened. A blast of cold air changed the temperature in the car. "Yeah, Joe?"

"Had no trouble picking him out."

"The tag numbers?"

"That was the trouble. It was a motor pool car. Government tags."

"Internal Revenue?"

"He didn't look like any I.R.S. man I ever saw. This one's got a hard edge to him." Joe started the engine and pulled out of the spot. He headed toward the exit.

"Where can we drop you, Billy?"

"Where I found you. My car's there."

Wilt turned to Joe. "He see you?"

"I don't think he did."

But he made me, Wilt thought. That bothered him more than he wanted to admit.

A charcoal gray sky. Darkening and the clouds rolling and tumbling as they crossed into Webster County. The wind was high in the trees, bending and flattening tree tops in a motion like surf.

"That's not car trouble," Joe said. "That's my stomach growling."

"You can eat after you drop by the paper."

"What ...?"

"You're such an avid reader of the society pages. Right?"

"Aw, Wilt ..."

"Go by the paper and see if the society editor has a recent picture of Missy Plowden in the files."

"Okay."

"After you eat you, run that picture off to Gus Triffon. See if he thinks this is the woman who was with the man driving the Thunderbird."

"If he does, we pick up Thorpe?"

"Not yet," Wilt said.

"Why not?"

"We don't have a case. What we have is a red and white Thunderbird seen driving onto the Henshaw place the day Cathy Dobbs is killed. A couple of weeks before that, Gus sees a man who might be Thorpe in a red and white Thunderbird with a woman who might be Missy Plowden. No way to place Thorpe with Cathy Dobbs or Dana Moore. Even a friendly judge would have to laugh us out of his court."

Joe shook his head slowly. "Maybe Egan is right. Just blow the son-of-a-bitch away one dark night."

"You start believing that, you can leave me a goodbye letter and that badge on my desk."

Wilt closed his eyes and settled back in the seat. He smothered a burp. That was the Daniels talking back to him about his empty stomach.

Shooting Thorpe dead would be easy. But what if they did, and if the child killings didn't stop with him dead? Then it was all a bad mistake. A fatal mistake.

Wilt couldn't live with that possibility. And when he could, he'd resign and buy a bait stand at the lake.

By the time they reached Edgefield, raindrops as big as quarters splattered on the windshield and drummed on the roof.

The sky closed down on them like a black glove.

CHAPTER TWENTY SEVEN

Wilt slumped behind his desk. There was a crust of a burger on a tinfoil wrap and a few greasy fries in the paper package. He looked pained, as if he had the beginning of indigestion.

"It's time you got your toes wet," Wilt said. He got to his feet and wobbled to find his balance. The hip was bothering him again, and he knew it was obvious to Joe. He got his tweed jacket from the hook behind the door. He shoved his arms in and took a min-ute to stuff his shirt in and pull the sides back so the wrinkles didn't show. He adjusted the knot in his tie.

"My toes are already wet."

"Let's go by and see the Chief." Wilt said.

"Why?"

"That's usually a good question. Today, somewhat against my will, there's a very good reason. We want something from him. That means we've got to stroke his mangy hide."

"Why take me along?"

"That's in case you really have your eyes on being Sheriff. You might as well get acquainted with one of the powers that be."

"Whatever you say, boss," he said evenly.

Wilt led the way.

"You making progress, Wilton?" Amos had his elbows planted firmly on his desk blotter. His huge belly pushed out and downward, partly hidden by the desk top.

"Could be, Amos." Wilt tamped an end of one of the Chesterfields on the end of the desk. He lit it and sucked in the smoke. It poured from his nose in twin streams. "You still got access to the Law Enforcement Intelligence Network?"

"I've got it."

"This is between us. It doesn't go past that door."

"Whatever you say, Wilton."

Wilt drew a memo pad that was on Amos' desk toward him and scribbled for a few seconds. He pushed the pad across the desk. "How about running this man through the Network and seeing what you can find?"

"He a suspect?"

"He's right on the edge of being. Still, like they say in the courts, he's presumed innocent. That's why I want this kept quiet. You get me?"

Amos nodded. "You know how much I want this sucker off the street. Of course, I'll do it. If anybody's got anything on him, the Network will."

"How soon do you think ...?"

"First thing in the morning if I put a rush on it."

"A rush then. I don't want this man, if he's the one, out there long enough to kill a third child."

"Call me in the morning or I'll call you." Amos looked past Wilt and seemed to see Joe for the first time. Joe caught his eyes and nodded.

Wilt turned. He did the introductions. "I don't think you two have met."

"Heard good things about you. You get tired of working for this slave driver," Amos said, "you come over here and join me. I've always got a place for a good man."

"I'll keep that in mind, Chief."

On the street, in front of the Police Station, Wilt stopped and looked back. His eyes seemed to fasten on the second-floor window behind which Amos's office was, The rain they driven into on the way back from Raleigh had blown past. The wind was drying the sidewalks and the streets.

"You see yourself working for that load of pig shit?"

"It's no bed of roses working for you," Joe said.

"If you feel that way, you could do worse than working for Amos. All you'd have to do is sit back and wait for him to have the heart attack and he's going to have one as sure as God made gnats. You step in and become Chief."

"It's a good plot."

"Well, you're a plotter, aren't you?"

"Some people say that."

They walked to the cruiser. When Wilt swung his left leg up to place it inside, his shoe sole caught on the bottom of the doorframe. "Damned leg," he grunted through clenched teeth. His face contorted.

Joe caught his shoulder. "You all right?"

"It's that fucking leg." Wilt rubbed the hip, rubbed it and clubbed it softly with a fist. A slick of perspiration covered his face when he closed the car door and settled in for the drive.

Joe drove the short distance across the town square and pulled into the lot behind the Sheriff's Station. He parked and waited.

"You make your report to the widow Charlotte yet?" Wilt asked.

"Maybe tonight."

"While you're there, do a bit of investigating. Find out what she's got against this Thorpe. I mean, it's no skin off her ass what Missy Plowden does. Why is she pointing the finger at Thorpe?"

"She probably thinks Thorpe is a fortune hunter."

"What's she got against fortune hunters? She likes you."

Joe felt stung. It showed like a slap across his face. "Come on, Wilt. You know I'm attracted to the lady."

"And not her money?"

"Hold off on that until I take my first dollar from her," Joe said.

"How'll I know?"

"I'll put it on a chain and wear it around my neck."

"You're going to look silly," Wilt said. He opened the cruiser door and got out carefully. He limped across the parking lot, leading the way to the Station.

By ten of nine, Wilt was at the Blue Lagoon. Before Wilt reached the bar, Kyle had a glass with a couple of ice cubes in it and was pouring the black Jack. "You're becoming a regular."

"I like looking at strange titties."

"Most men do." Kyle waved Wilt's money aside. Wilt stuffed it in the tip jar and looked around from the doorway of the main room. The stage was dark. The dancers wouldn't start for a few minutes. He had a swallow and tasted the Daniels. His eyes did a sweep, right to left. He'd done about three-quarters of the room when he stopped. His head locked.

Diane sat at a table there, in profile for him. A young man sat across the table from her. Good-looking. Dark curly hair, even bright teeth. One more look and Wilt backed toward the entranceway.

It wasn't the young man that stopped him. Handsome was a dollar a dozen. And he could get unhandsome fast if Wilt wanted to ugly him some. If there was reason.

What Wilt saw stopped him. Diane had her left arm extended, her hand resting on the young man's arm. And she was laughing. That she was laughing bothered Wilt as much as the hand on the man's arm. The time he'd known Diane he'd seen very little laughter from her.

One final look and Wilt turned and reentered the bar room. Kyle saw him coming and reached behind him for the Daniels bottle. Wilt shook his head. "And, on the other hand, some days strange titties bore me."

Kyle sliced through that lie. "Diane busy?"

"How'd you know?"

"Second sight."

Wilt drained the glass down to the ice cubes. He tapped the glass on the bar. "See you."

"Stay around, Sheriff. Keep me company. It's a slow night."

"Some other night."

"Sheriff, it's not what …"

"Screw it." A wave and Wilt was through the door and into the parking lot.

CHAPTER TWENTY EIGHT

Wilt stopped at the Inside Out Lounge. It was one of the new "in" places where the singles spent their time. He had three quick drinks and watched the men and women bouncing around like the steel ball in a pinball machine. He considered coming on to a blonde a couple of stools down from him. The bartender knew Wilt and saw his interest and offered to make the introductions. But Wilt shook his head.

By a little after eleven, he was back at his apartment. He checked in with the Station. Floyd said it was slow and under control. He undressed and fell into his bed. It was a drunk, deep sleep.

It was a sleep without dreams.

He awoke. The telephone was ringing.

Or was he dreaming that the phone was ringing?

He clawed at the phone on the table beside the bed. He fumbled, found it, lost it and heard it hit the floor with a bang.

The alcohol fog lifted. The receiver was on the floor and it was still ringing. Therefore, the ringing wasn't the phone. That wasn't possible. He sat on the edge of the bed and lifted the receiver. All he heard was the dial tone.

Not the phone. He slammed the receiver on the base and grabbed his bathrobe. The lighted dial on the bedside clock gave the time as three-fifteen.

The doorbell. He switched on the lights as he moved through the apartment. He put on the robe and belted it. The floor was cold. He realized he'd cut back the heat when he left the apartment and had been too drunk to remember to switch it on when he returned.

"Coming," he yelled at the door. He stopped and gave the thermostat a push that got the furnace rumbling.

"What the hell is so important …? He jerked the door open.

Diane stood there, wet and cold and shivering.

"It's raining?"

"Yes."

"How'd you get so wet?"

She shook her head. "Coffee. You have any coffee?"

Wilt put an arm around her shoulders and drew her into the apartment. He put the water kettle on. He returned to the living room and found her standing over one of the floor vents. Her head was down, her eyes closed. He shook his head and went to the closet where he kept the towels. He found a large soft one.

"Let me have your coat." He said.

He handed her the towel, she gave him the soaked coat. He carried the coat into the bathroom and draped it on the shower rod.

The water was hissing in the kettle. He put in the filter and readied the drip pot. He threw a couple of handfuls of coffee beans into the grinder. A few seconds and the coffee was ready for the filter. He left the kitchen and went into the bedroom. He dressed in tan pants and a pullover sweater. He carried the robe into the living room.

"The boots," he said. He knelt and pulled them from her feet. He put them aside and pressed the robe on her. "Out of those wet things. All of them."

He returned to the kitchen and dampened the grounds, waited and then poured the water into the filter holder. He walked to the doorway. He found she had the robe on and the wet things were in a heap next to the vent. While the water settled, Wilt carried the wet clothing into the bathroom and added those to the shower rod.

He passed her and couldn't see her face. The towel covered her head completely. The water had settled. He fixed two cups and added a strong slug of cognac to both of them. It wasn't the way he liked his brandy. He didn't like to think that all those fumes rising above the cup were, in fact, most of the alcohol.

He handed her a cup. "Drink it fast before the booze gets away."

A swallow and she coughed. "Too strong."

"Drink it down," he insisted. He sipped his. He knew he didn't need it. Back in bed he'd be asleep in seconds. He gave her a close look. The brandy and the hot coffee had brought some of the color back into her face. "What brings you out on a wicked night like this, little Nell?"

"You … you mule."

"Me?" Wilt backed away from her and eased down into a stuffed chair. "Why me?"

"Because … because you're so wrongheaded."

"You're talking about dependable, steady John Law."

She stood on one leg while she held the other foot over the heat rising from the vent, "You came to see me, didn't you?"

"Yes. Or to see Rachel."

"You came to see me and you didn't stay to see me."

"I saw you, lady." He limped into the kitchen and grabbed the cognac bottle. He came back and poured a trickle into his cup and added about half a shot to hers. "You were busy."

"That wasn't my fault." Her lower lip trembled.

He realized that she was a little bit more than chilled. She was high. "You have a few drinks tonight?"

"I had more than a few."

"Why?"

"You walked out without trying to see me. That hurt my feelings. You don't think I have feelings? So I had a lot of drinks. I had as many as I wanted."

"How'd you get here?"

"Kyle dropped me."

"That was smart of him."

"He said he didn't want me to drive," she said.

He sipped his drink. The brandy overpowered the coffee. "How'd you get wet?"

"Standing … outside."

"Why'd you stand out there?"

"Well," she flared at him, "I couldn't come up here. You might be with a woman."

"If you couldn't come up to the apartment, why come here at all?"

It was getting stupid. He was sober but groggy. She was drunk but sobering up from the chill. Until he started pouring brandy down her again.

"Why didn't you stay and see me?"

"I didn't feel like competing for your time."

"Noble of you."

"I didn't like standing there and watching you with another man. And there's nothing noble about that."

"That wasn't another man. That was Williard, my husband Jimmy's brother. He heard about the divorce and came by to see how I was, if I need anything."

Wilt placed the cognac bottle on the table next to the stuffed chair.

"I told him he didn't have to worry. I was fine. I was being taken care of by a mean bear of a man. An upright man. That I thought this mean bear of a man might even love me."

He smiled. "I know this man?"

"Do you know this …?" The cup shook in her hands. A violent wave of trembling and shivering racked her. The coffee and brandy splashed around her. She continued to shake and when she lifted her head, he saw that she was crying.

He took the cup from her and put it aside. He put his arms around her and held her with her face deep in his chest.

"I'm so cold, Wilt."

"One cure for that." He lifted her and carried her toward the bedroom.

Her arms tightened around his neck. "Your poor hip."

"You're not as heavy as you think you are."

He placed her in the bed and pulled the covers up around her neck. He stretched out beside her but on the outside of the covers. His warmth, even from outside, would warm her.

"Aren't you…" Her eyes flickered. She fought against the weight of her eyelids. "Aren't you going to take advantage of me?"

"Not tonight."

"Poor man." Her voice was so low he had to lean close to her to understand the words. "Poor man, I'm in your bed and I'm so drunk you don't want me."

"Go to sleep." He stroked her face.

"I don't want to go to sleep. I want you so much, you poor man."

"Go to sleep," he said. "I think I love you."

"You do?" A child's radiant smile moved across her face.

"You won't remember I said it in the morning."

"I will. I will." Then she passed out.

He stayed with her, against her, warming her, until he was sure that the worst of the chill was over. He tested her forehead and found no sign of fever. One last tuck at the covers and he carried a pillow and a couple of blankets into the living room. He slept the rest of the night on the sofa.

CHAPTER TWENTY NINE

H er clothing was dry by morning. He placed them on the chair next to the bed. He had a shower and a shave. The noise didn't awaken her. Before he left for the Station, he made a pot of coffee and had a cup and a half and left the rest for her.

He placed a clean cup on the kitchen table. It anchored a note.

I knew you wouldn't remember so I'll tell you again: God, you're great in bed.

Almost fresh coffee in the pot on the stove.

Let's do this again on some dry night.

It was almost nine when he reached the Station. Joe was already there. He'd relieved Charlie and was seated in Wilt's chair as if testing it for a good fit. Wilt watched him for a time and finally said, "You're going to have to cut back on all that exercise. You haven't got the right spread back there yet."

Joe jumped, Wilt thought, as if he'd been surprised in the act of playing with himself. "Is that why it feels so uncomfortable?"

"That and the job," Wilt said. He peeled his heavy coat off. When Joe didn't leave his chair, he sat in the straight-backed one at the corner of the desk. "Your friend, Amos, call?"

"Not yet."

Wilt nodded at the telephone. "You mind if I use my phone?"

Joe jumped from Wilt's chair. There was a startled and even a guilty look on his face. "Hell, Wilt, I guess my mind's ..."

Wilt smiled at him. "You got heavy thoughts in your mind?"

"A gentleman never kisses and tells."

"Who said anything about kissing?" Wilt circled the desk and eased into his seat. He pulled the phone toward him. "So you had a date with Charlotte." Joe nodded. "You get any sleep?"

"Not much. She's a tiger."

"Try to stay awake." Wilt punched in an outside line and dialed the Police Station. The switchboard patched him into the Chief's office.

"This about Raymond Thorpe?" Amos asked.

"Yep," Wilt said.

"It just come in on the printer." There was the rustle of paper. "The sum of it all is that there ain't nothing on any Raymond Thorpe."

"You sure?"

"Not even a traffic violation. This one's so squeaky clean he don't sound like any prime suspect to me."

"Maybe it's under another name," Wilt said.

"You got another name you want me to try?"

"Not yet. The well's dry."

"Call me if I can help."

Wilt heard the click as the connection was broken. He looked at the phone and eased it onto the base. He made his guess that Amos wanted one of those instant solutions and a closed case. The inquiry about Thorpe hadn't reassured him.

"You ask the lady the question I wanted you to before the action started?"

"First thing," Joe said. "Charlotte said she dislikes Thorpe because she thinks he's using her friend's infatuation to take advantage of her."

"How?"

"He's got the guest house rent free. He takes some of his meals with the Plowdens and he borrows money from both of them, from Jonathan and Missy."

"That all?"

"One more thing. It wasn't said in so many words. More like it was implied. The using might be acceptable if Missy was getting as much of what she'd expected of a young blood like Thorpe."

"In bed?"

"That's how I understood all this talking between the lines."

Wilt yawned and covered his mouth with a hand. He left the hand there. "Like I said, that's a hard way to make a living." The hand covered a smile.

"Aw, Wilt, it's not like that with me and Charlotte."

The boy was too thin-skinned. He got his feelings hurt. Wilt sent Joe off to serve papers so he wouldn't have to watch him sulk around the office.

After Joe left, Wilt asked Susie to get someone from Motor Vehicles on the line in Raleigh. While he waited, Wilt opened the notebook that Joe usually carried during an investigation and flipped pages until he found the right notation.

Susie put the call through. The man with Motor Vehicles gave his name as Bob Goodman. Wilt wrote down the name. He read off the tag numbers they'd copied down at the Plowdens, the ones on Thorpe's black BMW.

"Your machine break down?" Goodman asked.

"I need more than an I.D."

Goodman said he'd make the check and call back. The callback was standard: Goodman wanted to be sure the call really came from a Sheriff Drake in Edgefield. He'd be sure if he called the Sheriff's Station.

"I don't see anything odd about the registration," Goodman said when he returned the call. "He bought the BMW in Raleigh. The papers on it are good."

"What you have on Raymond Thorpe's license?"

"He had a New York permit. Took the test and passed it here, got his North Carolina license."

"When was that?"

"May, this year."

Wilt thanked him. He'd run out of questions. He had another cup of coffee and leaned on the counter in the lobby and talked to Susie while he decided what his next move was. In the end all he could see was one open avenue.

"Susie, get me Special Agent Harriman at the district office of the F.B.I. in Raleigh."

Harriman said, "Of course, I remember you, Sheriff."

"I thought you might." Wilt lit his first Chesterfield of the day. "I need some information. This could concern a suspect in the child-killings over here. That's why I need the facts."

"I'll do what I can, Sheriff."

Wilt walked through it slowly. The name he had. The job Thorpe had with Wiegard & Timmons. The fact that Thorpe's old driver's license had been from New York. To this he added a fairly long description of Thorpe.

"What do you need?"

"Anything. Everything. Don't cull it at all."

"I'll push it as urgent," Harriman said.

Wilt wasn't fooled. This wasn't a new Special Agent Harriman. The visions of sugar plums, the chance to steal the credit for a big and important bust, still danced in Harriman's head.

Usually the credit-hogging bothered Wilt. This time something turned over in him and it didn't matter anymore. He'd trade away more than the credit if he could prevent one little girl from having to suffer that ordeal and that awful death.

Wilt dialed the phone at his apartment at noon. There was no answer. Which meant she'd left or she didn't want to answer the phone at his apartment. It was a no-win situation. A mistake.

There was a minor wreck on the Raleigh highway, a mile or two outside the city limits. Wilt sent Joe to investigate it. By the time that was closed out it, was after three.

He sent Joe to the grammar school to make sure all the kids boarded their buses. And while Joe was there, what Wilt wanted him to was to talk to each of the drivers. He was to tell them that Sheriff Drake held each of them accountable. They were to watch for strangers at the bus stops. If they had to, to ensure the safety of the children, they were to take each little girl by the hand and walk them to their doorsteps.

Special Agent Harriman called around four. "I ran the check you wanted, Sheriff."

"Find anything?"

"There's nothing on Thorpe in the Bureau files in Washington."

"That's no help."

"The New York state license was valid. Thorpe has no record there."

"That doesn't bother you?"

"Some people have neat lives."

"That must be it," Wilt said. "A neat life."

It didn't smell right. It smelled of rotten fish and dirty jock straps.

Wilt stalked the office until his hip complained and bitched at him. He sat in his chair and lit a Chesterfield and blew smoke rings at the closed window.

He had Susie put through another call to Bob Goodman at Motor Vehicles. Wilt explained the favor he wanted – all the details on Thorpe's New York license.

Goodman wanted to be sure it was really important. He wasn't supposed to use the long-distance lines unless it was a big, important matter. Otherwise, his boss came down hard on him.

"You read about the two child-killings here in Edgefield?"

"This is about that?"

"Yes," Wilt said. "It is."

Goodman said he'd call back just as soon as he got through bothering New York.

Goodman called back at a quarter of five.

"I'm on overtime now," he said.

"Think of it as your good deed."

"I had a long talk to the guy in Motor Vehicles in New York. Some odd business there. Thorpe had a new license. It goes back only to April. That's a month before he traded that in for a North Carolina one. I asked if there was anything in the file about Thorpe having a license from another state before he asked for the New York permit. He had no record of that. There's a blank in that part of the form. Here's how it looks: one day there's no license and the next day there is. And one more fact. They keep copies of the written exam. In this case they can't find the exam, only a notation that Thorpe passed it. No score or anything."

"What do you make of it?"

"It all flew past me."

Wilt thanked Goodman for his overtime work. He sat and stared at the wall. The information from New York meant something, but he didn't know what that was.

He was still stewing about the gaps, the holes, the blank places in Raymond Thorpe when the outside, private phone number was dialed. He caught it after the first ring.

"I do remember." Her voice was hoarse, throaty.

"How do you feel?"

"Don't change the subject. I do remember."

"That you're a great lay?"

"The other. Don't you try to play with me."

He laughed. "What do you remember?"

"I won't say it. I'm going to make you say it to me again."

"When do I see you?"

"Tonight." It was a fact the way she said it. There was no hesitation.

"Stay out of the rain. Don't get wet. The fever'll go away and you'll be rational in no time at all."

"I do remember."

"Is that right?"

"And your robe smells like you. Tobacco and booze and sweat."

"All those wonderful odors that all women love and can't live without."

"Yes." She giggled like a schoolgirl and hung up on him.

CHAPTER THIRTY

Wilt stood it as long as he could. He was as gentle as he could be when he lifted her arm from his shoulders and moved it. His left leg was cramped all the way from the hip to the ankle. The pain, when he moved the leg, set his teeth into a clenched position. His eyes watered.

Diane murmured something. He leaned toward her but she didn't repeat it. He eased his legs over the side of the bed. The pain was even worse then and he bit into his bottom lip and waited to see if it would ease or go away. A minute or two passed. The pain didn't change. It remained constant.

He leaned forward and pushed himself to his feet. He stood there, swaying slightly, until he found his balance.

He limped to the window and drew the drapes away so that he could look down at the street. He leaned on the window sill. The street was empty. Not even a car passed. There was a stillness of the early morning and he tried to guess the time. There was no hint of light and it was a darkness that could have been two a.m. or four a.m. It was dark as an armpit.

In the bed behind him Diane stirred. Her hand patted his side of the bed. Searching for him, he knew. An animal sense told her he was missing, that his warmth was gone.

They were in his bedroom. That was the main argument they'd had the night before. Where they should go. The rest of it was a foregone conclusion. He'd only won and taken her to his apartment because they struck a bargain.

"I don't care where we go," she said, "as long as you say to me what you said last night."

"All I did was ask if you were warm enough."

A shake of her head, "No."

"After I had my fill of you, I said you were great in bed."

A more impatient shake from her head.

"Okay. When we get there, I'll say it in the dark. That way, you won't know if I'm lying."

"You weren't lying. Not last night."

"What do you remember anyway?"

"That you put me in your bed. That you stretched out on the bed next to me, on the outside of the covers. And you said something important to me."

"Important or important to you?"

"Don't chop up words with me, buster."

"You're trying to lead me." Wilt said. "You don't remember and you're trying to trick me into saying it again so you'll know what I said ... if I said anything."

"Mule."

"Yes." He nodded, admitting it.

"You're a wrongheaded mule."

He grinned at her.

But later in his bedroom he said it for her.

"I love you."

Her face flushed with a new color. A warmth touched him, all the way to the pit of his stomach. An emptiness had been there for years and now he was full.

He said it a second time, just to see if she could be even more beautiful and he saw that she was. The amazement grew and choked him and he turned away and tried to control himself while he poured the wine, a Muscadet, a glass for her and one for him. By the time they finished the glass of wine, the old furnace had huffed and groaned and warmed the room. They undressed facing each other.

In bed, when he reached for her, she stopped him. "Let me see the merchandise." But she meant the hip. She crouched over him and studied the puckered scar and said, "That must have hurt, Wilt." She rubbed a cool hand over the scar. "I wish this was a healing touch."

"Maybe it is."

"And this is healing too."

They made love. And it was love. Two kinds, the violence, the harsh need, because she wanted him and her appetite was strong. And there was the want that had been growing in him from the first time he saw her.

Later, there was a time for gentleness, a slow dance to a kind of music that floated somewhere in the back of his mind. And the way she moved with him, he knew that she heard the same music.

Breath back to normal, raised on elbows, his hand on her hip. There was an impish way about her. "Now that you've had your way with me, what exactly is your intention toward me?"

"To continue to have my way with you."

A mock sadness. "And nothing more."

"Certainly not anything less," he said,

"It's a lot but it's not enough."

He put his arms around her and drew her to him. Soft warm skin the length of him. He stroked her hair. "That and everything. Everything in the world."

"That's too fancy. Maybe you'd better calm me again."

"God, I love you."

"That doesn't calm me," she said.

"Tell me your thoughts, Wilt."

He kept a hand on the window sill to steady himself and turned. She was awake now, sitting with pillows behind her head.

"Thoughts about you. All good thoughts. But I won't tell you."

"But they're all good?"

"Good and beautiful."

"Then why are you out of my bed?"

"*My* bed," he corrected her. "I guess it's something I have to get used to. I've been sleeping alone too long. It's hard to adjust."

"Poor badass," she said.

"When you're a teenager you spend all your days and nights dreaming about sleeping with a beautiful woman. And when you're older, you discover you feel that somebody invaded your territory."

"The first man I've wanted to go to bed with in years and I find he doesn't want to sleep with me. That's disappointing."

"We'll work it out." He padded into the kitchen and got two cans of Bud from the refrigerator. He opened one and had a long swallow. He carried them back into the bedroom and pulled the tab on hers. "Thirsty?"

She gulped the beer. "All that wine …"

He kissed her. She tasted of sleep and the sourness of the wine.

He took a deep breath and felt the pain going away. Perhaps there was something to the healing touch, though it was slow-acting.

"I talked to Wes tonight," she said, "just before I met you."

He waited.

"Don't you want to know what he said?"

"You'll tell me," he said.

"He said if I was going to waste my life on some man, I could do worse than you. That you'd been to the top of the mountain and looked at what was on the other side."

"Nice of him. But the truth is that there's nothing there. There's nothing to see on that side of the mountain."

"Me?"

"No." He wrapped an arm around her and put his face deep in her hair. "You're on this side of the mountain."

CHAPTER THIRTY ONE

Wilt held the receiver to his ear while he waited for Susie to place the call to Judge Baldwin's office. Joe frowned down at half a cup of coffee across the desk from him.

"I'm tired of pussyfooting around Thorpe," Wilt said.

"Past time." Joe looked rested and fresh.

Wilt had his guess that Joe hadn't spent the night with Charlotte Winters. A second bit of proof: there was a glow to Joe's skin and that meant he'd had his early morning workout.

The call went through. The Judge's secretary said he was due in court in half an hour. Was this so important that it couldn't wait? If it couldn't wait, could it be handled in five minutes?

"I need a search warrant," Wilt said.

"How soon can you be here?"

"Three minutes," Wilt said.

The secretary said the Judge would expect him.

Judge Jason Baldwin was thin and short and dapper. He had an out-of-date pencil thin mustache and wore his hair combed over so that it partially covered a bald spot on top of his head.

He was University of North Carolina and Harvard trained and there was, often, a confusion about which accent he wanted to use.

"This Raymond Thorpe, you have reason to believe he is involved in the death of the Dobbs child and the Moore child?"

Wilt argued the patchwork, circumstantial evidence he had. Even as he rushed through it, he saw clearly how thin it really was.

Judge Baldwin listened politely, his head canted to one side. "It doesn't sound like you have much to go on."

"I know that. Let's just say that I wouldn't mind if Thorpe knew that we were thinking about him."

"Wouldn't that have the adverse effect of warning him?"

"Maybe that's what I want. Let's say we scare him. It might keep him away from school bus stops until we have a case against him."

"This goes against my grain, Wilton. I don't want this to be a fishing expedition."

The secretary, a dowdy woman with her hair in a painful tight bun and with a sour pursed mouth said: "Ten minutes, Judge."

"I want it specified what you're looking for," The Judge said.

"Women's underpants, unworn."

The Judge nodded but looked confused.

"Also children's underpants, worn, belonging to Cathy Dobbs and Dana Moore."

"You think the killer kept them?"

"Maybe. They're missing. And we want to look for false identification, credit cards, driver's licenses, social security cards in any name other than Raymond Thorpe."

"That's all?"

"I wish I could say 'and anything else that helps.'"

"You can't." The Judge's head was down. He scribbled on a pad and turned and handed the pad to his secretary. He paused at his desk to sign the search warrant. "Miss Marsh will type in the particulars."

Five minutes later, Wilt and Joe were on the highway headed for Old Oak Terrace Road and the Plowden estate.

⚜ ⚜ ⚜

Missy Plowden was upset after she read the search warrant. She followed them to the cruiser, still arguing. She was dressed in riding pants and tight brown boots that reached her knees. The riding pants were a mistake, Wilt thought. In them, she looked like she had a rear-end like a draft horse.

They'd stopped at the main house to get a key to the guest house. She rode with them the quarter mile to the house where Thorpe lived. She wanted them to hold off their search until she called Thorpe and he arrived from Raleigh. Wilt insisted that it was not necessary for Thorpe to be there while the search was conducted. They were, he said, on a tight schedule and they couldn't spare the time for Thorpe to drive over from Raleigh.

That settled, Missy relaxed. She would go with them and oversee the search. With the anger and outrage dying, she appeared to notice Joe Croft for the first time. From the passenger seat in front, Wilt saw the calculated interest and he considered how he could use it.

The guest house was a single floor. It wasn't huge but it wasn't small either. It was a bit larger scale than what a single man or woman got in a studio apartment or a one-bedroom place.

There was an expensive oriental rug on the living room floor and a leather-covered couch near the fireplace. The living room had windows on three sides and thick, heavy drapes that shut out the light. Chairs placed here and there and an entertainment center with closed wooden doors that enclosed a color TV and a tape deck.

Wilt sent Joe to search the living room and the kitchen. He would do the bedroom. His calculation was that Missy would remain with Joe, trying to seduce him away from Charlotte, and he would be left alone to turn the bedroom inside out if he wanted to.

He was right.

Wilt started with the closet. He didn't expect to find anything. A sly man knew that was where the search began and made sure there was nothing to be found. There was a full rack of clothing, several suits and expensive jackets in tweed and flannel. A dark raincoat and a light-colored one. Perhaps two dozen pairs of trousers. He checked the clothing. He found a few coins. Next, he checked the suitcases. Empty except for some shirt wrappings and a plane ticket stub for a flight from New York. He replaced the suitcases and checked the closet shelves. Nothing but dust and a pair of shoes that needed new heels and half soles.

On to the small bookcase. He shook each book to make sure nothing was hidden there. Next the dresser. He found stacks of shirts and boxer shorts in one drawer. Socks and starched handkerchiefs in a second. He checked everything but took care not to disturb the order.

The bathroom was next. The usual articles in the medicine chest. Shaving things, razors, lotions and a couple of prescription drugs. Aspirin. Bromo. As a final, foolish gesture, he lifted the top from the toilet water tank. He found nothing but rusting water.

He returned to the bedroom. The night table first. He raked through the contents of the table drawer. A couple of packages of rubbers. The ones with ribbed tips. A roll and a half of breath mints. An opened package of Tums. A plastic bag with what was probably half an ounce of grass in it. A pack of rolling papers next to that. He replaced the grass. It wasn't on the search warrant and there wasn't any reason to worry about it. Any hassle about the grass could only bring up the possibility that the search had gone past the limits set by the warrant.

The floor was highly polished wood. Another oriental rug, used like a throw rug, was beside the bed. He lifted it. Nothing.

He stood in the center of the bedroom and felt the failure and the disappointment and just a bit of anger.

Now what? Fuck it. He attacked the bed and tore the covers from it. The heavy bedspread, the blanket, the top and the bottom sheets. He tossed them one after the other into a pile on the oriental rug.

Wilt started on one side of the bed and ran his hand between the mattress and the box springs. He lifted the mattress as he went. Then his hand touched something. A push and the mattress was raised.

It was pair of women's underwear. They looked unused.

He left the panties where they were and went to the door that led to the living room.

"Joe, come here."

Joe entered and stood beside him.

Wilt lifted the mattress and pulled out the single pair of panties. "You're a witness where I found these."

"I see them, boss."

Wilt lifted the mattress and flipped it over and away from the box springs. Nothing else. He was disappointed. He wanted to find the children's underwear. That would tie a knot in Thorpe's tail.

Missy Plowden stood in the doorway. "What did you find?"

Wilt held up the woman's panties.

"Oh ..." One look and she whirled away from the doorway and went out of sight, into the living room.

Wilt checked the waistband. "Same brand, same maker, same size."

"Still not enough," Joe said. "Not enough so he's got a choice between electricity and a lethal injection."

That was true. "You find anything?"

"Nothing. No false I.D. or credit cards."

"Was Missy helpful?"

"Only to my ego. I must be the greatest stud since sliced bread."

"That's a mixed metaphor."

Joe shrugged. "You know what I mean."

CHAPTER THIRTY TWO

Wilt had lunch at the Corner Cafe, a soup and sandwich shop. He didn't taste the bean soup or the tuna salad sandwich. Head down, he kicked the facts around in his mind like a soccer ball. But there were no goals and the score was zip to zip when he left and headed back to the Station.

As soon as he entered the lobby, he knew something was wrong. Susie was flustered. Wilt stopped at the switchboard and leaned on an elbow.

Susie's voice was a breathless whisper. "There's a man in your office to see you."

"In my office?" That was against the rules. His first law was that no one got admitted to Wilt's office while he was out.

"Joe's with him."

"Who is he?"

"I think he's a Federal man," Susie said.

"He give a name? He say who he's with?"

"Not to me. Maybe he told Joe."

Wilt straightened up. He tucked his shirttail in. "A Bureau man?"

"I don't think so. Usually they tell you right away who they are. This one ... well, this one is different."

"Let's have a look at him." Wilt winked at her and marched into his office.

Joe looked up when he entered. A look that might have been relief washed across his face. He stood and pushed back

Wilt's chair. They passed each other as Wilt circled the desk and stopped behind it.

"Sheriff, this is Enos Bottoms."

The chair to Wilt's right was occupied by the tall gray-haired man, the one with the long, lean face who'd been with Raymond Thorpe in the Bird and Bottle.

Bottoms turned very slowly in his chair and stared at Wilt. He didn't stand or offer his hand. He reached into his jacket pocket and brought out a small leather case. He opened it and dropped it on Wilt's desk with the badge showing.

Wilt sat down and pulled the chair forward and grabbed the I.D. case. He lifted it and read it slowly. Not Bureau. Bottoms was a Federal Marshal.

Bottoms reached for the case but Wilt ignored the gesture. He read the I.D. a second time and even spent another minute or so studying the badge.

Just when Bottoms lowered his hand, Wilt dropped the I.D. case on the desk. "What can we do for you?"

"First of all, you can back off on Raymond Thorpe. That's for beginners."

Wilt looked past Bottoms to Joe. "What do you think of his manners? Not even a comment about the weather or a how's the family? *Bam.* Right to the point."

"You want manners," Bottoms said, "Read Emily Post."

"And witty too, huh, Joe?"

"I don't have time to dance around with you farmers. All I've got for you is a message. Leave Raymond Thorpe alone. You've already mixed too much in things you don't understand."

"You want to explain them to me?"

"Explanation is not part of my job."

"I liked that line about us being farmers," Joe said. "He's cute, Wilt."

Wilt nodded. "What do you think we ought to do with him?"

"I think we ought to show him where the door is."

Bottoms whipped his head toward Joe. "You're not man enough."

"One way to find out," Joe said.

Wilt planted his elbows on the desk blotter. He turned his hands so the palms were up. The hands were slightly cupped. He looked at Joe. Joe nodded.

Joe passed behind Bottoms, unlocked the gun cabinet and reached inside. He came out with a 12 gauge pumpgun. Turning, all in one motion, he swung the pumpgun and released it.

The pumpgun flew past Bottoms' head and shoulder and landed, with only a slight adjustment, in Wilt's upturned hands.

Wilt tilted the barrel upward and pumped a shell into the chamber. "Show him the way, Joe, I think he's lost way out here in the woods with us farmers."

Bottoms flinched when the shell chambered. It took good control but he relaxed and the tension didn't show.

"Keep working me," he said. "I can cloud up and rain all over you any time I want to. Try me. You see, all you hicks have got a common fault. You've all got sticky fingers. All of you *take*. And there's the matter of the Blue Lagoon."

"Tell me about it."

"The usual. You pressure and you take. It's called corruption when you violate the oath of your office."

"Prove it," Wilt said. He pumped another shell into the chamber. The discarded, unspent shell hit the desk and rolled across the surface until it lodged against a stack of papers.

"We don't have to prove anything. All we do is raise the question."

"You're talking in front of a witness."

"Him?" Bottoms snorted. "He's your man, your flunky. He's no witness."

Wilt collected the shell from the desk and shoved it into the slot. He checked the safety and tossed the pumpgun to Joe. The butt of the pumpgun missed Bottoms' chin by no more than a couple of inches. "You know what all this yelling and threatening is all about, Joe?"

"I can't say I do." Joe righted the shotgun and held it at high port.

"My guess is that this is one of the Federal Witness Protection guys."

The chair legs rasped as Bottoms pushed them away from the side of the desk. "I gave you your chance. You'll never know what hit you. A Federal Task Force will be in Webster County before a week passes."

"Is Thorpe, whatever his name is, really worth all this trouble?"

"It's the bargain we made."

"A devil's bargain."

"But still a bargain." Bottoms put on the Irish tweed walking hat and whirled and left the office. Joe followed him to the doorway and stood there for a few seconds. When he turned back to Wilt, he said, "He's gone."

"I don't think we've seen the last of him."

Joe closed the door. He carried the pumpgun to the cabinet and racked it and locked the door. "That was some threat he made about the Federal Task Force."

"It'll be here," Wilt said. "Resign now and avoid the rush."

Joe appeared to consider that option. In the end, he shook his head. "No, I'll stay around and see how you handle it."

Wilt nodded.

"You may not believe it," Joe said," but I'm in your corner."

"Warms my heart," Wilt said.

The prospect of having Joe underfoot all afternoon was more than Wilt could accept. Around two, he sent Joe over to the grammar school to make sure that all the children were safe and safely boarded on their buses.

Wilt locked the office door and switched off the lights and leaned back. There had to be somebody. Somebody in the right place who owed him a favor. The man at Motor Vehicles couldn't get the information he needed and Harriman and his bunch at the Bureau w probably in bed with the Federal Marshals.

Somebody not tied in, someone whose I.O.U. he held or someone who would hold Wilt's I.O.U. until he needed to call it due.

He dragged out a dozen names and rejected all of them. Wouldn't get involved. Wouldn't have the necessary access. Too much risk and this one wasn't a risk-taker because his job would be on the line. And on and on. Half a dozen reasons and one or the other or even two reasons disqualified each source.

Until he thought of Ellie Cooper.

Captain Charlie Cooper's widow.

Charlie Cooper who was dead because he'd taken two steps off the cleared trail to take a whiz and stepped on a mine. One minute alive and the next moment spread all over the trail and the woods and pieces of him hanging from the trees.

Later, in Washington, seeing Ellie again, Wilt hadn't told it that way. He'd gift-wrapped Charlie's death in self-sacrifice and honor. It was what Ellie needed then. And she'd cried on his shoulder in that fancy Washington hotel bar and believed him.

Wilt forgave himself that lie. An honorable death might be absurd but it wasn't as absurd as death with a full bladder, cock in hand, just about to whiz.

Every few months he had a letter from her and there was a yearly Christmas card. And still a widow. Because, she said, she'd never found anyone who measured halfway to Charlie or the benchmark he set.

She was a Washington career woman now. She put the time in and the movement was upward until she was executive secretary to Douglas Wingate, Chief of Planning of the National Security Office of the United States. It was a small but powerful shadowland that didn't have to be accountable to anyone.

Ellie could unlock Raymond Thorpe for him. If she would. If she thought his reason was as strong as the risk.

The two dead little girls, that might tip the balance for him.

He peeled back the cuff of his shirt to check his watch. Still too early. Two hours at least before he could call her. Better to call her at home. The home phone would not keep a record of the call. Home was better.

If Ellie would take the risk.

He thought she would.

CHAPTER THIRTY THREE

The National Security Office of the United States was created in the hysterical months that followed the death of John Kennedy. An influential Senator remarked, in passing, on a talk show that there should be an investigative arm of the government that had responsibility for keeping tabs on all potentially dangerous citizens, ones with grudges, with a capacity for violence. The N.S.O. would be funded by the government but it would not and should not be under the control of any party or any elected official. It would remain neutral. It would have primary access to all police and justice department files and records.

The fact that members of the House and Senate were told they might look upon themselves as likely targets in the future worked its magic: the N.S.O. was created and funding was almost immediate and more than generous.

Ellie Cooper had worked for the office for almost ten years. At first it was "for" and then, in time, it was "with." Ellie was bright and dedicated and, among her superiors, there was a sense of her that she wasn't interested in another marriage, that the work she took to her would occupy her for the rest of her life.

Wilt called her from the payphone at Guy Winston's gas station and reached her just as she entered her apartment. There was a breathlessness about her at first and pleasure when she knew who he was. That made it even harder to make his request. As he expected, she was shocked at first. What he wanted violated the loyalty she felt for N.S.O. Only after he told her what he was

up against did she soften and say that she would look into it quietly, if she could. She would have to do it by the numbers so that
it wasn't obvious that it was a private matter and not the usual
N.S.O. check she was doing. It would take a good cover lie if she
was found out.

"I don't want you in trouble," Wilt said.

She laughed. In his mind's eye he saw the red hair and the
freckles that even face powder couldn't hide.

"They won't fire me," she said. "I know too much. They'd
have to shoot me."

When she had a pen and paper, he gave her all the information he had on Raymond Thorpe.

When he was done talking, Ellie said, "I'll get on this early
tomorrow. There's one thing you might not know, Wilton."

"What's that?"

"If he's under the Federal Witness Protection Plan, and he's
pushed into a corner, they'll move him from North Carolina
without a minute's notice. He'll have a new identity and he'll be
settled in Fargo, North Dakota overnight."

"You give me all the good news."

The call ran longer than he'd expected, so the operator came
on and he had to add another couple of dollars from the fistful
he'd collected at the 7–11 store.

When the operator was gone, Ellie said: "What's wrong? You
don't trust your office phone or your home phone?"

"With the Feds involved?"

"Then we'd better set up a system for me to call you back."

They decided she'd call him at his office when she had information for him. They'd set a time for her to call back, and he'd
give her a phone number with the last two digits reversed.

There was almost a sad ending to the call. She said, "Come to
Washington and see me."

"When I can," he said.

"How's your love life?"

"Improving."

"Awww," she said, throwing it back at him, "now you give me all the good news."

A moments's hesitation, a pause, as if she wanted to say something more. What she said, finally, was a wistful goodbye.

The call from Ellie Cooper came in at one the next afternoon. Wilt hadn't left the office all morning. All the coffee had given him a gut ache and the chopped barbecue sandwich had him queasy after a hurried lunch in his office.

"I've got something for you." That and nothing more, not a name or what the information concerned.

As they'd arranged, he gave her the pay phone number at the gas station with the reversed last two digits.

"Ten minutes?" she said.

He said ten minutes was just about right.

He got her on the line and she began telling him what she'd learned.

Thorpe was Rayfield Bellows, a small-timer who'd grown up in West Virginia and moved to New York, just as soon as he could steal enough money for a bus ticket. He was sixteen and he never looked back. There was still family there in West Virginia but, as far as Rayfield Bellows was concerned, he was an orphan. Perhaps his family felt the same way about him.

At first, Bellows was at the edge of the crime world. A mugging here and an armed robbery there when the rent was due or when he needed some walking around money. He'd even flirted with pimping but girls were not exactly his strong suit.

"What was his taste?" Wilt asked.

"Young girls. Two arrests in the early days for molesting children."

"Convictions?"

"I think the parents were bought off or scared off."

"It happens," Wilt said.

"Bellows was on the way up." He caught the eye and attention of Carlo Bennedetti, one of the minor underlords of the Gambesi family. To Bennedetti, Bellows looked like a comer, a smart boy with a good criminal mind.

"That's a funny way to put it."

"Some people have a good legal mind and go into law. Some have a good criminal mind and take up crime."

It turned out that Bellows did have a good criminal mind, what might almost be called a creative criminal mind. Working for Carlo Bennedetti, he came up with several new wrinkles and devised imaginative ways to separate fools from their money. There was one food stamp scam that cost the government ten million dollars before they were even aware they were being taken. That was the big one, but not the only one, and Ellie listed half a dozen more cons that Bellows created.

"He was on his way up." He wasn't Italian so there would be a limit how far he could hope to go. But there was money and power and all that went with them. Then, a year and a half ago, it soured between Rayfield Bellows and Carlo Bennedetti.

"You know what happened?"

"Bellows was arrested again. He couldn't keep his hands off young girls. This time, as with the others, it was fixed. But although Carlo is a crook, he wouldn't tolerate attacks on little girls. Bellows had to go. Permanently. Bellows sensed what was coming and he made a run to the Feds. He made his deal. Protection for what he knew. And what Bellows knew would fill a phonebook."

With the information that Bellows furnished to them, the Feds broke Carlo and through him, the Gambesi family. Bellows testified and then he dropped out of sight.

"And surfaced in Webster County, North Carolina," Wilt said.

"It looks that way," Ellie said.

"The bastard."

"Which one?"

"The Federal Marshal, Enos Bottoms. He knew Bellows was a walking problem about to ruin some child's life."

"What now, Wilton?"

"I don't know. I've got to stir this soup and see what I come up with."

"Let me know what happens. I care about you and you know that."

"Likewise," Wilt said. "Thank you for sticking your neck out for me."

"No thanks necessary," she said. "This whole thing stinks and it needs to be set right. You're the man who can do it."

Wilt ended the call and headed for his cruiser. Before he got to the car, Guy Winston came to the door and wiped oil from his hands. "Guess you didn't pay your phone bill this month, Wilton."

"I can't afford to on the salary you people pay me."

Guy waved at him and closed the door against the cold and the wind.

One dangerous and tempting thought came to him as he drove back toward town. There was a safe way to rid the county of Rayfield Bellows. It was so safe and foolproof that the temptation filled the car as if it were a real shape with a real form and weight.

The Feds were hiding Bellows. That meant that the Gambesi family was still looking for him. It would be easy to find a channel in North Carolina that get the word to them in New York. He could just sit back and wait for them to act. Then he would take a drive to the guest house on Old Oak Terrace Road or to some field in the county where hunters had found the body of a man. A tortured body with a single shot to the back of the head when the sport was over.

It was safe but not completely clean. Three people would know.

He would know, and maybe he could live with that, but the second person who knew would be the channel to New York and it might cost him. It could be used against Wilt. It could give someone leverage against him. And the third person, that was the hard one. Ellie would know. She'd be sure that Wilt had passed the word to the Gambesi family. She'd see the weakness in him, and the frustration and, because she was human, she'd understand or think she did. But she would never feel quite the same about him again. As if she'd lifted a flap on his chest and taken a good look inside. At the rotten heart with the maggots crawling in and out of it.

No, that wasn't a choice. It was a last resort, if everything else failed. And it would be an admission that he couldn't do his job, that he couldn't nail Thorpe or Bellows or whatever his name was, within the law.

Time to line up the ducks. From the next roadside pay phone, he made three calls. The first one was to the Station. He talked to Joe and said that he had some of the information that he needed. Also, he would be taking a long lunch and he wasn't to be expected at any particular time.

"I'll be there when you see me walk through the door."

He called Diane at her home. "You doing anything for lunch?"

"I was staring at a can of soup."

"Put it back in the cabinet. How long will it take you to be ready?"

"Half an hour if you're picking me up."

"I am. Isn't that what a gentleman does?"

"I'll be in the lobby."

The third call was to the Willows Restaurant. It was the new, expensive one in the area. The word was the food and wine carried a heavy price-tag to discourage the ordinary diner.

Upstairs, entered from the rear of the building, there was an afterhours private club. In a public relations gesture to make sure there would be no trouble with the local law, both the Police Chief and the Sheriff were presented memberships. So far, Wilt had never used his card. It was, he knew, his stiff-backed way of saying that he couldn't be bought or even nudged.

He made a reservation for that afternoon at three. That was the main convenience of the Willows. It served late.

CHAPTER THIRTY FOUR

They sat over their coffee. The table had been cleared. He'd had steak cooked with a green peppercorn sauce and he could feel the beginning of a burn. Either the barbecue sandwich he'd had earlier in the day or the green peppercorns he'd just eaten. One or the other, it didn't matter which, might make the rest of his day uneasy.

Diane had used the half an hour well. Her dress was black and fashionably long but there was a hint of sleek, long legs. On the walk from the entranceway he'd heard the eyeballs clink like billiard balls. And the maitre d' seated her with a flourish that might have had a bit of a trumpet sound scored into it.

"You didn't tell me what I did to deserve this," Diane said. She held a cigarette and he reached across the table and lit it with a battered Zippo and flipped the cover closed.

"It's our farewell for a time."

Her eyes closed as if he'd struck her. Then they were open again and she blinked. "I don't think I understand your sense of humor, Wilton."

"It's a fact of life." He lowered his voice and told her about the visit from Bottoms, the Federal Marshal.

She relaxed. She still didn't understand him.

"Look at it this way. I won't let Bottoms play games with me. But he's going to play hardball because that's his way of getting what he wants. If the Task Force can't find anything, they go in for the best smear job they can put together."

"It doesn't concern you and me."

He shook his head. "That's where you're wrong. He mentioned the Blue Lagoon when he didn't have to. He's pointing. He knows something about you and me. I don't know what he thinks he knows. My guess is that he misreads it."

The waiter appeared behind Diane. He refilled her coffee cup and circled the table and topped his cup. Wilt waited until he moved away. "One thing you've got to do. You've got to keep complete control over what happens at your club. Nothing illegal. Nothing that can be pinned to you. No suggestion that the girls go off with the customers, no late alcohol sales. No drug deals in the parking lot or the men's room."

"I can't swear…"

"Put it to Kyle. He'll know how to enforce it."

"Why all this caution?"

"Lady, he wants my hide and if he can get at me through somebody I care about, then that's a Christmas surprise and bonus for him."

"How will finding something on me help him dirty you?"

"He'll try to turn you. If he gets something on you, he'll try to deal. He'll tell you you're looking at so much time in the slammer and then he'll ask you about me. What he'll want is some handle on me. And most people sell their grandmother when it comes to the crunch. I don't want you in that position."

"You think I'd sell you, Wilt?"

"No, I don't. But if the offer is made to you, and you turn it down, then there'll be no deal when it goes to court. No plea bargaining, no settling for a guilty on a lesser count, and no chance of probation. The Feds will push for the maximum the law and the codes call for. I don't want that to happen to you. I don't want you in that position."

"You're afraid for me?"

"Some." He didn't want her to know how worried he really was. The Feds, when you got on the wrong side with them, could grind you down from bones to dust.

"How long will it be?"

"Until I burn some tailfeathers. Until I get those slicks running back over the county line."

"My bed'll be empty."

"It better be."

"It would serve you right if it weren't."

"Fill it if you need to. What happens between you and somebody else doesn't have anything to do with us."

"You crazy, crazy man." Her eyes watered. She blinked and fought it back.

He reached across the table and placed his hand there, palm up. Her hand touched his and remained there. Her cigarette burned to the filter, forgotten. His coffee cooled.

Their waiter tapped his feet and checked the time on his watch. This last deuce of the day was taking the whole afternoon and the man looked like he was the type who thought *tip* was something you did with a canoe.

Joe Croft had a pout on. Maybe he felt he'd been left holding the main desk too long. The pout went away when Wilt brought him in his office and laid out what he'd learned about Thorpe.

"You've got sources." Joe said.

"A few."

"How do we use what we know?"

"This instant friendship between Jonathan Plowden and Ray Thorpe. Does that bother you?"

"Now that you mention it ..."

"What's the common ground between a small-time hood and Mr. Society? We need an answer to that before we can put pressure on Thorpe."

"Maybe we should ask Plowden."

Wilt got his heavy coat. "That's what I was thinking."

❧   ❧   ❧

There was no answer at the Plowden's front door.

Wilt led the way around the side of the house. He reached the top of the stairs that angled down to the patio. What he saw there stopped him.

The wheelchair was halfway down the stairs, wedged against the handrail. Just past the last step, Jonathan Plowden sprawled face-down on the patio. He was wearing pajamas and a heavy bathrobe. One foot was bare, the other covered with a brown leather bedroom slipper.

"Check him," Wilt said.

Joe went down the steps at a trot. He avoided the wheelchair. When he reached Plowden, he squatted and felt for a pulse, trying the wrist first and then the neck. After a few seconds he stood and stared up the stairs at Wilt.

"Nothing," he said.

Wilt turned away. The other bedroom slipper was there, in the gravel that had been used to surface the parking area. Wilt squatted over the slipper and gave it a close look. The toe was badly scuffed. The natural grain of the leather showed in a few places beneath the dye.

Standing again, he paced the distance to the stairs. Roughly six or seven feet. And, as Wilt faced the stairs, the slipper was to the left, about four feet from the edge of the shoulder.

Joe stopped at the head of the steps and looked at the slipper. "There's no answer at the house."

"Use the cruiser radio."

"Doc and the photographer?"

"Yeah."

After Joe moved out of sight, Wilt took his time getting down the stairs. He had trouble stepping around the wheelchair. When he reached the patio, he rested a few seconds to let the hip end its screaming at him. He limped over and stood staring down at the body of Jonathan Plowden. He noticed two details immediately.

One. The back of Plowden's skull was caved in. Blood matted in his hair but there was little pooled blood on the patio surface.

Two. The bare right foot was turned inward at some impossible angle, Broken, Badly broken, Wilt thought.

He'd leave the rest to Doc Simpson.

Wilt was on the steps, about even with the wheelchair, bracing himself to swing around it, when the back door slid open and Edna, the black maid, stood there. She froze in the doorway and stared at the body of Jonathan Plowden.

She reared back her head and screamed.

The scream peeled a layer of skin from Wilt's chest.

CHAPTER THIRTY FIVE

He could see the two women in the house, through the window. Charlotte was trying her best to comfort Missy in the breakfast room. He swung away and saw that the two men from the ambulance had wrestled the gurney to the top of the stairs and settled it on the ground level.

The photographer had come and gone. Wilt took time to direct his shots, what he wanted and from which angles. He sent Joe for a tape measure and charted the position of the single slipper and the distance from the slipper to the stairs and the ledge.

Doc Simpson, making some last notes, stopped next to Wilt and studied the two women inside.

Doc said. "It's murder, sure as hell."

"Glad you agree with me."

Doc tipped his head towards the house. "Was it the wife?"

Wilt shook his head. "She was out shopping and the maid was with her the whole time."

"You got other suspects?" Doc said.

"One or two," he said.

Wilt remained in the patio until Doc climbed the stairs and disappeared, obscured by the ledge. Another look around and he began his slow climb. The last ten steps or so were the hardest. The hip was playing out. He stopped and took a deep breath. Joe leaned over the ledge and grinned at him.

"You need help with the last few steps, Wilt?"

"Screw you." He gutted it up and climbed the last steps. "You must be happy. There's another empty bed in town."

Joe whirled away without answering him.

That makes us even, Wilt said to himself.

This time the maid almost bowed them into the living room. "Miz Plowden'll be right with you."

It was a high-ceilinged room, bright and colorful and perhaps a bit girlish for a woman Missy's age. Wilt had a sense that he'd walked into a teenager's dream of the perfect apartment to go with a matching bedroom.

Wilt dropped his outer coat and cap on the sofa next to him. He watched as Joe took a stuffed chair and eased into it and carefully arranged his crease.

"A hell of an accident, huh?" He kept his eyes level with Joe's.

"I didn't like that slope the first time I saw it," Joe said. "Should have had a rail of some kind around the patio."

"You buy accident?"

"Sure. Why not?"

"The bedroom slipper."

"That's easy," Joe said. "He dropped the slipper and couldn't or didn't want to bother to pick it up."

"Cold day to be there with a bare foot. How about the broken ankle?"

"He caught it somehow as he tumbled down the stairs."

"The caved-in back of his skull?"

"He struck it when he landed in the patio."

"And then rolled over and put his face to the tiles?" Wilt shook his head.

"You're saying it's murder?"

"I say it is. Doc says it is. Whoever it was started pushing Plowden toward the ledge. Plowden tried to use his right foot to stop the wheelchair. The man pushing it rams him forward harder. The foot caught and turned under and broke. My guess is that the fear and the pain had Plowden screaming. The man sapped him hard with something and caved in his head. Then a push that landed Plowden in the patio. If he'd landed on his back, maybe we wouldn't have noticed the head wound was more than it seemed. It's possible that the killer didn't care one way or the other. He thought we'd assume Plowden struck his head on one of the hand rails."

"You think it was Thorpe?"

"I'd sure like to know what he was doing a bit over an hour ago."

"That the time slot?"

"Doc says it's hard to say. He thinks a shade over an hour because of the weather, the old temperature."

Missy Plowden came in, pale and red-eyed, and the lack of makeup revealed the coarse skin and the sagging pouches under her eyes. Charlotte had an arm around her, bracing and supporting her. The way Charlotte cut her eyes toward Joe, Wilt knew it was hard on her. Here she was trying to be a good friend to Missy and what was singing in her blood was really how much she wanted Joe.

"Dr. Withers prescribed something to help her sleep," Charlotte said.

"I haven't taken it yet. I understand you want to talk with me." Missy eased into a stuffed chair across from Wilt. Charlotte patted her shoulder and stepped back.

"Just a few questions and we'll leave you to rest." Wilt looked over his shoulder. Joe had his pad in one hand, the pen in the other.

"Anything, Sheriff." She said.

Wilt checked his watch. "You left here to go shopping. What time was that?"

"My maid, Edna, and I left a little after ten."

It was twelve-twenty-five. Wilt and Joe had found the body forty-five minutes earlier. "Did you see Raymond Thorpe this morning?"

He and his car weren't on the property. It was the first thing Wilt and Joe had checked after finding the body.

"Usually we see Raymond either on the way to work or on the way to the guest house. This morning he stopped by while we were having breakfast. He had a coffee with us."

"Do you remember what you talked about this morning?"

"Is it important?"

"It might be," Wilt said.

"I didn't hear much of what was said. He'd hardly arrived before I had to leave and bathe. What I did hear was rambling, general... you know, business and the weather and things like that."

"I see."

"And when I came down twenty or so minutes later, Raymond was gone."

"Did your husband say anything that indicated they might have had a quarrel?"

"No. Why are you ...?"

"It's an investigation. I've got to cover all the possible angles."

"It was an accident. Why are you ...?"

Wilt ignored her question. "Did he say anything about Thorpe?"

Missy closed her eyes. There was a moment or two of deep concentration. "Well, Jonathan's mood had changed. He'd been ... well, happy... before Raymond dropped by. Now he was distracted. He seemed under a strain. I thought at the time it was his illness. You see, he didn't feel good after a heavy breakfast."

"He say anything?"

"He said he needed to go into town this afternoon to see Benjamin Wallace. Benjamin's his lawyer."

"Did he tell you why?"

Missy shook her head. "I thought it was because he didn't feel well. His illness had a way of getting him on edge. I remember several times it happened this way. He wouldn't feel well and he'd talk to Benjamin Wallace and they'd go over his will and make certain that everything was covered and they'd discuss his investment portfolio. He always appeared to feel much better after one of those meetings with his lawyer. So, to please him. I called Benjamin and made an appointment for two and ..." Her voice broke. "I've got to call Benjamin and tell him what happened."

"Charlotte will make the call for you." Wilt turned toward her. "Would you do that now, please?"

"Of course, Sheriff." Charlotte said.

Wilt waited until the door closed behind Charlotte before he faced Missy again. "One final matter. Where did your husband meet Ray Thorpe?"

"It's embarrassing."

"Go on."

"Jonathan got into trouble with the I.R.S. and the best lawyers in the state couldn't keep him out of prison. For six months he was ... there ... and he met Raymond. They weren't good friends but Raymond helped him get by and I guess Jonathan is grateful."

"Where was that?"

"Danbury, Connecticut."

"Why there?" Wilt knew that usually the Feds put a man in a minimum security prison near his home, in his home state, if it was possible.

"The case was heard in the New York courts. That's where ... what they called the fraud took place. Jonathan could have served his time here, in North Carolina. He didn't want to. He wanted to be away from the state, as far as he could be. That was how embarrassed he was."

"When was that?"

"That was 1979 ... no, 1980."

It was all coming together. They needed to talk to Thorpe. Wilt thanked her for her help and pulled Joe aside, out of Missy's earshot.

"You have the name and the number for the deputy we met in Raleigh?"

CHAPTER THIRTY SIX

The badge and the I.D. were in the open leather case on the counter at the front of the insurance office. The girl Billy Egan faced had bright red hair and a small hook-shaped scar on her chin.

"Mr. Thorpe's been out of the office all day," she said. "He's following up on inquiries."

Egan looked over his shoulder at Wilt.

Wilt stepped forward until he was shoulder-to-shoulder with Egan. "Did he come in at all today?"

There was a hesitation. "He called in. It happens that way when his schedule is full. He calls in and lets us know that he'll be out most of the day."

"Do you have a list of his appointments for the day?" Wilt watched as Billy Egan picked up his case, folded it and put it away.

"The agent makes his own appointments. A lead might come in through us but we pass them on to him and he sets up his own schedule."

"You have any way of getting in touch with him?"

"Not unless he calls in," the girl said.

"And he hasn't?"

"Not since he called in around…" The girl checked her watch. "I think it was just before my break. That would make it ten-thirty or so."

Ten-thirty or so. That would place it about the time Jonathan Plowden had gone over the edge and down into the patio, Wilt thought. The call could even have been made from the Plowden home. A check with Southern Bell could establish whether a toll call had been made from the Plowdens in Edgefield to Raleigh about that time. It would, if it checked out, be a small beginning in a case against Thorpe.

They stopped in the lobby downstairs. Through the doorway they could see the sky, the grayness there, the hint of rain or ice. A strong, gusty wind blew trash down the sidewalk past the doorway.

Egan lit a filter-tip. "A nasty day."

"You should have been around for our morning," Wilt said.

"You think Thorpe's coming back here?"

"Not if he knows we're looking for him. There's a good chance he's running."

"Where'll he run?"

"To a Federal Marshal who will babysit him no matter what." Wilt said. "And you won't make any friends if you get in that Marshal's way."

"That's one good reason to back you," Egan said.

Wilt nodded at Joe. He turned up the collar of his heavy outer coat. "I'll call you."

"Let me give you my home number," Egan said.

Joe turned and dug out his note pad. He took the number and placed it below the departmental number.

"Any hour," Egan said.

Wilt popped the lock on the back door of the Plowden's guest house. The place was empty. There was the smell of bacon grease in the kitchen and a crusty skillet soaked in the sink, along with the breakfast dishes.

"What are we looking for?" Joe asked. "I mean, without a warrant, nothing we find can be used in court."

"I want to find his getaway cash," Wilt said. "If it's still here."

They went inside and began a thorough search. This time, without a watchful Missy, they weren't as careful. They blew through the rooms like a storm wind down a narrow tunnel.

When Wilt finished with the bedroom, he shifted to the living room. Joe was still in the kitchen. He was checking all the containers, all the boxes and bags, everything but the canned goods.

Wilt left him to that and started on the living room. He dragged all the furniture to the center of the room and tipped it over to check for anything hidden behind or under or inside. He wrecked the home entertainment center in the process and came up with nothing. He manhandled the furniture back into place.

The fireplace was next. He tossed his cap on the coffee table, set the fire screen aside and tested all the stones around the fireplace arch, seeking a loose stone. He enlarged the search to the brickwork apron that extended from the fireplace base to the edge of the rug. He ran his fingers around each brick. He tested the mortar. One brick wobbled, near the center of the apron. It was held in place, he thought, by sand rather than mortar.

He called to Joe in the kitchen. "Bring me two kitchen knives."

Joe came out a moment later with the two knives and handed them to Wilt. He inserted the knives into the sand at both ends of the brick and it slid upward easily.

There was a hollow pocket beneath the brick. Wilt reached down and grabbed a package wrapped in several layers of plastic.

Joe stood over him while he opened the package on the coffee table. There was a banded stack of hundred-dollar bills and two stacks of twenties.

"How much?" Joe asked.

"I'd guess between eight and ten thousand dollars." Wilt rewrapped the cash and tossed it in the center of his cap. "That's number one. Let's see if he has a second one."

"What makes you think there's more?"

"He wouldn't put the whole nut in one hidey hole. What we're looking for is more cash or maybe the papers to back up the new, second identity he's put together since he moved here from New York."

"You act like you're sure."

"What's important to a guy on the run? Food, shelter, comfort and cash in the pocket." Wilt knelt at the fireplace and stared at split logs stacked on the grate. "You think he's had a fire in this?"

Joe stepped around him and ran a hand up, out of sight, into the chimney. He turned and showed Wilt the hand. There was a smear of soot. "It's been cleaned, maybe this summer. I'd bet a month's pay it hasn't been used since then."

Wilt leaned against the mantlepiece. "Say you had two stashes. Say you thought, on a bad day, that they might uncover one cache. What would you expect of them?"

"Huh?"

"If they looked for a second stash, where would you expect them to look?"

Joe understood. "Well, first of all I'd hope they believed the one stash was all of it."

"Or…?"

"The search would move on, to another part of the house. You wouldn't expect two stashes close together."

It took only two or three minutes to uncover the second cache.

Wilt unscrewed both knobs from the end rods of the fire screen. He dug around inside with a ballpoint pen until he felt a resistance. They turned the fire screen upside down. Small tight rolls of hundreds slid from the rods and plopped on the carpet. Wilt slipped the rubber bands from one roll and counted the hundreds. A thousand dollars. That times the six rolls. Six thousand dollars.

"He's broke now?" Joe asked.

"Except for what he's carrying or what's in the bank. I'd say little money in the bank. The Feds would monitor that and question him if his bank account got too fat." Wilt tossed the six thousand into his hat and nodded at him. "This goes in the trunk of the cruiser for now and then in the safe. I'll need a statement that you were with me when it was found."

Wilt lifted his heavy outercoat off a chair.

"We going somewhere?"

"I am," Wilt said. "You're not. I hope you don't have plans with Charlotte for tonight."

"Nothing that won't hold until tomorrow."

"I want you to nest in here and wait. If I miss him, my guess is he'll head straight here for his getaway cash. So the drill is you don't show lights, you don't move around. And this warning. If this guy gets an edge on you, he'll swat you like a fly."

"You worried about me, Wilt?"

"A good deputy takes a while to train. In time, if you keep learning, when I'm tired of this job, I might let you have it."

"Big of you."

He waved a hand at the bedroom. "Make your excuses to Charlotte while I'm still here."

Joe left to make his call. Wilt opened the front door and let the cold wind blow inside, sucking the cigarette smoke outside. He wanted the house cleared of any smell that didn't belong to Thorpe.

After a minute or two. Joe returned. Wilt picked up the cap with the stash money inside it. "Stay alert."

Wilt drove past the Plowden house. In the gray early evening, the bottom floors were dark. The only light he saw was on the top floor, three lighted rooms with the brightness dimmed by curtains.

The radio crackled at him. "You there yet, Sheriff?"

"I'm here, Susie."

"I've been trying to reach you for half an hour. You know a Billy Egan in Raleigh?"

"I know him."

"He left a number where you can reach him."

Wilt wrote down the number. "What's it about?"

"He said it was about Thorpe. In his words, he said that 'Thorpe just broke bad in my territory.'"

CHAPTER THIRTY SEVEN

At the first 7–11 store on the way to Raleigh, Wilt pulled off, found a pay phone, and dialed the number that Susie gave him.

"Deaf Smith's Bar and Grill." A man answered, hard to hear over the background noise of a busy dining room.

Wilt wondered if he'd got a wrong number. "Is Billy Egan there?"

"He expecting a call from you?"

"Yeah."

Egan came on the line. "That you, Sheriff?"

"The Station just reached me."

"Your boy, Thorpe, is now on my shit list."

"Tell me about it."

"Not over the phone," Egan said and gave him directions to Deaf Smith's.

It was dim in the bar. A long room that looked like a Boy Scout dining hall. A huge log burned in a crumbling fireplace at the back end of the room.

"It was a dumb play on my boy's part." That's how Egan began it.

As a favor to Wilt, Egan had a man drop by the insurance office every hour or so to see if Raymond Thorpe returned. About five-thirty, one of his younger deputies, Buck McSwain, walked into the insurance office and found himself face-to-face with Thorpe.

Like most of the young officers in a situation like that, Buck overstepped his authority and his orders. He'd been told to check and call in if Thorpe was there. Buck didn't follow orders. He told Thorpe he was wanted for questioning. Thorpe seemed docile enough. They left the office and entered the elevator. A witness who was in the lobby saw the elevator start down, then stop and go to the fourth floor. When the elevator returned to the lobby and the doors opened Buck McSwain was balled up in pain inside, bleeding from a deep slash in his right kidney. Thorpe was nowhere to be seen.

"How is McSwain?"

"He's losing the kidney. It's no good to him anymore the way it is."

"Was he conscious enough to tell you how it happened?"

"His version has him being real careful. Since he didn't cuff Thorpe, he keeps a safe distance. He gets on the elevator with Thorpe. Thorpe is too close to the door. Buck tells Thorpe to punch the lobby button. Thorpe just looks at him like he doesn't hear him. That should have been the warning. Buck was too dumb to see it. He has to make a quarter turn to reach past Thorpe and slap the button. The elevator starts to go down. That's when Thorpe seems to lose his balance and falls toward Buck. A split-second later Buck feels the pain and the next things he knows he wakes up in the hospital."

"I should have warned you. This one is deadly."

"I was warned. The kid wasn't smart." Egan tipped his beer bottle and took a long swallow. "That Federal Marshal you told me about …"

"Enos Bottoms."

"I got mad and put his tail in a crack."

"You might be sorry. You'll have a task force investigating you."

"Let them. See what they find."

At the huge fireplace the bartender used a poker to turn the log. Sparks flew upward.

"You heard of our D.A., Jarvis?" Egan asked.

"I have," Wilt said. Jarvis had the reputation as a man who'd walk barefooted through hell to get where he wanted to be and what he wanted.

"I called Jarvis. I told him about Buck and I told your story about the problems with Bottoms and how you think the Feds are protecting Thorpe. Jarvis got mad. You don't want to be around Jarvis when he's mad. He gets on the horn to the Governor, who owes him some favors. The Governor gets mad. Right away, he's on the phone to the ranking Senator in Washington. That's the last I heard of it. My guess is that the Senator is scorching ass over at the Justice Department."

"How long ago was that?"

"An hour ago. Maybe a bit more."

"When'll you hear?"

"It's my day off. As of four this afternoon. This is my office when I'm off. Jarvis has this number."

"I don't know if I can wait around with you. I need to be in my county to keep the lid on in case Thorpe returns."

"Billy." The bartender shouted and waved the phone toward Egan.

Egan took the call leaning on the bar, his back to Wilt. Wilt couldn't read his face. But when Egan left the bar and headed for the booth he was grinning. He sat and said, "Not Jarvis, but as good. That was Bottoms and he wants to talk."

"He tell you what he wants?

"A problem in communications. I think that was how he put it."

"That means he's talking and we're not listening," Wilt said.

❀ ❀ ❀

The trenchcoat Bottoms wore this time was gray, of an English cut, and he wore it with the belt looped instead of buckled. The Continental method, Wilt thought as he watched Bottoms remove it, turn it inside out and fold it carefully. He placed it on the seat of the empty booth behind them. His jacket was hounds tooth and the trousers fawn gray. The jacket and the trousers had the look of money and Wilt wondered what a Federal Marshal was paid.

Bottoms sat across the booth table from Wilt, gave him a grim look and then turned his head to Egan.

"You're mixing in matters you don't understand."

Wilt had a swallow from his longneck and smiled at Egan. "That's the Marshal's favorite song. When he's not singing it, he hums or whistles it."

Egan glowered at Bottoms. "I've got a man in the hospital missing a kidney. So I understand enough. And Drake here told me about his troubles with Thorpe."

"You've been a busy boy today," Bottoms said to Wilt.

"Thorpe's been busy too." Wilt said, then shifted his gaze to Bottoms. "Or should we call him Rayfield Bellows?"

Bottoms' face tightened. Wilt had scored a hit. Bottoms looked at Egan. "What proof do you have Thorpe assaulted your deputy? You got him red-handed?"

"He's red-handed now," Egan said, "unless he washed his hands."

"You got a witness?"

"The best kind. The one that Thorpe stuck the blade in."

"Your man sure of his assailant's identity?"

"Is that what this meeting's about?" Wilt said. "Your laughable defense of Thorpe? If it is, you're wasting our time." Wilt lit a Chesterfield and saw that his hand was shaking with anger. "I think Egan ought to call Jarvis again and Jarvis can talk to the Governor and we can bump this up to Washington once more."

"I don't appreciate people going over my head." Bottoms placed his hands palm down on the booth table top.

"Fuck what you like," Wilt said. "What makes it your birthday every day?"

Bottoms' face flushed. His mouth moved but he choked off what he started to say.

"What is it you want, Sheriff?"

"I want Thorpe and I want you to back off."

"I can't do that. I give you Thorpe and nobody'll trust the Witness Protection program again. We need guys like Thorpe to turn or we're powerless against the Mafia."

"That's your problem," Wilt said. "Not mine."

Bottoms gave Wilt a sad smile. "You're like every redneck who ever graduated from some mail order be-a-cop course. You can't see past your county line. There's a bigger world out there. Things are more complex than you can comprehend."

Wilt turned to Egan. "You take in all of this?"

"Every word."

"You hear enough?"

Egan nodded. "I'm calling Jarvis."

"I wouldn't make that call, boy," Bottoms said to Billy Egan.

Egan touched Wilt on the shoulder. "Let me out."

Wilt got to his feet. He took a step back to allow Egan to pass him. Egan was two steps past Wilt, headed for the bar, when Bottoms moved. The move was so sudden that it surprised him.

Bottoms, hardly seeming to move from the booth, hit Egan with a right to his adam's apple. Egan grabbed his throat and sat down. He'd have fallen backwards but two drinkers at a nearby table rushed to him and caught him by the arms and shoulders. Egan gasped for breath. For a split second, Bottoms took his eyes off Wilt and looked at Egan to see how much he'd hurt him.

Wilt took one step forward. He gripped the booth table top to brace him and give him a springboard. He hit Bottoms with his best shot. All his weight was behind the punch. The fist caught

Bottoms flush on the jaw and snapped back his head. The force of the blow threw Bottoms against the booth back and stretched him out on the seat.

Wilt dragged his right leg and tried to put his weight on it. Before he could settle the weight there, his left hip jerked and trembled. He lost a valuable second or two and when he leaned in to try to finish it, he walked into a left from Bottoms that staggered him and numbed the whole right side of his face.

He wobbled back a step. Hands, from a closeby table clutched at him and steadied him.

Egan was on his feet again. He tried to step in front of Wilt. "Mine," he said in a hoarse voice.

Wilt pulled Egan aside, "No."

Bottoms gripped the table top and drew himself into a sitting position. His jaw was hurt but he could still talk. "Both of you at the same time for all I care."

"Me." Wilt set himself. "Here I am, Bottoms."

He knew he was outmanned. The hip would fail him somewhere down the line and that would be it. Unless he could end it quickly and do as much damage as he could before Bottoms knew how bad the hip really was.

Bottoms pushed up from the booth. His eyes were clear now. He did a little slip-slip to one side, circling toward the cleared center of the bar.

Wilt moved after him. Bottoms retreated, flicking a left at him. Wilt hunched a shoulder and batted the fist away. He moved in. He saw the right coming. It seemed lower, he thought, than Bottoms wanted it to be. Wilt swung his body and let the right slide past his kidney.

The miss, the force behind it, threw Bottoms off balance. Bottoms leaned forward. It was more than Wilt could wish for. He threw a right and jammed it in the soft tissue under Bottoms' chin.

Bottoms staggered, his knees buckled. Wilt went after him. He threw another right, this one searching upward for the belly.

Wilt felt the stab of pain in his left hip. He had to make his move now or it would be too late.

He stepped in closer and grabbed Bottoms by the sides of his face. The moment Bottoms lifted his face toward him, Wilt jerked his head downward and butted him in his nose with his forehead.

Wilt heard the bones crunch. There was a blast of spit and breath against his face and a gasp of pain. When Wilt leaned away, he saw the first gush of blood from Bottoms' nostrils.

Once more. That would end it.

Wilt lifted Bottoms' face to him and butted him on the nose a second time. It wasn't a gasp this time. It was closer to a scream that poured from Bottoms' throat.

Wilt released him and staggered back. Bottoms didn't fall. He was dazed. The pain drew his mouth into a straight line. His hands fumbled as he tried to lift them.

"Go down, God damn it." Wilt threw a wild roundhouse right that struck Bottoms on the side of his face.

The Marshal's knees gave and he felt for the bar behind him. He caught the bar edge and hung there. He shook his head and blood splattered in a half circle in front of him.

Wilt cocked his right and took a step forward. That was when hands caught him and pulled him away.

"That's enough," Egan said. He supported Wilt to a chair and eased him into it. "Willis, bring me a big shot."

The bartender protested. "You know I don't have a license to sell hard stuff."

"Bring it," Egan yelled.

Wilt watched Egan walk toward Bottoms. He grabbed Bottoms under the arms and turned him and half-carried, half-dragged him to another chair that one of the customers pulled away from a table. Wilt and Bottoms faced each other across a space about six feet in length. Willis brought Wilt a beer glass with about four fingers of whiskey in it.

Egan leaned over Bottoms. "Bring me a wet towel and a towel packed with ice."

Wilt gulped the whiskey. It was cheap, raw bourbon. It tore his throat and hit his stomach like a fire ball. He stared at the hand that held the glass. It was swelling and puffing.

Egan used the wet cloth to wipe the blood from Bottoms' face. He tossed the stained towel toward the bar and pressed the ice pack against the broken nose. "Hold that there."

"How about some ice for me?" Wilt said.

"You?" Egan turned on him. "You didn't get a scratch."

"The hand." Wilt switched the glass to his left hand and held up the one that was swelling.

Willis didn't wait for the order from Egan. He brought a towel pack of ice to Wilt.

Egan stood in the open space between them. "I guess you two had your fun."

Bottoms lowered the ice pack and stared at Wilt.

Wilt took another swallow of the bourbon. "Let's not forget you wanted part of him, Billy."

"That was before I saw the error of my way." Giving Wilt a wink he turned to Bottoms. "What happens now? Do I call Jarvis?"

"You don't know the damage this can do to the government's fight against—"

"Thorpe molests and kills children," Wilt interrupted.

Bottoms was silent for a long moment. "I'll take care of it. He won't commit any more crimes in this state. You've got my word on it."

Wilt lowered his glass. "You move him somewhere else, right?"

"That's a judgment call." Bottoms wiped the ice pack across his face and trailed a smear of blood across his chin. "Above my pay grade. There's more testimony he needs to give on our ongoing cases, but he can't if he's on trial here. What happened here can wait."

"The hell it can." Wilt looked at his left leg and realized it was beyond his control, trembling and jerking with a life of its own. "He faces charges here and now."

"Maybe I stopped his fight too soon," Egan said. "I'm with the Sheriff. You're trying to jerk us around because of some deal you made with this asshole. If you keep that bargain, you're on the wrong side of me the rest of your life." He turned his right wrist and looked at his watch. "You've got one minute to step over and join the righteous. After that I call Jarvis again."

"You bastards. You gang up on a man." There wasn't any force in his protest. He was weakening.

"Where is he?" Wilt asked.

"I don't know. He missed a meeting this morning and he hasn't called in on the emergency number."

Wilt grunted. "He missed the meeting because he was busy killing a sick old man in my county, a man who might have known something that tied him to the child-killings."

"And he hasn't called because he's running after slicing the kidney of one of my boys." Egan said. "Lovely guy you're protecting."

"So find him. I'm out." Bottoms said.

"Then stay out, all the way." Wilt said. "If he contacts you, no new identity. No financial help. Nothing at all."

"Not my call," Bottoms said. "It's fine for you two to be righteous, but in my job, you have to make deals with the bad people to get the really bad people. That's the way it is out there."

"You don't like your job get out of it," Egan said. He put his back to Bottoms. "You ready, Sheriff?"

Wilt stood. The weight came down hard on the hip. The trembling, the jerking was gone.

CHAPTER THIRTY EIGHT

Wilt sat in the cruiser. He was hurting and he hadn't taken any of the worst of it, not by a mile. Now he waited for a surge of energy, for anything that would help him on the drive back to Edgefield.

Egan stood outside the cruiser, on the driver's side. A light misty rain, an ice spray, flicked at him and he blinked into it. The spray that stuck to the windshield had a glint like polished glass in the parking lot lights.

"What do you think about what Bottoms said?" Egan asked.

"He knows his criminal types. He knows that Thorpe will have a stash of getaway money. If Thorpe gets past me and he gets to another city, he'll be in touch with Bottoms and they go on their merry way."

"You don't sound too worried about that."

"I found his getaway cash. He's running on empty. He doesn't know that yet. He's got to make a try for it. Just knowing where he thinks it is gives me an edge."

"I wish I could be over there when it happens."

"I could always use good help," Wilt said.

"I'll see what I can do."

The door to the bar opened and Bottoms stepped into the parking lot. He walked upright, too upright, like a man who'd had too much to drink and was putting on his best sober act. He was a few steps from the door before he saw Egan and the cruiser. He stopped. He appeared to steady himself and then he paced very deliberately toward the cruiser.

He was a few steps from the cruiser when Wilt opened the car door and stepped out. He had some difficulty getting the leg straight and he had to grab at the door to keep from falling.

Bottoms watching his struggle. He said, "I hurt you and didn't know I did?"

"Not you. A sniper."

"Shit. You're a cripple."

"That's what they tell me," Wilt released his hold on the car door and stepped away from it. "You got more to say to me, Bottoms?"

"You're a son of a bitch," Bottoms said. "But I got to respect you for standing behind your badge."

"Let's all hug and cry," Wilt said.

"Have it your way." Bottoms took a deep breath that shuddered through him. "This Thorpe is a bad one. No guilt and no remorse. He'll kill you and his heart won't skip a beat. You get him under your gun there might be a temptation to relax, to say to yourself that it's over. Well, it's not. That one will tear out your liver and stuff it up your nose before you know what happened."

"I've got a move or two you haven't seen."

"Whatever. But you don't belong in any boxing ring and you sure as hell don't belong in a fight with Thorpe."

Bottoms turned and walked to his car.

Wilt and Egan stood beside the cruiser and watched Bottoms weave his black sedan through the parking lot. He drove like a drunk. On the way out the driveway, he almost sheared the sign post with his right bumper and fender.

"Like it or not, I'd better follow him," Egan said. "He might need help getting from his car to the emergency room. And I'd better be there to back up, as the law, any explanation he has for what happened to him tonight." He started away. "Don't ever get mad at me, Sheriff."

Wilt tailed Egan and his Firebird for a couple of blocks before he reached the turnoff that put him on the highway to Edgefield.

❖   ❖   ❖

About ten p.m., Joe Croft started to feel drowsy.

The heat in the guest house had him dried out and too relaxed. Both legs and feet were only a hair away from cramps and numbness. He got to his feet and bounced until he felt the blood circulating again.

He left the living room and opened the back door as quietly as he could. He didn't show a light and his eyes were used to the darkness. After a time, sure that the yard was empty, he eased the opening between the door and the frame wide enough so that he could slip through and out into the night. He soft-footed across the wet wood of the porch and stood on the steps for a time. He took deep breaths, listening to the hissing that was the sound of ice rain on trees and undergrowth.

A few minutes later, he'd settled into his nest again. What he'd arranged was a space between the armchair and the wall. There was a clear, unobstructed view of the fireplace. He settled his back against the wall, trying to get it right, comfortable but not too comfortable. His .38 Police Special on the rug next to his right knee.

Warm. Warm. The heat in the room lulling him. He decided that it was probably worse now, after his return from the fresh chill air. From that cold to the overpowering heat, that was a mistake.

He shifted his weight. His rump felt numb. Had he dozed off? He didn't think so but there was no way of being certain. Had he been alert and awake or had he dreamed he was alert and awake?

The real key was to keep his mind going. He told himself that. Think about something interesting. Like Charlotte? For all her foolishness, for all the conceits she had and for all the concern she had about her age, she was a hell of a woman in bed. In bed. That was a thought for you. It got him thinking about Charlotte in bed and then he was aroused and he sensed the change, the tightening, the lengthening...

The heat in the guesthouse and the darkness overpowered him and the dream came down over his head like a hood.

He awoke frozen in place. He heard breathing and, at first, he thought it was his own breathing. But he realized there were two different people in the room, the breathing not in stroke. His eyes remained closed at first. He opened them a slit and after an inner count of ten he widened the slit until he could make out the dark shape of Raymond Thorpe above him, one knee braced on the arm of the stuffed chair.

Joe knew he was one muscle pull away from death. Oddly, he didn't panic. Deep inside him, he accepted his death and in accepting it ,he could now try to make it as hard for Thorpe as he could. His left knee rammed hard against the stuffed chair. The chair moved and that unsettled Thorpe. As Thorpe fought for his balance, Joe grabbed the right wrist, the one that held the pistol. The muzzle blast almost scorched him. The grab and the force behind it had turned the pistol aside and the round plowed into the heavy stuffing in the back of the chair.

The sound of the gun blast in the closed room deafened him.

He held the wrist in his left hand. With his right hand he gripped Thorpe's left bicep, his fingers digging in. He pushed the barrel of the pistol upward. At the same time, he avoided a knee that was aimed at his face. He struggled to get to his feet. His legs, from the hips down, were numb and bloodless. He put his weight on his feet and realized that his concentration had wavered. The pistol edged slowly downward. He used all his strength to halt the movement of Thorpe's right hand. He searched even deeper inside himself and found a reserve of strength. The pistol edged upward again, until the barrel pointed straight at the ceiling.

At the apex, when his strength was the greatest, he did the unexpected. He released the right wrist and the left bicep and took a backward step. While Thorpe battled the surprise, Joe set himself and hit him with the hardest right he'd ever thrown, in the ring or in his workouts with the heavy bag.

Thorpe staggered. While he had the advantage, Joe rammed chest-to-chest against him and grabbed for the pistol. The pistol fell from Thorpe's hand and hit the floor. It got kicked away and skidded across the rug. Joe saw the direction it had gone and he pushed Thorpe away and dived for the pistol.

Thorpe saw his intention and stuck out a knee and threw him off direction. The impact stunned Joe and he hit the rug and rolled. He thought he was still near where he'd seen the weapon last. His hand slapped against the rug, feeling, clawing.

He felt rather than heard footsteps. He braced himself for Thorpe. It took him a couple of seconds to realize that the footsteps were moving away from him. He knew for sure when he felt the blast of cold air that entered through the back door.

Joe stood. He found the light switch on the wall and cut on the overhead light. He scooped up the pistol. He realized then that it was his .38 Police Special. He ran for the open back door and across the porch and down the steps into the yard. An ice crust broke under his feet. He felt it rather than hearing it.

A circling of the guest house and Joe knew that Thorpe was gone.

Long gone and running.

He went back inside and called the Sheriff's Station. He could barely hear Floyd. He gave a minimum account of the incident.

Thorpe showed at the guest house. There was a scuffle, a round fired. No one hurt. Get the word to Wilt. He'd wait for him.

CHAPTER THIRTY NINE

Wilt squatted over the brick apron to the fireplace. His fingers traced the lines of the sand that replaced the mortar around the central brick that had hidden the stash.

"I don't think he removed the brick." He stood and turned to Joe. "It's too neat. No sand's been spilled." He tapped the brass rods of the fire screen. "You know if he checked for the stash in the tubes?"

"He didn't get that far. I called him before he got started."

"Hearing getting better?"

"It's coming back."

"Good." Wilt walked to the overstuffed chair behind which Joe had nested. "Warm in here."

"I'd just been outside to let the cold blow on me. Right before Thorpe showed."

Wilt nodded.

"I wasn't sleeping, Wilt."

Calm eyes assessing him. "I didn't say you were. Don't get jumpy."

"It's the God's truth."

Wilt shook his head, abrupt at cutting him off. "We've got to assume that Thorpe doesn't know we've uncovered his getaway cash. That might keep him in the area. He might decide he can make one more grab at it. Otherwise, we have to figure him as gone, that he's leap-frogging across the country."

"Makes sense to me."

"Longer he stays the better. Next to nailing him right away, we'll settle for running him for a time. Until he gets tired and turns on us."

"I'll stay here and wait for him," Joe said.

"Naw, I've got better plans for you. We'll use King for the stakeout."

Nobody ever called the deputy by his given name. It was always King. He was a backwoods boy in his early twenties who spent all his off-time hunting and trapping or fishing.

Before Wilt hired him, he'd asked a few good old boys about him. One said, "That boy can track a tick through a pack of dogs and ten miles through a thicket and show you where that tick swam the creek." It was a reference that almost wasn't an exaggeration.

"Call him," Wilt said. "Tell him to bring a shotgun of his liking and his choice of shot."

Deputy King arrived twenty minutes later on foot. He carried a long shape under one arm and a battered gym bag in the other hand. He stood six-two and he appeared to be part Indian. His hair was shaggy, black as coal, and it looked like it had been cut with the garden shears. His uniform was wrinkled and it probably hadn't been washed for a week. But Wilt never noticed any bad body odor. King always smelled like fresh cut grass.

King nodded and peeled an oil cloth cover from his 12-gauge shotgun while Wilt talked. The shoulder butt had been replaced with a pistol grip. Head down, listening to Wilt, inserted four shells into the magazine.

"Four ought to be enough," King said.

Wilt cautioned him to take no chances with Thorpe. "If he moves after you, tell him to freeze or you'll cut him down."

"Hadn't planned to dance with him," King said. He placed the shotgun on the rug next to the stuffed chair. He reached into the gym bag and selected a shotgun shell. He tossed it to Wilt. "Load my own. These will tear a man apart."

King was backwoods enough not to be squeamish about making a mess of a man. Wilt had known a few like King in the field with the Corps. They'd been the real asskickers when the rough times came.

The pay phone was in the open. Wilt hunched his shoulders and put his back to the wind. The ice rain had stopped for the time.

Marshal Bottoms had called. Floyd had reached Wilt on the highway.

"Thorpe called me on our emergency line," Bottoms said. "He wants us to bring him in. He wants to be moved to another location."

"What did you tell him?" Wilt was surprised he was even getting this call from Bottoms.

"I said I'd need permission from someone higher up. He didn't like it. He said I was wasting his time."

"You give any reason why you needed permission?"

"I told him I'd heard there were charges out on him. And that broke his part of the bargain."

"Did he have you list the charges for him?"

"He didn't seem interested. My guess is that he knows what the charges are."

"How'd you leave it?"

"He's to call me between midnight and one a.m. By then, I'm supposed to hear from Washington."

"If I don't have him by then, set up a meet with him. And if the meet's in Raleigh, you'll need to contact Billy Egan. It's his territory."

"And you two will be there waiting to nab him," Bottoms' voice had a dry quality, like a scratching of dead leaves on cement. "That's asking a bit, isn't it?"

"Not as much as you think. We'll take him. Then you can come out and protest all you want to. I'll have you outgunned. That way your ass is covered.

"Maybe. I'll think about it. No promises."

"He raped and killed two little girls and he stabbed a cop. Is this somebody you really want to put yourself on the line for?"

Bottoms broke the connection.

Joe sat across the desk from him at the Station. He lifted a hand and hid a yawn behind it. Wilt stared at him for a time and said, "You ought to sack out for a few."

"An hour or two ought to do it."

"Here or home?"

"I'm afraid of my own bed. I get in there I might never get out again."

"Set my cot up in the locker room."

After Joe carried the bundled cot away and closed the door behind him, Wilt put his head on the desk blotter and closed his eyes. He dozed. He awoke. He dozed again.

A call came in for Joe at the front desk and he took it in the Records Room. He saw the way Floyd looked at him. He knew the word was getting around. The Chief Deputy was getting some and then, expanded, the Chief Deputy had himself an older woman and she was rich, rich and very rich.

"Yeah?" He threw it at her, hard and impatient. Time to let her know he didn't like these personal calls during his working hours.

"It's Missy. I'm worried about her."

"Why?"

"She doesn't answer her phone. No one answers at all."

"Come on, Charlotte, I was there when she said she'd been prescribed as a drug to help her sleep. That's probably what it is. She took the pill or the powder or whatever and unplugged her phone."

"You think that's what it is, Joseph?"

"Sure. And my guess is that she needs the rest more than she needs to talk right now."

She sighed. "You make me feel better already."

"It's natural to worry about a friend."

"I miss you. When do I see you again?"

"When this investigation is over. And it's close right now."

"You'll call me?"

"As soon as I can," he promised.

He went into Wilt's office. The Sheriff was awake now. Wilt squinted at him through a curl of cigarette smoke. "Anything?"

"Charlotte. I think she wants to hold my hand."

"Take a few minutes and run by."

"She'll keep." It wasn't the way Joe wanted to function. He didn't feel you had to reassure somebody all the time. A man knew who he was and what he was and that was all there was to it. A woman ought to have the same feeling about herself.

"Take the time," Wilt said.

Joe shook his head, "It's a bother."

Bottoms called Wilt around nine-thirty. The work day was running long. From the window behind his desk, Wilt could see the dark, cloudless sky. There was a beginning patter of rain.

"He's been in touch again." Bottoms said. Wilt lit another cigarette. His tongue felt cracked and grooved and sore. "He wants to come in. I told him to come ahead, the road was clear. He said he would as soon as he finished some business he had."

The stash. "He give you any idea what that business was?"

"No." Bottoms took a deep breath that seemed to suck air through the phone line. "Whatever it is, he won't leave until it's done."

"He calling back?"

"When he's ready to leave. He's talking about the west coast. Maybe California."

"He gets to make his own picks?"

"He thinks he does," Bottoms said. "If I had my say, if I was really moving him this time, I'd put him in West Jesus, Montana."

"Call me when you hear from him."

"I hope you find him first. Otherwise, my balls are in a nut-cracker no matter what I do."

"The shit comes with the job," Wilt said and hung up.

He rubbed his eyes. He felt dirty and tired and he needed a shave. He rubbed the whiskers, estimating if it was worth a layer thin run with the electric razor he kept in his desk.

"You know what?"

"What?" Joe heard his stomach rumble and slapped at it.

"That asshole, Thorpe, has got the guts of a highwire walker. He hardly gets past you the last time and he's still ready to make another attempt at the guest house."

"Maybe he's thinking we'll figure he tried and now we won't expect him again. Anyway, he doesn't know we know about his getaway money. He might think we believe he dropped in for a suitcase and some fresh clothes."

It made sense. "I'd give one nut to know where his hiding hole is."

Joe froze. His mouth opened but nothing came out.

"What?" Wilt said.

"Charlotte called because she hasn't been able to reach Missy. Of course, it's probably nothing. The sleeping pills Missy took. But what if it's not?"

"Worth a look." Wilt said. "Might explain how Thorpe disappeared so fast after his try at the money and why he'll make a second try." Wilt lifted the phone and placed it closer to Joe. "Call Missy."

Joe found the number in his notebook. He dialed and heard the phone ring a dozen times. He waited another five or six before he gave up. "Nothing."

"Call Charlotte."

"Huh?"

"Unless you know the complete layout of the Plowden house, call Charlotte. We get there, it might be good to know where the doors and windows are, the furniture and how it's set up in each room."

"Sure, Wilt."

Wilt left him to make the call in private. He crossed the lobby and leaned on the counter next to Floyd. "I want cars three and four to converge on Old Oak Terrace Road. Three from the east, four from the west. I want that road blocked off for a quarter of a mile on either side of the Plowden house. No sirens. Quiet drill. Nothing loud or sudden unless a car leaves the Plowden driveway. In that case, block that car. Shoot him if necessary."

He put his back to Floyd as he began to call in cars three and four. He found Joe standing in his doorway.

"She's expecting us," Joe said.

CHAPTER FORTY

Charlotte had dressed herself in a jumpsuit that was a high fashion rip-off of jungle warfare fatigues and short black boots. This was obviously a serious matter, Wilt told himself. The fur coat she'd selected to wear over the jumpsuit was a sensible compromise with the weather. For all that, he could see that she was excited. Here was a real-life drama. And best of all, she was being helpful to the man she was sleeping with.

Watching them, her sighing over Joe and Joe preening for her, Wilt wasn't exactly sure she knew he was in the room.

"I want the whole layout. Floor by floor. All the distances estimated. All the doors and windows noted. Closets, the way the furniture is arranged," Wilt said, handing her a sketchpad. "What I want is the best feel we can get for the house without a walking tour. I've got some calls to make. Where's the closest extension...?"

"In the kitchen," Charlotte said.

He left them huddled together over the sketch pad. He leaned against a kitchen counter and dialed the station. Floyd knew he'd call and he had his report ready. Cars three and four were in place. There had been little movement on the road. That was probably because the local forecast was for slick and icy highways. There was one problem. A black woman had been stopped. She said she'd come to check on Mrs. Plowden. She had a fit when they wouldn't allow her to pass the cruiser and enter the Plowden drive.

"That's Edna, the maid. Tell her I'll be there in a few minutes and explain it to her."

"Will do."

"I'll call in when I have something to report.

"Sheriff...?"

Wilt waited.

"Be careful. The county don't give Purple Hearts."

"Got mine already," Wilt said.

Before he made the next call, he found a glass and poured himself a milk from the gallon in the refrigerator. He gulped it down and picked up the phone again. He dialed the Blue Lagoon.

Kyle answered. "She's not here right now. She left twenty minutes ago."

"You think she's home?"

"That's my guess. Unless she found somebody she liked who doesn't wear a uniform."

"It's the uniform gets them every time."

"Navy myself," Kyle said. "Never could stand jarheads."

He ended the call and dialed Diane's apartment at the Towers. The ring was somewhere between the seventh and the eighth when Diane answered.

"Am I interrupting anything?"

"Just an affair between me and the shower. I'm dripping all over the rug."

"I'll call back some time when you're dry."

"Don't you dare hang up on me."

"Yes, ma'am."

"When will I see you?"

"Soon. If I'm lucky." He heard the soft purr of her breath. It raised the hair on the back of his neck. "Go back and finish your shower."

"Oh, Wilt..."

"Goodnight. I'll call when I can."

His final call was to Raleigh. He reached Billy Egan at Deaf Smith's. "You want to come to the dance, but just as a spectator, a wallflower?"

He explained the situation.

"What you need is a SWAT team," Egan said. "That's no game for men who aren't trained to do it."

"You ever tapdance through a mined rice paddy?"

"No."

"Come over and see how it's done."

"My problem is that I'm not used to going to a dance and not getting my feet sore."

"Let's say you're there as an observer. If Thorpe gets past Joe or me, he's your meat."

"That's a better invitation," Egan admitted.

Wilt said he thought it might be.

Twenty minutes after they arrived at the Plowden Estate, after all the planning and a slow floor-by-floor stealth, they reached the master bedroom. The entry was by the book. Joe the quicker and the first one in, crouched in the firing stance. Wilt behind him in the doorway, piece up and ready.

Raymond Thorpe wasn't there but the room wasn't empty. Wilt walked past Joe and stopped beside the bed. It wasn't pretty, what was there, but death wasn't ever anything Wilt wanted to write poetry about.

Missy Plowden was sprawled in the middle of the huge bed. Her face was battered and cut. A dental bridge was on the sheet near her right shoulder. Her face was black-blue and puffed and swollen.

Joe stood across the bed from Wilt. "How do you see it?"

"Beat her, strangled her."

"Why?"

"Pure meanness. Maybe frustration because he couldn't get to the money at the guest house. Maybe she whined too much. Maybe she cried and got on his nerves. Hell, we're not talking about anything that has to be rational."

Wilt walked to the door.

Behind him he heard Joe. "The rotten son of a bitch."

"Call Doc. He must be tired of hearing from us. Get the photographer. Close off the house until Doc's done in here."

Joe followed him down the stairs. "You'll be ...?"

"At the guest house with King."

"You want me there?"

"Soon as you make the calls," Wilt said.

Wilt left him in the living room. He walked outside. After the sweat, the tension of the stalk through the house, the ice rain and the wind beat on him and almost staggered him. He stopped on the steps and waved an arm at the cruiser that was parked, broadside, about fifty yards away from the front entrance. Charlie stood and revealed himself from the crouch he'd taken behind the engine of the cruiser.

"Charlie, call in and tell Floyd we missed Thorpe here at the Plowden ..."

In the distance they heard the slap-slap of a handgun. That was followed by a single boom of a shotgun.

"What the hell ...?" Wilt almost forgot the hip. He went down the steps at a run. He circled the cruiser while Charlie passed him his pumpgun and got behind the wheel. Past Charlie's shoulder, as they pulled away and turned onto the road that led to the guest house, he saw Joe on the front steps.

"You want me to stop ...?"

"Gun it. Get me there."

He listened for a second round from the shotgun. It didn't come.

❧   ❧   ❧

A hundred yards from the guest house Wilt said, "Far enough," and tapped Charlie on the shoulder. Charlie braked. Wilt stood in the road while Charlie got a second pump-action shotgun from the trunk and joined him.

Wilt held the shotgun at high port. "It charged?"

"Yeah. Double aught buckshot."

Charlie moved to the side, putting about half the width of the road between them. Wilt stopped after they'd gone twenty yards. "Best you stay here. Somebody comes running down this road and he's not limping you put him down. You hear me?"

"I do." Charlie said.

He jogged next thirty yards. Then he stopped and jogged another twenty. The running jarred the hip into a clawing pain. He stopped and took a few breaths to get his hands steady. Then he went into what he thought of as his Indian Country walk. That was for the times when you were in the open and it could come at you from any direction. Braced for the hit. And as they always said, with your asshole puckered.

Wilt stopped in the front yard of the guest house. There were no lights. He heard no sounds. He did a pivot, the whole 360 degrees and still heard nothing.

"King, you sing out."

He waited. Then he called out again.

"Here ... over here ..."

The voice was faint. He thought it sounded like King. But it was a very weak King.

The voice was from the darkness and the shadows of a thicket that faced the front door of the guest house. Wilt rushed in that direction. He stopped. "King?"

This time he heard coughing. He followed that and stood over King. The boy was on his back at the edge of the thicket.

Wilt got on his knees beside King. He needed a flashlight. He didn't have one. He'd left it in the cruiser when they prepared for the entry of the Plowden house. So he had to check King's wounds by touch. He found the gaping hole low in King's left shoulder first. The entry was high in the back and the exit hole low in front. Wilt wadded his handkerchief into the hole and pressed it there.

He found the second wound in the calf of King's right leg. As far as Wilt could tell from his touch-examination, the slug had missed the bone altogether. The bleeding was slow. That was the cold weather, Wilt thought. It probably helped with the coagulation.

King moaned and opened his eyes. "That you, Sheriff?"

"Yeah. What happened?"

"He got behind me. I don't know how he knew I was here."

"What are you doing out here anyway?"

"Couldn't stand the heat in there. Decided I had a better chance out here. Came out and got under a poncho. Lord, he must have smelled me. One second I was all alone, and the next one he was behind me and I got the feeling he was there and moved. He missed a back shot and got me in the leg."

"Doc's at the Plowden house by now. Or will be soon. I'll make sure he sees to you right away."

"I got turned around. I got the shotgun up. That was when he fired the second time. Hit me in the shoulder as I was turning. All I could do was cut loose in his direction with those wad cutters and hope they scared him away."

"Take it easy," Wilt said.

"That scudder tried to backshoot me."

Wilt heard footsteps in the front yard of the guest house. He stood and turned the pumpgun. He was about to fire when Joe said, "Wilt, it's me. Where are you?"

"Here. King's down but all right. Run a circle around the house."

Wilt stood in the shadows, pump-action shotgun at the ready, until Joe returned. He lowered the shotgun and stepped from the thicket.

"That man's a ghost," Joe said. He stepped around Wilt. "How's King?"

"Bad enough. Doc at the big house yet?"

"Ought to be there soon."

Wilt sent Joe to Charlie's cruiser. He wanted the word passed that Doc was to come straight to the guest house.

Wilt left Joe with King and entered the guest house. He switched on the overhead light and looked around. The knobs were unscrewed from the fire screen rods. The brick had been removed from the fireplace apron.

So now Thorpe knew that he was hanging in the wind. There was nothing left to him but the protection of the Federal Marshals.

Wilt switched off the light and returned to the yard. Joe waited for him on the porch. He carried King's cutdown 12 gauge.

"Doc's with King. He said to thank you for finding a live one for him."

Wilt eased to a sitting position with his back against the front door of the small house. His mind was running. Where would Thorpe go after learning his stash was gone?

Not back to the Plowden house. He'd left a corpse there.

So where?

Behind the house, the homeowners had banded together and bought that last big chunk of woods. It was a co-op. They didn't want some real estate guy to come in and put up ticky-tacky ranch houses or condos. It was about twenty square acres.

If he were Thorpe, that's where he'd run.

It was time to make a choice and stay with it. "Thorpe's in there."

"Huh?"

Wilt struggled to his feet. "He's in that twenty-acre square of woods." He walked to the edge of the porch and reached back and took King's shotgun. "I want you on the radio to Floyd. I want every man he can round up. See if he can borrow all Amos can spare at the Police Department. I want a line drawn on three sides of this wood. We'll handle this side, the fourth side. I want one cruiser to patrol until it finds Thorpe's BMW. I want it found and fixed so it won't run. Even if we have to take a sledgehammer to the engine. Give them the color and the tag numbers so they get the right one. Got that?"

"If you're wrong?"

"He'll run to Marshal Bottoms in Raleigh and we'll set a trap. You'll be with me if it comes to that. But I don't think it will."

CHAPTER FORTY ONE

Wilt sat with his back to the closed guest house door. It was cold but there was some warmth that escaped under the door. He eased himself into a relaxation he didn't really feel. He closed his eyes and drifted. He rested. He opened his eyes when he heard footsteps in the road nearby. He recognized the short, square shape of Charlie. Charlie reached the top step and waited.

"How you feel, Sheriff?"

"Got an ache. See if there're some aspirin in the bathroom. I need about a dozen."

Wilt moved aside to let Charlie pass him. Charlie returned with a glass of water and a handful of aspirin. It was more than a dozen. Wilt took six and washed them down with the water. He put the other aspirin in his trouser pocket. Wilt finished the water and put the glass aside. "You got a canteen in the cruiser?"

"Yeah." Charlie went back down the road to the cruiser.

Joe's cruiser passed Charlie on the road. Joe parked and came to the porch. "It's underway. I've got Bud cruising the road. Amos is sending a dozen men to help out. Floyd called in the off-duty crew and they'll be here in ten minutes."

"Wake me when it's in place."

Wilt willed himself into a limpness. He heard Joe's breathing but it was far away. He heard voices, Joe and Charlie talking, something about the canteen. Then he was in the deep darkness where he didn't feel the pain.

❧ ❧ ❧

He awoke when Joe's hand touched his shoulder. "It's in place."

"Where's the canteen?"

"Here. I filled it in the house."

Wilt stood. He seemed fresh, rested. "I need a dark poncho."

"I've got one in the trunk of the cruiser."

"Go get it."

While he waited for Joe to return, he entered the house and checked the cutdown 12 gauge. He jacked out the three shells. He picked them up from the floor and cleaned them. He inserted them in the magazine. He carried the cutdown to the chair and found King's gym bag. There were six more home loads in the bag. He inserted a fourth shell in the shotgun and dropped the other five spare in his pocket.

Ready. He walked outside. Joe shook out the poncho. Wilt put it on and snapped the sides. He hung the long leather loop on the canteen over his shoulder and across his chest.

"First light I want the lines of men to move into the woods from three sides. I want Thorpe driven in this direction."

"Where'll you be?"

"You and Charlie and another man, if you can find one, will guard this side. I'll be at center ground."

"The hell you say."

"I thought I'd surprise him. I thought I'd play some Jungle Jim games."

"Why?"

"I want him driven toward me. I don't want him to know I'm there."

"All night in there?"

"That's the game," Wilt said.

They walked around the house and stopped next to the back porch. The wood was straight ahead. Wilt lowered his voice to a whisper. "Keep a good watch. If he realizes I'm in there, he'll try to bypass me during the night and come out this way."

Wilt moved to the edge of the thick wood. Joe saw him. Then another step and he was gone. There was a rustle of brush and no sound at all.

"Crazy," Joe whispered to himself. "I work for a fucking crazy man."

By one a.m., Wilt reached what he estimated to be the center spot of the twenty-acre wood plot. He made his calculation by judging the relative distance between the lights at the Plowden house behind him and the lights of the estate on the other side of the wood.

It took him over an hour to reach that center point. It was slow going. And he was careful. He never moved more than a few feet at a time. After each movement, he stopped and listened. He planned as he went: no straight lines, no predictable jog left and then right and left again. He wanted nothing that would allow Thorpe to set an ambush on the assumption he would be at Point B at such and such a time.

He heard no sound of movement ahead of him. His main concern was not to move past Thorpe and let him get behind him. If he let that happen, he was chilled meat on the butcher block. But, careful as he was, he wouldn't know for sure until first light when the "beaters" uncorked their pinch movement from three sides. If he didn't then hear Thorpe moving ahead of the "beaters," if he didn't see Thorpe, he would know that the man had gone to ground and let Wilt pass him. If that happened, Wilt would have to turn and protect his back. His attention would be divided, his concentration shattered.

Wilt allowed himself to trot the last hundred yards. The ice rain increased in density and the crash of the ice on the fallen leaves and the undergrowth covered all the sound he made.

At least, he hoped so.

If he couldn't hear Thorpe, there was a better than even chance that Thorpe couldn't hear him either.

By the luminous dial of his old military watch, he saw that it was still five hours, give or take a few minutes, until first light. He was there, in place, and still alive.

He tried to think like Raymond Thorpe. He believed Thorpe, no matter how crazy he was, would expect the sensible approach from the law.

A sensible man remained warm and comfortable. He didn't follow a dangerous man off into a dark wood five hours before daybreak. Instead, he settled into an available bed and said, wake me half an hour before the sun's up.

He wouldn't be expecting Wilt to come at him like this.

Wilt chose a thick oak at the edge of a small clearing. The clearing spread before him in the direction of the section of the wood where he thought Thorpe was. He eased himself into a seated position with the oak trunk as a back rest. He reached behind him and scooped away rotting leaves and limb fragments.

He was comfortable.

At least as comfortable as he could be under the circumstances. Hip aching. Chilled to the bone, even under the poncho. Feet like blocks of soaked wood. Face numb from the cold. The ice rain pelting him like a thousand ice splinters.

Surprise. That was the element he wanted, that he'd bargained a comfortable warm morning for. At first light the beaters would drive Raymond Thorpe into a spot right under Wilt's gun. Maybe not at this tree. Thorpe's movement would alert him. He'd slide laterally, with the time the warning gave, and prepare himself.

When that happened, if it happened, he would learn a hard and important truth about himself. He would find out if he was really a lawman. Faced with Thorpe, would he give the proper warning? Would he try to take Thorpe alive? Would he deliver Thorpe to the courts for justice, no matter that there was no punishment on the books that could come close to setting a balance for the destruction he'd caused and the pain he'd handed out?

Or, that moment, that instant, would he swallow the *police* and *freeze* and blow Thorpe apart in a fury that was much closer to the old Testament sense of justice?

He didn't have an answer.

Stay Alert.

Wilt lifted his head and let the ice rain beat against his face. He could not allow himself to become accustomed to the discomfort either. He would use the weather so that he didn't fall into a deep sleep.

CHAPTER FORTY TWO

At four-ten the ice rain ended. A harsh, blade-edged wind whistled through the woods. He shivered against the wind and felt the muscle warmth inside his shirt.

Wilt took six aspirin and washed them down with gulps from the canteen.

At five, the minute hand straight up, he got to his feet and prepared himself. He couldn't stamp his feet to get the blood moving. He settled for wiggling his toes around in his soaked shoes.

He was as ready as he'd ever be. An hour to wait. Unless Thorpe decided he was cornered and wanted to slip back toward the guest house road before daylight made him vulnerable.

Waiting...

In the grayness of first light, Wilt began to think Joe Croft had gone home to bed and forgotten about the operation. But a few moments later, he heard the faint flutter in the distance. It grew louder and louder until it became the looping beat of a helicopter that flew in low out of the sun.

The helicopter was, by the markings, from the Air National Guard. It swept in low, barely above the tree tops and it passed directly above Wilt before it wheeled and angled away. It was so low that Wilt could read the numbers on the underside of the fuselage.

As the copter made a second run, Wilt saw the reclining figure of a man in the open hatchway. An automatic rifle was in this man's hands, pointed downward, and he wore the retaining harness.

Wilt knew that the pilot and the rifleman didn't know him from Thorpe. So, on both passes, he lowered his head and pressed against the oak tree until he was a part of it. He didn't want to be shot at and he didn't want the copter to point out his position to Thorpe.

The helicopter overflight was a good touch. That was the fancy trimming. Now to the meat of it. Where the hell was …?

As the helicopter moved away, as the clatter and beat dimmed, he heard the push off start. There was noise, voices and shouting, the equivalent of the tiger beaters who used sticks on metal tops and pans.

Maybe there was hope for that boy, Joe, after all.

Shotgun at the ready. Shell chambered. When the time came, he would have to distinguish between the two levels of noise. The careless noise created by the three lines of men who were pinching in and the secretive, muffled, almost silent footfall of Thorpe.

Unless Thorpe panicked.

That was what Wilt hoped for. He wanted Thorpe to break and run. If he ran, the warning would reach Wilt five or ten seconds before Thorpe was there.

Five or ten seconds would be enough.

Ten minutes passed. Wilt put a shoulder against the oak trunk. He wanted sun and warmth. Even in daylight he couldn't find a bit of sun.

The consolation was that the same need for sun and warmth that racked him with trembling and shivering also wracked Raymond Thorpe.

Wilt waited. He eased his breath, he controlled his heart rate.

His head jerked up when he heard the sound that didn't fit. First it was a scratching nearby. That was followed almost immediately by a soggy noise like someone squeezing water from a washcloth.

Where? He turned his head and heard the same sounds again.

There, toward the sun.

He lowered himself to one knee. He put part of the oak between him and the sun. He squinted into the brightness.

There was no third repetition of the sounds.

Thorpe, he knew it was Thorpe, had made one mistake and knew it and he'd checked himself. He wouldn't make the same mistake if he could avoid it.

Wilt thought of what he knew about Thorpe. That he had grown up in West Virginia. Had he learned the woods there before he moved on to the big city? Had he hunted and tracked? Did he have his face smeared with blood and lose a shirttail when he killed his first deer?

A core of silence in the middle of the noise created by the beaters. Wilt knew it was a man. A man who waited as he waited. A man who scented the wind. A man of cunning who heard the trap closing behind him on three sides and had to wonder what was waiting for him on the fourth side, where the guest house and the road were.

The cunning part of Thorpe had to suspect a trap. The operation was standard and straightforward except for the fourth side which hadn't moved at all.

Wilt could almost hear Thorpe mumbling, "What the hell is ...?"

Wilt's hip began to throb. A few aspirin might help. He knew he couldn't risk it. So far there'd been no accidental noises. Also, he couldn't lower the cutdown for even a brief time. Thorpe might make his move at any moment. He'd have to go one way of the other: toward one of the lines pinching in or toward the guest house road and into what might be the mouth of a trap. It was a trap, Thorpe would think, or somehow the law had screwed up.

The longer Thorpe waited the more his options were shaved down. The three lines of men moved closer and closer. Thorpe might not know it, but the choice was being made for him. The known was behind him, on three sides. Ahead of him was the unknown. In the end, willed or against his will, Thorpe would have to take his first step into the mouth of the trap.

Turn to face the known or run toward the unknown. Thorpe's choice. It was so limited that it was hardly a choice at all.

Wilt took in a slow, deep breath.

He knew when it came it would be sudden.

Another five minutes passed. Wilt didn't have to check his watch. His body clock ticked off the time for him.

About a hundred feet away, Raymond Thorpe stepped onto the fringe of the clearing and stopped. He was in the sun and the light for a brief time. The way he looked, he'd had a rough night in the wood. He hadn't been dressed for it. His trousers and shoes were soaked. The trenchcoat that was buttoned to the neck and belted was filthy with mud and wood's trash.

Wilt opened his mouth to give the order to freeze. He closed his mouth as Thorpe took one step back and vanished in the shadows of the bleak day.

Blood surged in Wilt. Thorpe had committed himself and stepped into the mouth of the trap. He'd tried the spring on the trap with that one step forward and hadn't seen it or felt it.

Ready. The cutdown lined up.

When Raymond Thorpe came, it was so sudden and unexpected that Wilt wasn't prepared at all. He realized that his reflexes weren't what they'd been a few years back.

Thorpe sprinted from the cover and his long-legged stride ate up fifty feet in a burst like that of a world class runner. At the beginning the angle was oblique, toward Wilt but shaded away. After those fifty feet, Thorpe swerved and came directly toward Wilt.

Wilt shouted, "Police ... freeze ..."

Thorpe's right hand blurred as it moved from his hip. Wilt saw the blue steel and the long barrel. His instant guess was that it was a Dan Wesson .357 with a six-inch barrel. There was a blast from the steel finger and the first round struck the oak trunk just above Wilt's shoulder. Damp wood sprayed into Wilt's face. The second round slapped the wet dirt a couple of feet past Wilt.

Wilt ducked when the damp wood struck his face. He lifted his head again and tried to turn the cutdown into a firing position. He almost had Thorpe in frame when Thorpe changed directions and put the oak between himself and Wilt. The hip restricted Wilt. He lost a valuable second in the struggle to turn around. Just as he was ready to fire, Thorpe reached the edge of the clearing and dived into the underbrush. The growth there closed over him.

Wilt stood. He moved so that the tree was between him and the point where Thorpe had disappeared. He waited for new sounds. A noise that would tell him that Thorpe was up and running. It came: a muffled pad-pad. Wilt pushed away from the oak and charged after him. He angled away and entered the undergrowth a good ten yards beyond the point where he'd last seen Thorpe.

His hip dragging now. His breathing ragged. The back of his throat was so dry he couldn't swallow. He'd run a few steps and stop, listening for the pad-pad that told him Thorpe was still running.

He'd covered about a hundred yards when he stopped a final time and didn't hear the running. With a shock, he realized that the trap had turned back against him. Somewhere ahead Thorpe waited for him.

He planted his feet firmly. He used the time to ease the rasp of his breathing.

All right, you asshole, if you don't move, I don't move. We'll stay here all day and all night and all week if we have to...

No, he wouldn't wait a week.

Wilt calculated where Thorpe had entered the undergrowth and the line he'd taken from there. He put that with the last place he'd heard the pad-pad of Thorpe's running.

Right there.

He held the cutdown at his hip and fired one round into the underbrush. The buckshot shredded everything in front of him. Even before that sound died, he swung the cutdown about ten degrees to the right and squeezed off a second round.

Complete silence followed the twin shotgun blasts. Even the men in the three advancing lines were quiet.

Wilt dug two of the spare handloaded shells from his pocket. His hands were suddenly very steady. He blew on the shells to make sure they were clean. Then he lowered the hand and turned the shells. He got the shells ready to insert in the shotgun's magazine.

His head remained up. He thumbed one shell into the slot. He was about to position the second shell when Raymond Thorpe jumped from the brush. He was thirty yards away and running for his life when Wilt saw him.

"Thorpe..."

Wilt lowered the cutdown to his hip. He tracked Thorpe and had him centered.

Thorpe looked around him. A wild look was on his face. He had let panic take over when he realized he was outgunned. But he hadn't given up. Even on the run he lifted his right arm and pointed the blue steel barrel at Wilt.

Wilt pulled trigger. The blast hit Thorpe in the side and he was in full stride when he seemed to be thrown high into the air. By some strength of will he continued to hold the .357. As he struck the ground, the barrel began to turn and tilt toward Wilt.

Wilt didn't hesitate. It was no joke being killed by a dying man. He dipped the angle of the shotgun and pulled the trigger again. The impact of the buckshot slammed Thorpe to the ground.

Approaching, Wilt kept the cutdown at the ready. He stopped a few feet away and lowered the shotgun. Thorpe was a bloody mess. The .357 was still close to Thorpe's right hand. Wilt stepped forward and kicked it away.

Thorpe had taken the first blast in the left side. The second round had hit him high, in the upper chest and the neck.

It had made mush of his neck and chin.

Wilt turned away and yelled as loud as he could. "Come on in. It's over."

He was seated twenty yards away from the body, head down, looking half asleep, when Joe Croft and Billy Egan reached him.

Egan stopped to have his look at the body. Joe rushed past him and stood over Wilt. "You hit? You all right?"

Wilt lifted his head and blinked at him. "Right as rain."

Joe put an arm around him and helped him to his feet. He took the cutdown from his hands and passed it to Egan. Egan took one arm and they walked him between them in the direction of the guest house.

Billy Egan leaned toward Wilt. "Damned good job, Sheriff."

Wilt coughed. He didn't have any words left.

CHAPTER FORTY THREE

Three days passed before Wilt returned to his office. He'd spent those three days in Diane's bed.

The brave Sheriff who'd gone hand-to-hand with a child molester and murderer was front page news for one day. The next day it was the subject of a short follow-up article on page three. The day Wilt returned to work, it wasn't news at all.

That suited him just fine.

Wilt settled in his chair and did paperwork. There was something relaxing and reassuring about falling back into the old drudgery. After a couple of hours, Susie buzzed him. Federal Marshal Bottoms, she said, was on his way back to his office.

Bottoms opened the door and stood framed in the doorway. The swelling had gone down, the nose looked about normal size, but his right eye was black and his left eye was a pale blue. A crust of scab had formed on his bottom lip where the stitches were.

Before Wilt said a word, Bottoms opened his jacket and revealed a rig with a tape recorder hooked to his belt. "Good morning, Sheriff. I was in the area and I thought I'd touch bases with you." Bottoms edged a chair close to the desk. He sat and leaned forward. He placed an index card on the blotter. It was neatly typed.

Have to cover my ass. Go along with me. Will explain.

Wilt read the card and pushed it back across the desk to Bottoms. Bottoms scooped it up and shoved it in his jacket pocket.

"I hope I haven't caught you at a busy time, Sheriff, dropping by like this."

"I'm always glad to talk to my friends in the Justice Department. No matter how busy I am."

"That's a good attitude. It'll make our talk a lot easier."

"What's the problem, Marshal?" Leaning back in his chair, Wilt gave Bottoms his go-to-hell grin.

"There's no reason for this to be kept secret between law officers. I assume you didn't know that Raymond Thorpe was in our Federal Witness Protection Program."

"He was? Lord, that's an amazement to me."

"If you'd known, I assume you'd have been in touch with us to see if we could work out some agreement that would have suited both of us."

"Exactly," Wilt said. "Heck, we both eat out of the same soup pot. No reason I know for either of us to poison the soup."

"It's good to hear that from you," Bottoms said.

"Of course, Marshal, if I'd known Thorpe was under your wing, I might not have done one solitary thing different. In this circumstance, the molestation and savage murder of two little girls, the murder of two adults, the serious attacks on two fellow law officers... I'm not sure much could be done to protect Raymond Thorpe from law and justice."

"But, at least, if you'd known our concern with him, we could have had a talk."

"Exactly," Wilt said.

"I believe we understand each other. Sheriff. I have to admit to you, just between us, that Raymond Thorpe was not the model of what the protected witness ought to be. I've read the record of your investigation and I have no quarrel with your conclusion that Thorpe was guilty as weekend sin."

"It's good to know that a lofty organization like the Justice Department approves of our investigative methods.

I'll quote you to my men, a kind of pat on the back, if you don't mind."

"Feel free," Bottoms said.

"It'll make them proud," Wilt said. "Peacock proud."

Bottoms scowled at him. Wilt's speech was getting more country every minute that passed. He stood. "It's been a pleasure talking to you."

"Enjoyed it myself."

"The next time I hope we meet under better circumstances." Bottoms pointed at the recorder and held up two fingers. He marched out and through the lobby. On the way past the switchboard he waved at Susie.

Bottoms returned a couple of minutes later. He smiled at Wilt. "Had to wait until I was outside before I switched off the recorder. Had to make it sound right." He opened his jacket. The rig and the recorder were gone.

Wilt shouted through the open doorway. "Susie, bring us in two cups of the fresh."

Bottoms settled into a seat across the desk from Wilt. "You really laid that hick crap on me."

"I thought it was what the Feds expected."

"It was cut thick."

"When it's typed it won't read that way."

Wilt watched Bottoms consider that carefully. He nodded. He would hope for the best. "It must have been rough out there a couple of nights ago. I don't envy you."

"Thorpe was good at all the wrong things."

Susie brought them two cups of coffee. She waited in the doorway. Bottoms looked at his coffee and frowned. "I'm now on sick leave. My boss thinks I shouldn't be on the job looking like I came out on the wrong end of a punch-out." He placed the cup on the desk blotter. "You tied down here for the day or can we get some breakfast?"

Susie answered Wilt's question before he asked it. "Joe's running late. He called in. He'll be here in five minutes."

Wilt got his heavy coat. Passing Susie, he said, "You drink the coffee for us like a nice girl."

"Where'll I reach you if I need ...?"

"You don't. We just disappeared. Joe's in charge. He makes all the decisions."

"If you say so..." Susie didn't sound happy about the arrangement.

"That's exactly what I say." Wilt stopped in the doorway next to Susie. He leaned over her. "Honey, that boy's got to grow up some day. He might as well start today."

Wilt tucked the covers around Diane and walked into the bathroom. He closed the door before he fumbled for the light switch. It was still very much her bathroom, a woman's bathroom. All he'd added to it was a card of disposable razors, a toothbrush and a tube of Alka-Seltzer. He even shaved with her scented soap and felt very much a dandy.

He removed his toothbrush, added water and dropped in two Alka-Seltzer tablets. He drank the fizz before the tablet dissolved. He chewed the thin, chalky disks that remained on his tongue after the liquid was gone.

That Bottoms was a drinker and that was no lie. After Wilt left the Brass Rail, he called in from his apartment and told Susie that Joe was still in charge. He curled up in his bed and slept off most of the alcohol before Diane called to remind him that he'd promised to take her to supper.

Now, back in her bedroom again, he stood beside the bed and looked down at her. Beautiful in light and beautiful in shadows. That he loved her both surprised and frightened him. It put a sense of wonder back in his life. His fear was that it wouldn't last, that love wouldn't stay as bright and shiny as a dime polished with mercury.

"Come back to bed, Wilt."

He hadn't known she was awake. "All you horny women want me in your beds now that I am a bona fide hero."

"Come to bed, old man."

"How old?"

"Just the right age," she said. "Slow enough for me to catch in the first place and too slow to get away if you change your mind."

"I don't have any intention of changing my mind. I especially wouldn't change my mind if I knew what you are talking about."

"I see," she said. "You are going to try to get out of it by pretending you don't remember what you asked me last night in the throes of passion."

"I'm an honorable man," he said. He sat on the side of the bed. "But I wish to hell I knew what you're talking about."

"A weaker woman than I am would cry now."

A cold wind shook the windows. He shivered and pulled back the covers and got into bed beside her. Her warmth soothed him.

"I think I'm remembering the question now," he said. "But I'm a little foggy on what your answer was."

"I'm an honorable woman," she said. "But I wish to hell I knew what you're talking about."

He twisted around in her arms. "Maybe if we were in the throes of passion, it would refresh our memories."

"Good idea," she said, and drew his head to her breast.

ABOUT THE AUTHOR

Ralph Dennis isn't a household name... but he should be. He is widely considered among crime writers as a master of the genre, denied the recognition he deserved because his twelve *Hardman* books, which are beloved and highly sought-after collectables now, were poorly packaged in the 1970s by Popular Library as a cheap men's action-adventure paperbacks with numbered titles.

Even so, some top critics saw past the cheesy covers and noticed that he was producing work as good as John D. MacDonald, Raymond Chandler, Chester Himes, Dashiell Hammett, and Ross MacDonald.

The *New York Times* praised the *Hardman* novels for "expert writing, plotting, and an unusual degree of sensitivity. Dennis has mastered the genre and supplied top entertainment." The *Philadelphia Daily News* proclaimed *Hardman* "the best series around, but they've got such terrible covers..."

Unfortunately, Popular Library didn't take the hint and continued to present the series like hack work, dooming the novels to a short shelf-life and obscurity... except among generations of crime writers, like novelist Joe R. Lansdale (the *Hap & Leonard* series) and screenwriter Shane Black (the *Lethal Weapon* movies), who've kept Dennis' legacy alive through word-of-mouth and by acknowledging his influence on their stellar work.

Ralph Dennis wrote three other novels that were published outside of the *Hardman* series but he wasn't able to reach the wide audience, or gain the critical acclaim, that he deserved during his lifetime.

He was born in 1931 in Sumter, South Carolina, and received a Masters degree from University of North Carolina, where he later taught film and television writing after serving a stint in the Navy. At the time of his death in 1988, he was working at a bookstore in Atlanta and had a file cabinet full of unpublished novels.

www.ingramcontent.com/pod-product-compliance
Lightning Source LLC
Chambersburg PA
CBHW020543020726
47494CB00006B/1903